All the ...

"Mr. Montclair," Philip... ...ing of kissing me?"

"*I*, kiss *you*! I did no such thing!"

"You were about to!" she charged.

He straightened with a jerk. "I would never force myself on a lady!"

"It would not have been—" In the nick of time she stopped herself. *It would not have been force.* That's what she'd nearly shouted in his face. *Kiss me, you impossible irresistible scoundrel,* had also been echoing inside her head.

Face burning, she clamped her mouth shut. The day felt suddenly hot and stuffy, and it seemed as though a swarm of bees were buzzing madly inside her head.

"It would not have been . . . welcome?"

She swallowed, unable to let that lie persist. "It—it *would* have been welcome."

His expression shifted. "In spite of all my efforts?"

Philippa blinked. "What?"

"You're not supposed to like me," he said, sounding almost frustrated.

"But I do," she protested, then frowned. "Why not?"

He glanced around, but they were still alone. "The more curious question is why you do."

Her frown deepened. "At times—like this!—I heartily wish I did not."

He laughed. "No doubt!" Still smiling, he shook his head. "I should have known."

"Known wha—?"

Her question, and her curiosity, went silent as he took her face in his hands and kissed her.

Also by Caroline Linden

A SCOT TO THE HEART
ABOUT A ROGUE

WHEN THE MARQUESS WAS MINE
AN EARL LIKE YOU
MY ONCE AND FUTURE DUKE

SIX DEGREES OF SCANDAL
LOVE IN THE TIME OF SCANDAL
ALL'S FAIR IN LOVE AND SCANDAL (novella)
IT TAKES A SCANDAL
LOVE AND OTHER SCANDALS

THE WAY TO A DUKE'S HEART
BLAME IT ON BATH
ONE NIGHT IN LONDON
I LOVE THE EARL (novella)

YOU ONLY LOVE ONCE
FOR YOUR ARMS ONLY
A VIEW TO A KISS

A RAKE'S GUIDE TO SEDUCTION
WHAT A ROGUE DESIRES
WHAT A GENTLEMAN WANTS

WHAT A WOMAN NEEDS

ATTENTION: ORGANIZATIONS AND CORPORATIONS
HarperCollins books may be purchased for educational, business, or sales promotional use. For information, please e-mail the Special Markets Department at SPsales@harpercollins.com.

CAROLINE LINDEN

ALL THE DUKE I NEED
THE I NEED

AVONBOOKS

An Imprint of HarperCollins*Publishers*

This is a work of fiction. Names, characters, places, and incidents are products of the author's imagination or are used fictitiously and are not to be construed as real. Any resemblance to actual events, locales, organizations, or persons, living or dead, is entirely coincidental.

ALL THE DUKE I NEED. Copyright © 2022 by P. F. Belsley. All rights reserved. Printed in the United States of America. No part of this book may be used or reproduced in any manner whatsoever without written permission except in the case of brief quotations embodied in critical articles and reviews. For information, address HarperCollins Publishers, 195 Broadway, New York, NY 10007.

First Avon Books mass market printing: April 2022

Print Edition ISBN: 978-0-06-291366-1
Digital Edition ISBN: 978-0-06-291367-8

Cover design by Guido Caroti
Cover photo by Glenn Mackay
Cover illustration by Allan Davey
Cover images © iStock/Getty Images; © Shutterstock; © Dreamstime.com

Avon, Avon & logo, and Avon Books & logo are registered trademarks of HarperCollins Publishers in the United States of America and other countries.

HarperCollins is a registered trademark of HarperCollins Publishers in the United States of America and other countries.

FIRST EDITION

Printed in Lithuania

22 23 24 25 26   SB   10 9 8 7 6 5 4 3 2 1

If you purchased this book without a cover, you should be aware that this book is stolen property. It was reported as "unsold and destroyed" to the publisher, and neither the author nor the publisher has received any payment for this "stripped book."

To Gretchen and Fred
Vive le HEA!

ALL THE DUKE I NEED

Prologue

❧❧ ❧❧

The wedding was small, as it should have been. The bride, after all, was long past the blush of youth, and the groom, even older, was a widower.

But this bride dearly loved a party and was not about to miss a chance to throw one. The wedding might have been small and private, but the celebration which followed was neither.

The bailey court of Carlyle Castle had been transformed, with tents and awnings and a parquet dance floor assembled by a crew of carpenters. A lavish spread of delicacies wrought rapturous praise from the guests, and a string quartet played under the dining room windows. As if to bless the union, the sun shone warmly in a crystal blue sky and a light breeze kept the dancers from becoming heated. When the sun began to set, footmen moved from tree to tent, hanging dozens of lit lanterns until they outnumbered the stars and illuminated the bailey almost as brightly as day.

Sophia Constance St. James, Duchess of Carlyle, presided contentedly over the scene from the largest tent. It was more like a village fair than a London ball, which was exactly how her daughter had wanted it. And there hadn't been a party at the castle in . . . goodness, years and years. It was good to hear laughter echoing off the stone walls again.

Her fond gaze found her daughter in the crowd, beaming into her new husband's face. From the far side of the lawn boomed Stephen's boisterous laughter. He was probably instigating a game of bowls or even an archery tournament. Her youngest son was like that. He had played a large part in planning the festivities, and he had been responsible for inviting the entire parish of St. Mary's, where he was soon to take the post of vicar. Every lord, squire, merchant, and farmer within ten miles was here.

As she watched, the bridal couple turned and started toward her. The duchess's heart almost burst with maternal pride. Her daughter might be old for a new bride—already thirty—but she was still beautiful and filled with joy. She wore a crepe silver gown that glittered in the twilight, and there were pink roses in her piled-high hair. But it was the luminous smile on her face that made the duchess's throat tighten with happiness.

"Here you are, Mama," said Jessica happily, sitting on the settee next to her. She held out her arms to her bridegroom. "Give her to me, Miles."

Miles Kirkpatrick was tall and somber, impressive in his army uniform, his dark hair gone gray at the temples. But his expression was warm and tender as he handed over the little girl he held. Only then did he turn to his new mother-in-law and bow crisply. "An exquisite day, ma'am, of intense happiness. Thank you from the bottom of my heart."

She raised her brows. "I only threw the party, Colonel. You and my daughter form the exquisitely happy part."

He smiled, and Jessica laughed. "Don't we, though?" She glanced around. "Where is Johnny?"

"He tired and went inside." The duke had been determined to see his sister wed. He had even walked her to the altar, but that had exhausted his strength. He'd lasted only half an hour under the tents before retiring to the castle.

"Ah," said Jessica. "I shall go see him tomorrow to thank him." Another burst of laughter made her look up, across the lawn to where her younger brother held court. "And I would thank Stephen not to start a riot!"

The duchess smiled. "He would never."

"Not where *you* could see him," her daughter murmured archly.

By now she had got the little girl settled on her lap, but at this remark the child opened her mouth and gave a wide yawn. Her father murmured in worry, but Jessica simply stroked the girl's hair and smiled. "Poor Pippa! We've kept you out here so long. Are you very tired, darling?"

The little chin set. The child shook her head.

"Now, Pippa, it is time for bed. Where is Asmat?" asked her father, naming the Indian ayah who was the child's nurse.

"Don't know," said his daughter. She put her arms around Jessica's neck. "Want to stay with Mama."

Husband and wife exchanged a glance. Across the grass, the musicians had progressed from stately dances to rollicking country ones, the very sort Jessica loved best.

"Leave her with me," said the duchess. "No doubt the nursemaid will come soon."

Hugging the little girl close, Jessica hesitated. "Are you certain, Mama?"

She gave a stern look. "As if I didn't raise four children. I think I shall be able to handle one small girl." She waved her hands to shoo them away. "Go! Dance and be merry!"

"If you insist." Gently Jessica deposited the child on the settee in her place. She bent down to speak to the girl, her fair curls brushing the child's dark ones. After a moment's whispered conversation, Jessica rose and took her bridegroom's arm. "We shall be right over there," she said—to the duchess or to the child, it wasn't clear.

"I know where you will be," said her mother dryly. "Have faith, my dear."

The colonel went down on one knee and kissed his daughter's forehead, her face so tiny in his hands. The little girl reached out and held on to a button of his scarlet coat. He murmured something to her, loosened her hand from his coat and kissed her fingers, then rose. "Thank you, ma'am," he said, bowing again as Lady Jessica made a face of amused impatience at her mother. "Send for Asmat if—"

"Yes, yes." She flicked one hand again. "One would think you don't trust me."

His face blanked with alarm, but Jessica burst out laughing. "Of course we do! We don't want to put you out. But since you insist . . ." She gave the child a cheery wave and took her husband's hand, pulling him back toward the dancing.

The duchess looked at the little girl, who gazed fearlessly back. Jessica had told her Colonel Kirkpatrick had a young daughter, but today was the first time she'd met the child. "You're Philippa," she said.

"Philippa Noor un-nisa Kirkpatrick," was the reply, with surprising confidence.

"Your father calls you Pippa."

She nodded. "Papa and Pippa." She was quiet for a moment. "And now Mama, since Ammi is gone."

Ammi must be her mother, who had died a year ago. Her Grace nodded gently. She knew what it was like to lose someone dear.

"What is *your* name?"

Her Grace's brows went up. "Sophia Constance St. James, Duchess of Carlyle." The little girl's nose wrinkled in disgust. "Perhaps you will call me something else," suggested the duchess, amused.

"Are you a daadee?" Philippa asked curiously.

"What is a daadee?"

"Ammi's ammi. She gave me this before we came here on the ship." Philippa patted the gold and jade pendant on a string of pearls around her neck. It was far too ornate for a child, but Jessica had been reading voraciously about India, and she said jewels on children weren't unusual there.

"Ah." The duchess nodded, but with a twinge. She was not a grandmother—not yet. "Would you like to call me Daadee?"

The little face brightened. "Yes!"

Her Grace was charmed. "Then I shall be Daadee."

"Daadee," repeated Philippa happily.

"Are you pleased to have a mama?"

Philippa nodded. "Mama's dress is lovely."

The duchess smiled in delight. "Yes, it is. So is yours."

Philippa slid off the settee and spun around, watching her yellow skirts bell around her. At the end she gave a couple of hops to make the ribbons flutter. "Papa gave it to me."

"That was very kind of him." It was clear the colonel doted on his daughter—surprisingly so, for a man of his age and profession. The duchess had never known army men to be sentimental.

Philippa climbed back onto the settee. "Your dress is lovely, too, Daadee."

The duchess looked at her own gown of deep blue silk, lavishly embroidered and dripping with Brussels lace. "Thank you," she replied, amused all over again.

The child sat so primly on the settee, her little feet dangling off the edge. Another yawn almost made her fall over.

"Are you tired?" asked the duchess.

Philippa shook her head. "No, no, no!" Then she ruined it by yawning again.

"Perhaps you would like a cup of milk."

Philippa regarded her with suspicion for a moment before slowly nodding. The duchess raised a hand, and a footman waiting nearby stepped forward. "Bring a cup of fresh milk for Miss Kirkpatrick." The man nodded and whisked away, returning in a few minutes. The duchess handed it to the child, who lifted the cup with both hands and drank it all. She gave a gusty sigh, and her eyelids drooped.

Of course she was tired. She was all of three years old and it had been a long day. Still, the duchess was impressed by her fortitude. At that age, Stephen would have been a howling demon, throwing a temper fit on the ground, and Johnny likely would have bitten someone by now. Her boys had been wild and energetic creatures.

But then, to Her Grace's astonishment, Philippa set down the cup and crawled right into her lap. She squirmed around, finding her preferred position, then turned up her head to gaze at the duchess. A little smile creased her plump cheeks, and then those big dark eyes closed and she went to sleep.

For a moment the duchess was frozen. Her arms had gone around the child instinctively, even though it had been a long time since anyone had crawled into her lap. But the little girl heaved a shuddering, sleepy sigh and nestled against her, and Her Grace's grip tightened.

She sat for some time, inhaling the warm scent of the little girl, marveling at the silky texture of the dark curls brushing her arm. Philippa slept so soundly, so trustingly. At times her mouth worked as if she were sucking her thumb, just as Jessica had done as a child. It brought a fond smile to Her Grace's face. It would be good to have a young one in the house again—and hopefully there would be more. Jessica was wed now, and Stephen would surely settle down soon.

She only gradually became aware of the whispers behind her. This tent was the most elaborately outfitted, but also now the quietest, as the duke had returned to the castle and most of the guests were clustered around the dancing area. The housekeeper had sent the maids out to start tidying up, and two of them were clearing the tables where guests had earlier dined on collared veal, lobster patties, and a fragrant dish called curry, made from the colonel's own receipt.

"Brown little thing, ain't she," whispered one of the maids.

"I heard her mam was one of those Indian concubines," whispered the other. "Fair strange for a man like the colonel to bring home a by-blow."

The first maid giggled. "Sticks out, don't she?"

"Wonder how long they'll keep her about," whispered the other. "Once Lady Jessica has a babe, and this one looks so different."

"You there," said the duchess sharply. With a clatter of china, both maids went silent. "Come here, both of you."

Deathly pale, the two girls hurried to curtsy in front of her. Her Grace looked them both up and down, allowing her displeasure to show. "What is your name?"

"Sarah Wood, ma'am," murmured the first one in a trembling voice, dipping another curtsy.

"Jane Carter, Your Grace," whispered the second. She held her apron in a white-knuckled grip.

"Have you so little to do that you can stand about gossiping?" The duchess raised her brow as they both shook their heads frantically. "Both of you think yourself superior to this child, I take it."

"No, Your Grace," said one in a tiny voice. The other girl merely shook her head again, her eyes wide and terrified.

The duchess stared at them coldly for another long moment. "Good. I will not abide that in this house. Sarah Wood, fetch a blanket for my granddaughter. Jane Carter, take those tablecloths to the laundry."

The maids stammered out apologies as they bobbed more curtsies and fled. Sarah Wood came running back a few minutes later with a blanket, and tucked it carefully around the sleeping girl. Her Grace dismissed the maid with a silent nod, still irate at their conversation.

No one mocked or belittled her guests, let alone an innocent child who was now part of her family. Her Grace studied the angelic little face resting against her arm and felt a piece of her heart melt. *Daadee.* Not a grandmother, but very nearly. Careful not to disturb her sleeping burden, she settled more comfortably in her chair.

At some point the bridal couple whirled back, Jessica's silver dress rumpled and the roses in her hair drooping but her face flushed with happiness. The colonel's own smile vanished when he saw where Philippa was.

"Oh, the poor little dear," cried Jessica softly.

"I'm very sorry, ma'am," said the colonel, reaching for his daughter. "Let me take her."

"Why?"

He flushed. "I should have found Asmat to put her to bed."

"I have her." The duchess raised a brow, looking between the two of them. "Go along and have your fun, my dears. Do not waste your wedding day. Don't worry about her—or me."

Jessica smiled. Lightly she brushed one hand over Philippa's dark curls. "Thank you, Mama."

"That is too kind, madam," murmured her husband.

"It is my pleasure," said the duchess serenely. "I will take good care of her for as long as you need me to."

Chapter One

❧❧❧

1787
London

You've done *what*?"

William Montclair grinned at his younger brother's incredulous expression. "Made you look up from the ledgers," he said with a wink.

The ledgers were a spot of contention. Jack fretted over them like an old woman, counting and tallying every column twice. Will, on the other hand, preferred not to look at the accounts at all, particularly not now, given the bad news they held.

Jack slammed the book shut and leapt to his feet. "Damn it, Will, stop teasing!"

"I'm not teasing." He leaned back and propped one boot on a corner of the desk, plucking a walnut from the bowl there. "I've been offered a position."

His brother stared at him. "You *have* a bloody job! This one!"

Will lifted one shoulder, cracking the walnut shell. "But this one is a good post. It pays well, and I shall make the acquaintances of important people." He nodded knowingly at his brother. "Thought I'd done a complete lark, eh?"

Jack glowered at him. "You have."

"Wasn't it you who told me just the other day that our accounts are running perilously low?" Will frowned thoughtfully as he picked the nut-meats from the fractured shell. "Or was that some other brother of mine?"

Jack flung up one hand in aggravation. "Of course we're low on funds, we've been here almost four months. But the best way to replenish the coffers is to build this business, not take an English-man's job."

"The quickest way to get money is to find some-one who will give it to us," noted Will.

"Instead of doing what Pa asked us to do?"

"All I have to do is manage a farm," said Will. He popped the walnut into his mouth.

Jack stared at him in amazement. "How well can that pay?"

"Better than you'd think," said Will, dodging the question. "I won't do it forever, just until we're on better footing here." His brother shook his head, muttering. Will played his ace. "Besides, I thought you'd be pleased to get me out of your way."

From the length of the following silence, Will knew he had him. Jack was the one with the head for this business, to say nothing of the passion and drive. Will was nominally in charge, but the truth was he didn't enjoy it.

In Boston he had. His father had put him in charge of maintaining the ships, and Will loved that—he checked every ship from prow to stern himself, climbing the rigging and inspecting the hulls. He'd been apprenticed to a shipwright for a few years, while Jack had been apprenticed to a merchant to learn bookkeeping. Those had been wise choices, as both took to their respective trades like ducks to water. And then Pa sent the pair of them to London, to establish their shipping firm there.

In theory they ought to have been a perfect team, yet somehow they hadn't quite managed to work in harmony. Jack always thought he'd been stuck with the dull parts, even though he didn't like being on the deck of a ship, and Will felt like he might suffocate if he had to sit at a desk all day.

So, after four months of butting heads and bruised feelings, he'd found a way out that would benefit both of them.

"But that's not what Pa told us to do." His brother still looked uneasy.

Will waved one hand. "How could Pa know how things would go once we reached London? We're just redistributing the work. You'll tend to this business, and I'll keep us afloat until then."

Jack drummed his fingers on his hip. He was weakening, seduced by the siren lure of having a free hand with Montclair and Sons. "How long do you plan to manage this farm?"

Will made a face. "How long will it take you to put us upright? I daresay no more than a few months. A year at the utmost."

"A year!"

"Make us rich sooner and I'll give notice." Will grinned.

Jack scowled. "What if I need help? Pa sent us both because it's a lot to do, Will."

"Hire a clerk. He'll work cheaper than I will."

His brother snorted. "And probably better, too."

"Probably," agreed Will, because it aligned with what he wanted to do. Now was not the time to defend his abilities.

For a long moment Jack stared out the window at the wharves below, teeming with sailors and dock workers, loading and unloading the vast number of ships in the docks. London hummed with commerce, and they both knew Montclair could thrive here. The long war with England was over, and any lingering hard feelings were best soothed by liberal application of profits on both sides.

"I don't like it," muttered Jack at last.

"Which part?" Will wanted to know. "The sudden influx of steady income? The end of our arguments over every expense?" He snapped his fingers. "It must be the loss of my constant company, and the dread of having our lodgings all to yourself."

Jack gave him a dark look. They'd been on top of each other since leaving Boston, first on board the ship, then in the cramped rooms they'd taken in Wapping. "Why are you so keen to do this?"

Now it was Will's turn to look away. He took another walnut from the bowl. "A change of scenery."

"Am I so dreadful to work with?" asked his brother in a low, strained voice.

"No!" Will shot to his feet and grimaced at Jack's doleful expression. "It's not that. It's . . . this." He waved one hand around the tiny office. "I don't like being trapped indoors. Sitting here every day, poring over ledgers and squeezing every penny, is going to drive me to drink. I want to *do* something."

Slowly Jack came back to his chair. "What will you tell Pa?"

"I don't see any reason to tell him at all. It's coming on to winter, and I don't have to take up residence at the estate until spring."

"So you'd still be here?"

Will nodded. "But able to afford better lodgings. And also able to do Montclair business, if needed."

Jack's eyes flashed his way. "You'd cede control to me, though?"

The words sent a funny ripple through him. He'd always been the leader, the instigator, the authority in everything they did, from smuggling a puppy into the house as boys to launching an office of the family business in London. He and Jack were barely a year apart in age, but their ranking had been unquestioned. What would it be like to take direction from Jack instead of give it?

"Yes," he said, shaking off that qualm.

His brother heaved a sigh. "I can't stop you, can I? So I might as well go along with it."

"Might as well," Will agreed.

"If it doesn't work, I *will* tell Pa," Jack warned.

Will made a face. "So he can cross the ocean to thrash us both? If we both do as we ought, everything will go smoothly. He won't even need to know."

"You don't *want* me to tell him." Jack's eyes narrowed in renewed suspicion. "Will, what are you doing?"

He reached for his hat, hanging on the back of his chair. "Exactly what I told you. But there's no assurance it will work out, you see? What if I'm no good at farming and get sacked?" He shook his head mournfully. "Put aside your own enjoyment of the prospect. I would prefer not to trumpet it about. If it should happen, I will come back with my tail between my legs, suitably humbled."

Jack gave a bark of laughter. "Humbled! You?"

Will wagged a finger at him. "But if I succeed . . ." He set the hat on his head. "Montclair will be profitable, free of debt, and I shall return to it, hopefully with a wealth of new connections in hand. That's what he charged us to do, isn't it?"

"Well—Yes . . ."

He grinned and spread wide his arms, waiting.

After a moment Jack sighed again. "All right. I won't tell anyone. But your word—no more than a year."

"I pledge it on my sacred honor." Will swept a bow. "Au revoir, mon frère."

Jack was still staring at him doubtfully as Will closed the door and clattered down the stairs.

The office they'd let was within shouting distance of the quays, in one of the innumerable little streets that formed a labyrinth along the waterfront. Will strode along the twisting lane, dodging the ragged boys waiting to pick his pocket, jumping over the sewer that ran through the cobblestones. To his left, masts of ships rose like a forest of bare trees above the rooftops, including the *Mary Catherine*, the ship which had brought him and Jack across the Atlantic. Behind him shone the gleaming golden dome of St. Paul's cathedral, and as he crossed Bridge Street he could see the hulk of the Fleet Prison looming darkly to the north. They'd both been warned about the Fleet, where debtors got sent. To the south was the river, the bright sunlight glinting off the silvery surface, teeming with energy and commerce.

He liked London more than he had expected to. He'd heard it was a dirty, crowded city, where squalor and crime crept right up to the elegant mansions of dukes and princes. That wasn't wholly wrong; the area near the quays was filthy, crowded, and dangerous at times. But Will had spent his free hours walking through the city, and thought it wondrous. As vibrant as Boston was, it was nothing to London, where the streets were lit every night by lamplighters, where the rattle of carriage wheels rang over cobbles until late at night. There were concerts and theaters and pleasure gardens and museums the likes of which he'd never seen. He and Jack had paid their two shillings to see the armory and menagerie at the Tower, and both had been dumbstruck by the Tower itself, seven hundred years old.

He walked up Fleet Street and turned into Chancery Lane, then into a small court. These houses were at least as old as the ones near the quay, but their stones were steeped in money and power, with nothing of the dirt of the rope works or the stench of the fish market.

He let himself in at one door and nodded to the clerk. "I'd like a word with Mr. Edwards. He'll be expecting me."

"Yes, sir." The clerk took his card and vanished through a door. Too restless to sit, Will hung his hat on a hook behind the door and prowled the room, which was well-appointed with wainscoting, a pair of elegant chairs by the fireplace, and the clerk's high desk by the window. It was much grander than the shabby office he and Jack had.

What *was* he doing? he asked himself for the tenth time. For all his confidence in front of his brother, he wasn't entirely sure.

It had been a lark, really, that got him here in the first place. He'd been strolling in the nearby Square, studying the houses and offices, when he literally bumped into Roger Edwards. After some apologies, the lawyer had asked about his accent. He'd been fascinated by Will's stories of America. Before Will knew it, the two of them had made several circuits of Lincoln's Inn, and then Edwards invited him to a nearby coffeehouse. They'd sat there and talked for another hour, first about Will's business and then gradually about Mr. Edwards's.

He was the lawyer for an old aristocratic family, in London to look for a new estate steward, as the prior one had been forced into retirement by old age and ill health. He spoke very candidly, even fondly of the estate and the family, as if they were his own. By the time they'd drunk several cups of coffee, Will was fascinated by the bucolic vision the solicitor wove, and when the man sighed about the difficulties he'd had finding a suitable steward, the words popped unbidden out of his mouth.

Sounds like something I could do.

He still couldn't believe he'd said it. Even less believably, Edwards had looked at him for a moment and nodded before asking, "Would you like the position, then?"

And for some wholly inexplicable reason, Will had replied, "I believe I might."

The door behind him opened. "This way, Mr. Montclair." The clerk ushered him down a short corridor to a larger, better appointed room.

The lawyer stood behind his desk. He was a tall, spare fellow in his late fifties with thinning brown hair, dressed all in black with round wire-rimmed spectacles perched on his nose. At Will's entrance, he bowed politely. "Mr. Montclair."

"Mr. Edwards." Will covered his growing uncertainty with an elaborate bow of his own. "Here I am, as promised."

The lawyer smiled slightly. "I am delighted by it. Please, be seated."

Will dropped into the chair. The shelves behind the lawyer were lined with tall ledgers and thick law books. He didn't particularly enjoy doing the ledgers for Montclair and Sons. God above, would he have to sit in an office like this, surrounded by books like that? What had he been thinking, to entertain this idea?

"Have you an answer for me?" Mr. Edwards resumed his own chair. Sunlight from the tall windows beside him reflected off his spectacles, hiding his eyes. His expression gave away nothing.

Will's heart thudded hard against his breastbone. He could still turn it down, walk away from this, go back to Jack and tell him he'd changed his mind.

"I have a few questions." His hands were damp, and he pressed them to his thighs before clasping them on his knee. "Regarding my residence at the estate . . ."

Edwards nodded. "Of course. There is a cottage reserved for the estate steward. It is not large, but perfectly comfortable for a single man." He paused, then gave a surprised smile. "Of course, I never asked, did I? If you have a wife and children."

Will shook his head. "I don't."

"Then I daresay you'll find it more than suffi-cient. There is also a gig reserved for the steward's use, with horses supplied by His Grace's stable. An allotment from the farms. I presume you have no staff of your own?" At Will's short shake of his head, Edwards went on. "I have confidence you will be able to engage any servants you require from the Castle or the nearby town, which may be most convenient as they will be familiar with the parish."

Will cleared his throat. "That all sounds accept-able." It sounded rather lavish, actually. "But you indicated the steward would be expected to re-main in London initially. Why is that?"

Edwards smiled again. "I've been managing the Carlyle estate for nearly two years now, since the former steward fell ill. I'm afraid I've developed my own particular methods and preferences, and wish to see them continued. After a few months' instruction, I expect you'll be ready to manage in person."

Will rubbed one finger over a scuff mark on the side of his boot. Did he really need months of in-struction? "Wouldn't it be better to begin in place?"

The attorney looked at him for a long moment. Will wished the sun would move faster, so he could see the man's eyes. "Alas. I must be here in London for most of the winter. It is more conve-nient for me to have you here."

There was no way around that, then. Will aban-doned the subject. "I assume the winter would be a trial of sorts, to see if you find me satisfactory."

Mr. Edwards's chin dipped. The glare off his

spectacle lenses vanished, and Will could see his dark eyes, sharp and assessing. "If you have changed your mind, sir—"

"No." He cleared his throat and sat up straighter. "But I don't wish to be out on the street in a few weeks. It takes time to learn any new command, and I would like some assurances."

"Ah." Again that faint smile crossed the attorney's face. "Shall we contract for a six month engagement? If you wish to give up the position sooner, I of course would not stop you."

"No," said Will almost before the man had finished his sentence. "You needn't worry about that. Six months it is."

He left after Mr. Edwards promised to draw up a contract with wages and conditions. After boasting to Jack that he would keep them in funds for the next few months, Will wanted to be sure he could do it. By spring Jack should have secured some contracts in time for the shipping season and established the toehold they needed in London. By spring, Will would probably have had his fill of managing a ducal estate and be eager to go back to sea.

And if not . . . Well, he would have satisfied his curiosity.

And that would be enough.

Chapter Two

❦

1788
Carlyle Castle

"The new steward has arrived at last," Mrs. Potter said, picking through herbs and ointments in the housekeeper's private pantry.

Philippa Kirkpatrick smiled. The saga of the new steward for Carlyle Castle had taken on shades of melodrama. The former steward had retired in ill health two years ago. Desperate for assistance running the estate, Mr. Edwards, the Carlyle attorney, had argued for months before Her Grace grudgingly gave permission to engage one last summer. The attorney had wasted no time, engaging a Mr. Montclair on his very next trip to London. All winter long the man had been working in town under Mr. Edwards's guidance, with the expectation that he would assume full command at the Castle in spring.

And now he was here. It was so rare that someone new came to Carlyle, Mr. Montclair's impending arrival had intrigued the castle's residents for weeks—including, it seemed, the housekeeper.

"Oh? What is your impression of the man?" she asked Mrs. Potter.

"Not what I expected," replied the woman primly. She selected some dried lavender and Epsom salts, and began crushing them in a mortar. The Duke of Carlyle had caught a cold, and the doctor had recommended hot bath soaks. Even now the servants were filling the tub. "I wonder what Her Grace will think of him."

Philippa turned in surprise. "What do you mean? How is he surprising?"

Mrs. Potter gave a tight shake of her head. "I don't like to say, Miss Kirkpatrick. You must decide for yourself."

Mrs. Potter was fond of saying that. *Decide for yourself*, she would charge, in such a tone and demeanor that made perfectly clear what conclusion she expected one to reach. The duchess said Mrs. Potter was simply seeking confirmation that her impression was correct, but then the duchess was the only one who dared contradict the housekeeper.

"Of course I shall," replied Philippa. "Has he been presented to Her Grace yet?"

Mrs. Potter snorted. "Only if Mr. Edwards is a fool, which he is not."

Her curiosity now truly piqued, Philippa removed her apron. "No, he certainly is not. Send the mixture directly to His Grace's rooms when it's ready, please." She let herself out and went in search of the attorney.

Philippa was mistress of the house in all but

name. She met with Mrs. Potter to plan the menus
and direct the kitchens. She approved the household accounts and oversaw the renovation of the
music room and dining room after a ruinous water leak. She supervised the gardeners and kept
track of which paintings needed to be rotated out
of the sunlight and held the keys to the silver and
tea chests. She didn't entertain, because there were
few if any guests at the castle.

It was an unusual position for her to have, but
she loved it. Carlyle Castle was the only home she
could remember, and the St. Jameses the only family she had left. The duke, gentle and frail, was
like a kindly uncle. The duchess had treated her
like a beloved granddaughter from the beginning.
Philippa returned this love and devotion in full,
and she suspected that she understood the duchess better than anyone else did.

And she knew that the duchess was already very
suspicious of this new steward.

Mr. Edwards had been singing the man's praises
since hiring him last year, becoming almost rapturous at the prospect of installing him in Stone
Cottage, the steward's estate quarters. The more
glowing his reports, though, the more certain
Her Grace became that Mr. Edwards was trying
to conceal something terrible about the man. "I
have never seen Mr. Edwards this complimentary
of anyone," she complained to Philippa. "One can
only imagine what defects he is trying to conceal!"

As usual, the duchess was not quiet about her
apprehension. Philippa had heard there were wagers on how long the steward would last. Between
the duchess's expectation that she would have to

sack the fellow on sight and the raging curiosity of everyone from the laundry maids to the butler, the poor man might well turn tail and flee, no matter how ardently Mr. Edwards welcomed him.

What on earth could this Montclair be like? Philippa very much doubted Mr. Edwards, who'd had to argue long and hard to get permission to hire any steward at all, would have chosen carelessly.

In the gallery she met Emily Calvert. Miss Calvert had been engaged to marry Lord Stephen before his shocking and untimely death. As the anniversary of that tragedy was approaching, the duchess had invited the poor woman to the castle for a few days, to pay her respects.

Philippa liked Miss Calvert. She still wore black for Lord Stephen, and had dedicated the year since his passing to ministering to the downtrodden. Lord Stephen had been the vicar at St. Mary's, and Emily would have made an ideal vicar's wife. She was kind, patient, and gentle, and the most sympathetic listener Philippa had ever encountered.

"Have you seen Mr. Edwards?" she asked Philippa. "I've just had a letter from my mother. A tree has fallen on the school in Kittleston, and there is a large hole in the roof. I don't wish to trouble anyone," she added hastily. "It is only . . . I suspect he might not *know* what has happened in the village, and yet His Grace has always been so generous with his support."

"Of course," Philippa assured her. "He will wish to know, and I'm sure His Grace will wish to help. He will remember how devoted Lord Stephen was to the pupils there."

Everyone always spoke as if the duke made all the decisions. In reality, it was the duchess who had the ultimate word. *She* would remember Lord Stephen's passion for teaching the children his favorite classics, how he would leap upon a chair to roar at the ceiling like a demented King Lear, or creep around a door with a cloak over his head to portray the temptation of Doctor Faustus. He had been a great favorite in the village of Kittleston, especially among the children.

Emily wilted in gratitude. "I do hope so. His Grace is kindness itself, as is Mr. Edwards."

Philippa smiled. "I was in search of him myself. When I find him, I will tell him you wish a word."

"Thank you, Miss Kirkpatrick."

A footman directed her to the south lawn. Centuries ago it had been the bailey, but the duchess had transformed it into a walled garden, with a broad sun-bathed lawn at the center of it. Philippa used to have picnics under awnings here with her stepmother and other children from the estate.

She shaded her eyes to survey it, catching sight of two men walking around the wisteria toward her. One was Mr. Edwards, sober and familiar, the sun glinting off his spectacle frames. The other must be the new steward.

And he made Philippa stop in her tracks.

In spite of the duchess's fears, the new steward had not inspired a very radical image in Philippa's mind. A tall sturdy fellow, she'd guessed, the sort of man people would instinctively respect. Spectacles, most likely, from poring over ledgers all day. A brown suit—perhaps gray, but somehow Philippa was most certain about this detail. He might be stiff and hawkeyed or round and avuncular, but he would be somberly, plainly dressed.

This man looked like a pirate. His long dark hair, held back by his hat, flowed loosely to his shoulders. He wore a bright blue coat with white facings and a sea captain's boots. His waistcoat of rich yellow brocade wouldn't have been out of place at the French court. There was even—she almost gasped—a golden hoop in one earlobe.

And he was young, so much younger than she had expected. The duchess had muttered about Mr. Edwards engaging a "ramshackle young fellow" but "young" to the duchess meant forty, perhaps forty-five. This man could not have been more than thirty.

Mr. Edwards caught sight of her and raised one hand, causing his companion to look up. Philippa's breath stopped as she got a direct view of his face. Lean, tanned cheeks, a long nose, a sensuous mouth already quirked in a mischievous grin, and brown eyes that surveyed her with blatant interest.

He was handsome. Rakishly, devilishly, *dangerously* gorgeous.

Oh, the duchess was not going to like him.

"Miss Kirkpatrick," said Mr. Edwards as they drew near. "Allow me to present to you Mr. William Montclair, Carlyle's new steward. Montclair, this is Miss Kirkpatrick, Her Grace's dear confidant and companion."

Flustered, Philippa curtsied. "It is a pleasure, sir."

"Most decidedly mine, Miss Kirkpatrick," he murmured, sweeping off his hat in a grand bow.

"I was showing Mr. Montclair some of the grounds," Mr. Edwards went on. "He is already familiar with the plans of the estate, of course, but nothing compares to seeing it in person." He looked thoroughly pleased with himself.

"Ah." She tried to keep her attention on the attorney, but her gaze kept flitting back to Mr. Montclair despite her desire not to. *Do not stare,* she reminded herself sternly—something he had clearly forgotten, from the way his attention was openly fixed on her. "How do you find the castle, sir?"

One corner of his mouth curled, as if they shared a private joke. "Magnificent, of course. Mr. Edwards's descriptions barely came close." His voice was a rich, rolling tenor, tinged with a hint of French.

He dressed like a pirate, he looked like a rake, and he sounded like a Frenchman. The duchess was not going to like him *at all.*

"You shall have plenty of opportunity to judge for yourself," she replied with a smile, smothering that warning thought.

"I look forward to it." He winked at her.

Winked.

She jerked her gaze back to Mr. Edwards. "Miss Calvert hoped to have a word with you."

His brows went up. "She did?"

"Yes." Philippa could feel Mr. Montclair's eyes on her, which brought a responsive warmth in her face, and in consequence she kept talking when she should have let it go at the single word. "I met her in the gallery just now, and she was searching for you. On an important matter."

"I see," said Mr. Edwards in surprise. He turned to the man beside him. "Montclair, would you excuse me? I must see to this."

Philippa flushed harder, realizing she had portrayed Miss Calvert's errand as an emergency. "I am not sure where she was going from the gallery," she babbled. "She may have gone into the garden or toward the—" She stopped, biting her lip. *The crypt,* she'd almost said. Where Lord Stephen was buried.

"Of course," said the solicitor after a pause, now faintly puzzled. "I shall look in both places." He gave a brief smile, bowed, and walked off.

"Not a sweetheart, I take it," said Mr. Montclair in the silence.

"Sweetheart?" she repeated, startled.

He gave her a lazy, intimate grin. "That was the most animated I've ever seen Edwards. For a moment I thought to myself, *It must be his sweetheart he's pining to meet. The man has a heart after all.*"

She stiffened. "Of course he has a heart! He's a kind and compassionate man, very mindful of his duty—"

He shrugged. "He's a lawyer."

Philippa frowned at him.

"Is Miss Calvert the housekeeper?" Immune to her disapproval, he fell in step beside her as she turned back toward the house.

"No. She is a guest." She didn't look at him. Up close he was even more startlingly attractive, and a devil seemed to be smirking out of his dark eyes.

"A guest!" He made a soft noise of astonishment. "I was told the castle was virtually sealed to outsiders."

"Who told you that?"

"Edwards."

"He did not!" she exclaimed. "He would never say such a thing—"

"Not in those precise words," he conceded, "but I understood it just the same."

Never mind the duchess; Philippa didn't think *she* was going to like Mr. Montclair. "Then you understood wrongly, sir. The castle is merely remote. His Grace does not receive callers, and Her Grace prefers a quiet life."

"And?" he asked.

Philippa frowned again. "And what?"

"What about you? Do you receive callers? Or do you also prefer a quiet life?"

She stopped and gave him a severe look, one that would have done the duchess proud. "How on earth could that possibly concern you?"

He smiled at her guilelessly. "I merely wondered. The duke and duchess aren't the only people who live here. I'm responsible for the estate, you know, including maintaining the roads and buildings on it. How much abuse and wear do they take?"

For a moment she could only stare at him. The *impertinence.*

Ignorance, she decided, was the only excuse— extreme ignorance, which was not a good omen. He was not English and did not know how things worked here. He had only just arrived at the castle, which he *really* knew nothing about, and was already prying into things that were not his concern. She simply shook her head, thinking that he wouldn't last long after all, and walked on.

He stayed beside her. "Was that out of bounds?"

She said nothing.

He flashed his pirate's smile again. "I do beg your pardon, Miss Kirkpatrick. I meant no offense. It was just such a surprise to me."

"What was?" she couldn't keep herself from asking.

"Well . . . You."

She stopped in shock, staring at him again with wide eyes. "I, Mr. Montclair? Why on earth would *I* be a surprise to you?"

Again that innocently humble expression. Already Philippa didn't trust it. "Mr. Edwards told me only that Miss Kirkpatrick was the duchess's companion."

Her spine stiffened. "And you have already judged me lacking."

He put up both hands. "Not at all! You're . . . not what I expected."

Ah. "Of course. You must have expected someone older, someone more mature and dignified."

His head had begun nodding gently as she spoke, and now he gave a wide, relieved smile. "Just so."

"I understand," she replied. "I expected exactly the same of the new steward." His face blanked with surprise. She smiled in victory. "Jarring, indeed. Welcome to Carlyle, Mr. Montclair." She bobbed the faintest curtsy and walked away, leaving him alone in the garden.

Chapter Three

⸙

Mr. Edwards rejoined Will at the other end of the garden. "I beg your pardon, sir," he said as he came hurrying through the bailey yard.

Will smiled politely. Edwards *ought* to apologize for leaving him to Miss Kirkpatrick's mercy. It had been a long time since someone had put him in his place with elegant brutality—and even longer since such a beautiful woman had done it.

Oh, she did not like him at *all*.

"Miss Kirkpatrick kept me company," he said.

Sunlight flashed off Edwards's spectacles as he turned toward the castle. The woman in question was long gone.

"You might have warned me," added Will. "I fear I didn't make the best impression upon her."

"Why not, Mr. Montclair?" Edwards clasped his hands behind his back, looking for all the world like a tutor bent on making him explain a passage from Cicero.

"I didn't expect the duchess's companion to be such a young woman." He gave a guilty smile. "I couldn't hide my astonishment well enough."

For a moment Edwards just stared at him. "Yes, well." He coughed and cleared his throat. "Miss Kirkpatrick is not merely the duchess's companion. Her father married Lady Jessica, the duke's only sister, when Miss Kirkpatrick was a small child. Miss Kirkpatrick was raised here at the castle, and is very dear to both the duke and the duchess."

Will heard the message loud and clear. Miss Kirkpatrick was a member of the family, and Will had best treat her as such if he wished to remain.

Which he did. But curiosity was still gnawing away at him, and he might as well ask now while he could get away with it.

"And she left her parents to remain here? That's uncommonly devoted. The duchess must be very dear to her as well."

Mr. Edwards paused again. "Yes. Lady Jessica died eight years ago. Colonel Kirkpatrick was killed in India the following year."

"Good Lord," he said, taken aback. "How terrible."

Edwards was watching him. "Yes. She and Her Grace were a great comfort to each other in those terrible, terrible years, and ever since."

Chastened, Will nodded. "Is Miss Calvert also a family relation?"

Now Edwards turned away. "She was engaged to marry Lord Stephen at the time of his death. She is naturally dear to the family, and you may regard her almost as one of them."

"Of course," he murmured, thoroughly sobered. Such a lot of death.

Edwards picked up the pace. They walked through a gate and down a sloping road. "The stables are that way." The attorney indicated a path branching to the right. "They used to be within the walls but the third duke had them moved and expanded. He built an impressive stud farm."

"Is there?" Will was startled. He'd seen nothing about horse breeding in months of studying the Carlyle ledgers and estate plans.

"No." Edwards sighed. "It was all sold off over twenty years ago. But the stables remain. I will arrange to have the gig brought around to Stone Cottage for your use."

Will's gaze lingered on the cupola of the stable, visible over the ridge. It seemed a great many pieces of the estate had been sold or shrunk over the last twenty years. He'd seen the transactions but didn't know why. He'd thought Englishmen lived to expand their estates, not shrink them.

Stone Cottage was nearly a mile away. Next to the castle it was tiny, but to Will's eyes it was exactly right. Broad and squat, built of honey-colored stone with a thatched roof, it looked like a natural part of the landscape. Two peaked gables rose on either side of the front door, each housing three small windows on the floor above. A garden rambled in front of it, already bursting into verdant life.

"Mrs. Grimes, the former steward's wife, was very fond of this garden," said Edwards as he opened the gate in the stone wall. "I promised her I would put in a good word for its care."

Will looked ruefully at the plants, which were neatly clipped and tended for all the impression of wildness. "I've no idea what to do in a garden."

Edwards smiled briefly. "Perhaps Miss Kirkpatrick will continue her efforts, then. She has tended it since the Grimeses left."

That name pricked up Will's ears. "Please assure her she is welcome to do so as long as she pleases. I would be very grateful and solemnly pledge to stay out of her way and not harm a single plant."

Edwards still wore that curious little smile. "You may tell her so yourself, at tea tomorrow."

"Tea?"

"Yes. Her Grace wishes to see you. One o'clock."

He'd expected to meet his employer sooner or later, but only now realized he'd thought it would be later. Which was foolish, because he'd been in the duke's employ for more than six months. "I'll be there," he said heartily to cover his sudden qualm.

Edwards paused with one hand on the sturdy wooden door. "Be prompt, and be fastidious," he said, quiet and serious. "If you do not make a good impression upon her . . ."

"Shall I leave my trunk packed, just in case?" Will joked.

Edwards's mouth flattened.

Will's grin fled. "Yes, sir."

The attorney hesitated. "I have been very pleased with your progress so far," he said, with an air of choosing each word carefully. "Her Grace knows that, and she values my judgement. She is a canny and intelligent woman. However, she wished to have an older, more experienced steward, and if you give an impression of impulsive, ramshackle manners—"

"Right." Will nodded. "I understand."

"She will scrutinize every aspect," Edwards pressed. He paused, thinking. "Prepare as if you are about to meet the father of the lady you've fallen in love with, and desperately need to win his approval to marry her."

Will looked at him askance. As serious as all that? "I see."

For a moment Edwards searched his face, then sighed. "I hope you do."

On that encouraging note, he opened the door and stepped inside.

Will followed, feeling more apprehensive than he had since that day last summer when he accepted this position.

The cottage was simple, clean, and bright. The corridor ran straight through the house from front to rear, where the kitchen garden led to the kitchen itself. The sitting room was to the left, the dining room to the right. A comfortable office lay behind the sitting room, one wall lined with bookcases and cabinets. Edwards handed him a ring of keys, which unlocked the desk and cabinets. Upstairs there were three bedrooms, one large and two small; only the large room was furnished. All the windows had been opened, and the scent of soap lingered on the air.

"That's the sum of it," said Edwards when they had concluded the brief tour. "I will have the ledgers and other records sent down now that you are in residence. Mrs. Blake and her niece Camilla will do for you until you engage other staff."

Will nodded. The women were cleaning the kitchen still, and both had curtsied and eyed him with surprise. He supposed they'd also expected someone older. It was becoming apparent that he would need to make a concerted effort to win the confidence of people at Carlyle. "Thank you, Mr. Edwards. I shall ride out and see the estate tomorrow morning."

This seemed to please the solicitor. "I'll tell Ned at the stables to have your horse ready at eight."

"Make it seven." Will squinted at the sky. It was almost summer. The days were long, and began early. "My father would toss me out of bed for sleeping so late," he told the attorney.

Edwards visibly perked up. "Early rising is an excellent habit to instill in one's son."

Will laughed. "It only happened because he keeps the same deranged hours! My brother and I used to wish he drank more, and would need to sleep it off now and then."

"Ah. Your father is an abstemious man, then?"

Pa was active and driven, with the energy of five men. He didn't drink to excess because he always had something important to do, and no time to lie about in a stupor. He expected his sons to keep pace with him.

And thinking of him reminded Will that his activities were still a closely guarded secret from everyone in his family but Jack. It had been easy enough to conceal while he was still in London, but now he was ninety miles away. If Pa found out he was here instead of there . . . Lord help him.

"It's good for one's health," he said vaguely. "Ned is the groom?"

"Yes." Edwards's expression reverted to bland and dispassionate. "In a few days the stable here will be ready. It has been under repair, which took longer than anticipated, but for now, you have the Carlyle stables at your disposal."

"Excellent."

The attorney left and Will went back to the kitchen and set about making himself agreeable. Mrs. Blake was reticent, but Camilla was openly curious. She was a bright-eyed girl of about fourteen whose words tumbled out in an eager rush. It took only half an hour of amiable conversation, answering her questions about America and London, for Camilla to regard him with respectful awe. Will remembered being that age, and how enthralling any adult's attention was. Mrs. Blake's manner thawed dramatically as she listened to him and Camilla. She promised to leave a pot of stew for his supper.

"And I could come back in the morning, if you'll be needing breakfast," she offered.

Will waved that away. "There's no need to trouble yourself. I can feed myself."

She eyed him up and down. "Can you, now? Well, there's plenty to eat at the castle if you change your mind. Mr. Grimes always used to stop in there for a bite to eat."

He grinned. "An excellent idea. Thank you."

Helping himself to an apple from the basket by the door, he walked through the cottage again, making a more leisurely appraisal. It was the first time he'd had a house to himself, and even if this one didn't belong to him, it would be home for the next few months.

The sitting room was painted a cheery yellow and simply furnished. The office was less cheery, clearly designed for work, but just as bright. Most of the shelves were still full of books, as if the previous resident had only recently left.

Mr. Grimes, Edwards had told him, had been steward here for thirty years, and before that a tenant farmer himself. He had been born and reared on Carlyle ground and only retired when old age and ill health caught up to him. Edwards had waxed poetic—for him—about Grimes's breadth of knowledge, his experience, his acumen. Will eyed the thick tomes on animal husbandry with mild alarm before resolutely turning away.

He walked to the window, munching his apple. There was a splendid view of the western side of the castle. The late afternoon sunlight turned the weathered stone walls silver, making the crenelated towers look like points of a crown, rising in height to the easternmost tower.

Will's mouth quirked. Carlyle Castle, the crowning glory of the highest hill in the county.

He dropped into the chair and leaned back, propping his boots on the desk as he polished off the apple. What had he got himself into?

For over six months Edwards had been teaching him the structure of the estate and how it ran. Will had studied a multitude of maps, historical records of harvests and production, the family's history in the county, and lists of every tenant and servant on Carlyle property. He knew where all the family's income came from, what land they owned, and how much they spent. It had been more interesting than expected, but he was very glad to be at the castle at last. All that study had intrigued him until he was virtually bursting with curiosity, impatient to see for himself.

So far it had exceeded every expectation. The castle was magnificent, like nothing he'd ever seen in America, second only to the Tower in London. He'd spied a mere sliver of the vast grounds, rolling fields of emerald green with ancient forests and sparkling rivers, under dazzlingly blue skies. Only ninety miles from London, but a whole world apart from the city. Yes, he had been astonished at every turn.

Not least by the duchess's companion. Will had imagined Miss Kirkpatrick as a practical woman of fifty or so, always directing four or five activities at once and unwilling to put up with any nonsense. In hindsight he realized his mental image bore a distinct resemblance to his Tante Emilie.

The actual Miss Kirkpatrick was about the same height as Tante Emilie, but that was where the resemblance ended. She was probably a few years younger than Will, with glossy black hair and luminous brown skin. Her eyes sparkled golden brown and green under swooping dark brows, and her full mouth was soft and pink and tempting.

Will flung the apple core out the window and folded his hands behind his head. A faint smile touched his lips as he remembered her astonished expression at the sight of him. *And the same to you, mademoiselle,* he thought appreciatively.

Not that it mattered. He wasn't here to flirt with a pretty girl. Before he left London two days ago, Jack had reminded him of his promise. "You gave your word," he'd called as Will mounted his horse. "Only five months more."

If he survived meeting the duchess tomorrow, that was.

Chapter Four

❧❧❧❧❧

The new estate manager incited considerable curiosity at the castle.

From an upstairs maid, Philippa heard he looked like a pirate and was probably here to loot the castle. One of the girls in the laundry was sure he was a Frenchman, come to kill some Englishmen. The groom who brought her horse thought he had an air of the highwayman about him, from the way he rode.

Philippa thought all that was nonsense, but she did agree with the underlying principle. No one thought it possible that William Montclair was a mere steward.

One charge especially worried the duchess. "A Frenchman," she moaned over breakfast the following morning. "I knew nothing good would come of Mr. Edwards's inquiries in France! He has opened the door to charlatans and imposters, and we shall be deluged by them."

"Mr. Edwards says he has been perfectly honorable." Miss Calvert's face flushed pink. She did not usually contradict the duchess. "And he would never allow anyone he did not trust to have so much as a peek at Carlyle. I am sure Mr. Montclair cannot be disreputable, even if he is French."

The duchess harrumphed over her tea. "Pippa, what did you think of him? You have actually spoken to the man."

Philippa had been thinking about how to answer this question since yesterday. On the one hand, she was certain the duchess would not like him. But at the same time, she didn't want to poison the duchess's mind against him any more than it already was. Perhaps the man would recognize that he hadn't made the best impression yesterday, and adjust his behavior. "I agree with Miss Calvert that Mr. Edwards has had far more opportunities to observe Mr. Montclair. If he isn't concerned about nefarious motives, I'm inclined to wait and see."

The duchess's forehead creased in worry. "Are you?" Fretfully she sighed. "You are usually right. I shall keep an open mind about this young man—he *is* very young, is he not? Mrs. Potter said he looked almost a boy."

Philippa tried not to picture the steward's wicked, knowing smile. "I assure you, ma'am, he is a grown man."

Very handsomely grown, at that.

Flustered, she put down her teacup. "He is old enough to be capable of doing excellent work. That is surely the most important thing."

The duchess sighed. For a moment she looked tired and careworn, though her erect posture never faltered. Philippa wondered in alarm if the duke's health had taken another bad turn. The last year had been very precarious for His Grace. He'd been plagued by a dry cough for weeks now, much as had happened last fall, but everyone hoped the spring weather would revive him.

"I shall withhold judgement," said the duchess at last. "I suppose I have no choice! But at least we are to meet this man at last. I have invited him to tea this afternoon."

Philippa glanced up, startled. "Have you?"

"Yes." The older woman's spirit seemed to revive. "At one o'clock in the Blue Drawing Room. Will you come?"

"Of course." She hoped Mr. Edwards had advised the man how to prepare for this interview.

Emily Calvert's hand fluttered nervously. "I—I do not think I should attend. Please forgive me, Your Grace, I—"

"Of course, Miss Calvert." The duchess waved one hand to forestall her.

The visitor heaved a tremendous sigh of relief. "Thank you, ma'am."

The duchess rose from the table. "I must see to the duke. If it continues fine, we may want the carriage for a drive later. Fresh air would do him good."

Philippa nodded. It probably would, but the duke rarely agreed to go, despite his mother's hopes.

The duchess left, and Emily turned to Philippa. "I didn't offend her, did I?"

Philippa smiled and reached out to pat the woman's hand. Emily had lost weight; her fingers were thin and cool. "Not at all. You've no need to meet the new steward."

Emily bit her lip. "I don't wish to seem ungrateful . . ."

"Of course not! You are very welcome at Carlyle."

This did not appear to comfort the other woman. "I am out of place here," she said in a low voice. "While Stephen lived, it was easy not to think of the castle much. He assured me he meant to stay on in Kittleston, even after—" She stopped, flushed and miserable.

Philippa looked down at her plate. *Even after the duke's death,* she meant. If Stephen were still alive, he would be heir to the estate, still visit every month and bring laughter to the castle corridors. If Stephen still lived, the duchess would not need to spar with Mr. Edwards over the new steward; she would leave that to Stephen, and occupy herself with the duke's care, or perhaps with spoiling a desperately wanted grandchild.

"But now that I've been here and seen it, I know that would have been impossible," Emily went on. "He would have been needed here, and I would have come with him and done my best to step into Her Grace's shoes, yet . . . it would have been a disaster." Her gaze flitted helplessly around the duchess's sitting room, with the elegantly carved furniture unholstered in sapphire silk, the lush carpet on the floor, the fine paintings on the walls. "I would make a terrible duchess."

"I've no doubt you would have risen to the challenge," said Philippa stoutly.

Her companion gave a thin smile. "I would have despised every moment. I miss Stephen dreadfully, and always will, but . . . Not this."

Emily would make a wonderful vicar's wife, kind and patient. Managing a household the size of Carlyle, however, was a very different matter. "I doubt anyone could ever fully replace Her Grace," she replied, trying to be diplomatic.

Emily smiled ruefully. "You're the only person who could ever come close."

Philippa gave a soft *tsk*. "Alas! Both Captain St. James and Mr. St. James are already wed. I have missed my chance." Captain St. James was the current heir presumptive, and his cousin Maximilian stood next in line behind him.

Finally Emily laughed. "That is their loss."

Philippa rolled her eyes, but with a smile.

"I'm returning to Kittleston," Emily told her. "This afternoon. Her Grace was very kind to have me, but I should go home."

"I understand." Philippa couldn't resist adding, "Would that I could go with you! That's the perfect excuse not to meet the new steward."

This time Emily's smile was tinged with mischief. "I did think of that benefit as well."

WILL URGED GRINGOLET faster up the hill, past the turnoff to Stone Cottage, past the stables. He was going to be late.

The horse's hooves clattered on the stones as he rode through the archway into the courtyard. He flung himself out of the saddle and scanned the area even as he tore off his coat and tossed aside his hat. He knew the kitchens were behind him, but he wasn't sure about the rest. Good Lord, this place was enormous.

And he was definitely late.

He fumbled his watch out of the saddlebag, where he'd tucked it for safekeeping. His father had presented it to him before they left Boston,

with an admonishment never to make others wait
for him. Only twenty minutes before meeting the
duchess. *Be prompt and be fastidious,* echoed Mr. Edwards's words ominously in his head.

Will tucked the watch back into the bag with a
grimace. He would be lucky to be either of those
things today.

There was no one about. Stomping his boots in
an effort to shake off most of the mud, raking open
his neckcloth and stripping off his waistcoat, Will
strode to the pump and worked it furiously. When
the water gushed he bent down and ducked under
it. He pumped again and splashed his arms, scrub-
bing at the blood. He stood and flipped his hair out
of his face with one hand, and beheld a maid, staring at him with astonished round eyes.

He grinned uneasily. "Ahoy there. Do you
know where Mr. Edwards can be found?" Her
mouth opened in a perfect *O,* but no sound came
out. "William Montclair, at your service," he said
quickly, with a brief bow. Water ran down into his
eyes and he swiped it away. "Have I met you yet?"

The basket in her hands hit the ground with a
thud. "M-Mr. Montclair?" she stammered, her eyes
flitting up and down him.

Will kept his smile even as he realized he looked
like a murderer on the run, covered in blood and
mud. "The very one. Mr. Edwards . . . ?"

She blinked. "Oh. Oh my, sir! Yes, I—I'll fetch
him." She bolted toward a door across the courtyard, leaving her laundry spilled on the flagstones.

Christ. He was going to be both late and un-
kempt. He looked down at himself; his shirt was
soaked, clinging to him even though the water

hadn't washed out the blood. He yanked it from his breeches and began wringing the tail.

"Mr. Montclair!" Mr. Edwards was almost running toward him, his expression set in furious disbelief.

Will held up one hand. "The bridge four miles from here—"

"Did I not tell you to be prompt and *fastidious*?" The lawyer's words cut like a whip. "What in the name of God do you mean turning up like this? Her Grace is expecting you!"

"That's why I came here." Will continued wringing out his shirt. "Going back to Stone Cottage would have taken too much time. There was an accident on the bridge, and a wagon on the way to market tipped and fell in. I came upon the farmer and his wife trying frantically to save their pigs."

Edwards paused. "The bridge on the south road?"

Will nodded. "Near the Smith farm."

Edwards swore, which astonished Will. He'd never heard the lawyer say such a thing. But then Edwards sprang into motion. He rushed to the nearest door, opened it, and shouted, "Frank! Come at once!" He turned and spied the laundry maid, lingering in the background, watching avidly. "Tell Mr. Heywood I need a fresh suit of clothing for Mr. Montclair immediately. And shoes. Go! Run!" he barked at her when she hesitated, eyes flickering toward Will. She fled, and Edwards turned back to him.

"We have only a few minutes to make you presentable," he said grimly. "Take off that bloody shirt."

Will yanked the sopping shirt over his head. "Someone must be sent to bar the way," he tried to say as Edwards herded him into the laundry. The two maids within looked up from their ironing, goggled at Will in shock, and rushed out at Mr. Edwards's furious gesture.

"I will see to that," snapped the lawyer, shutting the door. "First we must prevent you from being dismissed. The boots, man."

By the time a footman rapped on the door and brought in a clean suit of clothing, Will was standing in nothing but his breeches, drying his hair with a towel Edwards had snatched from a nearby cabinet and thrown at him.

"Here." Edwards handed him the clothing. "You're much the size of a footman, let us hope it fits."

Another footman came in with a pair of shoes in each hand. Edwards motioned at him, and without a word the two servants advanced on Will.

Edwards watched them dress Will in silence, only once speaking. "Is that blood on your face?"

His chin raised for the footman to tie the neckcloth, Will croaked, "Yes, sir. Some of the planks splintered, and the horse—"

"Wash it off," Edwards ordered one of the footmen, who did so in silence. Will hadn't been manhandled like this since he was a child and his mother scrubbed him.

But in a matter of minutes, he was once more clean and dressed, in shoes that were only a bit too small.

Edwards looked up from his pocket watch to inspect him. "It will have to do," he said on a sigh. "Come."

Will scrambled to catch up as they crossed the courtyard toward the front of the castle. "The horse had to be put down. It was their only horse, though, and I want to lend them one from the stables—"

"Yes, yes." Edwards opened a door and waved him through. "To do that, you will have to retain your post." He led the way into a corridor of such beauty and elegance, Will would have stopped and stared if he'd had time.

Hustling along, Will wondered if this wasn't a little ridiculous. Surely the duchess would understand. It was her tenant farmer he had stopped to help. "I thought it more important to help in a moment of crisis. Mrs. Smith was up to her waist in the river—"

"We will deal with that later." Edwards turned up an enormous stone staircase and took the steps two at a time. Will followed, wincing as the pinch of the shoes became a little more strident. They raced down another corridor, through four connected rooms until, in front of a tall, ornate door, he stopped, and Will plowed to a halt as well. The lawyer lowered his voice. "Mr. Montclair. This is not a moment for levity. I am not exaggerating when I say your employment depends entirely upon this interview. Do you understand?"

He cleared his throat, suddenly wary. "Yes, sir."

Edwards gave him a searching look. "Very good." He rapped at the door, straightened his shoulders, and a moment later a footman swept it open.

Chapter Five

❧⚶❧

Even before the doors opened, Will told himself not to gawk—only to stumble in awe the moment he stepped into the chamber behind Mr. Edwards. It was magnificent beyond anything he'd ever seen or imagined in his life.

The walls were covered in a pattered blue silk, but mostly covered by paintings, right up to the ceiling—which was a work of art itself. Twenty feet above, it was carved and embellished with shields and animals and things Will couldn't even identify. A pair of stone pillars stood like guardian sentinels at the sides of the room, dividing it, and Will realized that, unlike the other rooms he'd seen, this one ran from outer wall to inner wall, with windows looking over the countryside to the east and windows facing west into the courtyard. Those windows, arched and deep set, were the only hint that the room had been built hundreds of years ago.

At the far end was the fireplace, a massive chimneypiece of white marble with ornately carved wood surrounding it. In front of the hearth was a low round table, with a delicate sofa and three chairs arrayed around it. And in front of the sofa stood the duchess.

Will spotted Miss Kirkpatrick as well; she was to the duchess's left, breathtaking in a jade green gown. He could have happily gazed at her more, but today he dragged his attention to the elderly lady who would decide if he stayed or went.

Judging from her expression, his chances were not good.

She was very petite, no higher than his chest, but plump. Her gown and her hair were, he recognized, in the latest London fashions, but both were also unrelieved gray, save for the white lace at her neck. Her dark eyes narrowed as she looked him up and down, and Will realized at once that Edwards had not exaggerated: he was in very deep trouble for arriving to this appointment with his hair wet, wearing a footman's clothes.

Mr. Edwards stopped and swept a formal bow. "Your Grace, allow me to present Mr. William Montclair."

The duchess's lips pursed as Will made his own bow. "Your Grace," he murmured. "Miss Kirkpatrick."

The old lady regarded him for a long moment, then turned and fixed an icy glare on the attorney. An entire conversation seemed to pass in that look. But all she said was, "Won't you sit down?" as she sank onto the sofa.

Will hesitated, but Edwards stepped back, indicating with a slight tip of his head that Will should take the chair directly opposite her. Feeling like he'd just been shown into the dock for his trial, Will sat down. He tried to catch Miss Kirkpatrick's eye, desperate for any sign of encouragement or help, but she was arranging her green skirts around her. A plump orange cat strolled from beneath her chair, back arched, and she leaned down to shoo the animal gently away.

He sat upright, shoulders squared, and met the duchess's gaze directly. *Face your fate like a man*, Pa would say.

The duchess stared right back at him, ignoring the other two people entirely. "Miss Kirkpatrick," she said, "will you ring for some tea?"

"Yes, ma'am."

Will had forgotten how lovely her voice was. His gaze strayed her way as she rose and went to the cord pull hanging at the side of the hearth. A long curl of dark hair draped over her shoulder, calling attention to her neck. Delicate, slender, her skin warm bronze against the white ruffle of her gown. She did not return his gaze.

"Mr. Montclair."

He snapped his gaze back to the duchess. "Yes, ma'am."

Her head had come forward as she scrutinized him. "Are you wearing livery?"

He cleared his throat. "Yes, there—"

"And your hair is dripping wet," she continued.

As if on cue a drop slid down his temple. Will didn't dare wipe it away.

The duchess's eyes narrowed. "Were you not apprised of this appointment, Mr. Montclair?"

"I was, ma'am—"

"Have they no manners in America? No, I am sure they do not," she answered herself before he could even open his mouth. "Do you not possess suitable clothing of your own?"

He darted a glance at Edwards, whose expression was unhelpfully blank. "Yes, ma'am," he tried, but again she cut him off.

"And yet you have arrived looking like a footman. You have been employed as the steward here for seven months, sir, and I *believed*"—she shot another dagger-like glance at Edwards—"that you were being adequately instructed on every aspect of the position. If this is how little care you take with your own appearance, I do not care to consider how you treat your responsibilities to this estate."

This time he waited a moment to be certain she was done. Then he leaned forward and met her gaze evenly and defiantly. "My own garments were ruined in the course of rushing to the aid of a tenant farmer who tried to cross an unsafe bridge. The planks broke, injuring the horse and tipping a load of young pigs into the river. I had to change into this"—he gestured at his clothing—"because my own perfectly appropriate attire is lying in the courtyard, soaking with mud and covered in blood."

"Blood!" she gasped.

Will nodded. "The horse was fatally wounded, and Mr. Smith was too shaken to do what needed doing. I had to put down the poor suffering beast before jumping into the river to help save the pigs. Mr. Edwards did warn me to be prompt and tidy, but I could only achieve one of those goals, and—as you can see—I chose to be prompt." He bowed his head. "I hope such accidents are not routine on this estate, but I could not leave Mr. and Mrs. Smith in such distress merely to arrive in clean garments. Ma'am," he remembered to add.

Then he sat back to await judgement.

Thunderous silence filled the room. The soft click and whir of a clock made everyone start.

"Were the pigs saved?" asked Miss Kirkpatrick.

He darted a glance her way. "All but one."

She was finally looking at him, her expression contemplative. "I am glad. Thank you, Mr. Montclair, for helping them."

His temper was still in full flow. "If that bridge had been kept in good repair, none of it would have happened."

That would probably get him dismissed, even if the rest didn't. Will didn't care. If the duchess expected him to put more care into dressing for her approval than into the actual job he'd been hired to do, then it was only a matter of time before he got sacked anyway.

"Well." The duchess didn't seem to know whom to glare at first. She chose Mr. Edwards. "Were you aware of this bridge, which is obviously a danger?"

"I was not, ma'am. I believe it is a little-used bridge—"

"And yet now it needs significant repair." She turned back toward Will. "Can it be repaired, or must it be rebuilt?"

He flexed his hands on the arms of the chair. "I wouldn't trust it without a thorough examination by a surveyor. The stream beneath looks like it's grown since the bridge was put up, and there is considerable erosion around the piers. I suspect relaying the planks will be no more than a temporary measure."

"Hmm." She was still watching him sharply, but now it was more measured. "Let that be your first task."

He nodded once. "I would also suggest a prompt survey of all the other bridges, on Carlyle land and in the village of Kittleston. I don't recall any recent engineering reports in the estate records, and the failure of a bridge can have dire consequences—as this one did."

Her brows went up, but she sat back. "Yes. Do that."

"And I wish to send a horse from the stables to the Smiths," he continued. "Until they can procure another of their own. The loss they suffered today was . . . deeply distressing." Mrs. Smith had sobbed and called the doomed animal Billy. Mr. Smith's hand had been shaking so badly he couldn't pull the trigger, and Will had had to take the pistol and end Billy's agony.

Her brows rose further. "A horse?"

"If they have no horse, they cannot take their goods to market or clear their fields. If they cannot do those things, they cannot pay their rents. Leaving them without a horse is the same as expelling them from the property." Will set his jaw. "And their horse was killed on Carlyle grounds by a bridge Carlyle maintains—or ought to have maintained. So, yes, ma'am, I believe we owe them a horse."

The duchess's wide-eyed gaze moved to Mr.

Edwards. The attorney shifted in his chair. "It is a reasonable and compassionate thing to do, Your Grace. I agree with Mr. Montclair."

"Yes." For a moment the duchess said nothing. The sunlight glittered off her jeweled rings on her fingers as she picked at her skirts.

Thankfully the maid came in then with a large tray of tea. Everyone seemed grateful for the interruption. Mr. Edwards cleared his throat and sent Will a piercing look, which he didn't know how to interpret. Miss Kirkpatrick smiled warmly at the maid as she arranged the tray on the table. And the duchess frowned down at her hands, still fussing with her dress.

For his part, Will felt as though the weight had lifted off him. He'd spoken his mind, and if she dismissed him, well, at least he'd done what was right.

Miss Kirkpatrick prepared the tea. Will watched in silence, oddly interested in the ritual. The tea dishes were a vivid, glowing red with gold rims. They looked like fine jewels instead of mere cups and saucers. She poured a splash of milk into one cup, then the tea. This she handed to the duchess. For Mr. Edwards she poured more milk and added a piece of sugar from the bowl. The attorney thanked her quietly.

Then she glanced at Will. "How do you take your tea, sir?"

He stirred uncomfortably. "Any way you please, Miss Kirkpatrick."

Her brow quirked, but she didn't press. She poured no milk and added sugar before handing him the cup and saucer. Will held it gingerly while she prepared her own the same way.

The duchess had been watching him. "Mr. Montclair," she said, raising her cup for a sip. "You are from America."

"Yes, ma'am."

That seemed to restore her. Her gaze grew sharp once more. "This must be very different to what you are accustomed to there."

Without thinking his gaze flitted about the room. "It is," he said wryly.

Again she shot a furious look at Mr. Edwards. "Perhaps you will do me the courtesy of persuading me you are up to it."

What followed was more probing than any examination he could remember by a tutor or even by his father. She quizzed him on details of the estate, principals of management, everything from how to set rents to how to select tenants. For the first time Will was glad Edwards had kept him in London for seven months—studying for this encounter, he now realized. It seemed to go on forever, but it was surely no more than half an hour before the duchess sat back with a faint "Hmph," and held out her cup.

Had he passed? He glanced at Miss Kirkpatrick, but her expression was pleasantly bland as she took the cup and set it back on the tray.

Of a sudden, the duchess rose, and Will and Mr. Edwards leapt to their feet as well. Her Grace gave him one more up-and-down look, then said, "I will see you again in three days, Mr. Montclair. I expect to hear more about these bridges. Good day."

The men set down their cups—Edwards's empty, Will's untouched—and bowed. When they reached the corridor and the door was safely shut behind him, Edwards exhaled.

"I think that went well," said Will, his heart still racing. "She expects me to be here still in three days."

Edwards gave a startled huff of laughter, and clapped him on the back. "Yes, my good man, I think you did well enough. Though I wouldn't recommend repeating this entrance."

Will grinned and looked down at the livery he wore. It was at once grander than anything he owned—fine green wool with gold lacing and gleaming buttons—and humbler, the garb of a lower servant. No wonder the duchess had looked down her snub little nose at him. "Next time I'll be bringing word about those bridges, which might not make me any more welcome."

Edwards's smile lingered. "No, no, bring the survey. I believe you have impressed Her Grace more than you know."

THE DUCHESS WILTED the moment the door closed behind the men. "Oh, Pippa," she said with a worried sigh. "What am I to do?"

Philippa fixed her another cup of tea before she answered. "It sounds to me as though he did the right thing, helping the Smiths. I'll visit them tomorrow."

"Do, do." The duchess sipped her tea. "But to arrive here like that! Where did he get a footman's livery?"

"Mr. Edwards must have procured it for him."

Her Grace made a noise of distress. "One can only wonder how he appeared before that!"

He'd mentioned blood. Philippa's stomach dropped at the thought.

"Still, he does appear well-informed, doesn't he?" The duchess sounded anxious again.

Indeed, he did. Philippa was as surprised as the duchess at his quick and easy responses to her every question about the estate. His appearance, in footman's livery with his dark hair slicked back, dripping wet, from his face, had thrown her, but obviously had not shaken him. His outrage at the accident had been evident, as well as his concern for the Smiths.

"I approve of his concern for the Smiths," she said. "He could have ridden back and sent others to help, instead of staying to help himself."

"Do you think it was an excuse?" The duchess frowned.

"I shall ask Gerald and Jilly what happened."

"Yes, do," said the duchess in relief. "If he is a liar—"

"I doubt it," said Philippa. "Much too easy for him to be caught out."

Somehow she knew it would be as he said. William Montclair was much more than he appeared.

Chapter Six

❦ ❦

Everyone had been curious about William Montclair before. Now that he had walked through the courtyard shirtless and dripping wet, he was all every female at Carlyle could talk about.

"Whipped it right off, ma'am, over his head! Daisy and Phyllis said they'd never seen the like," marveled Marianne, Philippa's maid. "It's the most excitement they've ever had in the laundry."

"As well-made as one of them wicked Greek statues," reported Josie from the kitchens. "We were all pressed up against the glass, trying to spy a look."

"A very healthy young man," even Mrs. Potter allowed, obviously forgetting her previous disapproval.

Philippa heard all this with a mixture of skepticism and irritation. How had every woman in the castle somehow managed to be present for the sole minute of near-nudity in the courtyard? And how was it possible they all agreed that the improper, sinful sight had been entirely worth it?

It must be the novelty and surprise, she decided.

Any other servant who stripped to his skin would be dismissed without a character. There was a dearth of young and attractive men at Carlyle, and the newcomer, handsome even when fully clothed, had already seized their attention.

Philippa did wish they would stop talking about it, though. It was enough to make her wish she'd seen it herself.

She set off in the gig. The Smiths were a young couple, only married last year, but their families were longtime Carlyle tenants. Philippa had known Jillian and Gerald for years. They had both come to the picnics years ago, when the duchess had worried that Philippa didn't have enough contact with other children.

On her way she passed Stone Cottage. Only the chimneys were visible over the hill and trees, and she wondered what Mr. Montclair was up to today. Perhaps he would spy a drowning child in the course of his bridge inspections, and plunge into yet another river. If he arrived back at the castle courtyard dripping wet for a second time, there would be open cheers and applause from the kitchens and laundry.

She blew out a breath, annoyed with herself. He had acted nobly. At least, it appeared so. It would be very disappointing if the Smiths told a different story.

A pair of chickens came out to greet her as she climbed down from the gig, followed by Jilly Smith herself. A smile lit up her face when she spied Philippa. She shooed away the chickens and dropped a curtsy. "Good day, Miss Pippa."

Philippa returned it. "And to you, Jilly. We heard

of the terrible accident yesterday, and Her Grace wished me to inquire how you and Gerry are."

"That's very kind." Jilly's smile wobbled.

Philippa touched her arm in comfort before asking carefully, "Mr. Montclair was there, I believe?"

"Thank goodness he was!" Jilly's face shone. "He come flying 'round the bend right after it happened. Gerry took a hard knock on the head, miss, he were still shaky, and Mr. Montclair, he jumped straight into the river and come out with a pig under each arm." She shook her head. "He stayed until all the pigs were out of the water, and Billy—" She stopped, her eyes welling.

"Yes." She clasped Jilly's hands. "The duke has ordered an immediate survey of every bridge on the estate. No one had any idea it was so dangerous."

Jilly nodded. "Gerry's been worried about it for a while, but we were already late, because two of the pigs got loose. It's the fastest route to Kittleston, and so we thought, we'll chance it. But then—" Her chin trembled, and she snatched up a corner of her apron to dry her eyes.

Again Philippa pressed her hand. "You shall have a horse from Carlyle as long as you need one."

Jilly nodded. "Mr. Montclair brought 'un this morning. Gerry—please, ma'am, don't be angry," she added anxiously. "Gerry was in a rare temper about that bridge."

"I don't doubt it."

"I told him to mind his tongue," Jilly pressed on. "Mr. Grimes didn't like to be spoke to that way, but Gerry wouldn't listen. He was proper angry when Mr. Montclair arrived. I—I don't want there to be any offense, Miss Pippa."

So the steward had got an earful from Gerald Smith. Philippa pictured the pirate who sat forward in his chair, wearing a coat borrowed from a footman, telling off the Duchess of Carlyle. She wondered how he had taken being challenged himself by a tenant farmer.

After her visit with Jilly, she decided to see the bridge for herself. It was out of her way, but she knew she was on the right road when she encountered a board nailed to a tree with *Bridge Out* hastily painted on it. With a cluck to the horse, she continued down the road.

Two men stood on the bridge. Gerald Smith was unmistakable, from his sturdy farmer's build to the mop of brown curls that shook as he brought down an axe on the planks of the bridge. The other man was taller and leaner and had his back to her, a stack of broken planks on one shoulder. Gerry put down his axe and shaded his eyes as she drove nearer, and Mr. Montclair turned around.

Philippa's heart jumped a little. He had only discarded his coat today, but his sleeves were rolled up past his elbows, and the white shirt certainly made his shoulders appear broad. At the sight of her, he walked to a waiting wagon and heaved in the planks, then waited for her to reach him.

"Miss Kirkpatrick." He made one of his sweeping bows. Philippa wondered if all Americans did that. "Have I forgotten, and missed, another vital appointment with Her Grace, and you've come to scold me for it?"

"No, Mr. Montclair." She set the brake. "I came to see the bridge myself."

A slow grin curved his mouth. "Excellent."

She secured the reins and took his hand to step down. His hand was bare, and Philippa felt the warmth of his grip through her gloves. Without thinking she gave her hand a little shake as soon as he released her. He noticed and looked away, still grinning.

Gerry bowed as she came near, and she greeted him warmly, still irked at Mr. Montclair. "Dear Gerry. How lovely to see you again, even if for such a terrible reason. I'm so relieved you and Jilly weren't injured."

He blushed bright red. "Aw, Miss Pippa— Miss Kirkpatrick—no, we weren't hurt, but this bridge—" He stopped abruptly. "It's been in need of repair for some time, Miss."

"It's falling apart." Mr. Montclair picked his way back to the hole in the bridge deck, reached down, and wrenched up a board with one hand. He held it up. "I ought not to be able to pull off pieces with my bare hands."

Philippa was trying not to look at his bare hands, or his bare forearms, or the way they flexed when he ripped the bridge apart. "I imagine not," she managed to reply. "What must be done?"

Gerry cleared his throat and shuffled his feet. "It could be repaired . . ."

"It ought to be torn down and rebuilt of stone. This stream is too variable for a wooden bridge." Mr. Montclair came back to the ground and threw the broken board atop the pile in the wagon.

She nodded. "Mrs. Smith said you've already brought them a horse."

He nodded toward a pair of horses hobbled and

grazing some distance away. "The gray. Jemmy in the stables calls him Atlas."

"He looks very strong," she agreed.

"He'll pull this back for us, then go home with Smith for a month or so." He slapped the wagon.

She nodded. That was generous for him to propose, but no less than the Smiths deserved.

"Miss Kirkpatrick."

She looked up at him. He was staring toward the bridge, face screwed up against the sun. Tiny wrinkles fanned out from his eyes, as if he smiled a lot. Perhaps he wasn't as young as she'd thought. "Might I ask a direct question?"

"Oh, haven't you done so all along?" she murmured. He shot her a sideways look, and she returned a bland smile. "By all means, sir."

He gestured at the bridge. "Does the duchess expect me to examine every other bridge on the estate in three days' time? There are nine thousand acres, miles of road, and at least a dozen bridges."

She raised one brow. "Do you think she didn't mean it?"

He went still. "That's not what I said."

Philippa's other brow went up. "If you happened to be *thinking* it, let me assure you that yes, she did mean it. She will expect to hear something about all dozen bridges, if for no other reason than to prove you know where they all are and visited each one. Are you not up to the task?"

He listened in silence, his jaw flexing once or twice. Then he turned and looked directly at her. For a moment they just stood there, locked in some kind of silent combat, until he leveled that dangerous pirate's grin at her. "Never say that, Miss Kirkpatrick. I'm up to any task you set me."

Philippa thought she might go up in flames. "Excellent," she said breathlessly.

Gerry Smith joined them with another armload of planks to toss into the wagon. "That's the broken ones. Shall I nail some up to bar the way?"

Mr. Montclair finally looked away from Philippa. "Aye. It won't stop boys from climbing across it, but I don't want another horse going through."

Gerry's throat worked as he took the unbroken boards. "No, sir."

"I'll be inspecting every other bridge on Carlyle land to be sure none are dangerous."

"The one on the Northampton road," supplied Gerry, to Philippa's surprise.

Mr. Montclair nodded, listening.

"There's one two mile north of here. I don't trust it, either." He scratched his chin. "And south of Kittleston, over the Nene. I don't think it's on Carlyle land, proper, but if the castle were to put in a word—"

"So many?" exclaimed Philippa. "Are they all in disrepair? How can that be?"

Gerry went silent. His gaze dropped and his neck turned red.

"It's a fairly simple process," said Mr. Montclair, folding his arms. His bare forearms were bronzed by the sun. Apparently the man regularly walked around without all his clothes on. "You begin by ignoring them, and then continue not repairing them, and sooner or later any bridge will begin to crumble."

She flushed. "But why so many?"

He raised his brows in an exaggerated haughty expression. That, she supposed with growing irritation, must be how he thought she looked at him. "You ignore them *all*, and then they *all* begin to crumble—"

"Yes, I understand," she snapped. "But Mr. Edwards . . ." She stopped, remembering Mr. Edwards spent half his time in London. "Mr. Grimes would never allow such neglect, and he was here only two years ago!"

Mr. Montclair slowly raised his shoulders, then his hands, regarding her expectantly.

Philippa's temper ignited. "Are you saying *Mr. Grimes* neglected them?"

Gerry shuffled his feet. "He were getting on in years, Miss . . ."

Yes. He had been. The duchess held Grimes in very high regard, though. "And Mr. Edwards?" she demanded, changing attacks. "Did he also neglect the estate?"

"You speak of the Mr. Edwards who spent most of these past seven months in London?" Mr. Montclair fired back.

She wanted to hit him—even more so because he was right, curse him. "I cannot believe it's so bad as that," she said through her teeth. "This estate is well tended!"

Mr. Montclair rocked back on his heels. "And do you inspect it frequently, Miss Kirkpatrick?"

Her hands were in fists. It was a wonder he hadn't burst into flame from the fury in her stare. "I live here, sir! And unlike you, I am not just arrived from God knows where!"

"You know where," he said, clearly enjoying how angry he'd made her. "America. Where, I strongly suspect, bridges require much the same care as they do here."

"As if you would know, since you've been here all of two days!"

Gerry cleared his throat. Both Philippa and Mr. Montclair started. The farmer had shuffled backward, his head down like a turtle's. "Miss Kirkpatrick, perhaps you ought to show Mr. Montclair about. You knowin' the estate so well, and him with fresh eyes to see it . . ."

From the surprise on Mr. Montclair's face, this was not a welcome suggestion to him. In part of her brain, Philippa knew it wasn't welcome to her, either. It wasn't her duty to show him around.

But her temper was roused, and she was furiously indignant that he would cast such aspersions upon Carlyle. She faced her nemesis and spoke before he could. "Perhaps I should. As a stranger here, Mr. Montclair cannot know the estate and its people, no matter how many ledgers he has read. He is no doubt sorely in need of the advice of someone who does know Carlyle." She smiled at the frown that flickered across his face. "Or perhaps he doesn't need anyone's advice. After all, he *has* seen bridges in America."

His mouth thinned. He faced Gerry. "An excellent suggestion, Smith. Miss Kirkpatrick's wealth of knowledge would be invaluable." He slapped the side of the wagon. "Take the debris back to the stables. They'll be expecting it."

Gerry nodded and fled. Philippa guessed he'd regretted coming off the bridge to speak to her at all, from the way he began pounding nails into boards blocking the bridge.

Mr. Montclair headed toward the hobbled horses. Philippa blinked at the blatant dismissal. "I have no desire to punish you with my presence, if you find it so distasteful," she called after him.

He stopped, turned, and strode back toward her until she had to tip back her head to meet his gaze. "Not at all, Miss Kirkpatrick," he said in a low voice that sent ripples of awareness over her skin. "I would be delighted to have the honor of your company, and extraordinarily grateful for the benefit of your extensive wisdom about Carlyle. Shall we ride out tomorrow morning at seven?"

Philippa blinked. "Seven?"

"As you said, there is much to inspect, and not much time to do it." Something of his devil-may-care expression came back, and his voice dropped even lower, until she could feel it resonating inside her chest. "But I've no desire to punish you with my early hours, if you find them so distasteful."

This man. Her shoulders went back; her chin went up. "Seven," she agreed.

He bowed low, but Philippa sensed he did it to hide another pirate's smile. Trying not to feel as though she'd just walked into a trap, she stalked to the gig, climbed in, and drove back to the castle without once looking back.

WILL UNDID THE hobbles and harnessed Atlas to the wagon, reviewing the conversation inside his head and finding three different ways he could have responded to Miss Kirkpatrick's barbed words that didn't result in her accompanying him on his tour of the estate.

He had set himself some strict guidelines for these months at Carlyle. Mind his own counsel. Do what he was paid to do. Eyes and ears open, to learn what he could, but mouth closed, to keep his own secrets.

Ha. He blew out a breath, annoyed at himself. Yesterday he'd all but told off the duchess and now he'd provoked Miss Kirkpatrick.

The trouble was, he'd seen the way she smiled at Gerry Smith. Her face seemed to glow when she was happy, her dark eyes shining, her eyebrows arching gracefully, her perfect, gorgeous mouth curving to display the little dimple in her cheek when she greeted him . . . That smile had upset at least two rules inside Will's head. He wanted to see it again.

Smith came back and hooked his hammer on the edge of the wagon. "I hope I didn't cause trouble."

Will did the last buckles on the harness. "Not at all. I welcome Miss Kirkpatrick's insight." He began rolling down his sleeves. "You seem well acquainted with her."

The man flushed again, but with a hesitant smile. "Aye. My wife, Jilly, was often invited to the castle, so the young lady would have some other girls as companions. Now and then they'd have a picnic or some such at the castle, too, and invite all the tenant children."

Will fastened his cuffs. "I've got on her cross side, unfortunately."

Smith coughed. "Aye."

Will waited, but the farmer said nothing more. "Have any advice for me, then?"

The other man put on his coat. "Don't slight the estate management. She won't take it well."

He looked up in surprise. "Is she that devoted to Grimes and Edwards?" From what he could tell, Grimes should have retired several years before he did. Edwards regularly remarked how pleased he was to delegate the responsibility to someone else, which Will interpreted to mean he had never wanted it in the first place.

Smith shrugged. "She's fond of 'em, aye, but . . . Her Grace is why Grimes lasted so long as he did, and why it took Edwards two years to hire another steward. When you speak ill of them, Grimes and Edwards, Miss Pippa hears a condemnation of Her Grace, and there's few things more likely to stir up her temper. She's fiercely devoted to Her Grace."

Will pulled on his coat. That explained how infuriated she'd been. She was gorgeous in a temper. She'd looked like a flame today, in an apricot-colored dress with vivid embroidery that made her skin glow like polished copper—and like a moth, he seemed to spiral around her in fatal fascination.

"Besides . . ." The other man's tone softened. "I 'spose none will tell you, but you ought to know— Miss Pippa runs this estate. Aye, Her Grace has final say," he acknowledged at Will's startled glance. "But Miss Pippa knows Her Grace's mind better than anyone, and Her Grace trusts her entirely."

Ah. "What of the duke?"

Smith's expression shuttered. He climbed aboard the wagon. "Don't know, sir."

Will had been trying for months to find out why the duke was never involved in any decision about the estate. Edwards had said His Grace was unwell;

Will was beginning to wonder if he actually existed. There were no letters from him, no list of instructions, not even word passed through Edwards. Even here at the castle, he'd seen nothing at all of the man's presence. Edwards avoided every mention of him, and now Smith did, too.

"About Miss Kirkpatrick," he said, to forestall Smith driving away. "Why is she so devoted? She's not a blood relation, I believe . . ."

Smith smiled. "Nay, dearer than blood. When Lord Stephen died last year, there was no more chance of an heir from the family. Miss Pippa's the nearest thing to a granddaughter Her Grace has got, or ever will have. And since her father died, she's got no one else here in England. Her Grace is all the family *she's* got."

"I see," murmured Will. "Miss Pippa?"

Smith flushed. "That's as we called her years ago, when we were young." He released the brake and tipped his hat. "I don't advise *you* call her that, though."

Will laughed. "That, I already knew."

Smith grinned and drove away. Will went to retrieve his own horse, who had wandered along the banks of the stream in search of tender spring grass. He couldn't let himself be caught off guard by her again.

A very interesting day lay ahead of him tomorrow.

Chapter Seven

❦ ❧

When he reached the castle the next morning, she was waiting.

A groom held a pretty brown mare. Gringolet tossed his head and nickered, and the mare responded with a flick of her tail, turning away. Will grinned. Even her horse disdained his.

"Good morning, Mr. Montclair." Miss Kirkpatrick stepped forward, tapping her crop against her dark orange riding skirt. "I had begun to despair of you."

"I never leave a lady disappointed, Miss Kirkpatrick." He jumped off his horse and swept a grand bow, just to see her lips twist. She thought him ridiculous and he took an irrational amount of pleasure from it.

"Well. As you said, there's a great deal of land to cover, and no reason to stand about." She headed toward the mounting block, and Will took advantage of the chance to admire her as the groom helped her mount.

She looked exceptionally fine this morning, which caused him equal shares of appreciation and consternation. Her saffron yellow riding coat nipped in snugly around her waist, which looked very small in comparison to the fullness of her skirt. Elaborate scarlet embroidery decorated each cuff, and followed the bottom of the jacket. There was a fluff of gauzy fabric at her throat, sheer enough to give a glimpse of her skin. A star-shaped gold brooch set with rubies and pearls secured it. He'd seen ladies riding in London, pale creatures in dark green and brown. The cut of Miss Kirkpatrick's garments was unmistakably English but the vibrant colors had to be Indian, and they suited her.

What was he supposed to do when she walked around looking like that?

At the sight of him standing staring, she raised that imperious brow. Her dark eyebrows were more expressive than any others Will had ever seen. He fancied he could tell her mood just from the set of them.

"Are we not to go on horse, sir?"

He blinked. "What?"

She turned her head and sighed impatiently. It fluttered the ribbons on her hat, a black ruffled thing tilted above her dark curls. "Do you intend to walk?"

"No." He shook off his fascination and vaulted back into his saddle. "Off we go."

Last night he had pored over maps of the estate until he was confident he knew where every bridge was, from the wide stone archway in the road leading to the castle to the meanest footbridge over a trickling stream. He turned the horses north.

"Aren't we going to see the bridges Mr. Smith

mentioned yesterday?" asked Miss Kirkpatrick in surprise.

Will smirked. "I went to see both of them yesterday, since Smith thought them in urgent need of repair."

"And?" she prompted a moment later when he said no more. "Are they?"

He nodded.

"How much repair? Are they a danger to anyone? Did you have to close them? Have you already sent men out to work on them?"

He pretended to be taken aback. "My word, Miss Kirkpatrick, I was not prepared for this level of examination!"

She flushed, her dark eyes snapping. "Forgive me, sir, I presumed you would know the answers to such obvious questions."

"I do know the answers," he said with dignity. "I did not expect *you* to demand them."

He was fairly certain she wanted to use her crop on him. "And why not? As you took the trouble of getting me to ride out with you at sunrise—"

"The sun rose nearly two hours ago," he murmured.

"And insisted you would welcome my company as well as my *extensive wisdom* about the estate, I trusted that you would behave like a gentleman and speak honestly and courteously."

"A gentleman!" He laughed. "I've no idea what the English consider gentlemanly. Is answering every question one is asked an important part?"

She pulled up her horse. "Mr. Montclair. Is this all a monstrous waste of my time?"

He circled around her to keep his horse moving.

"Another riddle I cannot solve. Am I now to place a value on your time and how you spend it?"

She closed her eyes. Her eyelashes were dark sweeps across her cheeks. Her mouth was a thin line of aggravation. When she opened her eyes and glared at him, he thought he might be singed. "Permit me to offer a small piece of well-meant advice. It may sound witty to your own ears to parse every word I say, but if you treat Her Grace with such impertinence, you will be sacked on the spot—deservedly so."

Will stopped his horse and leaned over the saddle toward her. "Forgive me, Miss Kirkpatrick, but do you speak for my employer? No one warned me of that, and in any other circumstances I would be reticent indeed to discuss my employer's business with anyone but the employer himself."

She took a deep breath and slowly let it out. With great effort Will kept his gaze on her face, and not on the rise and fall of her bosom. Damn, she made a handsome figure on horseback. "Carlyle is a vast estate. Her Grace naturally relies upon trusted people for independent views and thoughts."

"It is a large estate," he agreed. "Was Grimes not trusted?"

Miss Kirkpatrick blinked. "Of course he was."

"And Mr. Edwards?"

"Very much so!"

Will nodded thoughtfully. "Then how can it be that neither of them told the truth about these bridges?"

Her perfect pink lips parted in astonishment.

"Smith is correct. Repairs should have been made years ago, and on many buildings as well. The mill two miles from here—I understand that serves the estate?" She nodded warily. "It also needs extensive work. At least half the tenants I've met are in need of something or other, and most of them confess it has been needed for some time. You're about to ask if they told Grimes or Edwards," he said as she opened her mouth. "Several of them did, and all were put off. Next year, they were told, and then another year. Patch it back together and go on as best you can. So they have been, but eventually things fail, and when they do, there can be terrible consequences, as we both saw yesterday."

She bit her lip, her expression troubled.

Will recalled what Smith had told him. If Miss Kirkpatrick was effectively in charge, he'd just called *her* derelict, which he hadn't really meant to do. *Let that go*, he told himself. He folded the reins into one hand and sat back to disguise his next query. "Why doesn't His Grace undertake personal oversight of things?"

Miss Kirkpatrick still appeared deep in thought. "She does," she murmured. "I—I suspect, perhaps, people didn't tell her the worst because no one wished to worry her overmuch." She looked up sharply. "Were repairs not done for want of funds?"

He wondered if she hadn't heard him, or if she had deliberately answered about the duchess instead of the duke. "No. The estate is prosperous. You must ask Edwards why nothing's been done." He wondered why himself. Edwards was neither foolish nor lazy.

She looked at him, no longer piqued or impatient, but honestly, her brow wrinkled in real concern. "How much must be done?"

He hesitated, soothing his horse as Gringolet
restlessly tossed his head, straining to reach the
grass at the side of the path. "Shouldn't I discuss
it directly with the duke? It's his estate. If people
have shied away from burdening the duchess,
perhaps—"

"Mr. Montclair, there's no reason for you to speak
to the duke."

"Why not?" Will leapt on the chance. "Is he completely disinterested?"

She reared back as if he'd struck her. "Why
would you think that?"

"Because I have yet to hear anything directly from
him in seven months, either in person or in a letter.
It seems passing strange that he wouldn't want a
look at the man hired to administer his estate. The
duchess, after all, had me in for inspection the day
after I arrived, and that after the steady stream of
letters of instruction she sent me in London."

The letters had been sent to Mr. Edwards, but he
had passed them on to Will after the first month.
They appeared to be in the duchess's own hand,
with her small, neat signature at the end. They
were always couched in the language of *His Grace
desires* or *His Grace wishes*, but from the duke himself, there was nothing.

Miss Kirkpatrick's horse chose that moment to
become restive, prancing to one side and shaking her head. The lady ducked her head to run
one hand along the horse's neck, murmuring and
clucking to her. It took a few moments to settle the
animal, even though she'd stood calmly enough as
they spoke. By the time the mare was under control, Miss Kirkpatrick was as well. Will wheeled

his horse to fall in beside her, wondering if she had jarred her mount to avoid answering his question.

"You needn't worry about His Grace," she said just as he decided she meant to ignore it. "Nothing is done without his approval."

"And he doesn't wish an introduction, even briefly?"

Her poise was back. She looked at him, one eyebrow arched. "Why would he, sir?"

Will said nothing.

"You were engaged to manage this estate. By your own account there is a great deal that needs doing. I advise you to get to it, instead of pining for an interview with His Grace." She darted another glance at him. "After your astonishing appearance before the duchess, I wonder that you desire another such meeting."

His mouth flattened. She knew perfectly well why he'd arrived in footman's clothing. But he heard the real message in her words: he wasn't going to meet the duke—ever. And no one was going to tell him why.

He touched his heel to his horse's flank to pick up the pace. "As you say, ma'am."

PHILIPPA GRIPPED THE reins so tightly it was a wonder Evalina hadn't bucked her off. Why did he want to meet the duke?

Mr. Edwards must have told him how things stood, but Mr. Montclair apparently didn't believe it. Every chance he got, he brought up His Grace, all but prying for information he didn't need. Philippa made a mental note to tell Mr. Edwards he must deliver the message more forcefully.

This was a bad beginning. Mr. Montclair had blown into Carlyle like a hurricane, upsetting the long-standing equilibrium of the entire estate. He'd made a terrible hash of meeting the duchess. By now everyone in the county probably knew how he'd stripped almost naked in the courtyard and gone to meet Her Grace wearing a footman's coat and breeches. The fact that he'd still managed to look like a pirate captain in them was probably not as well-known, but Philippa knew. No one would ever mistake this man for a servant.

But she had to admit he did seem to know what he was about. They reached the first bridge after half an hour's ride. It was a sturdy stone structure and looked perfectly sound to her. The steward, though, jumped off his horse and climbed all over it, even shucking his boots and stockings to wade into the river to study the underpinnings.

"I did not think to bring a towel," she said as he clambered back up the muddy bank.

"Fortunately, I did." Feet bare, he went to his horse and rummaged in the saddlebag. "Learned a thing or two from my adventure the other day," he added with a wink.

Philippa looked away, wishing he couldn't make her blush with just a look. He must be a rake, or a rogue—one of those London creatures who exerted a deadly pull on innocent women and made them forget themselves. She'd read the lurid stories in the newspapers but had never met one. She stole a quick glance at him as he bent down to pull on his boot. Her gaze lingered on his backside; the coattails had fallen to the side. She wasn't in the habit of staring at men's posteriors, but it must be true, what the girls in the laundry said, even if he'd still had his breeches on then—

With a start she jerked her head around. He *was* a devil; all he'd done was stoop to put on his boot and she—a respectable, modest woman—couldn't stop staring at him inappropriately.

Shod once more, he went back to his horse and took a notebook from the saddlebag. He flipped it open and began to write with a stub of pencil.

And he wrote. And wrote.

"Goodness, sir, what do you see?" she finally asked.

"What do *you* see?"

Philippa looked at the bridge. "It's old," she said cautiously.

"Not so very old." He scribbled away.

She frowned and stared hard. It was a simple stone bridge with three arches, only wide enough for one wagon. The path over it had probably once been stone but was now packed earth. "Is it something hidden beneath that caught your attention?"

He closed his book. "Not hidden. Look closely."

She urged Evalina forward, beginning to feel very stupid as she got closer and closer and still saw nothing wrong. She could feel him watching her. His gaze felt piercing and hot upon her back as she searched for the weakness that had apparently been so obvious to his eye.

Their argument of yesterday echoed in her mind. *This estate is well tended,* she had insisted, but with no good reply to his taunt: *And do you inspect it frequently, Miss Kirkpatrick?*

She did not. She managed the castle and oversaw

the accounts. She read Edwards's reports to the duchess and answered his questions about what was to be done—which had never included requests for significant repairs. She visited the tenants once a quarter, and no one had said anything to her.

Clearly what she did wasn't good enough; her inattention had led to disaster. If Philippa had taken the time to tour the estate more often, she might have realized more work needed doing. The duchess was resistant to radical innovation, but she did believe in keeping things in good repair.

Philippa paused on that point. Had the duchess's opposition to improvement kept Grimes and Edwards from suggesting them?

She dismounted and walked onto the bridge, determined to see what Mr. Montclair had seen. She had already disappointed the duchess's faith in her, and wasn't about to let it happen again. She ran one hand over the parapet, and mortar crumbled away. "It's coming apart!"

"A bit." He was right behind her. Philippa started in spite of herself. He reached around her and dug out a bit more with the tip of his finger. "This can be replaced. It's the cracks in the pier that worry me more."

"The pier?"

He rested his elbows on the parapet beside her and leaned forward to look down. Gingerly Philippa did the same. Several feet below rose one arch of the bridge, with the river running docilely through it.

Mr. Montclair took off his hat and leaned over more, until he was more upside down than right-side up, one arm outstretched as he pointed. "See the cracks snaking up the side, between the stones? I fear they run deep and threaten the soundness of the pier. If the pier fails, the whole bridge will fall."

Philippa leaned farther. Her toes were barely touching the ground. She did see the cracks, but they wouldn't have caught her eye if he hadn't pointed them out.

But Grimes or Edwards should have noticed, or at least tasked someone with monitoring them.

"Grimes's records show only minimal repairs to anything in his last several years as steward," Mr. Montclair was saying. "There were floods a few years ago in Northumberland that swept away several bridges. I don't want that to happen here."

Yes, she'd heard about that. It had seemed apocalyptic, and very far away. "What is to be done?"

He rested his chin on one arm and regarded her. "Hire an engineer to inspect the lot, and then surveyors and workmen to make the repairs. And have it inspected regularly, to keep it in good condition."

She turned to look at him. Hanging over the edge of a bridge was far from dignified—his long hair had escaped the tie and was in a tousle over his face. She must look as disheveled. "Excellent plan," she said on impulse. "I daresay no one anticipated you would need to undertake such a large task immediately."

One corner of his mouth went up. "Why wait to make your mark?"

Why, indeed. Without thinking she touched his hand where it gripped the parapet. "Thank you for your kindness to the Smiths."

For a moment his gaze met hers. He was very still, his expression unreadable. Then he gave that sly pirate's grin, his brown eyes glittering with mischief. "Don't suggest I'm not a worthless cretin after all."

Philippa snatched her hand away and lurched upright, smoothing her hair back into place and re-pinning her hat. "*That* is still in question. I merely acknowledged that you displayed some compe-tence, which is all the more welcome for being so unexpected."

He laughed as she marched back to her horse. "'Tis the kindest thing you've ever said to me, Miss. I shall treasure those words in my heart."

Philippa said nothing. The moment she started to respect him, even perhaps *like* him, he had to ruin it.

Evalina had wandered toward Mr. Montclair's horse, and now the two of them were side by side munching grass. When Philippa collected the reins and tugged her away, Evalina tossed her head and tried to prance sideways into the geld-ing. Both horses nickered at her irritably. Philippa fumed silently. Even her horse was taunting her. She clicked her tongue and tugged again, and Evalina came away with a saucy swish of her tail.

Then Philippa realized she had a problem. There was no mounting block, nor any stump or stone nearby. This bridge was at a wide point in the river, connecting two level expanses of grass.

She flushed. She could mount her horse from the ground, but it wasn't the most graceful pro-cess and involved hiking up her skirts an indecent degree. The very last thing she wished to do now was flash her legs at Mr. Montclair, who would no doubt stand there smirking at her.

"Shall we?" He had gone to his horse and swung atop it with disgusting ease.

Philippa glared at the pommel on her saddle. "Just a moment." Hopefully he would ride on and she could mount while he wasn't looking.

"Ah." There was a thump, and then he peered around Evalina's head. "A bit of a problem, eh?"

"No," she snapped. "I can manage."

He ducked his head. "Of course. I apologize for making light." He cleared his throat. "May I?"

To Philippa's surprise he went down on one knee and extended his hand. He caught sight of her face and turned away, but not before she saw the flush on his cheekbones. When she didn't move, he tapped his knee. "Step up."

It was the most dignified solution. She gathered her skirt and crop, gripped the saddle, and set her foot on his knee before springing up. "Thank you," she said without looking at him as she settled her skirts.

"It was my honor, my lady."

"I'm not a lady," she said evenly, nudging Evalina forward. "Do not address me that way."

He rode up beside her. "I was raised to treat all women as ladies. I'll not take a whipping because the English have some rule about who is and who is not a lady."

She glanced sharply at him. "Who would whip you?"

He grinned. "My mother, if she discovered it. If I vow never again to be so respectful, will you promise not to tell her?"

Philippa's mouth set. "Is everything a joke to you, Mr. Montclair?"

"No. I am mercilessly somber about putting this estate back into good form."

"Back!"

"It's been neglected," he said, unrepentant. "I do apologize if that offends you, or the duke and duchess, but it's the truth. If the duke wants someone who will lie and assure him all is well, he's got the wrong man and might as well sack me now."

She gaped at him. "Lie!"

"I won't," he said firmly. "Not when it comes to the safety and well-being of the people and creatures who depend on the castle."

"No one has asked you to lie!"

"Good."

By the time they returned to the castle several hours later, she was more than ready to bid him farewell. He leapt down and was at Evalina's side before she could maneuver away. Silently she let him help her down. Philippa was cross and out of sorts even before he made another flourishing bow and gave her a cocksure grin. With a curt nod, she handed Evalina's reins to the groom and went inside.

She tried to cool her temper while she changed. The duchess would expect a report on the excursion. What could she say without losing her temper and ranting about Mr. Montclair?

She could praise his work ethic and energy. In just a few days he had been all over the estate; numerous people hailed him as they rode, and most seemed admiring. At every stop he made copious notes in his book. Philippa hadn't questioned him after the first time, because he had already impressed her by spotting things she had not, and because she didn't think he'd tell her anyway. And she did give him credit for freely admitting he was still learning, despite his obvious familiarity with Grimes's records—lacking though they clearly were.

The thought of Mr. Grimes made her hesitate outside the duchess's sitting room door. Her Grace had been fond of the man, who had been at Carlyle as long as the duchess herself had been. When he had first broached retirement, the duchess had urged and cajoled him to stay, until two years ago when his health irretrievably broke down. Philippa remembered the dismay that event had caused; now she wondered if the duchess ought to have listened to the man and allowed him to step aside when he first asked, several years before.

No, she wouldn't mention any of that today. Nothing could be done about it anyway, as Grimes was comfortably pensioned off at a cottage near the coast, and Mr. Montclair was attacking the problems with his shocking but effective blunt force manner. She tapped on the door and went in.

"Oh goodness, there you are at last." The duchess was pacing the room, wringing her hands. "Come in, Pippa dear."

"What is wrong?"

"France." With that dire pronouncement, Her Grace plucked Percival, her big ginger cat, off the sofa and sat down. The cat curled up on her lap and stretched up one paw to touch her chin, making her smile reluctantly.

"Oh my." Without being asked, Philippa rang the

bell. Word from France necessitated tea. "There is . . . progress?"

The duchess gave her a fulminating look. "Progress would be hearing nothing at all!"

Philippa asked the maid to bring extra cakes with the tea.

"I knew this would happen," said the duchess after the maid had left. She flung out one arm in despair and pressed a handkerchief to her face with the other. "I knew it! And yet Mr. Edwards persists in poking into things. I hope he is satisfied when this entire estate is snarled in controversy and nothing can be done with any part of it!"

"So he's found someone?"

It wasn't an exaggeration to say that everything hung upon the news from France. The duchess had known since Stephen's death that there might be an heir to the dukedom in France, but she had stubbornly refused to confront the possibility, for several reasons.

First was that a French heir would revive one of the biggest scandals of the century. Nearly a hundred years ago, Frederick St. James had married a French heiress, Anne-Louise de Lionne, whose godparents included the French Queen Marie-Thérèse. The marriage between the beautiful but spoiled seventeen-year-old bride and the arrogant heir to the dukedom of Carlyle was an arranged one, undertaken in a complex and ultimately futile attempt to ease hostile relations between England and France. To no one's surprise, it was also a complete disaster. Anne-Louise bore three sons before fleeing back to France, taking her middle child, Thomas, with her.

Frederick vilified his wife as an adulteress and a thief before banning her name on his lands. On one infamous occasion, he'd had several servants whipped for spreading rumors that little Thomas was really the son of a French diplomat, and that Frederick had been cuckolded in his very own bed.

The duchess, who'd wed Frederick's eldest son, George, described Frederick as a cold and harsh man. She confided to Philippa that she sympathized with the long-gone Anne-Louise, who would have been her mother-in-law. What she could not forgive was the kidnapping of Thomas, whoever his actual father had been, because by English law Thomas was the next heir to Carlyle.

No one had seen or heard from him since he disappeared eighty-seven years ago. The duchess was sure that was proof enough that he was dead. Mr. Edwards relentlessly pointed out that if he had legitimate male descendants, they would also be heirs—what's more, heirs who would supplant the two English cousins already located and prepared for the inheritance, Andrew St. James and Maximilian St. James.

That was the second, larger, reason for the duchess's despair. She had slowly warmed to the idea of one of them inheriting the title and estate; despite initial low expectations, they'd both impressed her eventually. A French heir meant all that effort and work with them would have been wasted, and her hopes dashed again.

In response to Philippa's query, the duchess sighed and pressed both hands to her temples. "No, there is not definitive word from France. Only another possible lead, another possible connection.

It is a steady ominous drumbeat, approaching footsteps that never materialize into an actual person." She set aside Percival and lurched to her feet to begin pacing again. "If only that whole country would go up in flames!"

"No," said Philippa at once. "Surely not."

The duchess wilted. "Of course I don't wish that. I only want a definite answer!"

Philippa said nothing, knowing that she only wanted a *specific* definite answer. "What did Mr. Edwards hear?"

"There it is. I am sick to death of it." The duchess waved one hand at a letter on the table.

Philippa read the letter, which was a report from the investigator Mr. Edwards had sent to France.

"He survived," she said softly—amazed. Anne-Louise had returned to her father's home with her son and lived there for a few years. Her family had favor with the French king, but fell from grace after Louis XIV died. Anne-Louise and her son had disappeared for several years. But the investigator had found evidence that Thomas grew to adulthood; he was listed in a French cavalry regiment, when he would have been about twenty-two.

"Survived! Did he marry? Did he have a son? Those are the only questions that matter." Tea had arrived while Philippa read, and the duchess handed her a cup.

"It will take time to discover. It was many years ago."

The duchess sighed fretfully and drank her tea.

Philippa folded the letter and put it aside. "How is the duke today?"

"The same." Her voice trembled.

Oh dear. "I spent the morning with Mr. Mont-clair," she said to change the subject.

The duchess's head snapped around. "Yes, of course. Did he arrive in some sort of masquerade dress?"

She smiled. "No, he was dressed in a very ordinary manner."

"And was he insolent? I will sack him if he spoke one cross word to you!"

"No, ma'am. We visited several bridges today." She hesitated, reminding herself to keep her personal irritation to herself. The duchess didn't need anything else to worry about, including another argument with Mr. Edwards about the estate manager. "I believe he's working diligently and carefully. He worries that some aspects of the estate would have benefitted from more maintenance, and he wishes to remedy that as quickly as he can."

"More maintenance! Such as?"

"One bridge collapsed," Philippa pointed out. "It's hard to argue about that. I'm sure he will have a detailed list when he comes tomorrow."

The older woman sighed, stroking Percival. "No doubt. And when he has all in order, a Frenchman will wander in and take it all."

"Daadee." Philippa moved to sit beside her. "Let's not worry about that before we must."

The duchess clasped her hand as if it would save her from drowning. "I fear that day is fast closing in upon us, Pippa."

Chapter Eight

❦ ❧

Will soon discovered that the bridges were only the beginning of what needed attention at Carlyle.

Several roads had become dangerously rutted and overgrown. The mill needed work, all the drainage needed to be overhauled, tenant houses needed new roofs, new chimneys, new wells. At times it felt like he had traveled through some mystical veil and found himself in the middle of an estate untouched for thirty years, which was utterly perplexing.

He located a large map of the estate and put it up on the wall, pinning additional notes to each site of what needed doing there. He hired an assistant, the miller's youngest son, who had an aptitude for figuring and wrote a very neat hand. He set Josiah to reviewing Mr. Grimes's estate reports for any other repairs or improvements requested but undone, adding those to his large master map as Josiah found them. Before long the map was covered with notes, some spots bristling with three or four.

His report to the duchess on the bridges kept him up late, checking and double-checking his notebook and various records left by Grimes. This time he made certain to arrive in his own clothing, scrupulously clean and early.

Mr. Edwards gave him a severe scrutiny before his shoulders relaxed. "I am relieved to see you met with no death and destruction on your way to the castle, Mr. Montclair."

"As am I," Will replied.

This time he felt much better prepared. A friendly maid in the laundry had been all too happy to answer questions when he brought his clothes for washing, so now he knew that the duchess had been a great heiress in her youth, that she had a kind heart even if her temper could be short, and that her word was law at Carlyle. He also learned that the duke was never seen, but that the duchess doted upon him. The maid Daisy freely confessed she hadn't seen him in at least two years. "Frail-like, I think he is," she'd said in a conspiratorial voice. "Phyllis says he can't walk on his own and needs one of them chairs with wheels."

Will thought about this as he followed Edwards through the corridors. Today he was able to take in the grandeur of the place, from the ornately carved woodwork that covered the lower half of the walls to the enormous canvases that hung above it. The floors changed from black and white marble squares to polished parquet, with thick, beautiful carpets covering vast expanses of it all. Will had a feeling he'd only seen a sliver of the castle's splendor.

This time Edwards took him in a different direction. "This is the Tapestry Room," he said as they reached a closed door. "It is one of Her Grace's favorite rooms in the castle. You should count it a good sign that she wished to receive you here today."

Will grinned. "I count it a good sign that she's receiving me at all."

Edwards's lips twitched. "As you should, sir." He put back his shoulders and rapped at the door. Almost at once it opened in the gloved hand of a footman, who ushered them inside and then quietly slipped away.

This room was smaller, more intimate, but no less impressive than the drawing room. As befitted its name, the walls were covered in tapestry that looked ancient to Will. Knights on horseback jousted and hunted stags while maids in veils looked on. Leopards and roses, which Daisy had told him were the badges of Carlyle, were everywhere, meaning the tapestries had been woven for the family. The upper windows were stained glass, lending a jewel-like color to the light that was reinforced by the reflection in the large mirror above the fireplace. The furnishings were still fine, but less formal than in the drawing room. Tea was already waiting on the table.

As before, Miss Kirkpatrick and the duchess stood awaiting them. The duchess looked the same. Miss Kirkpatrick wore a string of pearls with a pendant around her neck, and a gown of pale green that looked soft and gauzy, as if she'd be very pleasant to hold in one's arms.

Will yanked his gaze away from her, unsettled by that thought. He bowed low to the duchess as Edwards made the greetings. Today, as before, he took the seat directly across from the older lady while Miss Kirkpatrick and Edwards moved discreetly but definitely to the sides. Miss Kirkpatrick poured tea.

"How did you find the bridges?" Her Grace fixed her small dark eyes on him.

"All of them in need of repair, to some degree." Will ignored her indrawn breath as he set his untouched teacup on the table and opened his notebook. "I would like to have a surveyor and an engineer appraise them to gain a more detailed assessment." He held out the list he'd prepared.

The duchess gazed at it as if it might bite her. Miss Kirkpatrick leaned forward in her chair and took it. She bent her head, a frown knitting her brow as she read.

Will cleared his throat. "In addition to the bridges, other parts of the estate require attention. I've begun a survey. Between the roads, the mill, and the farms, it will take some capital to improve."

The duchess recoiled. "Improve!"

"Yes, ma'am."

"I did not ask you to improve," she snapped. "Only repair."

Will gazed back unflinchingly. "It would be a waste of time and money to repair as they were, instead of bringing them up to modern standards."

Her eyes narrowed, and the look she gave Mr. Edwards was positively venomous. She sipped her tea and said nothing.

"Surely it wouldn't be a waste." Miss Kirkpatrick laid a delicate stress on the last word. "Perhaps . . . inefficient?"

"Highly inefficient." He sensed this was for the duchess's benefit and went along with it. "And still expensive. If it were my property, I'd never spend so much without expecting substantial improvements."

The duchess puffed up in outrage. "It is *not* your property," she said coldly. "It is the duke's and he wishes only to make repairs."

Miss Kirkpatrick sighed and closed her eyes for a moment. She folded the list and held it out. Will stared; was that all the attention it was to receive, after the immense effort of producing it within three days? Apparently so. He put it back in his notebook and snapped the book shut. "Very well. If that's all you wish done, that is all I shall do."

The duchess looked at him suspiciously. "And?"

He glanced at Miss Kirkpatrick, wishing she would help, but she only gave him a disgruntled look. "And . . . what, ma'am?"

"That's all?"

For a moment they stared at each other. Will had no idea what she wanted to hear. "Yes," he finally replied. "If you don't wish to discuss improvements, there's nothing else to say."

She turned her displeased glare on the attorney. "Mr. Edwards, a word. Mr. Montclair, you are dismissed."

For a moment he thought she meant permanently, but Miss Kirkpatrick cut her eyes toward the door. Hoping she meant to explain, Will rose and bowed, then left.

In the corridor he let out an aggravated breath. *Don't improve. Only repair.* Of all the idiotic ideas. What was the point of clearing drainage ditches when, with just a little more work, much better ones could be dug? Perhaps he didn't much care if he got sacked and went back to London early . . .

The door opened behind him. For a moment the duchess's voice floated out, high and angry. "—Not what we agreed! I asked for a sensible, mature man, and you bring me *this* fellow—"

Miss Kirkpatrick closed the door. Her cheeks were flushed—very beautifully, he thought. Now that he was about to be dismissed from Carlyle Castle, there was no harm in appreciating how lovely she was.

"Did you listen to a single thing I said the other day?"

Oh Lord. The flush was anger. Will clenched his jaw. "Every word, ma'am."

"Do you recall that I warned you not to be impertinent to Her Grace again?"

He straightened in real affront. "How was I impertinent? I delivered the report she requested, and it was cast aside with barely a glance."

"I read it!"

"And dismissed it."

Color suffused her face. "I have not!"

"Even so, you clearly are not making the decisions. *It is not your property, it is the duke's,*" he mimicked. "*Only repair.*"

Miss Kirkpatrick's hands were in fists. "I *tried* to guide you in the proper way to present it to Her Grace, but apparently you do not need anyone's advice!"

She had. Will began to regret not feeling his way along more carefully. He tapped his notebook against his thigh. "Why can nothing be improved?"

She took a deep breath and slowly let it out. "She was taken off guard by your assertion that nearly everything on the estate needs repair and improvement. I warned you—"

"Yes." He jerked his head once. "Yes, you did. I ought to have listened. I apologize."

That seemed to disarm some of her fury. The pink remained in her cheeks, but her scowl faded and she smoothed her hands down her skirts. Unthinkingly Will's eyes tracked their progress. He sensed he was about to be sacked—may already have *been* sacked, and Edwards would emerge at any moment to deliver the news—and recklessly thought he might as well savor his last sight of Miss Kirkpatrick.

"She has a great deal to worry about," she said, "and many competing concerns. This comes as a terrible surprise to her, not only on its own merits but because it means those she trusted have let her down."

Still annoyed, still helplessly entranced by the woman in front of him, Will shrugged. "I fear, if anything, I've understated the matter. This estate might have been stopped in time as it was thirty years ago."

Notably, she didn't argue. "How much can things have really changed? Perhaps, in the course of repairing, some improvements might be made that . . . well, that aren't so very obvious."

"Are you suggesting I act against her express orders?" Even through the closed door, he could still hear the duchess's angry tones, excoriating the attorney—or rather, Will by proxy. "Am I not being sacked soon enough for your taste?"

Wrath kindled in her eyes, but a housemaid chose that moment to hurry past. She paused mid-stride to curtsy, and Miss Kirkpatrick nodded in reply. As soon as the maid was gone, she made a sharp motion to Will, who followed her to a win-dowed alcove overlooking the formal gardens.

"Telling her it needs improvement sounds to her ears as a reproach, for letting things deteriorate," she explained in a low voice. "You must frame it differently. She isn't obstinate, only hesitant."

"Hesitant? She's scourging Edwards's ears right now. Miss Kirkpatrick, you must admit that is not mere hesitation."

She flicked one hand irritably. "She won't sack you. But you would make your own life consider-ably easier if you attempted to understand her, sir."

He stared. "How on earth am I to accomplish that? I've spent less than an hour in her presence and was defending myself every moment."

Her shoulders heaved in a sigh. Those expressive eyebrows pulled moodily together. "I shall have to teach you."

Will stiffened. "Pray do not feel obliged. If the duke is displeased with my work, I'm prepared to face the consequences."

She sent a dark look his way. "There." She stabbed one finger at him. "That. Always bringing up His Grace when it is *Her* Grace you answer to."

He leaned toward her. "Why is that?"

She was undaunted. "There is no reason for you to see him. Everything she does is at His Grace's request, with his express approval. Do you under-stand?"

Will suddenly realized the duke wasn't just

unwell in body, but also in mind. He jerked his head in a nod.

"You've been here only a few days, and already you've declared that the estate has been grievously neglected."

"It has been."

"Mr. Montclair!" Her eyes were snapping fire at him. "Have you no sense of diplomacy, or even manners?"

Reluctantly he smiled. "Now you sound like my mother."

"I—What?" Up flew those eyebrows as her mouth fell open.

"I take your point," he said. "I could have approached it differently. I admit to being swept up in"—*astonishment, indignation, a bit of fury*—"surprise that a ducal estate of this size is so lacking. It's not a matter of funds, as I saw in London when Mr. Edwards taught me the books. Now I see it's also not a matter of disinterest. That only leaves ignorance, don't you agree?"

She just stared at him, still wearing that flummoxed expression that so intrigued him.

"The duchess doesn't know how much has been let go," he said gently. "Of course it's not her fault. Someone—Grimes or Edwards, I don't know—must have assured her that all was being seen to, when it was not."

"Yes," she said after a moment. "They did."

Will shrugged. "I've no idea what Grimes's reason was, but Edwards isn't here. Even now he returns to London every fortnight. I presume he didn't reside here before he engaged me."

"No," she said, after a longer pause. "He was here often, but for other reasons."

Will wondered what those were; was the estate in legal trouble, too? "Shall we strike a truce, Miss Kirkpatrick?"

She tensed warily.

"For the sake of the estate," he added. "I meant what I said earlier. It's ridiculous to put things back as they were when they can be done better." He hesitated. "I suppose the duke might not know about these new and better methods, and perhaps that is preventing Her Grace from sanctioning improvements."

The glance she gave him was a very strange one—still guarded, but also assessing, as if weighing how much she could trust him.

Will opened his arms. "What possible trick could I be attempting?"

"Fraud, I suppose," she said slowly.

He laughed. "As if Edwards won't make me account for every shilling spent!" He sobered. "I was hired to do something. Now I've been told not to do it as well as I can. What would you do, in my place?"

She gazed at him for a long time. The dark lock of hair on her shoulder gleamed in the sunlight streaming through the windows, and made her gown glow like the ocean in the West Indies. Up close he noticed that her necklace wasn't a plain pendant, but a disc of gold wire spun into an intricate filigree. "I would still try to do my best," she finally answered. "Bearing in mind that my employer wouldn't be likely to notice smaller or less obvious improvements made in the course of repairs. I would present any such improvement as a happy discovery."

"So you think I should proceed without her approval."

She raised her chin. "She gave explicit approval for repairs."

"Hmm." Will wondered how much of this she did, managing the duchess and her interactions with everyone. "And if she discovers I authorized a repair which was technically a complete replacement of the item in question?"

Miss Kirkpatrick inhaled deeply. The blush went all the way down her throat to the swells of her bosom, visible through the gauzy kerchief covering her shoulders. Will yanked his gaze back up to her face—if he wasn't getting sacked after all, he had to keep his distance.

"Perhaps you could say . . . there was difficulty getting materials, and so different, newer ones will have to suffice." She paused suggestively. Will said nothing. "Or perhaps . . . if workmen cannot repair something, such as a bridge, and must rebuild it, then you might say they only know how to build in the new style."

"I see," he said at last. "Call anything and everything a repair."

"Something like that," she agreed. "I suppose . . . I could advise you . . ."

Behind them a door opened and closed, the solid thud of it reverberating through the still air. Will turned to see Mr. Edwards approaching.

Miss Kirkpatrick took a step back. "Pardon me, sirs . . ."

Will held up one hand. "Stay, please." He watched the attorney come toward them. "What is my fate, sir?"

The man gave him a harassed glance. "No good end, I'm sure."

He grinned. "Have I been sacked?"

Edwards glared at him. "No."

He felt a ripple of surprise. "I am faint with astonishment."

"As am I," muttered Edwards peevishly. He mustered a smile for the lady. "Might I have a word, Miss Kirkpatrick?"

There was no mistaking her relief. "Of course, sir."

Will bowed and turned to go, pausing only as she spoke again. "Mr. Montclair . . . if it won't inconvenience you, I would like to continue tending the garden at Stone Cottage."

"You shall never inconvenience me." He made another bow. "I would like it above all things, Miss Kirkpatrick."

She gave him a significant look. "Thank you. I will come tomorrow morning."

When she meant to teach and advise him about the duchess. Will hid his grin and left.

PHILIPPA HOPED HE'D understood her. Just because he hadn't been dismissed today didn't mean the duchess wouldn't reconsider and do it tomorrow. Which, she was somewhat surprised to realize, she didn't want to happen.

She tried to push away that thought and turned to Mr. Edwards. He still looked cross, and glanced over one shoulder to be sure Mr. Montclair was gone before he spoke. "I must beg a favor, Miss Kirkpatrick."

She nodded. "She wanted to sack him, didn't she?"

"Desperately," he said on a sigh. "It's my fault. I taught him the business of the estate, but not enough about the family who owns it. I must remedy that posthaste."

Philippa knew what he was going to ask. How strange that she had just suggested the very same thing to Mr. Montclair himself. "Perhaps I could help."

The attorney's face all but melted with gratitude. "My dear Miss Kirkpatrick, I did hope for exactly that. There's no one better able to explain things to him."

"Why do you think he's so direct?" she asked. "Is it because he's American?" Philippa had never seen anyone face down the duchess and brazenly tell her she was wrong.

Edwards sighed. "I'm not certain. However . . ." He ran one hand over his face. "Her Grace is under extraordinary strain. I ought to have told Montclair to be delicate."

Philippa's back stiffened. The duchess was not fragile. "I will speak to him," she said formally. "Hopefully he can learn. He doesn't seem a stupid fellow."

"Indeed he's not." Mr. Edwards smiled again. "Thank you, Miss Kirkpatrick."

Philippa went back to the Tapestry Room, where the duchess was standing at the window, teacup clutched in both hands.

"Have you all agreed I'm mad?" she asked moodily.

Philippa raised one brow and came to stand beside her. "Of course not. You've not even thrown the china at anyone."

A reluctant smile softened her grim expression. "As if I would!" She tilted the cup in her hands, watching it sparkle like rubies. Maximilian St. James, one of the heirs, had given it to her, and she was very fond of the scarlet tea service.

"If you ask me, I believe Mr. Montclair's fault lies in being too eager, rather than in scorning those around him as dim-witted," Philippa said. "I believe he wants to do well by the estate."

"By tearing down and *improving* everything," muttered the duchess.

"Well, if there's a better way to do something, why not seize the opportunity? Particularly when the old is in poor condition."

"The old ways have been reliable for decades. These new plans and methods have not."

"Yes," agreed Philippa carefully. "But at the same time, we embrace new fashions. Those cups were made with a glaze never seen before Bianca St. James created it. New roads are much smoother, and soon there will be canals bringing coal from all over Britain. Surely that's an improvement?"

The older woman gave a silent huff. "You're saying I'm a fearful old woman."

"No," Philippa protested.

"Well, I suppose I am. Let the captain or Maximilian decide to improve the fields. Even a Frenchman! Let *him* deal with Mr. Montclair." The duchess went back to the sofa and lowered herself with a sigh.

"Would it set your mind at ease if I kept an eye on him?" It was what Philippa meant to do anyway, but she wouldn't do it behind the duchess's back.

The duchess rolled her eyes. "My dear girl, I wouldn't wish that upon *anyone*."

She laughed. "Nevertheless, I'm happy to do it. It will sharpen my wits."

She said it lightly, but the duchess looked up, suddenly alert. "Yes," she said slowly. "Perhaps that is a good idea. And when you go to London, you will be accustomed to dealing with impertinent rogues."

Inwardly Philippa quailed from the mention of London, where the duchess had been suggesting she go to find a husband. *You must look to your future*, she would say, *and a home and family of your own.*

Because, of course, she could not stay at Carlyle forever. When the duke died, it would become someone else's property: Captain St. James's, most likely, or perhaps Maximilian's. The duchess would leave the castle when the duke died, and Philippa could certainly go with her, but she was nearing eighty. Eventually, Philippa would be left without home or family.

She would not be poor. Her father had left her a respectable sum, and the duchess had declared she meant to leave her fortune to Philippa—and the duchess had been one of the greatest heiresses of her day. Philippa would be well able to afford a home of her own.

It was the family she would be without.

She had lost her mother, her father, her stepmother . . . The duke's health was uncertain, and the duchess was elderly. She wanted to cling to them as hard as she could, not leave them, and certainly not for a London rogue who would have to be blinded by her fortune to overlook her distinctly un-English complexion.

"Yes." She made herself smile. "I suppose I shall go to London, at some point." It would please the duchess if she agreed, and between Mr. Montclair and the unsettling report from France, the duchess needed something to be pleased about.

The older woman visibly brightened. "I shall write to Lady Beauchamp immediately to arrange your visit."

"Won't you come, too?" Philippa was startled.

The duchess shook her head. "I must remain here, to see to Johnny. You'll be in much better hands with Diana. She knows everyone in town, and the best dressmakers, too."

Diana, dowager Countess Beauchamp, had been her stepmother's closest friend. If Philippa had to leave the duchess behind, there was no one she'd rather go to than Aunt Diana. "I would adore seeing her again."

The duchess beamed. "Excellent! Oh my dear girl. It would please me so much to see you happily settled." Her eyes grew a little misty. "I would like it above all things in life, to dance at your wedding."

"Well! I won't marry if you do not promise you will," exclaimed Philippa in mock severity.

The duchess laughed. She didn't laugh much

these days, and Philippa's heart leapt to hear it. They continued discussing London, with Philippa teasing that she would commission a new gown in London for the duchess to wear to her wedding, and the duchess laughing again and saying Diana would find that marvelous.

And Philippa made two vows to herself: first, she *would* go to London. As much as she shrank from it, her finding a husband would bring the duchess such joy. It felt selfish to deny her that.

And second, she was going to whip William Montclair into a proper, respectful steward who never gave the duchess another moment's dismay, so help her God.

Chapter Nine

❦⋆❦

The garden was a convenient excuse for going to Stone Cottage. Mrs. Grimes had been very fond of gardening, and she'd taught Philippa a great deal. When the Grimeses left Carlyle, Philippa had promised not to let Mrs. Grimes's work all go to seed.

For the last two years it had been her own private bower, the house quiet and empty, a peaceful retreat from the castle. As she drove the gig down the hill, she braced herself for it to feel very different.

To her pleasure, it didn't. The windows and door stood open, curtains fluttering in the breeze. A whiff of something baking drifted to her as she set the gig's brake, and she inhaled happily. Mrs. Blake was an excellent cook. Philippa's spirits perked up; perhaps she could inveigle an invitation to tea.

After going round to the back of the house and greeting Mrs. Blake and Camilla, she got to work. There was something so heartening, so rewarding about tending plants. The tulips never teased her, and the clematis never made her angry.

More than an hour later, she had made her way around the side of the house when she saw something that shouldn't be there. It was small and brown, a twisted little thing. She thought it was a piece of wood, until she poked it with her trowel.

Her nose wrinkled. It was an apple core. And—she began counting—it was only one of many. Some were wizened and brown, others were fresher; all were swarmed by insects. They littered the ground.

Right beneath an open window.

Philippa stood up. Mrs. Blake had told her he was here, working in the study, and inside she could see him bent over the desk, scribbling with a quill. "Mr. Montclair," she said.

He ignored her.

"Mr. Montclair!"

"Yes?" He turned a page and kept writing.

Philippa's temper began to boil. "Are you responsible for this?" She held up the core.

"Most likely," he called back in a distracted, dismissive way.

The core flew from her hand before she knew what she was doing. It bounced off a corner of the desk toward him, rolling across his paper. He jerked back with an exclamation. "Did you *throw* something at me?"

His insulted tone banished her astonishment that she had, in fact, thrown a rotten apple core at him. "I did," she retorted, lifting her chin.

"Why?" he demanded.

"Why are there a dozen apple cores"—she snatched up another one—"in my garden?"

He relaxed. The rogue even grinned at her. "It's my garden, if you want to be precise about it."

This time she meant to throw it, and he barely ducked out of the way in time. "Stop!" he exclaimed.

She threw another. "Don't—throw—apple cores—out—the window!"

He dodged them, arms over his head. "What are you doing?"

"This garden is swarming with pests now!" She threw another.

He glared at her, and before she realized what he meant to do, a handful of walnuts came sailing back at her. Philippa gasped. "You threw walnuts at me!"

He paused. Hands on hips, he scowled at a bowl on the side of his desk, presumably the source of the walnuts.

Philippa's wide eyes went from the walnuts, lying forlornly in the dirt, to the man inside, who refused to meet her gaze. In fact, it looked like he was blushing. She began to laugh, and couldn't stop.

"I'm sorry," she gasped between bursts of laughter. She had to lean against the side of the house, one hand holding her stomach. "Oh goodness . . ."

He came and leaned out the window, giving the scattered walnuts a black look. "I didn't like the look of those ones," he growled, sending Philippa into another gale of helpless laughter.

When she recovered enough to speak, he was watching, his elbows on the windowsill and a sheepish grin on his face. "Shall we call it a stalemate?"

Still breathless, she fanned herself and shook her head. "No! You've caused me a great deal of work, now that snails and ants have infested this section, *and* you wasted some perfectly delicious walnuts."

"I did." He rubbed his jaw. "I should order myself flogged." He hesitated. "There are more walnuts in here. Would you care to come inside and save them from my temper?"

"I would." She took off her gloves. "I did scheme to be invited to tea."

He laughed. "I'll ask Mrs. Blake to make some."

Philippa took her time going through the garden. She spotted another apple core among the mignonette, and tossed it into her pail of pruning and weeds. It wasn't hard to picture him working at the desk and carelessly chucking the cores out the window. Shaking her head, she made her way around the house, and found him already in the kitchen.

"And tea," he was saying as she reached the kitchen gate.

"Tea, sir?" Mrs. Blake sounded shocked.

"For Miss Kirkpatrick," he said.

From inside the kitchen came a chorus of "Ohhhh," as if that explained all.

Mr. Montclair turned and saw her. "This way," he said, gesturing toward the house. "Camilla will bring a tray."

Philippa let him lead her into the house. To her surprise, a young man jumped up from a narrow desk as they entered the hall. Short, skinny, his dark hair stuck up in a ruff around his ears. "Ma'am. Miss," he said, with a hasty bow.

"Master Josiah," she said. "I didn't know you were working for Mr. Montclair."

Nervously he looked past her, but the steward simply jerked his head. "Go on, Josiah. That's all for today."

With another bow, the boy fled toward the kitchen.

Philippa removed her hat and strolled into the study. On the opposite wall, directly beside the window and thus invisible from outside, was a large map, with innumerable small pieces of paper tacked onto it. "What is this?"

He came up beside her. "Carlyle."

"I know that," she said patiently. "What are these?"

The man beside her said nothing. Philippa leaned close to read the handwriting on one scrap. "Rethatch roof, repair chimney flue, rebuild fence," she murmured. "Is this what needs to be done?"

"Yes."

Her gaze swept over the map. "Is . . . is it really this bad?" she asked, taken aback. Some of the notes seemed minor—*cracked window glazings*—but others were significant—*all fields drainage*.

He shrugged. "It will take months to do all of this, but I wanted a comprehensive survey."

"Josiah Welby?"

"He's helping me collect and organize reports from the tenants."

Philippa nodded, silenced by the sheer number of notes.

He cleared his throat. "Shall we go into the parlor—er, drawing room? I suppose that's the proper place to have tea."

"Oh no, this is fine." She was transfixed by that map. She went around the large desk and pulled up a chair. Mr. Montclair returned to his own seat, brushing a stray apple core off the surface.

"I apologize for that." Her face grew warm.

"I'll take care to toss them on the fire from now on."

"They attract insects," she said. "Insects devour the plants."

He nodded. "My apologies to the garden, and to the gardener."

Camilla brought the tea tray, hesitating outside the door until Mr. Montclair waved her in. She set it on the table, and Philippa gasped in delight when she saw what was on the tray. "Oh my!"

"Yes, ma'am. Mrs. Blake remembers how you like 'em. She started baking as soon as you drove up."

"You must send her my fervent thanks." Blushing, Camilla curtsied and hurried out. Philippa caught Mr. Montclair eyeing the tray of glistening little buns. "These are the most delicious thing you will ever eat." She placed one on a plate and held it out.

He raised one brow. "Indeed."

She waited for him to take a bite, smiling triumphantly as his eyes widened in surprise. Philippa took a bite of her own gulab jamun. The soft milk buns were flavored with cardamom and fried in butter before being dunked in sweet rosewater syrup.

"What is it?" Mr. Montclair took another bite.

"Gulab jamun." It was hard to restrain herself from devouring it in two bites and then eating three more. "My mother was Indian, and my father said she loved them. I did, too. When we came to England, my ayah made them for me. She taught Mrs. Blake before she went back to India." She smiled wryly. "Asmat said it was not the same as in India, but better than anything the English had."

He grinned as he took another. "She's not wrong."

"Oh? Have you been to India?"

He shook his head. "I've had English cooking for nearly a year now."

Philippa laughed. The gulab jamun had put her in a much lighter mood, as usual. Unthinkingly she sucked the last of the syrup from her fingers.

Across the desk, Mr. Montclair choked and began coughing.

"Oh dear—" She started to rise but he waved her away, turning his back as he cleared his throat. When he faced her again, his face was red.

Philippa reached for the teapot. "Tell me something," she said as she poured a cup. "Why don't you drink tea?"

Mr. Montclair's gaze slid away from hers. "Why do you think that?"

"Because I've served you tea twice now and not seen you take a sip."

"Ah." He flipped one hand. "I'm not used to it."

"No? They don't have tea in America?"

He lowered his eyes. "Not as much in the last fifteen years."

"Oh yes. You Americans threw it into the harbor." She stirred a dollop of honey into the tea. "And now you don't care for it. What do you prefer?"

"Coffee. Cider." Another cheeky grin. "Rum and wine and beer."

"Will you try it?" She arched one brow, holding out the cup.

He hesitated a long time before taking it gingerly. "If it pleases you."

Philippa nodded. "It will endear you to Her Grace."

"Ah." A wry smile this time. "Of course."

She prepared another cup. The duchess preferred sugar, but Philippa liked the honey from Carlyle, and Mrs. Blake had thoughtfully remembered.

"Votre père est français?" she said, sipping her tea.

His eyes flashed her way, vaguely puzzled and somewhat wary. "Oui," he said after a moment.

She nodded. "Et votre mère?"

"Elle est québécoise," he replied. "De Montreal."

"The first thing you must know about Her Grace," she said, "is that she is not fond of the French."

On the verge of sipping, he lowered his cup. "What—the whole people?"

"In general, yes."

He stared in amazement. "Why?"

"An old family scandal," she said, waving one hand and leaving out the very current reason for the duchess's animus. "Your accent . . ."

"I don't sound French!"

"Perhaps not in America, but here you do." Philippa glanced pointedly at the cup forgotten in his hand. "Do you like it?"

He took a hasty sip. "Exquisite. But about the French—"

Philippa held up one finger. "It isn't rational. I grant that. But there's no chance of changing her mind." Not unless a messenger from France brought definitive proof that Lord Thomas had died childless. "The second difficulty you labor under is being new to the estate."

His eyes narrowed. "I see."

Philippa shook her head. "Mr. Grimes was born and raised here, and therefore she trusted him. Even Mr. Edwards, who's been the family's attorney for almost thirty years, still isn't entirely beyond suspicion in her eyes."

He put down his cup. "That's why nothing's changed in decades."

She nodded. "Yes. That also isn't entirely rational, but it's how she manages."

For a long moment he turned the cup on the saucer, a brooding frown on his face. "I see." He looked up. "Because the duke is unable to manage the estate himself."

Philippa nearly spat out her tea. "Mr. Montclair!"

He leaned forward, his gaze intent upon her. "It's true, isn't it? Sole responsibility rests on the duchess's shoulders, and she's wary of making a mistake, so she maintains everything as it has been."

She sat like a statue, which was surely as betraying as if she nodded her head and said *yes, exactly so.*

Mr. Montclair's face softened. "In that case, I understand better," he said, a note of apology in his voice.

Flustered, she reached out and seized his hand. "Then you must understand this," she whispered. "It is a *grave* secret. No one outside Carlyle can know."

"Why?"

Philippa bit her lip and glanced over her shoulder. The door stood properly, respectably open, but the house was quiet. Young Josiah had gone, and Mrs. Blake and Camilla were probably in the kitchen. Still, she lowered her voice even more. "If there were an inquiry made, and the duke found to be . . . to be"—a lunatic; that was the legal word, but Philippa hated it—"unequal to the title, the Crown would appoint a committee to manage the estate and have charge of his person. A dukedom is no ordinary estate. Surely you can understand why a mother would fight fiercely to protect her son from being taken into the care of strangers."

"What of the heir? Surely that fellow deserves better than to inherit an estate mired thirty years in the past."

Philippa hesitated. What to say? People at Carlyle had seen Maximilian and Captain St. James, the two nearest cousins, when the duchess summoned them a year ago. Indeed, the captain had spent two months here and made several rounds of the estate meeting tenants.

But Mr. Montclair was very much a stranger still, and he hardly needed to know every detail.

"He won't," she said. "That's your task, to set all to rights. Can you do it?"

His fingers flexed under her touch. Philippa realized she was still gripping his hand and released him with a start. "I can." She let out a sigh of relief. "But you'll have to instruct me all along the way," he added, some of his familiar sly smile returning. "So I don't mistakenly build an extravagant new barn."

She forced a small laugh. "I shall do my best, but if you don't heed my advice, it will all be for naught."

"I vow to listen attentively to every word you say."

"You'd better." She paused. "What was your last estate like?" Perhaps that was a good place to start. Philippa knew something of estate management, but not enough, obviously.

"My last estate?"

"The one you managed before coming to Carlyle. I presume it was smaller."

His gaze drifted. "Much."

"Surely you weren't given free rein there."

A strange smile crossed his face. "No."

She raised her brows and waited.

"This is my first position managing a landed estate," he said.

Her mouth dropped open. *No.* Mr. Edwards couldn't possibly have handed over responsibility for Carlyle to someone wholly inexperienced.

"I think it's going well so far, all things considered," went on Mr. Montclair. "What is your opinion?"

"I—I—" She took a hasty sip of tea. "What on earth were you doing when you accepted this position?"

She meant figuratively—what made him think he was equal to this? She would deal with Mr. Edwards's fit of obvious madness later. But he answered literally. "I was in London for business."

She blinked. "Business."

He nodded. "My family's merchant shipping company." He leaned closer, propping one elbow on the desk. "Between us, Miss Kirkpatrick, I prefer this."

Her brain still felt stunned. "You do?" she said stupidly.

"Very much so," he said softly. His gaze roved her face. "Particularly now."

Still thinking about his admission, she stared blankly back. Then, like a smack to the head, she realized what was happening. He was *flirting* with her.

A pulse of energy shot through her. There was something almost magnetic about him, the tempting curve of his mouth, the admiration in his eyes, the way he was looking at her. He was a handsome man, who could make her flustered just by rolling up his sleeves. Philippa felt suddenly very alert and very awkward.

She had no experience with flirting. All the tenants and servants knew her and knew her place here. Captain St. James and Mr. St. James were handsome men in their prime, but neither had looked at her like this.

It was . . . it was thrilling. It made her feel reckless and a bit wild, which must explain why she canted forward in her chair and tipped her head coquettishly to one side. "Then you must be eager to please."

His eyes gleamed with golden sparks. He rested his other elbow on the desk and folded his arms. "Very much so. How, pray, may I please you?"

"You should trust my advice." She plucked another gulab jamun from the plate and nibbled it. "Wasn't I right about these?"

His gaze dropped to her mouth. "Entirely."

Philippa almost choked on the bun. The way he watched her mouth was . . . intoxicating. His eyes turned dark and heated and his expression grew taut and absorbed. She managed to swallow and licked her lips. A muscle twitched in his jaw. She set down the remainder of the bun and watched his gaze track her hand, then up her arm to meet her eyes.

Her heart was thumping violently, half in panic, half in excitement. No one had warned her flirting was so exhilarating.

"How else?" he murmured. "What else do you desire?"

"I wish you would make an effort to charm the duchess." The words came out before she knew she was saying it.

Mr. Montclair froze. His face went blank for a moment, until he burst out laughing. "Good Lord," he exclaimed. "For a moment I thought you actually meant it!"

Philippa was rigid with mortification. She had misread him. Or, more likely, he hadn't been flirting with her out of attraction but in pursuit of some advantage. She wasn't his employer but she was very close to it. Perhaps he'd thought this was the way to avoid being sacked.

She rose. "Obviously not, Mr. Montclair," she said coolly. "Charm is clearly beyond your capabilities. If you send me a list of the work you believe most urgent, I will speak to Her Grace about it. It appears unlikely you could stave off dismissal a third time, should you attempt to present anything to her yourself. Good day." She collected her hat and gloves and swept out, cheeks burning.

WILL GRIPPED THE arms of his chair to keep from following her. If he opened his mouth he would apologize until he ran mute. If he looked at her, he'd forget all over again that he had vowed not to become entangled at Carlyle.

Only when he heard the gig's wheels rattle down the lane did he leap to his feet and pace restlessly about the office. He'd been here less than a fortnight and already he was breaking his own rules.

I know what I'm doing, he'd boasted to his brother. Idiot. None of his cocky plans had accounted for the duchess having a beautiful young companion, with a tart and exhilarating wit and a way of casting provocative looks from under her long dark eyelashes—

"Stop it," he said under his breath, squeezing one hand over his eyes. So he was attracted to her. So he wanted her. He was never going to *have* her, so he'd best stop flirting with her before he got himself into real trouble.

He opened his eyes and raised his head. The map on the wall confronted him. That was why he was here. Already he'd begun to care about the people of Carlyle, who were so loyal to the family and yet so grateful for his promises of help to come. It had become common for grown men to seize his hand, tears in their eyes, and barely manage to speak their thanks. They needed him. He couldn't let them down, even though he was apparently going about everything in the worst possible way. The duchess was already on the brink of sacking him, according to Miss Kirkpatrick.

With a sigh he braced both hands on the wall and let his head fall forward. Five months. In five months he would be done here, and then it would never matter what Philippa Kirkpatrick thought of him.

Chapter Ten

$\mathcal{F}$or the next few weeks Will kept strictly to his plan and did nothing but work. Rising at dawn, he rode every mile of the Carlyle estate and visited every tenant and resident on it. He went into Kittleston and spoke to everyone there, for Carlyle had a large influence on the village. When he returned to Stone Cottage for dinner each day, Josiah was waiting with more work—surveyors' and engineers' reports, bills from tradesmen. He had five months to put this estate in order and he meant to make the most of it.

Every Monday and Thursday he left a summary of the works in progress at the castle for Miss Kirkpatrick. He made sure to do it early, so early he often met the milkmaids and scullery girls just beginning their days. Every Monday and Thursday evening when he returned home, her reply was waiting on his desk.

He spent more time than was reasonable reading these letters. She wrote a very pretty hand, and in fact he realized now that the letters from the duchess, sent to him and Mr. Edwards in London, had been in her handwriting. He'd assumed it was a secretary, but of course, whom would the duchess trust with such sensitive details?

Her letters were long, filled with detailed rebuttals when she denied a proposal and explanations of how things had always been done. Frequently a spark of humor crept into them, as when she wrote that permission was granted to dredge the mill pond, *in the most efficacious manner, be it traditional or some revolutionary new method you have devised; no one cares much about dredging.* That made him laugh, and wish he could respond in kind.

But he couldn't. He'd taken too many risks as it was. Will ignored the wit and kept his own letters dry and dull.

Eventually, though, he had to visit the castle during daylight hours. Edwards was back from London and wanted a report in person. Will intended to make the most of it by getting authorization for the most expensive projects. Two bridges needed to be torn down and replaced, and there were good arguments for building two new ones. He rode up to the castle, armed with engineering reports and proposals from the builders totaling over two thousand pounds. For that amount, let Edwards face the duchess.

The attorney had an office in the castle, but Will wasn't certain where it was. He went in through the kitchens, following the smell of baking. The pastry cook was Mrs. Blake's sister-in-law, and there was something of a friendly rivalry between the two women. Will, perpetually hungry from long days of physical labor and riding, took full advantage of this. Today there were dainty cherry tarts, with a dollop of cream atop each.

"Dionysus himself would faint in ecstasy if he ever got a taste of your cooking," he told Mrs. Amis.

She shook her head, chuckling. "Flatterer! Have another, Mr. Montclair."

"To please you." He took the proffered tart with a wink. She waved one hand as he left.

The butler said Mr. Edwards was with Her Grace. Will nodded and said he would wait outside, wanting to avoid any chance of meeting the duchess. Summer had reached Carlyle, and today was exceptionally fine. It was rare he had time to spend in peaceful enjoyment of the sunshine. He found a door and went out, wishing he'd taken a third tart.

He wasn't entirely sure where he was. He hadn't seen much of the castle except the service courtyard. Whatever it was, this spot was beautiful, and must have been even more so a month ago; the fading remains of tulips were everywhere. He clasped his hands behind his back and turned his face to the sun, savoring the moment of peace.

Off to his right a door opened. Thinking it must be Edwards come to find him, Will opened his eyes and turned.

It was not the attorney. Two servants in livery were carrying out a suite of furniture: a chaise longue, a table, a footstool, an exquisitely painted screen. They arranged all this on a small terrace near the house, almost hidden behind manicured shrubs. A maid brought out a silver tray filled with china and crystal and laid it on the table.

He had obviously stumbled into one of the family's private areas. Hastily Will stepped back, not wanting to provoke the duchess's wrath, when the double doors opened again and two more servants came out bearing a chair on poles between them.

In the chair sat an old man. He wore a magnificent dressing gown over his shirt and breeches, and on his head was a velvet cap, of the sort old men slept in, with a thin coif of gray hair visible at his nape. The servants carried him down the steps, then helped him gently onto the chaise.

He had probably once been tall, but was now stooped and gaunt. When he raised one hand to lean on a servant's shoulder, his hand was like a spider, the long fingers spindly and crooked. A gold and emerald ring on his hand caught the light, dazzlingly bright.

And then he looked up and caught sight of Will.

"Ah! Lemuel," he cried, his voice raspy and thin. He extended his arms as if for an embrace. "Returned at last from Brobdingnag!"

Caught off guard, Will laughed. He knew that story; it had been a favorite of his as a boy. "And I bring you Glumdalclitch's compliments, good sir." He made a flourishing bow.

The duke's face lit up—for it could only be the Duke of Carlyle. He beckoned Will to come closer. The servant attending him bent to whisper something to him, but he waved the man aside. "Come," he called. "Come, and tell me of your adventures."

Will tensed. He'd answered without thinking,

and now didn't know what to do. He glanced over his shoulder, expecting—hoping—to see Mr. Edwards approaching, even if it meant a scolding.

But the duke was waiting, his hand still raised in welcome. Was it better to apologize and back swiftly away, or obey his actual employer's command? He would probably be sacked simply for being here. Damn it. Why hadn't he waited in Edwards's office?

Slowly Will crossed the grass.

As he came near, the duke's expression clouded, growing puzzled. Will stopped at the edge of the grass and bowed. "William Montclair, Your Grace. The new steward."

"What?" The old man sounded confused. "No, no, you are not." Will froze. The duke frowned at him. "But what do you know of Brobdingnag?"

Will darted a nervous glance at the duke's attendant, a tall, broad-shouldered Black man with spectacles, distinguished from the footmen by his gray suit of fine wool. The man flicked his eyes at the chair next to the duke, and so, despite feeling as though the duchess's sharp voice would ring out at any moment, ordering him from the property, Will made his way to the chair and sat down.

The duke leaned forward to scrutinize him. "Did you really see the giants?" he demanded, his faded eyes hopeful. "Glumdalclitch?"

Will smiled. Glumdalclitch was the young giantess who cared for Lemuel Gulliver on his sojourn in Brobdingnag. "The best natured female I ever encountered, sir."

He clapped his hands together with delight. "And are these the clothes she made for you?"

"Ah . . ." Will glanced down at his ordinary garments. "No, sadly not. Those were lost in the chest when I was put to sea off Brobdingnag."

"Ah, yes! I remember. A veritable coffin," the duke muttered.

Will nodded. "I received a great many suits of clothing in my travels. These are from . . ." His mind blanked. Where had Gulliver ended his journeys?

"The Yahoo?" offered the duke hopefully.

Will made a face. "Those are long since worn out. These are English."

The duke looked disappointed. "And are you reconciled to your family, after so many years away from them?"

The words stuck in Will's throat. He thought of his father, who had read *Gulliver's Travels* to him and Jack so many years ago. Of his mother, who had indulged their desires to recreate the fantastic worlds Swift wrote of, from letting them sleep in bureau drawers to building a giant chest in the woods. Of his brother, who had let Will talk him into those wild schemes and now another one here in England. Of his sister, who had wailed when told she couldn't come to England, too—because she had been convinced there *would* be some sort of adventure.

Will had been lying to all of them for months now. He had no idea how, or if, he would ever be able to rectify that.

"No, sir," he murmured. "Not yet."

"Ah, well." Carlyle patted the air as if to console him. "Someday, my good fellow. Never give up hope."

Will managed a smile. "Thank you."

A small cough made Will look up. There stood Mr. Edwards, his face grim and pale with fury.

"Who is there?" asked the duke irritably. He spied Edwards and rolled his eyes. "Oh, you. Unless you have brought news of Laputa, go away!"

"I'm afraid not, Your Grace. I have need of Mr. Montclair—"

"Who?" snapped the duke. Mr. Edwards stopped as if he'd been slapped.

Will cleared his throat. "Your pardon, sir, but I must go with this gentleman. He has the look of Munodi about him."

The duke's face cleared. "Munodi! Goodness yes, he does. Well, we must do better than the Laputians and listen to him. You may go." He tipped his head like a king dismissing a subject.

Will rose and bowed. "Good day to you, sir."

"And to you." Carlyle leaned back on the chaise, humming softly and looking pleased.

Will followed the attorney, who led the way to his office at a furious pace. Once inside, the door closed, he turned on Will. "What the devil were you doing?"

The sharp tone stiffened his shoulders. "I was waiting for our appointment when the duke came outside. He saw me and called me to him."

"Oh?" Edwards's brows shot up. Will had never seen him this angry. "And what did you say to His Grace?"

"We spoke of *Gulliver's Travels*." Edwards's furious expression didn't change. "The book," clarified Will. "It was a great favorite of mine when I was a boy. It seems to be a favorite of His Grace's as well."

"Is that all?" Edwards looked suspicious.

Will thought. "Yes. He appeared to think I had just come from Brobdingnag, the land of the giants."

The anger seemed to drain out of Edwards. His shoulders slumped, he raised one hand to his forehead, and he heaved a shaky sigh. "If he is upset, or discomposed, or even suffers a chill on the morrow, you'll be called to account by the duchess."

Stung, Will frowned. "He spoke to me first. Was I meant to refuse him? He *is* the duke."

Edwards scrubbed both hands over his face. When he looked up, his poise was largely restored. "Of course. Sit down." He went behind his desk and Will took a seat, still feeling unfairly accused. "His Grace's health is delicate at the best of times," the attorney explained. "Anything that unsettles him or shakes his equilibrium is cause for concern. You ought not to have gone into the Tulip Garden, but it sounds as though no real harm has been done."

"By all means speak to the man attending him," retorted Will, irked. "He saw every moment of it, and even indicated I should be seated and stay."

The attorney sighed again. "If I must, I will." Meaning, if the duchess demanded it. "Who is Munodi?"

"What? Oh." Will shuffled his feet. "The only man of sense and discernment in a land of fanciful fools."

Edwards gave a huff, a reluctant smile twitching at his mouth. "Should I be flattered, then?"

"I would say yes," said Will. "It was meant as a compliment."

"Very good." He cleared his throat. "What is your business today?"

Right. Will had almost forgotten. He pulled out the proposals and plans from his coat pocket and spread them on the desk. "I would like funds for these plans."

Chapter Eleven

Word reached them that Mr. Montclair had approached the duke almost as soon as Mr. Edwards left the sitting room.

"What?" The duchess's voice rang like a blade being unsheathed.

The footman bowed lower. "Mr. Amis sent me to inform you at once, Your Grace."

Philippa tensed in worry as the duchess inhaled so sharply, she trembled. "Thank you, Henry," she said hastily to the footman. "You may go."

When he had bowed his way out the door, the duchess turned to Philippa. "That man!" she hissed, her eyes flashing. "I should have sacked him weeks ago!"

Philippa said nothing. She hadn't told anyone about her visit to Stone Cottage. Every time she thought of that meeting, she tried to decide what she should have done differently, but never reached a satisfactory answer.

She had kept her word to direct Mr. Montclair, but only via letter. Twice a week there was a letter from him beside her breakfast plate. Initially she had been self-conscious about reading them in front of the duchess, but she needn't have been; he wrote of nothing more alarming than the need for a new floor in part of the stable. Still, it took her far longer than it should have to compose her replies. Too often she found herself getting carried away, lapsing into familiarity or asking if Mrs. Blake had made more gulab jamun, and then she'd have to recopy the entire letter.

The one thing that made her feel better was that he seemed to be doing an excellent job. She had done her own investigating, and was dismayed to find that he was entirely correct about the condition of the estate. Whatever had gone on before under Mr. Grimes and Mr. Edwards, Mr. Montclair was a much better steward.

If only he had the sense God gave a rabbit and confined himself to his duties. Of course, he might have known better how to do that if she weren't such a coward.

"Perhaps there was no harm done," she said to the duchess. "Where can Mr. Montclair have seen the duke? It must have been outside."

After a long winter closeted in his rooms in ill health, the duke had improved recently. The duchess, who believed fervently in the restorative powers of sunshine and fresh air, had long urged him to sit outside on fine days, and he'd done so twice, to her immense joy.

At this suggestion, the duchess perked up. "Let us go see. And so help me, if Mr. Montclair is pestering him—" She shook her head and bustled out of the room, Philippa following.

It took several minutes to make their way to the

family wing of the castle. The duke had a large suite of rooms there, which he rarely left. Years ago the duchess had created a private garden for him right outside it, hoping her son would go out more. Philippa and her stepmother had filled it with tulips, to surprise the duke in the spring, earning it the name of Tulip Garden, but the duke rarely went outside.

Today, though, he had. Mr. Amis, the duke's personal valet, caught sight of them. He spoke to the duke, who reclined on a chaise. Carlyle opened his eyes and lifted one hand to them. "Good day, Mother and Pippa."

The duchess clasped his hand. "What a pleasure to see you out here, Johnny!"

"Yes, yes . . ." He smiled, though his eyes drifted closed. "The sun is very bright, isn't it?"

The duchess looked at Mr. Amis, who silently shifted the screen. "I understand you had a visitor." The duchess sat down beside him.

"Hmm? Yes! Lemuel returned, Mother!" He actually laughed. Philippa couldn't believe her ears. The duke hadn't laughed in months. "Can you imagine it?"

"No," said the duchess, her voice hoarse. "I— How did you know him?"

The duke went still, his gaze distant as if thinking. "I don't know. He didn't look the same. Perhaps it's not Lemuel, but he did seem to know . . . But then that Munodi fellow took him away." He sighed. "I hope he will come again. I want to hear about Houyhnhnmland."

A spasm crossed the duchess's face. "I'm certain he will," she said gently.

"Mother." He reached toward her. "Will you tell Jessica? She will also wish to hear of Houyhnhnm-land."

"Yes, my dear," said the duchess more softly yet. "I know she would."

The duke relaxed. He looked at Philippa. "And you, dear Pippa. You should hear what he has to say."

She smiled. "I would like it above all else, sir."

They stayed half an hour with him. The Duke of Carlyle was a peaceful person; one didn't need to speak much or do anything. And he was in very good spirits today, humming quietly and even asking a question about the flowers. When his face turned gray and he stopped smiling, the duchess had the servants convey him back inside, leaving her and Philippa on the sunny terrace.

For several minutes the duchess sat in silence, her brow creased. "I am not pleased to admit this, but that man seems to have had a good effect upon Johnny," she said abruptly. "We must have him come again and see if he can replicate it."

Philippa nodded in understanding. "I will speak to him."

"He must be instructed," went on the duchess. "Nothing upsetting! Nothing of estate business! Let them talk of Lilliputians or other tales, whatever amuses the duke. Be very clear with Mr. Montclair, Philippa. If he causes anxiety or consternation, I will—" She broke off, looking away.

"Of course, Daadee." Philippa covered the duchess's hand with hers, and the older woman gripped it with surprising strength.

"Did you see how he laughed?" she whispered.

"He hasn't laughed in so long. If Mr. Montclair can make Johnny laugh . . ." Her eyes closed, her lashes glittering with tears. "I will find a way to endure that man if he can bring my son joy."

Philippa squeezed her hand. "I will tell him," she promised, and set off in search of him even though her heart felt like it was leaping into her throat.

She hadn't known Mr. Montclair would be here today. Marianne, her maid, reported that he still brought his laundry to the castle and was a frequent visitor to the kitchens in the early mornings. It appeared he was quite popular belowstairs, despite remaining fully clothed since that one shocking day.

He must have come to see Mr. Edwards, but when Philippa knocked at the door, she only found the attorney, frowning thoughtfully at his wall.

"Montclair? He's gone," he replied to her question. "I presume the duchess heard about his conversation with Carlyle."

Philippa nodded. "I'm to speak to him about it."

Edwards gripped his temples. "I already did."

"No," said Philippa ruefully. "I'm to invite him back."

Edwards's head jerked up.

"The duke was in the best spirits we've seen in a long time. The duchess wishes to see if Mr. Montclair has a lasting effect upon him—properly instructed on what to discuss, of course."

Edwards seemed astonished. "Well," he said. "Well indeed." He rose and paced the office. "Remarkable," he said under his breath.

"What do you mean?" Philippa hated that she

wanted to know what Mr. Montclair had been up to. His letters, mundane as their topics were, tantalized her—the droll descriptions of "a roof that would better serve as a fence" and requests to demolish a rickety shed "with all proper respect to the medieval craftsmen who built it." She hated that she flinched every time Marianne mentioned him, and she hated that she didn't have the nerve to go back to Stone Cottage.

"Hmm?" Edwards glanced at her. "Forgive me, Miss Kirkpatrick. What did you say?"

She felt too awkward to say it again. "Why was Mr. Montclair here?"

"Estate business. Two more bridges must be replaced and two new ones built." Edwards picked up a paper, covered in familiar handwriting.

She stared at that paper, the diagrams labeled with swooping arrows and the paragraphs so tightly knit, they seemed to form ovals and triangles. She pictured his giant map on the wall, covered in notes in his small, precise writing. She remembered how thoroughly he examined the bridge, and how he'd leapt to help Jilly and Gerald Smith. She remembered him at his desk, leaning toward her with a heavy-lidded smile that sent tendrils of heat through her.

She shook off that last thought. "Is he doing well?"

"Yes, and at a bruising pace. All the man does is work." Edwards laid down the paper. "I hope it has improved Her Grace's estimation of him. He can hardly have time to be impertinent."

"He never comes to the castle," Philippa murmured, knowing this was her fault.

Edwards was surprised. "Oh?"

"He sends a list of works each Monday and Thursday for approval."

"Ah," was all he said.

Philippa left in discontent, no wiser about Mr. Montclair's activities or whereabouts. She would have to seek him out.

She took the gig to Stone Cottage, bracing herself, but Mrs. Blake said he was out, and rarely returned before dusk. Camilla added that he left early, and she might catch him then.

So she tried. At seven the next morning she rode down to the house, only to learn he'd been gone an hour already. Irate at being up so early with no benefit, she left a note asking to speak to him. When she returned from her ride, Marianne informed her that he'd been at the castle that morning, laughing and teasing Mrs. Amis in the kitchens. Half the kitchen maids were in love with him, and all of the laundry maids, Marianne reported, which only made Philippa more annoyed.

The next day she expected him to call. He did not, although Mr. Edwards mentioned in passing that he'd seen Mr. Montclair at the mill that afternoon, overseeing the dredging of the pond and sluiceway.

Philippa sent a more pointed note to Stone Cottage, fixing a time when she expected to see him. The only thing that came to the castle was his reply, jotted underneath hers. *Regrettably unable to keep this appointment* —WM

By now she was angry. She told the coachman to ready a carriage and set a boy to watching from the top of the west wall, to notify her when he spied Mr. Montclair returning. As soon as Tommy came running through the courtyard to tell her, she set off.

When she reached Stone Cottage, he was in the stable. Philippa stalked through the twilit garden, wildly irate that she had to resort to this. "Mr. Montclair," she snapped when she reached the stable door. "There you are."

He glanced over his shoulder, then turned back to brushing his horse. Dust covered his coat and breeches, and his boots were caked with mud. "Aye, here I am."

"I've wanted to speak to you for several days now."

"I haven't had time. Apologies." He turned and gave her a mocking bow, slinging the brush into a pail as he did so. "Could it not be written?" He clucked to the horse and guided the animal into a stall.

"No. Why did you refuse my summons?"

"I didn't have time," he repeated, pouring water into the horse's trough. "What is it, Miss Kirkpatrick?"

"About the duke, and your conversation with him."

He paused, his back to her. Then he hung the bucket of oats on a hook, slid the stall door closed, and walked past her toward the house.

Insulted, Philippa stormed after him. "Do you *want* to be sacked?"

He stopped and turned. "Go on, then. Do it."

She recoiled, blinking. His voice throbbed with suppressed anger. It was dark enough she couldn't see his expression beneath his hat brim. But suddenly it came to her that he'd been avoiding her.

He spread his arms wide when she said nothing. "Tell me to pack my trunk and crawl back to London, all for saying a few words to a lonely old man. It seems hard punishment to me, but how dare I violate one of Her Grace's commands."

"No," she said softly. "No, I—I would like you to come speak to the duke again."

He stared at her for a moment, then turned and went into the house. A lamp had been left burning, and he carried it into his study. Philippa followed, uncertain.

He shrugged off his coat and threw it on a chair in the corner, followed by his hat. There was a plate on the desk, covered with a cloth, and a bottle of wine with a glass. "Sit down," he said, and walked back out. Philippa hesitated, and a moment later he came back with a second glass. "Please, be seated," he said again, dropping into the chair. He pulled the cork from the bottle and filled both glasses, offering one to her.

Philippa took it as a goodwill gesture. His lips twitched, as if he meant to smile, but that was all. He whisked the cloth from the plate to reveal roasted chicken, carrots, fresh peas, and mashed parsnips, with what smelled like gingerbread pudding on the side. "I beg your pardon, but I've not eaten since dawn." His eyes skimmed over her. "I would offer refreshment but it appears you've already dined."

She flushed. Her cloak had fallen open, revealing the gown she'd worn to dinner. "Yes. Please don't let me keep you from your dinner."

"Excellent." He picked up a chicken leg and took a bite.

She seated herself in the same chair where she'd sat last time. She wondered who else sat here and talked with him—flirted with him. Not that it mattered to her. "Her Grace was intrigued by your conversation with the duke."

He merely raised one brow and kept eating.

"*Gulliver's Travels*?" She tried a smile. "It was one of His Grace's favorite books."

"So I gathered."

"It pleased him very much," she forged on. "The duchess was delighted. She begs you to consider coming again, to discuss Gulliver some more."

He studied her as he chewed. He took a sip of wine. "Is that all?"

She blinked. "Well—if there are other stories . . . Perhaps *Robinson Crusoe*?" She tried to think of the tales boys might have read. There must be books up in the old schoolroom. She should have checked.

"Forgive me, but the last time we spoke about the duke, you told me explicitly that I was never going to meet him, and not to ask questions. Now you want me to come specifically to see him?"

Philippa looked at her hands. Of course he would throw her own words back in her face. "We have few visitors at the castle. He was rather taken with you. Your conversation seemed to strike a chord in him, and it brought him great pleasure." She looked up. "But you must understand—you're not to discuss estate business with him, or politics, or anything that might trouble him."

He smiled—not his rakish pirate's grin, sparkling with mischief and humor, but a flat, cynical expression.

"His mind is not whole," she said severely. "He called you Lemuel, didn't he?"

"What happened to him?"

Philippa bit her lip.

"Was he born like that?" prodded Mr. Montclair.

She took a fortifying sip of wine. "No," she murmured. "He was not born that way. He was . . ." She stopped.

The Duke of Carlyle had been a gentle but distant figure her entire life. Philippa had grown up listening along with the duke as her stepmother, Jessica, read to both of them. There had been much laughter then; Philippa had loved those sessions. When she was finally old enough to ask about the duke's health, Jessica had cried, telling her.

But she had also told Philippa about him in his youth, how he'd been reserved yet witty, dutiful and earnest but with a streak of deviltry in him. And sometimes the duchess told her more, of how the duke and his brother had nearly killed themselves racing their wooden horses down the hill, how they frightened her nearly to death by scaling the castle walls, how they'd adored Jessica and spoiled her as a child, carrying her between them on their shoulders and hanging a swing for her under the spreading oak. Stephen had been jealous of his sister, for his brothers were away at school by the time he was born and he'd missed their attentions.

Philippa had always wished she could have known him then, too.

"He was injured," she told Mr. Montclair. "As a young man. A horse . . . He was kicked." She touched her temple, on the left side. "His cap conceals it, but there's a dent in his skull. When it happened, he was insensible for nearly a week. The family feared he would never wake. And when he did, he was no longer capable of deep thought. He is kind and gentle and perfectly loving," she added fiercely. "But his memory isn't reliable. He cannot analyze problems or make arguments without tiring."

His expression had grown somber as she spoke. Now he bent his head, hiding his expression. "I'm very sorry to hear that. What was he like before? Do you know?"

"It happened years before I was born. I never had a chance to know him as he was. But my stepmother told me he was charming and amiable. His humor was keen, but subtle. His brother was fond of teasing him, but he always spotted the joke. Mama said the two of them were quite a pair." She smiled at the memory.

"The poor fellow." Mr. Montclair sat back, his face in shadow.

"You asked why this estate is mired thirty years in the past. That's how long it's been since there was a duke able to care for it. His Grace was injured only a few months after his father died. Lord Stephen would have inherited, but he was a clergyman and found more joy in that role. The duchess feels the weighty responsibility, and has done everything in her power to preserve the estate."

"For Captain St. James."

"Yes. When Stephen died, she summoned him

and another cousin, Maximilian, who would inherit if the captain didn't survive."

"Why isn't he here if this is all to be his?"

Philippa smiled slightly. "He's Scottish, sir, as is his wife. They prefer Stormont Palace near Perth. Mr. Edwards corresponds with him monthly about the estate."

Mr. Montclair grunted. "The duke deeded Stormont Palace to him. I saw the papers."

"A wedding gift." She chewed her lip, then added, "In truth, the duchess couldn't keep up with so much property. Stormont Palace was not entailed, and Mr. Edwards was advising her to sell it."

"But deeding it to the captain keeps it in the family," murmured Mr. Montclair. "And when he inherits the rest, it will return to the ducal estate."

Philippa nodded. "Yes. Will you come to see the duke?"

He seemed troubled, and went back to picking at his dinner. He'd devoured the chicken and vegetables while she spoke, and now took a bite of the pudding. "Begging your pardon, Miss Kirkpatrick, I'm not certain I should. I seem to have a rare talent for angering Her Grace despite my best intentions."

She moved to the edge of her chair. "I'll come with you. I promise to take full responsibility and warn you if necessary, as well as vouch for your conduct with the duchess." He said nothing. "She sent me to ask you," Philippa added. "She desires you to come and see him, not her."

His lips curved in a faint echo of his familiar rakish grin.

"It's perhaps the best of all possibilities," she said with an encouraging smile, sensing he was about to agree. "You needn't see her, but will have every chance to win her good opinion."

Finally he laughed. "As if dedicated labor on behalf of her estate would not?" He waved one hand as Philippa's mouth fell open. "Never mind. But his health must wax and wane from day to day. I don't have time to wait at the castle every day for a propitious moment to visit."

"I'll send you word in the morning if it's not a good day," she promised. "And such a breakneck pace isn't necessary. The estate has been here for hundreds of years."

His amusement faded. "No, there's not enough time," he muttered. "But perhaps it's worth the risk."

Philippa was so pleased she didn't ask what he meant. "Thank you. Would tomorrow suit?" The duchess had asked her every day if the steward had agreed to come. Philippa could see the battle inside her, her irritation at Mr. Montclair warring with her desperate desire to see the duke smile and laugh again.

He looked at her for a long moment. "I can't help but feel this is only another chance for me to displease her. One wrong word and I'll be sacked. I'm better suited to rebuilding barns and repairing roads, Miss Kirkpatrick."

"No, no." She set down the wineglass in agitation. "Please come. I promise to advise you."

Too late she realized she had promised that before, and failed. She flushed so red her face hurt.

Mr. Montclair obviously sensed what she was

thinking. He cleared his throat and looked down. "I apologize," he said quietly. "I offended you the last time you were here, and I regret it."

"Offend!" A burst of hysterical laughter escaped her. "No, I . . . I also apologize. I promised to guide you in your dealings with the duchess, and haven't done so." She hesitated. "I know," she said carefully, "that she is demanding. To me she is very dear, like a grandmother. To you, she is . . ." She hesitated again. Mr. Montclair arched one brow. "She is difficult to please," Philippa admitted. "*Very* difficult, at times. But I assure you that she *has* been pleased by your work. Mr. Edwards has praised your initiative and plans, and she trusts his opinion."

She did not tell him that Mr. Edwards's praise also had the power to alarm the duchess, nor that Philippa herself had been the one to see the sense of Mr. Montclair's proposals and persuade the duchess to approve them. She didn't want him to be sacked, for a variety of reasons she didn't care to examine too closely.

"I also was glad to see the duke happy," she added—truthfully. "I would be very grateful if you came and cheered him again. Please."

Finally a real smile touched his mouth. "In that case, I cannot possibly refuse."

Chapter Twelve

❧ ❦

One good thing about weeks of nonstop hard work: it had lulled Will's conscience almost to sleep.

This time when he rode up to the castle, he could barely hear the little voice inside his head—which sounded rudely like his brother's—reminding him that he was leaving in three months and wasn't to flirt with anyone. Today he was spending the day with Miss Kirkpatrick, and he was looking forward to it more than he should.

He hadn't realized until she appeared in his stable, cross and impatient and so beautiful he could barely look at her, how much he'd missed seeing her. No letter could compare; he'd hung on the way she spoke of the duke, the expression on her face when she asked him to come back, the way she beamed when he agreed.

That smile alone could lay waste to all his plans and intentions, if he didn't watch himself.

Today, instead of going to the service courtyard, he presented himself in the magnificent entry hall, with its display of antique arms. Heywood went to inform Miss Kirkpatrick, leaving Will to contemplate a rather brutal statue of Perseus holding aloft the severed head of Medusa. *That'll be your head, if you're not careful*, he could almost hear Jack say.

"Mr. Montclair!"

He looked up and the floor seemed to heave under his feet. Miss Kirkpatrick was hurrying down the stairs, an eager smile on her lips. She held up her bright yellow skirts as she came, and he caught a glimpse of slim legs in white stockings, scarlet embroidery tracing up her ankles.

He had to close his eyes and take a deep breath. One glimpse of her ankles, and his mind began plotting removing those stockings as arousal bubbled up inside him like a volcano boiling toward eruption. *Stop*, he told himself.

"Is something wrong?" she asked breathlessly, and he snapped to alertness.

"Never better." He grinned, and something inside him seemed to leap and burst like fireworks when she smiled back, so widely her dimple appeared again. Without thinking, he offered his arm and she took it, which set off another riot in his chest that drowned out the warning inside his head.

"I thought we might take a look in the old nursery first, to see if there are other books the duke might recall." She led him up the staircase.

Will looked at her askance. "Oh. I imagined . . ."

"What?" she prompted when he stopped.

"I thought a simple chat with the fellow would be enough."

Her glorious eyebrows swooped into a stern look. "That is the duke you speak of," she chided.

"And I promised to guide you. Better to be prepared with more than one topic, don't you think?"

"Right," he said, snatching his gaze from the splendid view of her bosom he had with her on his arm. Her breasts were so plump and tempting in the curved neckline of her bodice. A line of lace peeked out, pale and suggestive against the warm copper of her skin. "Of course."

She led him through elegant rooms with ornate plasterwork and salons hung with silk, past paintings twice as tall as a man and six times as long, past suits of armor and statues of marble. If she hadn't been leading him along, Will would have stopped and gaped like the provincial he was.

By the time they reached a fairly ordinary corridor, with only a plain woven carpet down the middle and no artwork at all, he was completely turned around. The south turret, he thought, but Miss Kirkpatrick opened a door and he forgot all about his bearings.

"This is the nursery?" The ceiling wasn't as tall as the finer rooms downstairs, but there were several windows, making the room bright. There were child-sized tables and chairs, shelves with books and toys. A carved wooden horse on wheels stood in one corner, glass eyes gleaming in the sun.

"Yes." She headed toward the bookcase. "I was the last child to use it, but only sporadically. My stepmama—Lady Jessica—didn't care for it and most of my lessons were elsewhere."

Slowly Will crossed the room to the horse. He touched the head; the mane, thin and scraggly from age, was real horsehair. "Did you ride him?"

"Him?" She came up beside him. "Oh. No." She

smoothed the threadbare woolen blanket under the saddle of real leather on the seat. "He was the duke's. Nestor is his name."

"The Argonaut," murmured Will, transfixed. He brushed the mane again. "Nestor fought the centaurs, hunted the Calydonian boar, and went to war with a shield of gold."

"Oh?" Miss Kirkpatrick smiled. "I never knew all that. Mama said her brothers used to race on Nestor and . . ." She paused, looking around. "There should be another one. I remember a story about a terrific crash when they were boys."

Will grinned. "I don't doubt it! My brother and I would have competed fiercely to see who could sail down the hill fastest." The broad path that led from the castle toward Stone Cottage was sloped but smooth.

She laughed in surprise. "Indeed! That was where they raced!"

He winked. "Boys are the same the world over."

"I wonder where the other horse went," she said, still smiling. "He must be here somewhere. Mama said her brothers were horse-mad and argued, well past childhood, about which horse was better, Nestor or the other one."

Will turned away from the horse. "A sporting family, I see." There were shelves and shelves of cricket bats, hoops, balls, pall-mall mallets, skittles pins, battledores and shuttlecocks, and archery equipment. A film of dust covered everything. The strings of the bows were loose, the racquets warped.

"Yes. The duchess believed exercise was good for children, and she encouraged them to be outdoors."

Will picked up a battledore and gave it a tentative swing. Miss Kirkpatrick grinned and tossed a shuttlecock into the air. Off guard, Will lunged and smacked it upward just shy of the floor. "How many children were there?" Will bounced the shuttlecock up and down off the sagging gut of the webbing.

"Four, but of a wide age range. The duke was fifteen, I believe, when Lord Stephen, the youngest, was born." She picked up another racquet and Will obligingly tapped the shuttlecock her way. She hit it harder than he expected, and he had to leap over a small chair to keep it aloft and hit it back.

"So, not a well-matched opponent."

"No," she said, darting around the table for her return shot. "The duke and Lord William were closer in age. Only two years apart."

"And Lady Jessica?" Will deliberately sent the shuttlecock toward the far corner for the pleasure of seeing her gasp and run after it, skirts held up in one hand.

"Eight years younger than the duke!" Her voice rose as she whacked the shuttlecock hard at his head.

Will threw up his racquet and gently flicked his wrist, tapping the shuttlecock more than hitting it. With a startled exclamation, Miss Kirkpatrick dove forward and swung, losing her grip on her dress. She missed the shuttlecock, and then lost her balance as her foot tangled in her skirts, and she pitched toward the floor. On instinct Will sprang forward and opened his arms.

"Oh!" She fell heavily into him, grabbing instinctively for his arms as they tumbled over backward.

Will landed hard on his back, but he barely felt it as she sprawled on top of him, soft and curved and smelling of flowers.

Time stopped. He had no rule for this situation, at least not one that he could remember. He had stopped flirting; he had avoided seeing her altogether. And yet somehow she was still on top of him, in his arms, her face inches from his, looking disheveled and flushed and so tempting he ached to forget who he was and why he was here, just for a few minutes.

He closed his eyes and tried desperately to remember that this woman was leagues out of his reach, that he was leaving Carlyle in a few months. And that even if those problems magically vanished, there would still be the matter of the lies he'd told everyone.

"Oh," she said breathlessly, struggling to get her balance. Her hair had come down and was falling around her face in silky dark waves. She tried to shove it back with one hand and ended up collapsing back onto him. Her breasts pressed against his chest. Her perfume filled his head.

"Are you hurt?" he managed to ask. All her wriggling was making his torment worse.

"No." Her cheeks were deep pink. The pulse throbbed rapidly at the base of her throat, almost as fast as Will's own. Up close her brown eyes glinted with flecks of gold and green, wide and dilated in surprise. Their gazes connected, and she went still.

He should help her rise. He should make a lighthearted remark about the accident. He should look away so she could right herself in dignified privacy.

Instead he thought: *Kiss me.*

She licked her lips before saying, "Thank you." Her voice was soft and husky. Like a lover's.

"For what?" His heart was hammering against his ribs.

"For catching me."

He shifted his gaze up to the ceiling. "It was more like breaking your fall than catching."

She smiled. "I am grateful, whatever you call it."

He managed to nod, staring fiercely at a spider-web above him. "It was my pleasure." *Kiss me kiss me kiss me kiss me,* begged the devil inside his head. Her lips were so close to his. His muscles were so taut he didn't think he could move, and he was so aroused he didn't think he should. He would be whipped from the property—hell, he'd probably be hauled off to prison in chains—if anyone knew that he was imagining rolling over this proper young lady, ward of the Duke of Carlyle, and kissing her senseless. Tasting the plump swells of her breasts. Sliding his hands up her silk-stockinged legs. Pulling out the rest of the pins and letting her hair tumble loose in a dark, silky waterfall . . .

She pushed herself up. Will's chest expanded as if he hadn't taken a breath in minutes as her weight lifted off him. Eyes still fixed on the ceiling, he offered his hand, and she clasped it for a moment as she clambered to her feet. She turned her back to him as she straightened her dress and fixed her hair.

And Will was glad. It gave him a moment to get himself back in hand, to roll up from the floor and adjust his own clothing, not so much to straighten it but to hide his erection. *You idiot*, seethed a voice inside his head. *Stay away from this one or you'll ruin everything.*

He knew that. He'd known it all along. And every time he thought he could safely bend one of his rules, it only ended with him wanting her more.

"Thank you," she said again, sounding far calmer and poised than he felt.

"It was nothing." He jerked his waistcoat down and strode toward the bookshelves. *Visit the duke and get out.* "Where are the books you said we might find?"

PHILIPPA'S HEART WAS hammering so hard she could hardly force the pins back into her hair. She'd fallen on him with all the grace of a sack of wheat and then nearly kissed him.

He knew that she'd been struck stupid by that contact, the crush of her body against his. She'd seen it in his eyes, when they went dark and hot, and felt it in the tension of his muscles. She could feel *everything* about him, lying on top of him, and shamefully Philippa had wanted to stay there.

She'd almost kissed him. That she blamed on him, because he was the one to look at her mouth with open desire. She tried not to think that *she* was the one whose pulse had leapt at the thought, who had felt a surge of euphoria, who had been on the brink of pressing her mouth to his when he— thanks be to all the saints in heaven—had looked away, giving her brain a chance to function.

Behind her he got to his feet and turned his back to her. Philippa was grateful for that. She pressed her shaking hands to her cheeks, unsurprised to feel how warm they were. She must be flushed all over; her skin felt scorching hot, crackling with every movement, and there was a faint buzzing in her ears.

He said something and went to the bookcase, as calm and collected as if they hadn't just been lying tangled around each other on the floor. His thigh had been between hers, and a thrill raced through her in memory—a delicious, dark, enticing thrill.

He stooped to see the spines. Today he wore somber ordinary garments of dark green and gray, the clothes she had once presumed a steward would wear, and it made him look even more dashing. That golden hoop in his ear looked just the size of her little finger, and she'd been appalled by how much she'd wanted to touch it—to lean down and press her face to his neck—press her body even closer to his. She'd wanted to kiss him and feel his hands on her, right here on the floor.

Philippa covered her mouth with both hands. She was lusting after the estate steward, and didn't know how to stop.

"Ah, here's our friend Gulliver." He took out a book and rested one foot on a small chair, propping his elbow on his knee as he paged through the book. "A duke's children merit a fine library."

Philippa kept her eyes averted as she went to join him. Never before had this schoolroom seemed so small, so warm, or so quiet. So intimate. He turned a page, and the whisper of his fingers over the paper made her quiver.

"The duchess insisted." She pulled out a book

at random and stared blindly at it. "I believe she read to her children every night when they were young."

"A devoted mother."

"Yes." Her thoughts were leaping around like a grasshopper. She had been lying on top of him. She had been six inches away from pressing her mouth to his. She had been close enough to see the streaks of gold in his eyes and smell his shaving soap.

For the first time in her life, she wished passionately that she'd been a laundry maid, and knew what he looked like without his shirt on.

"What was your passion?"

She started violently, nearly dropping her book. "What?"

"What stories did you enjoy?" He glanced up. "As a girl." His hair was loose around his shoulders, rumpled waves gleaming like polished mahogany in the sunlight. Hadn't it been tied back before? Had it come loose while she was lying on him on the floor?

"I don't remember," she whispered.

His eyebrow twitched. He had a way of tilting his head, just slightly, to the side, that made him look mischievous and tempting even though his expression was completely serious.

Or perhaps she imagined everything. Perhaps it was her complete inexperience with gentlemen that left her in such upheaval. Why else would she be turned completely upside down by this one infuriating man—a man she certainly had no future with. It was wrong for her to want to feel his body against hers and scandalous to dream of tucking her face into the crook of his neck and absolutely wicked to imagine his arms around her and his mouth lowering to hers . . .

Flushed, suffocating, Philippa jammed the book back onto the shelf. "The duke will be expecting us." She turned and all but ran for the stairs.

Chapter Thirteen

❧❧❧

Mr. Amis was waiting for them when they reached the duke's suite. "He's in good spirits today, Miss Kirkpatrick. He is outside again. Her Grace has sent down twice, asking if Mr. Montclair has arrived yet."

Philippa hastily hushed him; the steward was only two steps away. "Send word that he is here," she whispered. "Tell her I will come to her directly when he leaves."

"Yes, ma'am." He bowed.

Philippa led the way through the suite. A footman opened the doors to the sunny terrace, where the duke sat in his banyan and cap. At the sight of her, his face brightened.

"Dear Pippa!" To her astonishment he rose from the chaise—unsteadily, leaning on a cane, but standing. She hadn't seen him on his feet since last summer.

"Uncle, you look so well!" She went and took the hand he held out to her, pressing it affectionately to her cheek. "The sunshine is good for you."

He chuckled. "So says Mother! Well, perhaps she

is right." He was already looking past her. "Ah, finally, you've come again to see me."

Philippa watched Mr. Montclair sweep his usual flourishing bow. "With great pleasure to be invited back, sir."

"Invited back!" Carlyle shook his head. "You are welcome at any time." He sank awkwardly back onto the chaise and gestured at the two chairs. "Sit down."

Philippa took the seat next to the table as Mr. Montclair skirted the terrace to take the other. When he sat down beside her, she realized he had brought the copy of *Gulliver's Travels* from the schoolroom.

The duke noticed, too. "Brought along your diary?"

Mr. Montclair nodded. "In the event I need to refresh my memory."

Carlyle put out one hand, and the steward gave him the book. The duke opened the cover, and sighed happily. "Here we wrote our names and wagers." He blinked at the page, and his finger shook as he traced the words. "Pippa, do you see there? How many did I win?"

Surprised, she took the book. Her breath caught as she read the lines in childish script, the ink long faded. "John Frederick and William Augustus do hereby swear to record all their adventures and misadventures, and to share with the other, at all times of life." Her throat felt tight as she turned the page. "William wagers one shilling that John is taken as a pet by a Brobdingnag and John wagers one shilling that William—" She paused, stricken. The next words were *William is lost at sea in a chest.* "William is adopted by a Houyhnhnm," she said instead, plucking one of the few stories she remembered from Gulliver.

Beside her, Mr. Montclair shifted. "I'd call that one even, Your Grace."

The duke gave a faintly puzzled smile. "Alas! I thought I'd won . . . Never mind. Tell me how you fared with Munodi when he dragged you off."

"Very well," replied the steward easily. "It's fortunate for all that you've placed him in command of Carlyle."

Philippa went rigid. He had *promised* not to mention the estate.

The duke blinked. "Oh yes, yes . . . My mother approves of him, I believe. And what is he doing?"

"We're building a few bridges," went on the idiot man blithely. "Perhaps you would care to drive out in the carriage to view the sites."

The duke fell back, astonished. Philippa gripped the arms of her chair to avoid flying at Mr. Montclair and clapping her hands over his mouth. "I say," murmured Carlyle, looking bewildered. "Ought I?" He turned toward her. "Pippa dear, what would Mother think?"

She opened her mouth and froze. It had been the duchess's deepest desire for months to get the duke to ride out in the carriage. Did that outweigh her stricture that Mr. Montclair was not to speak of the estate? "I believe she would be very pleased to join you for a drive," she said carefully. "Shall I ask her?"

"An excellent idea," said Carlyle with relief. "Go now, that we might plan the trip."

Involuntarily Philippa's gaze flew to Mr. Montclair's, who gazed calmly back as if he had no notion of the upheaval he'd just caused. He widened his eyes and gave a minute shrug, as if to say *why not?* Philippa got to her feet. "I will, Uncle."

He caught her hand as she moved past the chaise. "Tell her I wish to go. And . . . tell her to invite Jessica." His voice turned wistful. "I've not seen Jessica in so long."

Philippa nodded, not trusting her voice. He hadn't mentioned her stepmother this often in months. She turned away and hurried blindly toward the house. She made it inside the doors before swiping at her wet eyes and then burying her face in her hands. How she too wished Jessica would come . . .

"Are you all right?" Mr. Montclair's voice made her start. He put his hand gently on her shoulder, and peered into her face. "I'm sorry," he murmured.

"You weren't to mention the estate," she said sternly, trying not to sniffle as she searched her pockets, to no avail. "And I want to be angry at you for ignoring everything I said but I cannot be, because Her Grace will be overjoyed if the duke rides out in the carriage."

Mr. Montclair held out his handkerchief. "Should I apologize for that, too?"

She took it and dried her eyes. "*No.*" She looked at him. "Why have you left him?"

His brow wrinkled and his smile was perplexed. "You were upset."

Philippa blew her nose, mortified that she'd fallen apart. "You shouldn't have."

"He gave me leave, and Mr. Amis is with him."

He paused. "He means Mr. Edwards when he speaks of Munodi. Perhaps he's more interested in the estate than Her Grace believes."

Philippa shook her head, not knowing what to think. "Say nothing more of it until I return."

He straightened. "And if *he* says something of it?"

She frowned at him. "Perhaps you could spy an eagle coming to carry you off and say you must flee for your life."

He raised one finger in counterpoint. "Gulliver was carried off by an eagle, yet lived to tell the tale."

"A vulture, then."

He leaned toward her. By now she knew that expression; he meant to tease and provoke her and take pleasure in her annoyed response. "Vultures only eat dead things."

Philippa smiled sweetly. "Wait until I return," she promised, "and there may well be something dead for the vultures to eat."

He gave her the sly, pirate's grin. "A dagger to the heart, I suppose."

Still smiling, she leaned toward him and tapped him on the chin. "Nothing so subtle, Mr. Montclair."

His eyes glowed like embers stirred to life. "I shall be on my guard," he breathed.

She raised her brows and tilted even closer, ignoring the clanging warning in her head that she was, for the second time that day, veering dangerously close to kissing this infuriating, enthralling man. "For what I have in mind," she vowed, "it wouldn't matter. You would be powerless to stop me."

His lips parted in delighted fascination. Now she thought he might kiss *her*, and the prospect only made her heart skip, hop, and soar with excitement. She smiled and batted her lashes at him, scarcely able to believe herself. "'Til later, Mr. Montclair." With a swish of skirts, she turned and went on her way, breaking into a giddy smile once she was safely out the door.

WILL WENT BACK outside, his heart thumping. God above, he liked that woman. She no longer looked angry at his teasing and impertinent replies; she looked exhilarated—though still irked—and answered him in kind. And he, idiot that he was, found that more arousing than anything short of her throwing herself on top of him.

God, what a day this had been.

The duke sat forward at his approach. "Was Pippa upset?"

"Only at me." He resumed his seat. "She cordially wished I would be eaten by a vulture."

Carlyle's chuckle was gentle. "No! Why?"

Will assumed a hangdog expression. "I wasn't to mention work about the estate."

The duke waved one hand. "It is tiresome. But it sounds more interesting when you speak of it than when Mother does . . ." His face clouded. "She does awfully well, but I'm no help. I ought to be, but I'm not."

"Everyone has different talents." Will sensed he trod on dangerous, employment-ending ground here. "I'm a slow hand at figuring the account books—always a shilling and tuppence off when I first do them, and then I've got to spend the rest of the day hunting for it. My brother, though, is top-notch at it."

"Did your father teach him?"

Will cleared his throat. "Our mother did, actually. My brother takes after her—sensible, orderly, a head for mathematics."

"Your mother," murmured the duke, his eyes growing distant. "How remarkable." For a minute he stared at nothing, then roused himself. "You're building a bridge?"

"Yes, sir."

Another thin smile crossed the duke's face. "I would like to see that." He closed his eyes and leaned back on the chaise. Mr. Amis stepped forward and spread a blanket over his legs. The duke didn't open his eyes, but patted Mr. Amis's hand.

"Shall I go, Your Grace?" asked Will quietly.

"Read a bit," came his faint reply. "I cannot remember Laputa."

Obediently Will picked up the book from Miss Kirkpatrick's chair and leafed through it. Mr. Amis moved the painted screen to block the sun from the duke's face, and Will began to read.

THE DUCHESS LEAPT from her seat as soon as Philippa burst into the sitting room. "Well?"

She held up both hands. "Mr. Montclair suggested the duke ride out in the carriage to see the bridge being built—"

The duchess inhaled and clapped one hand to her heart, her eyes flashing with fury.

"And Uncle said he would like that very much," finished Philippa in a rush. She held her breath, hoping. She found Mr. Montclair extremely aggravating . . .

as well as intriguing and amusing and far too
appealing for her own good. "He sent me to ask
if you would care to join him in the carriage."

For a moment the duchess seemed frozen, hand
still on her bosom. But now her eyes were wide
with dazed surprise, not anger, and Philippa
feared she would faint as she slowly wilted back
into her chair.

"He wishes to drive out . . ." she whispered. She
covered her mouth with one hand and closed her
eyes. Philippa wasn't surprised to see the glitter of
tears on her lashes.

Abruptly she bounded out of her seat and hurried from the room. Philippa darted after her, sus-
pecting where they were going.

The duke's sitting room had been the bedchamber before the duchess renovated the suite after
his injury. Now the large room on the ground
floor was the bedchamber, with a tiled bathing
room and dressing room, and up the corner stairs
was the study. It was a beautiful room, with soaring windows that offered an unequaled view of
the castle grounds. Sometimes the duchess would
coax the duke upstairs for tea, looking over Carlyle, but the room was little used by anyone else.

Today the duchess went directly to the windows
and unlatched one. Gently she pushed it open and
together they eavesdropped.

The terrace lay directly below, bathed in afternoon sunshine. Philippa peered out. Mr. Montclair, his hat pushed back on his head, sprawled
in the chair, one leg stretched in front of him. He
held the book in one hand and moved the other
as he read, describing shapes in mid-air. Carlyle

reclined on the chaise, his hands clasped on his stomach and a slight smile on his face. His eyes were closed. To Philippa's surprise, Mr. Amis now sat in the second chair, listening just as avidly as the duke.

"'We had two courses of three dishes each,'" read Mr. Montclair. For the first time Philippa realized the trace of French was gone from his voice. He sounded as English as she did. "'In the first course, there was a shoulder of mutton cut into an equilateral triangle, a piece of beef into a rhomboid, and a pudding into a cycloid. The second course was two ducks trussed up in the form of fiddles; sausages and puddings resembling flutes and hautboys, and a breast of veal in the shape of a harp.'"

"A harp," declared the duke in delight. "Charles, see if Mrs. Carter can truss a breast of veal as a harp."

Mr. Amis nodded. "I will, sir."

"I have every confidence she can," said Mr. Montclair. "You're blessed with magnificent cooks at Carlyle."

"Are we?" The duke sounded uncertain.

"Indeed, sir," said Mr. Montclair fervently. "There were some cherry tarts the other day fit for the gods."

"You enjoyed those tarts, Your Grace," murmured Mr. Amis.

"Oh . . . Yes, I remember." Carlyle waved one hand. "Read on, if you please."

Upstairs, the duchess gripped Philippa's hand. "He sounds so happy," she whispered. "And he wishes to drive out in the carriage?"

"To see one of the bridges being built."

The duchess nodded. "We shall go. Tell Mr. Montclair we will go tomorrow, weather permitting." She was silent for a few minutes. Mr. Montclair's voice drifted up to them again, but Philippa didn't believe the duchess was listening; she was thinking.

"How can it be?" she asked softly of no one. "Have I denied him something vital all these years?"

Philippa squeezed her hand. "No!"

"Not knowingly," said the older woman. "Not wittingly . . . but depriving him all the same."

There was no answer for that. Philippa thought of how Jessica had read to the duke for hours. He had listened, enjoyed it, smiled with her . . . but not this way. Through the windows came a shout of laughter—all three of them were howling at something. When she peered out, Mr. Amis was wiping his eyes, Mr. Montclair's shoulders were heaving, and the duke was chuckling, looking very pleased with himself. *He* had made the joke, she realized with a start. Carlyle.

They listened there for some time, until the sounds of conversation and merriment faded. "Bring him," said the duchess, and Philippa ran down the stairs to intercept the steward.

"WELL DONE," MR. Amis murmured as they left the terrace.

Will grimaced. "Don't be surprised if this is the last you see of me."

The Black man looked at him, a glimmer of

amusement in his eyes. "I *would* be greatly surprised by that."

"I spoke of things I wasn't to mention." He'd known that at the time and still had not been able to restrain himself. "I'll likely be sacked when the duchess learns of it." Miss Kirkpatrick had bolted off to tell her, and not returned. He couldn't help but take that as a bad sign.

The valet's smile grew. "Did you not hear the window above open? I believe Madam must have heard for herself."

Will let out his breath, imagining the duchess's expression at the jokes they'd made. He'd be back in London within days, if not hours.

"I have been here ten years, and rarely seen the duke so happily animated as he was today," Amis told him. "I expect she'll be greatly pleased by that." He paused. "I have been most curious to make your acquaintance, Mr. Montclair. My wife has told me of your visits to the kitchens."

"Ah, you are the fortunate husband of Mrs. Amis!" He grinned in delight.

Amis chuckled. "I am. You have impressed her, and that is not something most men can say."

"Someone at Carlyle who hasn't found me inferior to Mr. Grimes!" Will smiled halfheartedly.

"No, indeed," replied Amis. "It was time for him to go."

"Oh?" Will wanted to ask more, but Amis turned as footsteps sounded behind them. Miss Kirkpatrick came hurtling down the stairs, her skirts once again caught up in her hands. This time Will kept his eyes off her ankles and on her face. She looked anxious.

"Alas," he murmured to the valet. "Our acquaintance may be brief after all."

"Don't begin packing yet," came his reply. "Yes, Miss Kirkpatrick?"

"I would like a word with Mr. Montclair," she said breathlessly. She looked at him, and helplessly Will's heart leapt. Her face was as flushed as when she'd looked down at him, lying on his chest. With great effort he kept his face impassive. "Ma'am."

Her cheeks grew pinker. "Come this way," she said, turning and hurrying back up the stairs.

"Wish me luck," he said under his breath.

Amis chuckled. "Say and do as little as possible," he advised quietly, "and be excessively humble."

Will climbed the stairs. At the top waited Miss Kirkpatrick, and to his astonishment she took his arm and led him across the room, to where the duchess stood near the open window.

"Here he is, ma'am," said Miss Kirkpatrick brightly.

He glanced at her in shock. She sounded as if she were presenting a long-lost friend, even before she turned her face up to him and gave him a brilliant smile. "Thank you for sparing us a moment, sir."

This was why he was in trouble, Will thought. No matter how disciplined he tried to be, no matter how strictly he adhered to his rules, one smile like this threw him right back into the dangerous pit of longing. "Of course," he finally managed to say. "'Tis my pleasure." Her eyes lit, and she gave his arm a little squeeze. He'd answered well, and it gave him another jolt of pleasure. He bowed to the duchess, simply, as Mr. Amis recommended. "Good day, Your Grace."

A frown knit the duchess's brow. "Mr. Montclair." She seemed uncertain what to say. "The duke appears to relish your company."

Will just bowed his head.

The older woman looked disconcerted by his silence. "Well. Miss Kirkpatrick says Carlyle wishes to drive out in the carriage to inspect the building of a bridge. Is that correct?"

"As I understand it, ma'am."

The duchess nodded once. "What else did you speak of with His Grace?"

As if she hadn't been listening at the open windows. "*Gulliver's Travels*, ma'am. A bit about cherry tarts and a bit about horse racing."

The duchess's brows shot up. "Horse racing!"

"Yes, ma'am."

She drew breath, but then let it out. "I see." She plucked at the trimmings on her gown.

"If the weather permits, we could go tomorrow," said Miss Kirkpatrick. "Would that suit you, sir?"

"Whatever you desire suits me, Miss Kirkpatrick."

He thought he'd spoken evenly and calmly, no hint of emotion. But her lips parted and her eyes grew dark as she stared at him, and Will realized she was attracted to him. Even though it did not help him, and in fact should have sent him racing back to Stone Cottage, euphoria jolted through him so strongly he almost wavered on his feet.

"Excellent," she whispered. She cleared her throat, and hungrily Will watched her wet her lips. "Noon?" Her voice was higher than usual.

Unable to tear his eyes away from hers, Will nodded. "As you wish, Miss Kirkpatrick."

She smiled.

"Yes," said the duchess abruptly. "Until tomorrow, Mr. Montclair."

Tomorrow. His pulse thundering in his ears, Will bowed again, and left.

Chapter Fourteen

❧❦❧

Philippa woke the next morning in excellent spirits. The sun shone brightly through the windows; it was a beautiful day. The duke had stood up on his own and laughed. They were going driving today, which would please the duchess enormously.

And Mr. Montclair would ride along with them.

She dressed in her favorite gown, a soft chemise à la Reine, the muslin gauzy and airy. She wore it over rose-colored stays and petticoat, which made the dress appear to glow pink, like the garments her mother wore in the portrait on Philippa's wall.

As Marianne fixed her hair, Philippa faced it, as she usually did. It was a splendid painting; Papa had got one of the best painters in Hyderabad to do it. Noor un-nisa smiled back at her, her large dark eyes soft and yet somehow impish. Papa said she had appeared sweet and meek, but that she'd been fearless in pursuit of what she wanted—even when she wanted an English soldier of no particular importance. Her father had refused the first time Papa asked for her hand.

Only Noor's relentless efforts had persuaded her father to allow the marriage.

Philippa loved that story.

When she got to breakfast there was a letter by her plate from Frances Beauchamp, Aunt Diana's youngest and only unmarried daughter. She opened it with a smile, then was surprised to see that it was full of eager plans for her imminent visit. *We shall visit everything and everyone,* her sprawling penmanship declared. *I cannot wait to see you again, dear Pippa! I am so delighted you are coming soon! We shall keep you until the first frost!*

Philippa cleared her throat. "Fanny Beauchamp believes I'm practically on my way to London already."

The duchess looked up from feeding slivers of ham to Percival. "An excellent thought! I shall order the carriage for Thursday."

Philippa folded the letter. "Daadee, we agreed I wouldn't go now."

"*You* said that." The duchess offered a piece of cheese to the cat, who cocked his head and batted it on the floor. "I think you should go."

She was puzzled. "Why?"

The older woman shooed Percival from the table. "I know you, child. *Next month, next week, tomorrow,* you say, when you do not look forward to something. There is nothing to fear about London! The sooner you go, the greater the chance you will meet someone wonderful."

Again the reminder that she would be alone in the world if she didn't find a husband. "I expect anyone worth meeting would still be there next month."

The duchess clucked in disapproval. "I do not! Best go now, to give yourself time to sift the few who are worthy from the many who are not."

Philippa laughed. "You're very eager to be rid of me!"

The duchess did not laugh. "You were staring at Mr. Montclair very strangely yesterday."

The laugh caught in her throat. "Was I?" she asked like an idiot.

"I'm an old woman but I'm not blind," came the tart reply. "He's a handsome fellow."

Her face was burning, and her heart beat so hard her hands shook. She put them in her lap. "Is he?"

The duchess's stern expression melted into concern. "He is the only unmarried man between the ages of twenty and fifty on this estate, isn't he? My dear, I am so sorry. This is entirely my fault."

She was frozen, half-terrified, half-mortified. "What is?" She couldn't even form a coherent sentence.

The older woman sighed. "Go to London. Meet people your own age, instead of moldering away with an old lady and a castle of retainers." She touched Philippa's cheek. "In London there will be a flock of handsome, charming young men deserving of your notice."

Unlike Mr. Montclair.

The duchess didn't say it, but Philippa heard it all the same.

She looked away, biting hard on her lip. She knew it was wrong to feel so attracted to Mr. Montclair. He was the steward—a servant. She was an heiress, if not a lady. He was completely inappropriate and yet . . . she couldn't stop thinking about him.

Perhaps the duchess was right; perhaps in London she would meet someone else, *several* someones, who made her heart race in delight, and she would forget all about the mischievous glint in Mr. Montclair's eye, and the way he made her want to scream and kiss him into silence and possibly fall full-length on top of him again to see him look at her with that focused desire . . .

She took a deep, steadying breath. Was the duchess correct? She must be. Philippa was naive. She should go to London, where she would learn to flirt correctly and how to tell a rogue from a gentleman and meet someone who would make her heart leap and her stomach flutter—someone, as the duchess said, who was suitable.

Impulsively she clasped the duchess's hand. "Thank you, Daadee, for caring for me."

The duchess smiled fondly. "My darling girl. How could I do otherwise? Diana will keep you busy from morning 'til midnight, dancing and flirting. I fully expect you'll soon have a dozen gentlemen vying for your hand . . ." She stopped, her eyes suspiciously damp despite her happy expression.

Philippa laughed. "A dozen! One or two would be plenty, thank you. If there were a dozen, how would I ever choose?"

"Ah, now *that* I know something about." The duchess smiled in arch remembrance. "Eleven offers of marriage I received, when I was a girl. I don't even count the ones who asked my father when I was a child. Oh my, the things they said to me! Such liars." She sighed. "Whatever his failings, the duke was not a liar."

"But I haven't your charm," teased Philippa, trying to keep the mood light. "Nor your youth! I'll be twenty-four this year, ma'am."

The duchess shook her head. "You have far more sense than I did. I chose on ambition and vanity." She gave Philippa a piercing look. "You must choose someone who adores you."

The duchess hadn't. Her husband, the fourth duke, had been arrogant and tyrannical, and he'd married her—only child of a wealthy banker, barely sixteen years old on their wedding day—for her dowry. He'd been dead for three decades and absolutely no one missed him.

"I hope so, too," Philippa said to the duchess, choosing hope over realism. She scooped up her letter and rose. "I'll see you at noon."

She made her way to her room, her steps slowing as she went. The letter from Fanny indicated how desperately the duchess wanted her to go to town; she must have written to Diana the moment Philippa agreed to consider it, even before she'd noticed Philippa's attraction to the steward.

That was only a passing fancy, she told herself. It would fade the moment she met other gentlemen, or simply stopped encountering *him*. She would recover from the moment of madness—

Then she stopped and gave herself a shake. She had done nothing wrong. He was the one who constantly tried to provoke her and flirt with her and tempt her into silly behavior. He hadn't made her fall on him, but he *had* started the game with the shuttlecock and battledores, and she hadn't been able to resist.

Philippa inhaled deeply. That was the problem—

she had become too stern and serious. Between the
duke's health and the search for the new heir, the
castle had been gripped with anxiety. Mr. Montclair, with his teasing manner and willingness to
buck any tradition, had injected some levity, which
ought to be welcome, and Philippa saw no reason
to deny that she liked it.

Very well then. She would allow herself to have
some fun, even with him. Perhaps if she stopped
being so shocked and flustered by everything he
did, he would stop trying so hard to do it. Or perhaps her fascination would fade, once she was better able to take his jests and antics in stride.

Yes. She let out her breath with a smile. That
was it.

And that meant there was no reason to avoid
him.

Chapter Fifteen

❧❧❧

To Will's astonishment and relief, the duke's visit to the bridge works was a success, and from then on, Will was expected at the castle twice a week. In addition, the duke would drive out to view other works, usually with the duchess in tow. Will tried to beg off escorting them, but the duchess curtly ordered him to continue. Miss Kirkpatrick explained later that the duchess desired the duke to have as much "gentlemanly companionship" as possible. As a result, progress across Carlyle slowed considerably.

It was, Will thought wryly, a fitting consequence to his curiosity about the duke. He'd wanted to see the man, and now he couldn't get out of it.

In fairness, Carlyle was a marvelous old fellow. Will liked visiting him, reading aloud from a childhood tale and eating sumptuous delicacies prepared specially by Mrs. Amis. The duke wasn't much for telling stories, but he enjoyed hearing them, and made sly and amusing comments often enough to make Will wonder if he wasn't so much befuddled or confused as simply never given a good audience.

And of course spending time with the duke meant spending time with Miss Kirkpatrick. He liked that far too much, but now he had no choice; he had been commanded to visit the duke, and he could not stop her from being there as well. Neither of them ever mentioned the day in the nursery. He told himself they had both learned their lesson—he, not to get too close to her, and she, not to let him.

But all that meant he had less and less time for himself, and he was exhausted.

"What are you doing here?"

Will lifted his hat off his face and squinted up at Charles Amis. "I work here."

Amis grinned. "Are you employed to sleep on a bench in the sun like a cat?"

Will pushed himself up to make space on the bench. "I was not sleeping. I'm waiting for my laundry. Daisy promised to do it . . ." A huge yawn threatened to crack his jaw. He scrubbed one hand over his face. "Perhaps I nodded off for a moment."

Amis sat down. "I have no doubt." He gave Will an appraising glance. "Are you courting the girl?"

Will twitched, thinking of Miss Kirkpatrick, but then realized the valet meant Daisy. "Of course not."

"Maria tells me half the maids in the kitchens and laundry are in love with you."

Will frowned. "What?"

"The incident of the shirt." He flushed and Amis laughed. "You will have no trouble finding a wife."

Will made himself flick one hand. "I'm not looking for a wife."

"Hmm." Amis raised his brows. "Not from the laundry, you mean?"

Thankfully Maria Amis chose that moment to come out, a tray in her hands. Charles rose to greet her. "Something for you, good sirs," she said with a smile, offering up her face to her husband for a quick kiss.

"Blessed are you among women, Mrs. Amis," said Will, eyeing the tray hungrily.

"And blessed are we among everyone at Carlyle." Amis peeked under the cloth. "Queen cakes! You know they are my favorite, my dear."

"And mine," piped up Will.

Mrs. Amis laughed at both of them. "I know very well these are your favorite, Charles," she said pertly to her husband. "Why did I bring them out, when I saw you sitting here? And I know very well *your* favorite cake is the one in front of you, Mr. Montclair," she told Will. She went back inside.

Amis handed Will one of the tall mugs of crisp cider and set the plate between them. "I met my wife here at Carlyle," remarked the valet.

Will ate one of the cakes in two bites. "And you may stop boasting of it any day now."

Amis chuckled. "Perhaps you will also be so fortunate."

"I have indeed been most fortunate to meet Mrs. Amis at Carlyle." He took another cake. Mrs. Amis made them small and sweet, with almonds and a candied rose petal on top. "What brought you here?"

"Much like you, Mr. Edwards engaged me. The duke's previous valet was no longer able to lift him when necessary. A tall, strapping fellow, Mr. Edwards said he required, and there I was, looking for a gentler position. I was a pugilist." He nodded at Will's startled look as he reached for another cake, too. "Victor in eighteen of twenty fights."

"Why did you leave it?"

Amis's teeth flashed white in his grin. "It did not pay well enough to make me enjoy being beaten about the head."

"No doubt." Will stretched his legs out in front of him and leaned back. It was warm here in the sunny but sheltered courtyard. "And you're still here, ten years later. You must be well satisfied with the place."

The other man nodded. "I am indeed. Not merely for my Maria, but it is a very agreeable position. His Grace is a good and gentle fellow, and Her Grace is fair and generous." Will's brows shot up and Amis wagged a finger at him. "She is only impatient with those who provoke her."

He must have looked skeptical.

"She values ability, sense, and respect for tradition," Amis explained. "You displayed none, arriving late to an appointment and then arguing with her about how things should be done. She will listen to suggestion, if presented appropriately. Otherwise, she wishes you to do as she directs without questioning."

Will took another cake. "How would one present *appropriately*?"

Amis shot him a curious look. "Is this your first employment? You seem to know nothing of being in service."

He had to laugh. "So I've been told." He was quiet a moment, savoring the cider and cake. "It is my first, for anyone other than my father. But I want to do well at it while I can."

His companion's brows went up. "While you can? Waiting for a long-lost uncle to die and leave you his fortune, are you?"

Will nearly choked on a mouthful of cider. "Good Lord, no!" He wiped his chin and put down the mug. "Her Grace will lose patience and toss me out eventually. But until then . . ." He looked around at the service courtyard, the windows newly releaded and the stones scoured of moss. "Until then I hope to do right by Carlyle."

The other man nodded. "Then you have common cause with Her Grace. I sympathize with her," the valet added. "Managing all this for so long must have been a massive undertaking. Women are not trained for such things."

"Nor are many of the men," muttered Will, thinking of Grimes.

Amis laughed. "Those are the blokes who make you look good in comparison! Give them their due, my friend."

"I certainly do." Will gave a flourishing salute.

From their seat they had a view straight out the postern gate, and in the distance appeared the landau, heading back to the castle. The duke and duchess had gone out for a simple drive today, no escort needed. The sun glinted on the glossy yellow paint and silver lamps. The perfectly matched grays moved in unison under the postillion driver's command.

The cakes were gone; duty called. With a farewell wave, Amis left to meet the duke, and Will collected his laundry. He rode out the gate as the carriage drew near enough for him to see that Miss Kirkpatrick rode behind it. Will bowed his head as the carriage passed him in a jangle of harness. The duke raised one hand, and the duchess made a tiny nod. At least, Will thought she did.

Miss Kirkpatrick gave him a nod as she rode past. Once again she was bright and colorful in her saffron and orange habit. For some reason this prompted Will to sweep off his hat and fold over his saddle.

She slowed her horse, giving him a piercing look. Then a slow smile spread over her face, deepening her dimple until she looked almost smug—or coy—or flirtatious. She arched one brow, and then she *winked* at him.

Will reeled. She nudged her horse into a canter and didn't look back, but his eyes followed her until she was out of sight.

God above. His heart was thumping, his muscles were taut, and he was grinning like a fool.

Oh, he was in real trouble.

Josiah met him at the door when he reached Stone Cottage, a letter in hand. "This came for you, sir. An express rider brought it from London."

There went his smile. "Thank you. Anything from the builders on the Northampton Road bridge?" Will shoved the letter into his coat pocket and strode toward his study.

Josiah bobbed along beside him. "Not yet, sir. But Mr. Gaskin came by, sir, wanting to let you know the stone hasn't been delivered for the bridge on the castle road."

"That's the second week it hasn't come," muttered Will, pulling out his chair and searching through a stack of papers on his desk for the mason's proposal. The stone had been promised a fortnight ago, but the mason hadn't bothered to send any explanation or apology when it didn't arrive. "Send word to Mr. Dodds that if the stone is not there by Thursday next, he should not bother sending it, nor wait upon any future orders from Carlyle."

Josiah nodded. "At once, sir." He took some sheets of paper and went out to the desk in the dining room, where Will had set him up at the table to keep track of the papers coming in and going out. He never ate in there, and the room might as well have some use.

Will scanned the notes Josiah had left on his desk; despite being so young, the lad was becoming invaluable. He would soon make a fine secretary, or even a future steward, well versed in every detail of Carlyle.

Which the estate would need, when Will left.

Steeling himself, he took out Jack's letter. What necessitated an express messenger? *This had better be urgent,* he thought as he sliced through the seal, only to reconsider with the next heartbeat. No, he didn't want that. He hoped it was simply Jack being Jack, punctilious and exacting and annoyed that Will hadn't answered his previous two letters.

Only the first paragraph was devoted to scolding and telling him off. The rest was positive, even ebullient—Jack had a potential client lined up.

Not merely that. "A *significant* client," Jack wrote, with flourishes and underlines in case Will didn't fully grasp his meaning. "So large, Pa will be pleased if we can win it. You must return to London at once to help me secure the business."

Will leaned back, shoving one boot against the edge of the desk until his chair tilted onto the back two legs. That was a problem. He had neglected to secure permission to return to London if or when he needed to. He could hardly just leave. He also didn't want to go back to London, not yet.

Not for a long time, whispered a wicked little voice in his head. Not as long as he had things to do here at the castle, important things like repairing the roofs and chimney flues on tenant cottages, and building roads and bridges to make the estate easier to travel. Not as long as he got invited to read *Gulliver* to the duke and savor Mrs. Amis's pastries and spend an hour or two in the stunningly beautiful castle gardens. And most certainly not while Philippa Kirkpatrick kept winking at him and replying to his smart comments in kind.

Will ran one hand over his face. He was trying to keep his distance from her; it just wasn't working. Every time she came near him, it felt like some invisible force kept him from backing away, like a lost nail helplessly drawn to a magnet. The fact that he liked it so much would horrify Jack. His brother already thought him restless and impulsive; if Will admitted that he was breaking his solemn promise to return to London when asked because of a woman—let alone a woman who was too rich and too beautiful for the likes of him— Jack would quite possibly ride out to Carlyle and drag him back in ropes and chains.

He flexed his foot, rocking the chair gently back and forth on the rear legs as he thought. What to

tell Jack? What would buy him a few more weeks
of freedom?

At that thought, he let the chair down. God help
him. He *did* view this as freedom from Montclair
and Sons—supervising bridge construction and
dredging a mill pond and directing a regiment of
carpenters and stonemasons to repair the small
city's worth of buildings on this estate. Even aside
from the luscious Miss Kirkpatrick . . . Will preferred it here.

On one side of the balance was his family. The
company was his father's passion, and he'd entrusted it to Will. In return Will had dropped
the burden onto his brother's shoulders and lied
to all of them, just so he could pursue his own
curiosity—which could come back to haunt him
very painfully.

On the other side lay the chance to hide from the
guilt for a few more days, basking in Miss Kirkpatrick's smiles and winks and saucy comments.

Illness, he decided, snatching up a pen. A cough,
with fits of fever. Blisters and headache. A touch of
vomiting as well. That should stall Jack for a fortnight.

And at the end of the fortnight . . . Either he
would have thought of a new excuse to stay, or
grown resigned to going.

Chapter Sixteen

❧❦❧

The duke's health and spirits continued to improve. Not only did he drive out once or twice a week with Philippa and the duchess, he even came to dinner from time to time. He still tired easily, but until then he was more animated and engaging than ever.

This brought the duchess a mixture of joy and deep guilt. She fretted about having denied and cheated him until Philippa suggested gently that it was better to devote herself to continuing his improvement. Tactfully Philippa made no mention of the *cause* of this recent improvement, and the duchess had given her a rueful smile and said, "Of course you are correct, my dear."

And so Mr. Montclair kept coming to the castle.

She never would have admitted it aloud, but Philippa liked him more every day. The air seemed to grow lighter and more festive every time he strode into the room, rubbing his hands and sitting down to tell some amusing story, making the duke chuckle and sending Philippa herself into gales of laughter. He was a born performer, and took to his task with relish.

Of course, he also broke every rule Philippa tried to lay out, per the duchess's instruction; he told jokes about the king and mocked the prime minister, he asked the duke's opinion of issues about the estate, and he managed to find shocking or inappropriate selections in every book he read aloud. Some of them made Philippa's eyes go wide, but Carlyle would lean back in his chair and listen with a faint smile. He was enjoying Mr. Montclair's antics, which was what mattered. So that's what she told the duchess.

"He's not being impertinent?" the duchess asked after hearing Philippa's account of a reading from *The Adventures of Roderick Random*. "That book is excitable nonsense."

"The duke requested it."

The duchess cast her eyes upward and sighed. "I suppose I cannot argue, if it amuses Johnny."

"It does," Philippa assured her. "Mr. Montclair reads with great spirit." It made her smile even now as she remembered the gleeful way he had read the revenges of young Roderick upon callous schoolmasters and cruel cousins and other tormentors.

The duchess's mouth twisted at mention of the steward. "I've had a letter from Diana this morning."

Philippa tried to hide her guilty start. She bent her head over her embroidery. "I trust she is well?"

"Very well, and eager to receive you. We must set a date, my dear. I vow, if we do not, she will come all the way to Carlyle to fetch you herself," said the duchess lightly.

Philippa laughed. She had agreed to go to London, but still hadn't managed to feel eager about it. She kept trying, putting on a happy expression every time it was mentioned and agreeing to all the duchess's plans for a new wardrobe. She had corresponded with Diana, hoping the proposed events and outings would stir some excitement in her.

She *was* excited to see the Theatre Royal, and the acrobats at Astley's Amphitheatre, and the menagerie at the Tower. She did look forward to visiting Ranelagh and the Royal Academy and seeing a concert in Westminster Abbey. She was even intrigued by Diana's stories of the shopping to be found in London, from fine glovers to the most exquisite milliners.

But Philippa couldn't bring herself to look forward to the social demands of town. Diana wrote of balls and masquerades and all manner of entertaining, which struck a fair amount of anxiety in Philippa's heart. She had been well educated, but she had never been in society. She feared she wouldn't have the social grace and charm necessary to succeed in London.

At Carlyle she was confident and at ease, in familiar and beloved surroundings, with people whom she knew and who knew her. In London she would be just another young lady from the country, naive and unsure, the sort of girl who routinely fell prey to frauds and fortune hunters in novels and brought dismay and disappointment to her relations. Here she wasn't uncertain—excepting where a certain estate steward was involved, but who *wouldn't* be thrown off balance by Mr. Montclair?

The thread snapped in her tense fingers and she burst out with a quiet "Damn!" before she could stop herself.

"My dear, have you hurt yourself?" asked the duchess in concern.

Philippa closed her eyes and summoned up a smile. "I broke my thread. These flowers will have a knot behind them."

The older woman smiled. "Alas! I was never a hand at embroidery. All my attempts had knots behind them. In London everything is done by the modistes, and my dear, their work is exquisite. You shan't need to do it, if you don't wish to." The fat ginger cat, Percival, leapt into Her Grace's lap, and was rewarded with a scratch under his chin. "Shall I tell Diana to expect you in another week?"

Philippa paused, her scissors poised over the strand of silk. *No, not yet . . .* The weather was so fine, and once she left she would be gone for months. She would miss summer at the castle, her favorite season. She wanted to hear more of Roderick Random. And she wanted to see more of the infuriating, appealing Mr. Montclair.

She had promised the duchess she would go. But on the other hand, she didn't want to go *now*.

"Not just yet, ma'am," she said, her heart thudding. "I hoped to take this jacket and it won't be done for at least a fortnight."

The duchess cast a surprised eye on the jacket. Philippa had marked an elaborate design on it, a

copy of a pattern of lotus and poppies her grandmother had sent her from India. It was only half-
done. "You've been working on it for some time
now."

"I shall pick up speed," she promised. "Let's not
write to Diana yet. Another week."

There was a moment of silence. "Is there any reason you're reluctant to go?" inquired the duchess
in a studiously neutral voice.

To her disgust Philippa felt her face heat. Did the
duchess mean Mr. Montclair? Or was that Philippa's guilty conscience, because Mr. Montclair *was*
part of the reason she didn't want to leave? She
thought she'd figured him out now. He delighted
in shocking her, so she refused to be shocked. He
delighted in flirting with her, so she responded
with impertinence. He delighted in teasing her, so
she teased him back.

She no longer felt flustered and cross around
him. Now she came away from their encounters
exhilarated and ready for more. That might be
even more dangerous.

"Of course not." She laughed to disguise the lie.
"Other than the fact that I shall miss Carlyle at its
most beautiful, and the duke, and *you*, since you
will not come with me—"

The duchess flicked one hand, although her expression eased. "Nonsense. Diana will keep you
so busy, you shan't have time to think of anyone
here."

Such as Mr. Montclair. Philippa tried not to think
of him. "Oh, no, I shall be too busy gawping at the
splendid sites like a country simpleton, blundering

through soirees in blithe ignorance of everyone's name and status, wearing something offensive like a two-year-old hat—"

"Stop!" The duchess pressed her lips together to keep from laughing as Philippa grinned. "Diana will guide you and protect you."

"From all the rakes and rascals and fortune hunters and jackanapes looking to make sport of a naive country miss," she teased. "Poor Aunt Diana! She will send me home within a fortnight, sorry she ever invited me."

Finally the older woman laughed. "Never say such a thing." She paused. "Diana wanted me to send you to her when your mama died."

Philippa started in surprise. "She did?"

The duchess nodded. "She begged to have you. And perhaps I should have agreed. You would have had the company of girls your age and the excitement of London. But I . . ." She sighed, and her voice grew rough. "I could not be parted from you. Not so soon after Jessica." She petted Percival as Philippa gaped at her. "And now I must pay the price," the duchess went on more briskly. "Johnny and I shall miss you, but you should go. Diana will be overjoyed to have you, and she will see to it that you have a splendid time."

Philippa reached out and took her hand. "I shall do my best, but Daadee . . . I fear I may be a sad failure in society."

"Never!" The older woman gave her hand a shake. "You have beauty, wit, elegance, and stand to inherit a handsome fortune. *That* is enough to ensure success in London."

Philippa cast a hesitant glance at their clasped hands, the duchess's pale and delicate with blue-gray veins visible beneath the finely wrinkled skin. Her own hand looked so much larger, younger, and browner. She wasn't sure the duchess had an objective view of things in London.

"Let me write to her that you will arrive in a fortnight," the duchess urged.

She forced a smile. "If you wish."

Chapter Seventeen

❦

When the duke announced he wished to go fishing, Will was not surprised that it happened within two days.

He was surprised by the scale of the outing, though.

The first carriage to arrive disgorged four servants who unloaded a rolled-up carpet, a chaise, several cushions, and a pair of low tables from the wagon that followed them, which they set up beneath a spreading willow tree. One of the servants brought out a large hamper, another a crate which turned out to contain plates and silver.

Wearing patched old clothes and a battered straw hat, fishing gear piled at his feet, Will watched in silence. The sound of another vehicle made him look up.

Miss Kirkpatrick stepped down. She at least was appropriately attired, in a faded blue dress that still looked very fetching. Will looked away; everything made her look very fetching.

When he raised his head again, she was standing in front of him, an impish smile on her face. "What is so amusing?"

"I thought we were fishing, not planning a garden party fit for the king."

She laughed. "Her Grace's suggestion."

Will watched the servants lay out a picnic large enough to feed twenty, even though only four people were planning to fish.

"The duke cannot go into the water," Miss Kirkpatrick explained. "Or he may tire. This is to ensure he's comfortable."

Will said nothing. He watched Charles Amis help Carlyle down from the carriage and across the grass. The duke leaned heavily on his valet, a cane in his other hand. "Good morning," he called to Will as they drew near. "Are they biting today?"

It was cool and misty, the exact sort of day Pa would have chosen. "I spied some carp earlier," he replied.

Carlyle nodded, looking pleased. Amis murmured to him, and the duke glanced at the furnishings with surprise. "What, what? No, I will not sit here," he said indignantly. "A man cannot fish from an armchair, Amis. We must find a spot on the riverbank."

Will shot a gleeful look at Miss Kirkpatrick. She pressed her lips together. "Your mother was thinking only of your comfort, sir."

Carlyle cackled. "And she's not here, is she, Pippa dear? Amis, help me find a good spot . . ."

So the comfortable furnishings were left behind as they made their way down to the riverbank. Will carried the fishing tackle while Miss Kirkpatrick brought the woven creels to hold the fish they caught. Carlyle studied the bank and finally chose a spot under the willow, where the bank protruded a bit and offered deep waters. Mr. Amis took a rod and settled a short distance away. "I trust His Grace's judgement," he said with a twinkle in his eye. "I want to sit upstream of him, to have first chance at the fish." And Carlyle chortled at that.

To Will's surprise, Miss Kirkpatrick peeled off her own shoes and stockings and proceeded to pull up the worn linen of her skirts through her pockets. "Where are you going?" he asked.

"To the river, sir."

"What if you fall in?"

She frowned in affront. "How dare you suggest that?"

He grinned. "Just wanting to know how likely it is that I'll have to dive in and save you." The water swirled and eddied around boulders in the stream, indicating a brisk current.

With a final yank, she secured her skirts. "Not likely at all, sir, because I know how to fish *and* how to swim."

He shook his head. "English ladies are far more accomplished than I ever imagined!"

"Oh?" She tightened the ribbon of her flat straw hat. "Who told you English ladies did nothing but sit in their parlors embroidering tablecloths?"

"Someone who never met you," he parried. "Shall we make a wager, Mistress of Rod and Line?"

"Why not?" She smiled sweetly, practically forcing him to look at her mouth. And her dimple. By God, that dimple tormented him.

He cleared his throat. "Right. A shilling to the one who catches more."

"A cherry tart to the person who catches the larg-est fish," she countered.

"Done, on both counts." He held out his hand, and she took it. His fingers closed around hers, and his heart jumped as she leaned close. "Good luck," he murmured with a wink.

She arched one dark brow. "Luck has nothing to do with it." She took her rod, bait, and creel and waded out to climb onto a large flat rock jutting up from the stream as he stood there reeling.

She no longer blushed and grew irate at his teas-ing comments. No, now she answered him in kind and Will didn't know how to react. It went to his head like whisky, so potent and bewitching that it took him a moment to realize she'd beaten him to the best spot. Shaking his head, he shucked his boots and stockings and waded right out into the main rush of the current. He was going to get wet, but the cold of the water might shock some sense back into him.

Fishing was a quiet activity. It gave one time to think, or peace not to think at all. The day prom-ised to be warm but the morning fog hadn't yet burned away. Shrouded in mist, away from the noisy bustle of the castle, Carlyle felt positively primeval.

Yet instead of fishing in silent contemplation, Will felt primed and restless. Miss Kirkpatrick was only ten feet behind him, and he swore he could feel her gaze on him. Every time he peeked over his shoulder, she was looking another way, but he was sure he wasn't imagining it.

Why would she stare at you? he asked himself. *Just because you wish she might? She's not. Don't look.*

A splash sounded behind him. Will whipped around, careless of his fishing line, only to see her pulling in a wriggling perch and stow it in her creel. "That's one for me," she called. "How many have you caught, Mr. Montclair?"

He grimaced, feeling the empty basket bang against his hip. "Plenty, ma'am!" he called back, to which she laughed.

Will imagined Jack slapping him in the face, hard. *Don't make her laugh. Don't look at her. Don't talk to her.*

"How did you learn to fish?" The question popped out before he could stop it. At least he kept his eyes on his line.

"My father taught me." She was grinning when he glanced back in surprise. "Who taught you?"

"My father." His line caught, finally, and he carefully pulled in a silver-gold carp. "How old were you?"

"Hmm." Her line jerked, but the fish escaped with a flash of shiny tail and she exclaimed in frustration. "About six. Papa loved fishing. He was a Scot, and claimed there was no better fishing anywhere in the world than Scotland, although he allowed Carlyle might be second best. He would go early, and carry me on his shoulders when I begged to go with him." She smiled. "I say *begged*. It was more like crying and wailing until he gave in. He took me, but said I must learn to fish. He was very serious about it. For years I thought it was strictly forbidden to speak at all whilst fishing."

Will nodded. "It ought to be."

"Yet here you are, asking questions. I was sitting in perfect fishing silence."

"You were." He grinned. Again his pole bent toward the water, and again he pulled a fish from the water, this time a perch. "When did you realize it was possible to catch fish and talk at the same time?"

A shadow flickered over her face. "After he left."

The hook missed the worm and slid into his thumb. Wincing, Will put his hand into the cold, rushing water. "He went to India," he said, watching the drop of blood dissipate into the gray of the stream.

"Yes." Her voice was sad, wistful, tinged with anger.

Her father had died there, Edwards said. In London Will had met a number of sailors who went to the East Indies. It was a long and difficult voyage; not less than seven months, which sounded endless to Will, who grew wildly impatient if the trip across the Atlantic took more than four weeks. Why had the colonel gone, leaving behind his wife and daughter? "What did he think of India?"

That brought a smile to her face. "He thought it was magnificent. He was the third son in his family, no expectations at home, and wanted to see something of the world, so he joined the army and was promptly sent to India. Most of his regiment hated it, but he thought it wonderful."

"I didn't know the army offered pleasure trips."

She choked on a laugh. "It was not! Hot and miserable at times, he said, and ravaged by fevers that cut through regiments like a scythe. But also . . . beautiful, with animals he could barely describe, food that made everything in England tasteless in comparison, flora and music and art that dazzled the senses. The people were so different from the English, he said. It was not unusual to meet a man who spoke four languages, and the ladies were so colorful and pleasant. He wanted to stay forever." She scrunched up her face. "Not in the army, though."

He dared a glance her way. Her lips were tight, and she was glaring at her fishing line.

"The East India Company began attacking towns allied to the French, and when they got into trouble they cried out for the British army to come save them," she said abruptly. "The company had gone beyond trading by then, building their own forts and taking over tax collecting, and Papa thought that they were becoming tyrants and looters instead of mere traders." She paused. "That's not only Papa's belief. The India governor, Mr. Hastings, has been impeached for corruption."

"So why did your father return?" he asked softly.

"Asmat, my ayah who came with us from India, wanted to return," she said, staring at the ripples of the current. "I was about fourteen, old enough not to need a nursemaid and Asmat wanted to go back, she had always said she would return. Papa didn't think it right to send her on the long journey alone, so he escorted Asmat home. And then . . . Then he got there and heard what the company was doing. He was a senior officer, a colonel, and he hoped to persuade his fellow officers that it was not the army's place to conquer India for one company's benefit. He felt that if the India Company didn't have the British army at its back, they would be forced to moderate their behavior." She huffed in disgust. "He was wrong. Too many lords in Parliament profited from the Company, and they sent more soldiers to protect it, with foolish, in-

competent officers who paid little heed to their
Indian sepoys or even their own commanders' orders and marched into a slaughter—" She stopped,
her mouth trembling and her face pale.

Good God. Heedless of the fish, Will strode to
her rock and jammed his fishing rod into a crevice.
"Miss Kirkpatrick." He touched her elbow, startling her so much she almost dropped her pole. "I
apologize. I never intended—"

"No." She pulled a handkerchief from her sleeve
and dried her eyes. "I never get to talk about him.
It took eight months for word of his death to reach
us, and . . . I miss him." She paused, looking over
the river. The sun was starting to burn away the
mist, and the water sparkled brilliantly, making
her screw up her eyes. "And at times, I have hated
him," she said in a low voice. "How dare he leave
me and Mama here? She tried to persuade him
against it. *Stay here*, she would urge him. *We need
you.* And he would look at me, and—and—" She
swiped at her eyes. "I know he saw my mother
when he looked at me. He went back for her."

Will glanced askance at her. Hadn't her mother
died?

"Her father was a wakil, a highly trusted agent
in the Mughal court. They were educated, capable
people, and the Company forced them out so the
English could take over. There was a famine, and
instead of taking steps to feed people, the Company made starving people pay ruinous taxes.
Papa was disgusted. He thought Ammi—my
mother—would have wanted him to try to help,
if he could." She paused, her gaze distant. "And
that's noble, isn't it? If you see a wrong, should you

not try to right it? But I was so angry at him. It was wrong to leave me, and Mama. *We* needed him. And he failed anyway. No one listened to him, and they got him killed."

Without a word he took her hand. She seized it. His heart ached at the grief in her voice.

"He sounds like the very best of men," he said quietly.

Tears sparkled on her lashes before she dashed them away. "He was. When Ammi died, he wanted to bring me to England himself. Plenty of army men had Indian wives and children, but Papa had seen men separated from their families until they lost contact altogether. His commander refused him leave, so Papa threatened to resign his commission on the spot." Some of her grief subsided, and a faint smile curved her lips again. "He meant to take me to his sister in Aberdeen, but I took ill, which delayed our departure from London, and then he met Lady Jessica, who became my mama. He used to say their marriage was all due to me, for keeping him in London, but it was really due to him—not every father would have delayed his journey because a child had a cold."

Her hand still nestled trustingly in his. Will tried not to think of how good it felt.

"Mama was a force of nature," she went on. "A whirlwind of cheerful determination! She always said she fell in love with both of us, me and Papa, and we—we both adored her. She had all of the duke's love of adventure, plus Her Grace's humor and generosity." She stopped and glanced warily at him, but Will wasn't about to argue. He merely nodded, and her fingers relaxed in his.

"Papa loved fishing." Her face grew brighter with every word. "He would carry me on his shoulders and say if I couldn't bait a hook, I couldn't eat the fish. Of course he was teasing but I didn't know. Mama didn't like to fish, so it would be just the two of us." She smiled. "I fell in so many times. Once, not far from here." She shaded her eyes and looked left and right, finally pointing downstream. "Over there, I think. He jumped in after me, and we both had to walk home soaking wet . . ."

Will sensed the moment of confidence was over, and let her change the subject without resistance. "It's not a true fishing expedition unless someone falls in."

"Did you?" She tucked the handkerchief into her sleeve.

He laughed. "All the time! Especially on hot summer days. My brother and I would slip right off every rock and branch we sat on . . . It was quite a mystery, how poor our balance was on hot days."

"I hope you took care to catch some fish for your dinner before you grew so feeble in the sun."

He winked. "Always. We were also hungry lads, never ones to neglect our stomachs."

She laughed. "As you've done today!"

"I think neither of us has made a good effort at winning our wager."

She cocked one brow. "Are you canceling it?"

"Indeed not." He rested his elbows on the rock and squinted up at her. "But the conversation was far more interesting."

Her blush was as pink as a rose. "You listened very patiently."

"Raptly," he replied, truthfully. He could listen

to her talk all day, let alone confide in him about things dear to her heart.

"Tell me about your father."

Ah, he should have seen that coming. Will waved one hand. "He enjoys fishing and good stories."

"Is he kind and affectionate?"

Until we disobey him. "Mmm-hmm," replied Will.

She raised her brows. "You sound uncertain. Are you hiding from him here?"

It was so near the truth he didn't have to affect his astonishment. He jerked backward, clapping one hand to his chest. "Bless my soul, Miss Kirkpatrick! What do you accuse me of, that I must hide from my own father?"

She dipped her toes into the river and flicked water at him. "If I knew, I wouldn't ask, would I?"

He laughed and plucked his fishing pole from the stones that held it. "And were I hiding, I would never tell! But now you have reminded me that I have a wager to win."

This time he went further downstream. By the time Amis called to him that the duke was tired and wished to go home, the sun had burned away the morning mist and the icy water had rendered Will's feet completely numb. The other servants had returned to pack up the furnishings sent by the duchess and unused by anyone.

"What a feast we shall have tonight," declared the duke as everyone put on their stockings and shoes. He sounded pleased but exhausted. "Amis, where are you?"

Mr. Amis stepped forward and the duke put an arm around his neck. Carlyle's legs buckled after a few slow steps, and Will leapt to catch him. He and Amis lifted the duke and carried him to the carriage.

Settled on the leather seat, Carlyle smiled and patted his arm. "Thank you, my boy," he murmured. His face was gray, and Will remembered Edwards's warning, that if the duke took ill, the duchess would blame him.

"Drive on," he called to the groom as soon as Amis took his seat.

"Is he unwell?" Miss Kirkpatrick asked, watching the barouche trundle off.

"Tired, and perhaps a bit overheated." He ran one hand over his head, and the tie slipped out, letting his hair loose. He'd been meaning to cut it, but hadn't yet found time.

Miss Kirkpatrick watched, lips parted. Her expression was open, wondering—more than friendly. Her eyes grew dark. Fascinated.

He tried to imagine Jack punching him; it did no good. He imagined facing the duchess in a fury; his heart still raced with anticipation. In desperation he turned his back to her, lashing the thong around his hair with suddenly clumsy fingers, only to see . . .

The bare grass where the carpet and furnishings had been.

The equally empty spot where the wagon had stood.

The servants had efficiently loaded everything into the carriage and wagon and gone home, leaving behind Miss Kirkpatrick.

Alone. With him.

Chapter Eighteen

❧❧❧

Philippa had been so distracted by the sight of Mr. Montclair with his hair loose, it took her a few minutes to realize everyone else had left.

"They forgot us," she said in surprise, and began to laugh.

Mr. Montclair was tying back his hair with a grim expression, but now his shoulders eased. "They didn't forget me. I walked."

She gasped, and laughed harder, flinging one hand to her forehead dramatically. "Only me, then! Oh, the indignity!"

"If you swoon from it, I would be forced to pour a bucket of water on your head to revive you."

Still laughing, she held up both hands. "Thank you, no! I shall also walk home."

Mr. Montclair grinned and they set out.

It was barely two miles, not a long walk. The duchess would cluck in dismay, but Philippa wasn't upset at all—because of the man ambling beside her.

There was really no denying it anymore. All her

attempts to repay his sly winks and teasing comments in kind had only made things worse. Now instead of just finding him infuriatingly attractive, she liked him far more than she should.

She could hardly believe she'd told him all that about Papa and Ammi and Mama. Even if she told herself it was because she had no one else to tell about them, she knew it was also because it felt right—safe, somehow—to tell *him*. He didn't laugh or shrug in disinterest. He offered his hand in comfort and listened. Sitting out there on that rock with his hand warm around hers, she had opened her heart and allowed herself to feel all the love and grief and even anger inside her. And he didn't tell her she was wrong to feel any of it.

He was so kind with the duke. He'd begun to follow her advice regarding the duchess. Everyone on the estate admired and liked him, from Mr. Amis to Gerry and Jilly Smith to the maids in the laundry. And he was bringing Carlyle into a state of polished good repair that Philippa had never seen. How had she not noticed the leaks in the roof or the buckling paving stones in the courtyard? He had and he had seen them fixed.

He was exactly what Carlyle needed. And perhaps what Philippa needed, despite what the duchess thought.

"We forgot to count the fish and settle our wager," she said.

He gave a soft *tsk*. "Alas. I shall graciously call it a draw."

"A draw!"

"By the time we reach the castle, the entire catch will have been jumbled into one large basket and cleaned for dinner. There's no way to settle it now."

"A gentleman would concede," she pointed out.

He laughed. "Would a lady wager in the first place?"

"I'm not a lady."

Another impertinent wink. "Well, I'm not a gentleman."

She was trying not to laugh. "I'll never trust your word again, sir. You're too slippery by half."

"What did we wager in the first place?" He scratched his jaw. "Must not have been very tempting."

"A cherry tart." She knew he liked them very much.

"No, did we really?" He heaved a sigh. "Alas. My day is ruined."

"There's still time for something wonderful to occur."

"How you do tease me, Miss Kirkpatrick. What could possibly happen?"

She clasped her hands behind her back and gazed at the sky as she fought back a grin. "You might discover a stray pup, who will become your dearest and truest companion."

He made a thoughtful noise. "That is appealing. But the little devil would chew my boots as well."

"You might return home to find a letter from someone dear."

He made a face. "It would be from my brother, annoyed over something."

Philippa folded her arms and tapped one finger on her lip. "Let me think . . . Perhaps you shall arrive home to find a large basket from Mrs. Amis awaiting you, with a despondent note saying she's made too many cherry tarts and begging you to take them."

He laughed. *"Extremely* tempting! However . . ." He stopped, and Philippa stopped, too. Hands behind his back, he leaned forward and whispered, "Perhaps it's already happening."

Uncomprehending, she stared at him.

"A leisurely stroll with a charming woman, talking of pleasant surprises one might have." His voice was low and warm. "What more could I want?"

She forgot to breathe. *Oh yes,* whispered a small voice inside her. This was why she didn't want to hurry to London. *He* was why.

And right now he looked like he wanted to kiss her.

Which Philippa thought she would like very much.

He leaned nearer, so close she could see the glints of gold in his brown eyes. Philippa inhaled unsteadily and then nearly swooned at the smell of him—clean linen, fresh air, shaving soap, something else that made her want to press her nose to his neck and breathe deeper to try to identify it.

Her chin tipped up. Her eyelids fell. Her heart skipped a beat and the breath stopped in her throat as she waited for him to—

He stepped back. "That tree needs to be cut down. It's dead."

Philippa blinked out of her daze of anticipation. He had put back his head and shaded his eyes to peer into the branches above them, but at her indrawn breath of surprise, he darted a quick look her way.

A wary look. Checking her expression.

Her temper began to simmer. "Mr. Montclair," she began.

"Yes?" He began walking again, frowning studiously at the trees.

She advanced on him, hands in fists. "Were you thinking of kissing me?"

"*I*, kiss *you*!" He affected astonishment. "I did no such thing!"

"You were about to!" she charged.

He straightened with a jerk. "I would never force myself on a lady!"

"It would not have been—" In the nick of time she stopped herself, breathing hard. *It would not have been force.* That's what she'd nearly shouted in his face. *Kiss me, you impossible irresistible scoundrel*, had also been echoing inside her head.

Face burning, she clamped her mouth shut. The day felt suddenly hot and stuffy, and it seemed as though a swarm of bees were buzzing madly inside her head.

"It would not have been . . . what?" he asked cautiously.

Philippa shook her head angrily.

"It would not have been . . . welcome," he said, his voice softer still.

She swallowed, unable to let that lie persist. "It would not have been force," she said stiffly. "It—it *would* have been welcome."

His expression shifted. "In spite of all my efforts?"

Philippa blinked. "What?"

"You're not supposed to like me," he said, sounding almost frustrated.

"But I do," she protested, then frowned. "Why not?"

He glanced around, but they were still alone. "The more curious question is why you *do*."

Her frown deepened. "At times—like this!—I heartily wish I did not."

He laughed. "No doubt!" Still smiling, he regarded her, then shook his head. "I should have known."

"Known wha—?"

Her question, and her curiosity, went silent as he took her face in his big, warm hands and kissed her. Not the delicate brush on the lips she had been expecting—anticipating, with girlish jitters. No, this was so much more, so unexpected and so unexpectedly wonderful that she had to grab his arms to keep her balance.

That seemed to encourage him; his fingers pushed off her hat and plunged into her hair, nestling more securely around the nape of her neck and tipping her face as he tucked her under his arm and deepened the kiss. Philippa's heart jumped inside her chest. Of their own volition her hands crept up his arms to wind around his neck and grip his hair.

William Montclair could kiss like . . . like . . . pure seduction.

It was so far outside of her experience—even outside of what she'd heard of, in giggling whispers among young ladies at the assembly or after church. It made her feel soft and hot, wild and restless, and wanted. Treasured.

"Mr. Montclair," was all she could gasp. Her

head spun like a top and she had to cling to him to stay on her feet.

He didn't let go of her, which meant she *had* to hold on to him, but oh goodness, she didn't want to let go.

He laughed quietly, his face against her hair. "After a kiss like that, you ought to call me Will."

Flustered, she nodded, because his lips were on her ear and he was still holding her indecently close. "*Will*. Kiss me again . . ."

"With pleasure, Miss Kirkpatrick." He captured her mouth and Philippa moaned, feeling as if she'd fallen into the river at high flood, in danger of being swept away except for the strength of his arms around her. This time when he licked her lips she opened, and he made love to her mouth, tasting of coffee and cherries and making her shudder with desire.

"You—" She gulped for air as his lips moved over her eyelids, her burning cheeks, her brow, skimming, lingering, sending sparks through her at every contact. "You called me Miss Kirkpatrick . . ."

She felt the silent rumble of his laugh in his chest. Her arm was around his neck, fingers caught in his hair; her other hand gripped the lapel of his coat for dear life. "What ought I call you?" he breathed, the scruff on his jaw rasping against her cheek.

Philippa bit her lip to keep from moaning. His body was so intriguing and tantalizing she could hardly think of anything like names. She released the lapel and slid her hand inside the coat, pressing her palm to his soft linen shirt. His heart throbbed as rapidly as hers did. He ran the tip of his tongue along the curve of her ear, and her knees all but gave out as she sagged against him.

"You scolded me for calling you *my lady*," he went on, as if his languid sensual caresses hadn't befogged her brain. "*Ma'am* seems very formal for such a situation. Do you prefer *miss*?"

"Oh!" She tugged at his hair. "Stop talking if you're going to spout such nonsense."

He pressed his lips to the corner of her jaw, just below her ear. "As you wish."

She melted into him with a contented sigh. "My name is Philippa." She rubbed her cheek against his chest, breathing deep. Sun-baked linen, she guessed, stored in lavender.

"Philippa." He made it sound like a dying man's prayer. It caused a strange feeling inside her—warmth, contentment . . . yearning. The duchess was the only person who called her by that name, and it sounded very different in Mr. Montclair's—*Will's*—deeper, rougher, American voice. She liked it very much.

His fingertips swept up her spine, slowing as they reached the top of her bodice. Only her kerchief separated his skin from hers. She could feel the heat of his touch, delicate though it was. She thought about whipping off the kerchief so his hand would fall on her bare nape. Like a lover's touch.

He inhaled unsteadily. "People would talk if I were to call you by name."

She didn't want to think about that, or about the fact that she wanted to keep on kissing him, and certainly not about how she would keep her composure when she went back to the castle, where the duchess would be watching suspiciously for any signs of interest, ready to separate them at a moment's notice by sending Philippa to London.

"I don't care," she said into his shoulder.

"You know what they would think, and what they would say." He tipped back her head, twirling a wisp of her hair around his finger. "I can't use your name, love," he whispered.

Love. She did almost swoon then, a glorious smile on her lips. She went up on her toes and kissed him. "Call me that."

His eyes closed. He rested his forehead against hers. He was still playing with that stray lock of her hair. "How I wish I could."

"When we are alone," she bargained. "Like this."

One brow twitched and his mouth curved in that mischievous way. "Philippa," he whispered. "Love."

"Yes, like that."

"But only," he said between kisses, "when no one is near." He smoothed back her hair and turned serious. "The duchess—"

She put one hand over his mouth. "No."

A faint frown creased his forehead. He reached up and clasped her hands in his. "I should go."

Philippa blinked. "Now? Why?"

He smiled a little as he kissed the knuckles of her left hand, then her right. "They've not forgotten you."

He released her and stooped to pick up her hat. Now Philippa could hear the jangle of harness and the creak of wheels. As Will stood and offered her the hat, the landau came bowling briskly around the bend in the road.

"You were right about one thing." His pirate's smile had returned. "Something wonderful *did* happen to me today, my love." He swept one of his ridiculous bows and strode down the road that led to Stone Cottage.

And Philippa could only stand watching him go, hat clutched in both hands, feeling dazed and ebullient.

Chapter Nineteen

❧ ～ ❧

As rash, reckless, even downright dangerous as it was to kiss Philippa Kirkpatrick, Will wasn't sorry.

He'd thought she was beautiful in a temper, appealing even when stern, and mesmerizing when she laughed with him. None of it compared to the breathtaking sight of her with head tipped back, eyes half-closed, waiting for him to kiss her.

He thought about that kiss every day, sometimes every hour. He'd be standing on a riverbank, listening to the stonemason about the progress of the bridge construction, and the light on the water would remind him of that day they went fishing, and her bare toes in the water. His mind would replay their conversation about her father and teasing over that silly wager until he'd missed every word the mason said.

There were only a few more weeks he could enjoy her company. His year was almost over, and based on Jack's increasingly hectoring letters, he would be held very strictly to his promise to leave. He knew nothing could come of his fascination;

she would forget him, and he would walk away
and forget her, too.

It was one of many lies he was telling these days.

When one of the castle pointers whelped a lit-
ter, he sent her a note inviting her to the stables to
see the puppies. She appeared an hour later, wide-
eyed and interested. Will led the way across the
stable courtyard to the empty stall boxed off for
the pups.

"Oh, the little darlings!" Philippa sank to her
knees in the straw, heedless of her peach silk gown.
"How old are they?"

Will knelt beside her and scooped up one to put
it gently into her hands. "About three weeks. The
mother is growing a bit tired of them as they begin
crawling about."

Philippa laughed, snuggling the puppy in her
lap. "No wonder, with seven of them!" The pup
nipped at her sleeve, and she held him up to her
cheek. "I wish I could take one and keep him."

Will glanced at her. She was effectively the
daughter of the castle. "Why don't you?"

She rolled her eyes and gave him a look. "Can
you imagine the duchess's expression if I brought
a puppy into the castle? Percival would never be
seen again."

Will guessed Percival was the fat ginger cat who
patrolled the drawing room. "A pity." He held up
one of the more adventurous pups so he was face-
to-face with the dog. "Would you chase a large but
very genteel cat?" The puppy gave a little yip and
licked his face, and Philippa broke into peals of
laughter.

"That means yes. You've cost yourself a life of

ease," he told the dog as he searched his pockets for a handkerchief. "Sleeping on silk pillows by the fire, fed choice bits of meat . . ."

"Here." Philippa stood up, dusting her skirts, and took out her own handkerchief. Instead of taking the handkerchief, Will simply raised his head to look at her.

God above, she was beautiful. Her eyebrows were perfect dark crescents, no quirk of displeasure now. Her eyes were like gold, he thought, dark in one light and glowing bright in another.

Now her eyes were dark, with only glints of the fire inside her. She leaned down and dabbed gently at his face. When her fingers brushed his face, Will inhaled, decimated by longing. "Am I supposed to like you today?" she whispered, stroking her handkerchief over his face. It smelled of her, flowery and warm.

"I hope you do," he murmured.

She surprised him by leaning down and kissing him lightly. He hauled her into his lap, his hands spanning her waist to steady her as he fell back onto his heels and then onto his arse. She laughed, and Will grinned, and then he brought his mouth down on hers.

He could kiss this woman forever. She tasted of tea and honey and almonds, intoxicating and delicious. She opened her mouth with a breathy moan that nearly undid him, and he almost lost his mind. He gathered her close and gave in to every temptation and kissed her until he could hardly breathe.

She curled against him, her arms still around his neck. "If you're still trying to make me dislike you," she said, her voice muffled against his chest, "you're doing a terrible job of it."

He laughed to hide the uneasiness her words stirred up inside him. "It was the puppies, wasn't it?"

"Of course," she said without hesitation. "What else could it possibly be?"

Will rolled his eyes.

She raised her head. Her hair was charmingly tousled from his hands, and her eyes glittered, heavy-lidded and golden. She looked like a woman ready to take her lover by the hand and lead him to her bed. "It's more than that," she murmured, running one finger along his jaw. "I have never felt this way about puppies before."

The stall was well away from the horses and its door was closed, but a groom might walk by at any moment and see her in his lap, in his arms. He should stop this. Instead he ran his hand up her side and touched his lips to hers and breathed, "How *do* you feel?"

A slow smile curved her lips. With a twist she turned to straddle him, her skirts billowing around them. His stomach tensed as he pictured her legs around him—white silk stockings—pink ribbon garters—smooth bronze skin—

She clasped her hands at the nape of his neck, an impish smile on her lips. "I feel like I have you where I want you. How do you like that?"

Too damn much. "It depends what you mean to do with me," he rasped.

"Hmm." She took a deep breath, and his gaze flew helplessly to her breasts, plump and tempting and right in front of his face, barely concealed by the gauzy kerchief tucked into her bodice. He tried feverishly to block out the devil whispering in his ear that if he rolled her over and pulled her skirts out of the way, he could make love to her. "What would you let me do?" Her voice was warm with laughter and laden with flirtation, and it sent shocks of electricity crackling through him.

He caught her face in both hands, to keep his hands away from the rest of her. "Anything," he said, his voice so rough and hungry he barely recognized it.

Her gaze dipped to his chest. "All the kitchen maids say you are very handsome without your shirt."

Will nearly expired at the thought of stripping off his shirt and having her hands on his bare skin.

"I wondered," she said, her voice barely a thread of sound. Her finger traced down his throat, over the knot of his neckcloth, onto his chest. "I wish I had seen it, when you walked through the court-yard without it . . ."

He calculated he could tear off the jacket, waist-coat, and shirt in less than a minute. He could show her, and offer himself up for her inspection. He could let her have her way with him . . .

No, he could not. He closed his eyes and focused on breathing, which was harder than it ought to have been. She didn't know what she was asking—and even if she did, he had to save her from it.

He caught her wandering hand and raised it to his lips. "What would you let *me* do?"

Excitement sparkled in her eyes. "Anything."

He raised one brow as he rolled her over until they were face-to-face, side by side. "Anything? What would you *like* me to do?" He dipped his head and brushed his lips over the curves of her bosom, teasing aside the loosened kerchief with one finger. Her breasts were splendid, and he ran his tongue along the edge of the bodice that confined them.

"Yes," she gasped, clutching his head to her chest. "*Yes*, that."

He listened for one moment for any approaching footsteps, and then gave in to temptation. She dug her fingers into his hair and whispered gasping encouragement as he made love to her skin. By the time he surfaced, drunk on the taste of her, her bosom was mostly bared and she'd thrown her leg over his hip, clinging to him. His jacket had come off and she had her hands inside his waistcoat.

Will smoothed back her hair. It had fallen out of the pins, loose dark curls everywhere like in his fantasy, full of bits of straw. "You bewitch me," he murmured against her lips.

Her answering smile was partly amazed, partly elated. "Tell me more," she whispered, tugging on his sagging neckcloth.

A sound from the aisle made Will freeze. Flushed and mussed, Philippa's eyes went wide. He touched a finger to her lips. She gazed saucily at him, then pursed up her mouth and kissed his fingertip.

He shuddered. Just because she wanted him to kiss her didn't mean he ought to, here, like this. He was a thief, stealing these moments with her—but he couldn't seem to stop himself.

He helped her to her feet, brushing straw from her dress as she smoothed her hair into some order and tucked the kerchief back into her bodice.

Now the clatter of hooves was louder and nearer, and the rumble of grooms' voices. Will glanced warily through the bars at the top of the door.

"Thank you, Mr. Montclair," said Philippa. She gave him a mischievous little smile. "For showing me the puppies." The puppies had long since gone to sleep in a mound in the corner.

Her whole face glowed. He could still hear the soft gasping sounds of her pleasure and taste the warm silk of her skin. Some of his satisfaction may have shown on his face, for she blushed. "It was entirely my pleasure, Miss Kirkpatrick," he said, loudly enough for anyone to hear.

She brushed past him on her way out of the stall. "Not *entirely* yours," was her parting whisper, and then she was gone, speaking to the grooms as calmly as ever while Will held on to the railing and wondered how on earth he was ever going to leave.

It was Charles Amis who told him she was leaving.

The duke reclined on a carpet and a pile of pillows under a large awning in the bailey yard, his face wreathed in smiles as the pointer pups climbed over him, little tails wagging. Philippa was busy corralling wayward puppies back onto the carpet. Her face was flushed pink from running after one straggler after another, and she was out of breath from laughing at them.

Will had arrived after the puppies; he stood at the side of the tent, watching in amusement as the little dogs tumbled about. Two kept hiding beneath Philippa's skirt, then bounding out to topple a sibling. She seemed to encourage it, sitting very still for a moment then flipping up the skirt and scooping up the puppy to nuzzle the soft head, laughing when they tried to nip her hair.

He remembered the feel of that dark silky hair in his hands.

"This is the most laughter at the castle in years," remarked Amis beside him.

Will grinned. "Have there been no puppies before?"

The valet shook his head. "It's not the puppies." He gave Will a considering glance. "It's your fault."

He scoffed uncomfortably. "Surely not. See, they're laughing now entirely apart from me."

Amis chuckled. "I've not heard His Grace laugh like this since before Lady Jessica passed. You began it, with talk of Gulliver."

Will snorted. "I was nearly sacked for that."

"And this is why you weren't." Amis gave him a pointed look. "Her Grace is no fool. She's not seen him this happy in years, either."

"I don't know why that would be," said Will stubbornly. "Miss Kirkpatrick is amusing him very well on her own."

"She is," his companion agreed. "But who will amuse him when she's gone?"

For a moment Will didn't understand. The words didn't make sense—Philippa leave the castle? No, she belonged here. Everyone at Carlyle depended on her.

"She's off to London," continued Mr. Amis. "Her Grace wishes her to have a chance to meet people."

The meaning hit Will like a hammer. Meet someone . . . to marry. He watched her, pink-cheeked with laughter, a puppy in each arm, and felt the air grow suddenly thin around him.

"I thought you ought to know." Amis, the damned perceptive fellow, clapped one hand on his shoulder. "In the event she hasn't yet mentioned it."

No, she had not. Not after he'd kissed her, nor after they lost themselves in each other in the stables. They'd sat with the duke in the Tulip Garden, taken turns reading *Roderick Random*, discussed estate business, and shared cherry tarts in the kitchen courtyard. She'd found him there one morning, tarts in hand, and said she'd decided that he'd won the fishing wager and deserved them.

Even without kissing, awareness hummed between them, like a soft, suspended note from a cello. They talked easily now, since that day at the river. Her eyebrows arched and quirked and scrunched up at things he said; she rolled her eyes and laughed at him, and with him, and teased him. Never once had she said a word about London.

Will's jaw ached from being clenched so hard. "There's no reason I ought to know," he said curtly. "What Miss Kirkpatrick does, and why, is none of my concern."

Amis didn't say anything, but he gave Will a look of such sympathy it physically hurt.

Without a word he walked away, circling the awning. A beautiful young woman with fortune and connections would want an eligible match. The best place to find one was in London. If anything about this surprised him, it should be that she hadn't already been to London and married one of the elegant fops there. In fact, he wished she had, for then . . . for then . . .

Then you never would have done such wicked things to her, whispered his conscience. He never would have seen her look at him with interest, even desire. He never would have been alone with her, or caught her in his arms, or dodged apple cores she threw at him. He never would have flirted with her and kissed her and had his mouth on her breasts. The mad, dangerous ideas never would have taken root in his head, because she would have been utterly unattainable from the start.

But then, she'd always been so. He was the fool for forgetting it.

When he reached the other side of the awning, the duke spied him. "There you are," he called. "See what Pippa's brought today." He lifted one of the puppies against his chest to show Will. The small dog spied the tassel hanging from his cap and began wriggling furiously, trying to bite it. The duke reared back, startled, which set the tassel to swinging, and the puppy scrabbled his paws and lunged. His claws raked across the duke's jaw, opening scarlet scratches, as his teeth sank into the tassel, pulling the cap free.

Carlyle gave a pained cry. Philippa looked up, eyes wide with alarm, as Will swooped in and plucked the pup from the duke's grasp. Amis was already on the other side of him, handkerchief in hand, dabbing at the scratches.

"Oh, Uncle, I'm so sorry," cried Philippa, rushing to his side.

Carlyle waved one hand, but he had gone very pale. "'Tis nothing," he said faintly. "Only a scratch."

Philippa turned to one of the footmen hovering nearby. "Run to Mrs. Potter and tell her to prepare an ointment." The fellow nodded and took off.

"Perhaps we should return to the castle, Your Grace," suggested Amis.

The duke closed his eyes as the valet pressed the handkerchief to his cheek again. "Yes, perhaps so . . ."

Will waved at the two other footmen, already inching near with the chair on poles. Together he and Amis lifted the duke from his bower of cushions and helped him into the chair. The valet led the way across the bailey yard.

Philippa pressed one hand to her chest. "I hope he doesn't get an infection."

"It didn't look deep. I have full confidence in Mrs. Potter." Will looked around. All the servants had gone with the duke, and the puppies were wandering freely across the grass. "These little devils should go back to the stables."

"Oh, yes, of course." She flipped open the lid of a large woven basket and put two puppies inside. Will added another and loped after one who was digging a hole in the grass. Philippa retrieved a puppy who had climbed atop the cushions and Will fished the last two from beneath the shrubbery.

"That's all of them," said Philippa, counting with her finger before closing the basket lid. "Whew!"

Will secured the lid, igniting a chorus of yips and growls from within.

"Did you see how they amused His Grace?" She smiled eagerly at him.

He had—right before Amis told him she was leaving. "Yes, Miss Kirkpatrick."

At his tone, she started in surprise, still flushed from running after puppies. Her hair was coming unpinned, and several wisps brushed her shoulders, just as they'd done in the stables. Will had to look away to resist the temptation to wind them around his fingers, smooth them back, pull out the rest of the pins as he laid her down beside him onto the carpet under this cloudless blue sky—

She's going to London.

To find a husband.

A proper Englishman, suitable for an heiress.

And then: *Two months,* whispered Jack's voice. *Does she know you're leaving?*

I'm leaving because I cannot stay.

And that was the real issue—the real reason he was a fool. He wanted what he could never have, and every time he started to forget it, the next reminder was more painful than the last.

"Good day, ma'am." Without looking at her he hefted the basket and started toward the stables.

PHILIPPA WATCHED HIM stride away, speechless with surprise. He was angry at her, his words clipped and formal. But why?

It had been six days since he kissed her by the river and three days since she kissed him in the stables—beautiful, glorious days in which her imagination ran wild every time she thought of him. At random times her mind would wander back to the first moment he cupped her face in his hands, smiling his rogue's smile, and she would wonder what had been going on behind his eyes. *You aren't supposed to like me,* he'd said, and then managed to distract her every time she tried to ask why. She knew he meant the duchess—and he was correct; the duchess would be horrified to know Philippa enjoyed spending time with him, let alone that she thought of little except kissing him again—but at the same time, Mr. Montclair didn't seem to care much for the duchess's opinion.

Then she would remember: *Will*, she was supposed to call him, and she would drift into a daydream about the strength of his arms around her, the feel of his fingers on her skin, the taste of his mouth on hers. Which left her feeling restless and warm, prone to leaping up to take brisk walks through the castle in increasingly brazen attempts to run into him. She had stopped denying it to herself: she wanted to see him, even if just for a passing moment in the courtyard.

Today she thought she'd planned it perfectly: they would take the puppies back to the stables together, via the long winding path through the garden where the wisteria would provide the privacy for her to call him *Will* and for him to call her *love* and for much more kissing.

It took a few minutes for her elated excitement to turn to bewilderment, and then to indignation as he rounded the corner of the castle and disappeared from view, as if he meant to carry that hamper of puppies all the way back to the stables without a word.

What had happened? Had Mr. Amis upset him? She couldn't think why. The duke was doing well. The duchess was satisfied.

She ran after him. "Mr. Montclair! I want a word with you!"

He didn't stop, only turned around and walked backward. "On what matter, Miss Kirkpatrick?"

"On the matter of your behavior!"

He raised one brow. His stride was longer than hers, but between her anger and him walking backward, she easily kept pace. "Pray continue, Miss Kirkpatrick."

His repeated use of that name set her teeth on edge. This man had held her in his arms and kissed her halfway into a swoon. "Why are you being so formal?" she demanded, flustered just thinking of that. "I thought we had become . . . friends."

His eyes flashed. "A man in my position must remember his place, Miss Kirkpatrick."

"But not his manners, I suppose," she snapped.

"I beg your pardon, ma'am." He spun on one heel and picked up speed.

Philippa picked up her skirts to walk faster, too. "I do not grant it! I want an explanation. What has changed?"

"Nothing."

"Something must have," she insisted.

"But nothing has," he said evenly, adding under his breath, "unfortunately."

She frowned. "What do you mean?" She was breathing hard now, rushing to keep up. "Will. Please tell me."

He gave her a dark look and turned into the stable courtyard. Philippa paused in the shade of the archway, resting one hand on the stone wall for balance as she rubbed the stitch in her side. Across the courtyard, Will disappeared into an open door. When he emerged a few minutes later, his hands were empty, and Philippa's resolve had solidified.

Things were splendid between them. She thrilled to see him striding through the door. Her heart glowed with delight every time she made him laugh. Her bones quivered every time he sent her a swift scorching glance, behind the duke's back or over a plate of tarts. And her heart seemed to somersault inside her chest when his eyes lit at the sight of her or his arm brushed hers. With him there was no mention of her leaving Carlyle, or of facing London society. There was no talk of how her fortune would lure someone into marrying her, or of how she needed to begin preparing for the day the duke and duchess died and left her alone. She loved being with Will, and she thought he felt the same.

In fact . . . she was perilously close to loving him. Even to thinking of *him* as her future. And she wasn't about to let him walk away without telling her why.

When he reached her, she stepped into the center of the arch to block him. "Explain yourself," she demanded, unconsciously adopting icy, duchess-like tones.

He bowed, low and obsequious. "I forgot myself, madam. That is all."

"In what way?"

He wouldn't meet her eyes. "It's best if we *both* forget how." As Philippa reeled, he slipped past her and walked on.

"No!" She ran after him, abandoning every shred of dignity. "Why? What happened?"

He skirted the stable block and turned into a stand of trees. They weren't hidden, but they weren't arguing in the middle of the road.

"Tell me," she pleaded again. "Please."

He moved back when she took a step toward him. Shocked, hurt, she stopped.

He took a deep breath. "Don't blame yourself. I'm at fault. I should never have kissed you, or . . ." He gave a short, angry shake of his head. "Her Grace would dismiss me on the spot if she knew of my actions."

Philippa flushed. "No, she wouldn't approve, but . . ."

"I'm not good enough for you," he said in a low voice.

She froze. *I'll decide that*, cried a little voice in her brain. "Is that what you meant when you said I wasn't supposed to like you?"

Something flickered across his face—surprise, unease, remorse. "Yes."

"Rubbish," she blurted. "You didn't mean Her Grace when you said that. You said you'd *tried* to make me not like you."

Now he went still, his gaze guarded. "Did I?"

"Were you toying with my feelings?"

"*No*. I was trying to avoid that."

Her eyes narrowed. "Because I was such easy prey to a scoundrel like you?"

He said nothing. But Philippa had been studying him for weeks now, and she could see the anger seething inside him.

"Was it a game?" she asked again. "An amusing respite from the tedium of building bridges and repairing fences? Seduce the naive spinster?"

Her voice broke on the last word, and so did Will's control. With a curse he lunged forward and caught her against him. Her heart nearly stopped as he kissed her, desperately, hungrily, and then she wound herself around him, kissing him back, feeling a bone-deep certainty that he *did* care for her, he *did* want her, and she—she—

She suspected she did love him.

"Don't," he whispered harshly against her mouth before another frantic kiss. "Don't ever think so little of yourself."

She clung to him. "Why did you kiss me?"

"Philippa—"

"Why?" She dug her fingers into his jacket, watching him closely.

For a heartbeat, despair flickered over his face. "Because I wanted to. I wanted you. God help me, you fascinated me from the moment I met you."

Joy sparkled inside her, as sharp and bright as diamonds in the sun. "Then why are you angry?"

He went still, then stepped back, tugging her hands from his jacket. "What do you expect to come of this?"

She opened her mouth, but no words emerged. What had she expected? That it would continue. That they would keep sharing smart comments, amused glances, quiet moments of perfect under-standing, and delicious, bone-melting kisses. That he would make her body sing and her heart soar. She never wanted all that to end.

But *all that* sounded almost like marriage. If Will confessed that he was deeply in love with her, and the duchess was so moved by their mutual affec-tion that she relented and decided she approved of Will after all, they could be married and live at Stone Cottage. In Philippa's fantasy, the duke lived another twenty years at least, and when Captain

St. James finally inherited, he would be so impressed by Will's work that he begged him to stay at Carlyle. And then Philippa could have a loving husband without having to face London, and also get to remain forever at Carlyle, surrounded by everyone she loved, who loved and respected her in turn.

The breath rasped in her lungs. Dear God. She was thinking of marrying the estate steward. The duchess would faint in horror, right before she woke up and absolutely forbade it.

At her silence Will nodded and released her. "Precisely."

Panicking, she shook her head. "No—no, wait—"

He retreated from her outstretched hand. "Nothing *can* come of it. We both know it. I'm a servant and you're going to London to find a suitable husband."

She jerked. "Who told you that?"

"Amis." He waited, daring her to deny it.

Which she could not do.

"Philippa," he prodded, "do you see any future for us?"

Her thoughts flitted wildly, seeking something solid to cling to, some reason, some hope. But every slender chance she thought of wilted in the face of his expression. Even if she was willing to grasp at straws, he wasn't.

Will closed his eyes at her silence. "Good-bye." He walked off, and this time she made no effort to stop him.

She stood in the shelter of the trees for a long time. His words echoed endlessly in her head. *I'm not good enough for you . . . you fascinated me from the moment I met you . . . Do you see any future for us?* Each echo grew louder and louder until they drowned out the hopeful, happy thoughts she'd been nursing—the silly and naive thoughts about desire and love and belonging. The wild, thrilling attraction to him. The feeling that he was like her, that he saw her as she was and found her bewitching, and that they suited each other perfectly.

None of that mattered.

When she made it back to the castle an hour later, she went to the duchess's sitting room.

Mr. Edwards was there, looking grave and grim. The duchess was pacing, and at Philippa's entrance she almost shrieked, *"There* you are!"

"What is wrong?"

"France!" The duchess threw herself into a chair and reached for Percival.

Normally Philippa would have rushed to comfort her. Today she barely listened as Mr. Edwards talked, frequently interrupted by the duchess. Lord Thomas had married. Two sons born in France. One dead in childhood. One survived. Signs that Lord Thomas had fallen into ruinous debt and might have fled to New France with his wife and son.

Today she didn't care who inherited Carlyle. It didn't affect her. In fact, at this moment she wanted far away from Carlyle and its steward.

"Pippa?"

She jumped. The duchess was watching her with concern. "Oh—Er. When was this?"

"Some fifty years ago," murmured Mr. Edwards.

"Fifty years! He must be dead, mustn't he? Oh, are we never to have an answer?" The duchess was almost hysterical. "Shall we scour the entire world for this infernal man and his descendants?"

Edwards gazed at her sadly. "I must send someone, madam."

The duchess buried her face in Percival's fur and said nothing.

"I am sorry," the attorney added in a low voice.

The duchess raised her head. Her eyes were dry, but her mouth trembled. "Aren't we all, Mr. Edwards."

The attorney rose and bowed, and Philippa went to sit beside the duchess and take her hand. "As if a Frenchman wasn't bad enough," said the older woman bleakly. "A provincial! One of those at Carlyle is more than enough."

At this reference to Will, Philippa flinched in physical pain. "I came to tell you I'm ready to go to Aunt Diana. But if you would rather I not, given this news—"

"What? Oh my, no indeed." The duchess perked up with a wide smile—of relief, no doubt. "Of course you must go! When shall I tell her to expect you?"

She had been deluding herself. The duchess would never agree to let her marry Will, an estate agent, an impertinent provincial. What's more, he didn't even want her, not if it would take effort and persuasion. It was time for Philippa to face reality. "As soon as it can be arranged."

Chapter Twenty

❧ ❧

If Will thought he would feel more peace after parting from Philippa, he was wrong.

She left two days after their confrontation. He heard the other servants discussing the uproar that had ensued. She'd been planning to go for several weeks, but it was strange for her to leave so suddenly, they all agreed. Miss Kirkpatrick was usually very considerate of the servants and the work they must do. It had taken three maids to pack everything in time.

Now you've done it, he told himself. *You've chased her from her own home.*

His desire to remain at Carlyle plummeted. He tried throwing himself back into work, as before, but now he could barely concentrate on it. Without Josiah's puzzled and worried questions, he would have lost track of the lumber meant for new barns and missed a report of a crater opening up in the mill road that needed immediate attention.

Instead his thoughts veered too often to London, where Philippa was no doubt dancing in the arms of a wellborn Englishman, a man who didn't jump at the whim of a cantankerous duchess, a man who wasn't running out of time in England. He imagined her smiling up at that man, her dimple showing, and he imagined that man pulling her close and kissing her until she made that breathy moan of contentment and forgot all about William Montclair, presumptuous idiot.

It was the way he knew it had to be, but it made him miserable and surly. He'd been right that putting it off would only make it harder to bear.

In the doldrums, he missed an appointment with the duke. Charles Amis sent a note to Stone Cottage, and Will cursed out loud when it arrived.

"What, sir?" piped up Josiah.

"I was supposed to call upon the duke yesterday." Will propped his elbows on his desk and ran his hands over his head.

"You might go now, sir," suggested Josiah. "I can write the rest of the letters and reports."

Will didn't move. He dug his fingers into the taut muscles at the back of his neck. For the first time he didn't want to see the duke. Philippa wouldn't be there, but he would think of her the entire time.

"I'll go tomorrow," he muttered, and dropped Amis's note into a drawer on top of all the other letters he was ignoring from Jack.

The next day poured rain, and he got caught up in the account books. Edwards had been spending more and more time in London and had entrusted Will with most of the estate finances. He did not go to the castle.

The following day he rode up the hill feeling a twinge of remorse. It wasn't the duke's fault, and the old fellow had no other visitors. He ought to go and read a few chapters of *Roderick Random,* or perhaps begin a new novel, one lacking any association with Philippa Kirkpatrick. He wondered if she would ever pick it up and finish it on her own, or perhaps suggest her adoring fiancé read it to her. She was an attentive and engaged listener.

Mr. Heywood intercepted him. "Her Grace would like a word, sir."

Will paused. He hadn't seen the duchess except in brief passing moments for weeks, and even during those, Philippa or the attorney had been present as buffer. "Immediately?" he asked, hoping he could put it off.

The butler gave him a rueful look. "It always is, when Her Grace sends for someone. Best go now, before she hears you're at the castle."

He took a deep breath. "Of course. Thank you, Mr. Heywood."

Heywood showed him to the same drawing room where Will had had his first disastrous interview with the duchess. What a brash idiot he'd been that day, full of himself and certain that his employer would see the sense of his explanation, even applaud his actions. But he'd also been full of curiosity, fascinated to see a real duchess and the inside of a real castle.

Today he didn't care. He walked in and simply bowed.

"Sit down," she said without pleasantries. She wore her customary gray with white lace, a deep blue shawl around her shoulders.

Will took a seat.

"You did not keep your appointment with the

duke." She turned toward a tea tray on the table and poured a cup.

"My apologies, ma'am. I've come today to see him."

"Today he is unwell."

Will nodded. "Then I shall come again another day, when he is able to receive visitors."

"Why did you not come?" she demanded. She held out the cup of tea.

Will stared at it. Philippa had urged tea on him often enough that now he didn't mind it—at least the way she prepared it, with a spoonful of honey and no milk. The duchess had added milk and no honey. "Thank you, ma'am, no."

Her eyebrows shot up. "What?"

His mother would box his ears for refusing, but Will stubbornly shook his head. "I don't take tea, if you please."

She drew it back with a rattle of china. "Don't take tea! Whyever not?"

"We don't drink much of it in Boston."

She frowned at him. "Of all the cheek." Absently she took a sip from the cup in her hands, then set it down. "Why did you disappoint the duke?"

Will's jaw tensed. "That wasn't my intent, ma'am. I'll arrange things with Mr. Amis and be more attentive in the future."

She sniffed and took another sip of tea. "Are you pouting over Miss Kirkpatrick's absence?"

Caught off guard, he stiffened. "No."

Her gaze ran up and down him, distinctly unimpressed. "I certainly hope not."

"Why would I, ma'am?"

"Indeed I do not know," she said in mild surprise, which managed to sound like disdain. "But if you were to harbor feelings in that vein, I would strongly advise you to disregard them. She has gone to London to mix with good company—including eligible gentlemen of family and fortune. I daresay she has not spent a moment thinking of you."

He was grinding his teeth so hard they hurt. "Why would she, ma'am?"

"No reason at all, of course. I spoke out of kindness, to remind you where your duty lies."

He said nothing.

"However, the duke still enjoys your company." She sounded as if she couldn't understand how anyone might stomach that, let alone enjoy it. "As long as you are employed here, you are requested to visit him twice a week."

"Requested," he repeated flatly.

Her eyes narrowed. "Expected."

He sat in rigid anger for a moment. "I've never thought of visiting him as a *duty*, ma'am. His Grace was kind and welcoming to me, and I was pleased to call upon him."

"Good," she exclaimed. "Then continue doing so!"

Will smiled without humor. "Or I'll be dismissed."

Her face turned dull red and her lips pursed tight. He could tell she was desperate to say the words and be done with him. Recklessly, he wished she would. "Perhaps."

The last little thread of his temper frayed and broke. Without a word he rose and headed for the door. Behind him there was a clatter of china and a rustle of silk. "Mr. Montclair! What are you doing?

Stop! Of all the insufferable insolence! Do you *wish* to be dismissed?"

He stopped and turned. She was on her feet, her plump little hands in fists at her waist. She looked irritated and shocked and frustrated. He told himself she was simply trying to protect her beloved Philippa; he told himself she was a rich old woman, set in her ways and accustomed to people bowing to her wishes in everything.

It didn't matter.

"Au contraire, madame." He swept the most formal, obsequious bow possible. "Je m'en fous."

He turned on his heel and walked out.

WILL DID GO to the duke, but it was a waste. Carlyle was glad to see him, but he was wan and lethargic, and Will wasn't in the right mood to cheer him. After a quarter hour, the duke said he was too tired. He asked Will to come again another day and simply nodded when Will apologized for being out of sorts.

Charles Amis showed him out. "What troubles you?" he asked quietly.

Will shook his head. "I had an unpleasant interview with Her Grace. My fault."

Amis peered at him. "Is that all?"

"What else could there be?"

Amis cocked his head. "Mrs. Amis says you are never in the kitchens anymore. She asked if you were ill, not to come around stealing tarts. And now you've forgotten His Grace."

"I have a great deal to do," Will told him. "I've been busy."

Amis nodded. "And Miss Kirkpatrick has been gone over a week."

He looked away. "Has she? I've no knowledge of the family's plans."

"*Will.*" Amis lowered his voice. "I know you care for her, and that she thought rather fondly of you. But you must understand, it was never meant to be."

"Right," said Will through his teeth.

"You must forget her," said the valet gently. "She will likely return from London with a fiancé, if not a husband."

Will looked at him for a long moment. The man spoke out of friendship and sympathy. "Thank you, Charles." He went out before Amis could dig the knife any deeper.

After that he worked himself to exhaustion, pausing only to visit the duke on the prescribed days. The two new bridges were nearly done, and most of the repairs were well underway. It was astonishing how much work could be accomplished when Edwards opened the castle's purse wide. Will had a reliable system arranged now with Josiah on all other matters, for reports of problems and routine administration. He'd always kept one eye on the calendar, anticipating the day he would decamp for good and wanting to leave everything in reputable order. By now the estate could almost run itself.

Therefore, when another letter arrived from his brother, laden with expletives and underscores, Will did not ignore it like the others. Jack wrote, no longer begging but demanding that Will come to London to help him win the Frenchman's business. *He has begun to say he might prefer a different company, and if he abandons us I will write to Pa and tell him you refused to say even a word of persuasion,* Jack threatened.

He thought of what his father would say if he learned that Will refused to help Jack. Then he thought of what his father would do if Jack retaliated by revealing where Will was. He took out a sheet of paper and dashed a quick message to his brother: *I will arrive within three days.*

He went back to the castle to tell the duchess, fully expecting to be turned off on the spot and not caring one bit if she did. It didn't really matter now; he'd promised to return to Montclair and Sons in a few weeks anyway.

To his surprise, she did not dismiss him.

Her mouth screwed up in displeasure when he explained that he was needed in London on a family matter, but she only said, "How long would you be gone?"

"No more than a fortnight." It was two days' journey to London, one if it were a punishingly long one. Ten days was long enough to win the business, or consider it irretrievably lost.

She sipped her tea. Today she hadn't offered him any, which suited Will. "And you will leave tomorrow?"

"Yes, ma'am."

She sipped again. "What of the duke?"

"Mr. Amis knows the books we've been reading. He can carry on until I return." *If I return.*

A little frown pinched her brow. "Apparently he prefers you."

Will didn't know what to say to that, so he said nothing.

The duchess sighed. "You must attend to your family, of course. I expect you will take the opportunity to call upon Mr. Edwards there to confer about the estate."

"If you wish, ma'am."

She shot him an irked look. "I do wish. Absenting yourself for a fortnight is extraordinary."

Wait until I resign the post, he thought. He ought to do it right now and go back to London for good. But then he would have no reason to come back, and somehow he couldn't say those words yet. "Yes, ma'am."

"Go, then," she said stiffly. "And I do hope the family matter is resolved happily."

He paused at this unexpected sign of kindness. "Thank you, ma'am."

The main hall of the castle was nearer, so he went down those stairs. As he rounded the turn, his gaze fell again on the statue below, and when he reached the ground floor, he paused to study it for a moment.

Carved of pure white marble, Perseus held aloft the head of Medusa, her features twisted in rage and pain. Killing the Gorgon had been a remarkable feat, achieved only with the help of three gods and a goddess. But Perseus's face was averted, because looking upon his prize would mean his own death.

Will understood that feeling. He'd come to Carlyle on his own quest, and he'd accomplished what he set out to do. And like Perseus, he didn't dare look at what he'd done.

He turned and walked out, perhaps for the last time.

Chapter Twenty-One

❧❧

From the moment Philippa stepped down from the carriage in Hertford Street, she told herself to enjoy her visit to London.

Diana and Fanny came out of the house as the luggage was being unloaded. "At last," Fanny cried, pulling Philippa into a warm embrace. "You're here!"

"And so happy to see you." That much was true. Fanny was like a younger sister to her.

The countess stepped forward to inspect her. "Even more beautiful than ever," she declared. "But no roses in your cheeks! We shall fix that as soon as possible."

Philippa smiled. "It was a long journey, Aunt! I'm merely tired." Diana had been Jessica's dearest friend, her bosom companion, her constant correspondent, and Philippa had called her Aunt from the beginning.

Diana laughed and took Philippa's hands and drew her toward the house. "Then we shall let you rest before we dazzle you."

"But, oh, we've made such plans for your visit!"

Fanny squeezed her hand. "I've been waiting for ages . . ."

Diana led the way up the stairs. Her house was exceedingly elegant. That was no surprise—Diana was exceedingly elegant, and the house was in a fashionable new part of town. It was a marked change from the centuries-old castle, thought Philippa.

"I thought you would like this room." The countess opened a door into a bright, sunny room done up in pale yellow and white, with delicate mahogany furniture. "Elinor always stays here when she visits. She likes the view of the park from the windows."

"Oh, yes. You know how that would appeal to a country girl like me." Philippa took off her hat as she went to the window and peered out. The house sat on the corner of Park Lane and Hertford Street, with a clear view into Hyde Park. "How lovely that it's so near."

"Extremely convenient for carriage rides and strolls on the arms of handsome gentlemen," teased Fanny.

Philippa kept her smile in place even though the thought of that made her want to crawl under the bed. She'd had enough of handsome men. "I was thinking more of escaping society from time to time, but yes, it shall also be convenient for carriage drives."

"Escaping society!" Fanny looked scandalized.

"Yes," said Philippa with a laugh. "When I make a faux pas and cannot show my face for three days."

Diana smiled, but Philippa saw scrutiny in her gaze. "I have no fear of that. We'll leave you to rest until dinner. Her Grace warned me you would need a complete new wardrobe, so we will begin tomorrow in Oxford Street."

Fanny gave a happy chirp, and Diana shooed her out the door.

Philippa told Marianne to unpack only enough for dinner, then to take herself off to rest as she wished. The maid thanked her and Philippa lay down.

It had been a week since Will said she'd bewitched him; four days since he told her they had no future. She had been trying to forget it, but her brain kept picking at the moment, searching for something she could have said or done to change the outcome.

She wasn't sure why she did this to herself. She had spoken honestly; there was nothing she had to regret . . . except how it ended. And now she was in London, away from him but unable to stop thinking of him.

Lying on her back, staring up at the beautifully embroidered canopy, she told herself that it was over—indeed, it had never *been*. It couldn't be love, because he didn't love her back.

Don't think of him, she told herself, and rolled over to try and rest so she didn't cause Diana any distress.

LIKE A GENERAL preparing for battle, Diana had drawn up a list of merchants they needed to visit. Philippa must have shoes, stockings, new shifts and petticoats and gowns, kerchiefs and hats and caps and gloves. There were ribbons and shoe buckles and jewelry to coordinate, and that was before Diana began talking about the hairdresser.

Philippa put her head in her hands and laughed. "I never knew I was so hopelessly outmoded!"

"Oh no," cried Fanny. "We would spoil you even if you arrived with trunks full of the very latest styles. Tell her, Mama!"

Still smiling, Philippa shook her head. "But where will I wear such finery? I'm only here for a month or two, and then I shall be back in the country, where no one notices if my skirt is too wide or too narrow, or if my bodice has exactly the right cut."

Fanny snorted with laughter. "Pippa, we shall be out nearly every evening. Mama is relentless."

Philippa looked at Diana. She gazed back innocently. "I shepherded two daughters to excellent matches in their very first Seasons, you know."

Philippa reached for her tea. Elinor and Henrietta had indeed made very happy matches. Elinor— now Countess of Darby—and Henrietta—now Lady Sanbourne—each had a handful of children and a devoted husband.

"If you doubt her, ask Beauchamp," piped up Fanny, invoking her older brother. "Can you imagine? Mama even found *George* an adoring wife!"

Philippa raised her brows in amusement. "Even George?"

Fanny made a face at her. "You know George—he fancied himself such a rake, it was a miracle anyone would want him, let alone someone as charming as Anne."

"Fanny," said her mother in mild reproof.

"I did not doubt you." Philippa concentrated on buttering her toast. "But I suspect I shall be a far greater challenge than Elinor or Henrietta, or even Lord Beauchamp."

Silence descended. Philippa ate her toast. The cook here made excellent bread; she must take the receipt home to Mrs. Amis.

"Why is that?" Diana asked carefully.

The duchess would have written and warned her, of course. Philippa wiped her lips. "The duchess told you about the steward."

Fanny's ears visibly pricked up.

Diana flicked one hand. "My dear, who among us hasn't developed a tendre for an inappropriate man at some point? It only means you're a healthy young woman. When I was a girl, I fancied my older brother's tutor." She laughed as Fanny gasped in shocked delight. "An admission which never fails to humble me! He was pompous and silly but he *did* have a way of reading Latin . . ."

Philippa smiled wistfully. She had a feeling if Diana ever met Will Montclair, she would not think him pompous or silly.

"The best cure for a girlish fancy is to meet a great many other gentlemen," Diana went on. "I forgot the tutor two days after I came to London. I've accepted an invitation to Lady Powell's soiree in three days' time. We shall be hard-pressed to assemble your wardrobe by then, but I believe we are equal to the challenge."

"Indeed we are!" Fanny echoed.

Over the next two days they traveled the entire length of Oxford Street, visiting merchants and buying more clothing than Philippa had ever owned in her life. By dinner every night, Philippa's feet ached and her head spun. Oxford Street was amazing. There wasn't anything one couldn't find there, from the shop that seemed to hold every possible style of women's shoes, including for dolls, to the shops whose windows were covered with engraved prints, tinted to lifelike colors and always attended by a crowd of onlookers. There were linen shops filled with delicate white wear. The confectioners and fruiterers displayed pyramids of fruits Philippa had only read of, especially pineapples. One shop had a cunning display of bottles of spirits illuminated from behind by candles, presenting a brilliant multicolored glow. The bustle and noise were overwhelming; glossy carriages bowled down the wide street side by side, drawn by splendidly matched pairs of horses.

As soon as her new wardrobe was in hand, the events began. A soiree in the large walled garden of a stately mansion. A box at the theater. A picnic on a hill outside of town. A leisurely sail down the Thames aboard some lord's yacht.

And the people. Diana thrived in large groups of people, and they never went anywhere without a party of ten or more. To Philippa, used to the quiet of Carlyle, it felt like being on a public stage.

Or rather, standing on the block to be bid upon. Papa had left her three thousand pounds; a very respectable sum for the daughter of an army officer with no other family to speak of. But the duchess had promised her almost ten times that, and everyone in London seemed to know it.

There was the Countess Mabry, who made a point of being introduced and sat next to her at the opera, chatting nonstop and dropping in little questions about her background and education. Diana mentioned with a smile that Lady Mabry had a handsome son—not the heir, but her second son.

Philippa was introduced to Lord James at a picnic. When his mother finally coerced him into walking with her, she impulsively asked if his mother was trying to marry him off.

"Obvious to all, ain't it?" He grimaced. "She's paraded one heiress after another in front of me."

Like her. Philippa smiled. "And you haven't liked any of them, I take it."

His face softened. "No offense to any of them, nor to you, Miss Kirkpatrick . . . but my heart is already taken. Mother will come around. She'll have to."

Three days later Lord James Mabry eloped with Mrs. Ferguson, a wealthy widow eight years his senior. "Never mind him," said Diana when she heard. "I never meant him for you."

"Meant?"

"Not that I would have prevented it, if you had wanted him." Diana patted her hand. "I thought you might want to practice a little flirtation on him."

Philippa smiled halfheartedly at that. Once she had thought of Will as a bit of practice flirtation, and look where it got her.

That turned out to be the high point of her London debut in society. There was a charming baronet, whom Diana whispered was deep in debt, and the eldest son of an earl who called on Philippa twice before Diana heard rumors he had the French pox. There were the rakes who asked her to dance with sly, predatory smiles, the rogues who tried to tempt her into shady garden walks alone with them, and even a gentleman who claimed to be an Italian count and professed his desire to show her his villa near Venice. Diana chased him away with a smile, but apologized later to Philippa.

"My dear, I have never seen such a poor showing by the gentlemen of London! It must be the fine weather luring all the best specimens to the country. We are left with those of no means and no manners."

"I don't mind, Aunt, really I don't." Philippa took her hands. "In fact, *I* never thought I was coming to London to find a husband. It's not like ordering a new gown, where you can specify exactly what you desire. I came to see you and Fanny, and enjoy myself."

Diana sighed. "And all the soirees and picnics aren't allowing that."

"The pressure to find a suitor isn't," Philippa admitted. "May we just . . . see London? I've heard so much about the sights here, and I would like to see them."

"The duchess will be disappointed in me," murmured Diana.

"Nonsense! I'll tell her I must return earlier next year, to have a better chance of meeting someone, and then I shall have another visit with you." She gave a cheeky smile to hide the pang that thought gave her.

The countess laughed. "Clever girl! Of course. I want you to think of this visit with nothing but delight."

Privately Philippa didn't think that very likely. As hard as she tried, it was impossible not to think of Will. While she strolled in the park on some stranger's arm, she wondered if he had completed the bridge near the Smith farm, and which

of the young horses he would persuade the duchess to give Gerald and Jilly. While she sat through
an elaborate Venetian breakfast in a viscountess's
garden, she wondered if he had finished reading
Roderick Random to the duke. And as she sat in Diana's box at the opera, her mind drifted to imagine Will sitting beside her, his hand touching hers,
tracing up her wrist and arm, caressing the back of
her neck until the curtain closed and he could pull
her to the back of the box for a passionate kiss, his
mouth open on her skin, his hands moving on her
body, while the audience cheered and paid them
no mind . . .

"Did you enjoy it?" whispered Diana under cover
of the applause. "You look very pleased."

Philippa was thankful it was still dark; her face
must have flushed six shades of pink at what she'd
been thinking instead of following the opera on
stage. "Who could not?"

She followed in the countess's wake as they made
their way from the box, through the corridors,
down the stairs, into the salon. As usual, a dozen
people greeted Diana, slowing their progress tre-
mendously. Even Fanny was whisked away by a
pair of young ladies her own age. Philippa was
very accomplished by now at nodding and murmuring polite nothings.

A flash of bright blue coat caught her eye. A tall
man with long, unruly dark hair and a swagger
unlike any London gentleman. For a moment her
heart leapt in such hope—without thinking she
took a step in his direction—

The man in blue turned; not Will Montclair, but a
much older man, his face weathered and lined. He

was smiling at a young woman in pale pink who was obviously his daughter. Cringing at herself, Philippa spun around just as Lord Ranley, one of Diana's dandyish acolytes, cried out, "Miss Kirkpatrick! It's the most marvelous thing, I've just met a relation of yours." He stepped aside with a flourish, and Philippa came face-to-face with a man she'd never met, but instinctively knew.

Matthew Kirkpatrick, baron of Balmedie, stared back at her, seemingly as astonished as she was. He was tall and broad, though slightly stooped. His once-dark hair was mostly gray, but his blue eyes still snapped. He looked so much like her father, as Papa would have looked now if he'd lived, that Philippa sucked in her breath, unable to move.

Her uncle recovered first. His gaze turned icy as he scanned her up and down. "Don't be ridiculous, Ranley," he said, in the exact same soft Scottish inflection Papa had had. "This woman is no kin of mine." With only a dark glance at Diana, he turned and walked away, his gait steady and quick despite his cane.

Philippa wanted to sink through the floor—and yet, she wasn't surprised at all. Thanks to Diana's sponsorship and the duchess's money, she had been received very politely in town. If she'd just been plain Miss Kirkpatrick, Anglo-Indian daughter of a humble army colonel, she knew it would have been otherwise. In a way, she had almost been waiting for someone to snub her for being different.

How mortifying that her own uncle had to be the one to do it, though—and in front of a theater full of people.

Dimly she felt Diana's arm slip through hers, and

saw Lord Ranley hastily clearing a path for them through the curious crowd. Somehow the Beauchamp carriage was nearby, and then they were inside.

"My dear." Diana's face was pale in the dark carriage. "I'd no idea—nor did Ranley—I am appalled."

Philippa closed her eyes and didn't pull away when Diana grasped her hands. "It's not your fault."

"Can you ever forgive me?"

She mustered a smile. "Of course."

The countess bit her lip. "I had forgotten . . . Jessica told me he was a cruel man."

Philippa said nothing. Jessica had called the baron a bitter and prejudiced brute, and Papa had not disagreed. Philippa hadn't been supposed to hear that, but she had known for a long time that her uncle wanted nothing to do with her. He never had. He'd told Papa to give her to her Indian relations and start anew with a proper English wife. She'd only discovered that when she read Papa's letters after his death, but it merely confirmed what she already knew: her father's relations didn't want her.

Diana seemed reassured by her stillness and silence. "There—we will never speak of him again, and I shall tell all my acquaintances he is abominably rude and hateful. And tomorrow we shall do something so diverting, we shall forget all about him. Will that serve?"

She looked at the older woman, waiting so anxiously for her reply. Diana loved her and wanted so much to please her. If only she knew there was

nothing—no party, no outing, no acquaintance—
that could lift Philippa's spirits.

She had thought coming to London was the best
way to deal with heartbreak, but that had been
wrong, or perhaps there was no good way to face
heartbreak. Everything she enjoyed, she thought
of telling Will about, and everything she disliked
made her wonder how Will would make sport of
it. Now all she could think of was the way he held
her hand as she talked of Papa, and how comfort-
ing it was.

No matter how many times she told herself to
forget him, something always reminded her. She
didn't *want* to forget him.

Lord Ranley finally delivered Fanny to the coach,
and she and Diana chattered on about the exciting things they might do on the morrow. Philippa
barely heard any of it. She nodded when it seemed
appropriate, and went to bed, not to sleep but to
ponder what to do, and what she wanted.

She wanted to go home.

"I'm simply not in the right spirits for London,"
she told Diana in the carriage the next day, on the
way to a tea garden she had apparently agreed to
visit. Fanny had been invited to go shopping in
Bond Street with her friends, so it was just the two
of them. "I wanted so much to be, but it isn't working. I cannot allow you to waste another month or
two ferrying me to soirees and events when I feel
so detached from everything around me."

Diana's face was a study in sympathy and upset.
"Is there nothing I can do to help?"

Philippa smiled ruefully. "If I knew, I would
ask it."

The countess sighed and gazed out the window for a long moment. "Of course I would not keep you, if you wished to go home. I only want your happiness, my darling girl."

"I know." On impulse Philippa added, "And please don't blame yourself. It's not because of my uncle's actions."

"Horrid man," muttered Diana. She was silent for a moment, then faced Philippa again. "Will you tell me about him?"

Philippa frowned. She didn't want to discuss her uncle.

"The steward," said the countess gently.

She sat in shocked—and anxious—silence.

"I understand Her Grace's fears," Diana went on. "But I also saw your dear mama fret the same way, when she met your papa. Jessica did not want to upset her mother." Diana sighed. "The duke had suffered his injury by then, and the duchess had taken over the estate. Jessica thought she would never find a gentleman who understood that she felt a duty to remain at Carlyle, to support her mother and brother and care for the estate. And then, here in London where she'd come at my urging for a visit, she met the colonel, who was the least likely man to suit her."

"She—" Philippa stared. "She thought Papa was inappropriate?"

"A military man, fifteen years her elder, a widower with a small child? I daresay *he* didn't think himself worthy of her. But she said her heart simply knew, and could not be denied." Diana raised her brows. "It did not have an auspicious beginning!"

"Oh?" Philippa sat forward eagerly.

"Goodness, no. He had gone to the theater with a group of friends, who were all dreadfully foxed. He was leaving; we were arriving late." Diana gave a dimpled smile. "My fault, I'm afraid. The fashions were rather extreme then, and I was somewhat vain. She teased me about it." Her smile grew wistful. "So there we were, rushing in after the performance had begun, and there he was, storming out in high dudgeon, and he knocked into her, forcing her into a deep puddle that muddied six inches of her skirt. He was horrified.

"But he was a true gentleman, your papa, and when he arrived the next day to apologize again, she received him. And then . . ." Her face softened. "He mentioned that he needed to hurry home to tend his little daughter, who was ill, and she was intrigued. And when he finally brought you, well, she was smitten. She fell in love with him, but also with you." Diana paused as Philippa closed her eyes. "And they would both wish you happiness, even if it crossed Her Grace."

She breathed unsteadily. Her parents' marriage had defied the social order; an English gentleman might take an Indian bibi as a mistress, but not actually marry her. Papa's brother had not approved at all. Noor's family had also been reluctant to allow the marriage. But Papa loved her, and Ammi loved him, and they had persevered.

"And once Jessica realized he was the one for her and put her foot down that she would have him," Diana added, "the duchess decided it was a splendid match after all. So you see, Her Grace is not immovable."

Could that happen again?

"When I first met Will, I thought he looked like a pirate," Philippa said haltingly. "He acted like one, too, brash and forward. He arrived to his first interview with the duchess wearing a footman's clothing because he had gone into a river to save a farmer's pigs when their wagon overturned."

Diana's brows shot up.

"He does nothing by halves," she went on. "Thus far he has argued and cajoled her into building bridges and repairing roads and completely changing the drainage system. He is dragging the estate into the modern age in spite of all of us, who had settled into habits of doing things and didn't realize the need for improvement. He's made everyone see the need, and then he's accomplished it. I believe every servant at the castle knows and admires him. And . . . he's even won the duke's affection."

The countess blinked. She was one of the few people outside the family who knew how badly the duke had been injured. "Carlyle?"

Philippa nodded. "They met by chance, but the duke is very taken with him, and now Mr. Montclair comes several times a week to read *Gulliver's Travels* and talk about estate matters and make sport of the king." She smiled wistfully. "He's not supposed to do any of that. But he does it all anyway, and Uncle has never been better."

"Goodness," murmured Diana. "If Her Grace ever dismisses him, please tell me at once so I can employ him."

Philippa laughed, but it caught in her throat and came out as a sob. "And I'm falling in love with him. Aunt Diana, what should I do?"

In a rustling crush of skirts, the countess moved

to sit beside her and hold her. "My dear, I cannot tell you. I only know that you must find a way to balance the demands of your conscience and your heart."

Philippa leaned into her embrace. She knew what her heart wanted: Will. Not merely for stolen kisses in the stable, but for always. He'd asked if she could see a future for them, and she'd said no . . . but now she realized there could be one, if she was brave enough to seize it.

Her conscience quailed at disappointing the duchess, whom she loved dearly. Every few days brought a letter from her: about the duke, the estate, Mr. Edwards's outrageous request to send men halfway around the world in search of the elusive and unwanted Lord Thomas, and of the weather. Not one word of Mr. Montclair. She despised the man, even before she'd suspected Philippa was attracted to him.

And yet, the duchess had blessed her only daughter's marriage to a humble army officer, third son of a Scottish baron. Not only that, she had welcomed Miles and his motherless daughter into her home and her heart. Surely she could do the same for the man who had won over everyone else at Carlyle—including Philippa.

"Yes," she said softly, to Diana and to herself. "Yes, I must."

Chapter Twenty-Two

❦

"Where the devil have you been?" was Jack's greeting when Will arrived.

Tired, hungry, and covered in dust, Will dropped his saddlebags. "It looks like we're doing very well in England after all."

Jack flushed. The office was a vast deal more elegant than it had been when Will left. The armchairs were leather, the battered old desk had been replaced by one with carved legs and a glossy top, and there were velvet drapes at the window.

"The old appointments made us look like a slipshod bunch of smugglers. Now we look like what we are—the finest merchant ship captains in New England."

Will raised his brows. "Are we?"

His brother's eyes flashed. "I told you about it every step of the way. You did read my letters, didn't you?"

Will didn't answer that. "Have we also got luxurious new quarters, too? I left before dawn to reach London in a day, there had better be a comfortable bed for me somewhere."

Jack sighed. "Upstairs."

Will heaved the saddlebags onto his shoulder and went upstairs. Already he was tired of this visit. His brother followed at his heels, talking all the while. "Why haven't you answered any of my letters? I was about to ride off to whatever county it was and reassure myself that you still lived."

Will's room was as he'd left it, although with a layer of dust and the hot, musty smell a room got when shut up for a long time. Nothing like the fresh breezes through Stone Cottage, with the fragrance of Philippa's garden drifting in the windows . . . sometimes even a hint of her perfume . . .

"I was busy." He peeled off his coat. "And it didn't appear you needed my counsel."

Jack opened his mouth, then frowned. "But we agreed . . ."

Will shrugged. "We agreed you would keep me informed. I read the letters and thought you had it all in hand."

His brother leaned against the door as Will sat down to shuck his boots. "I wondered how things were with you. In all these months you never said."

"Everything was splendid," said Will evenly. "You received the funds I sent, didn't you?"

"Yes," admitted Jack, "and they were very useful."

Will squinted at him. "Useful?" He'd sent every penny he could spare, assuaging his guilt by pouring his earnings into the company. He'd sent Jack over a hundred pounds, and his brother had obviously had no trouble spending it.

"Beneficial. Even vital." His brother waved one hand. "Tell me about it."

Will peered into the pitcher. Bless Jack; it was filled with tepid water. He unbuttoned his waistcoat and stripped off his shirt so he could splash himself clean.

"You've been outdoors a lot," observed Jack as he bent over the basin.

"It's the country. Have you got anything to eat, or must I go back out?"

Muttering, Jack left and Will poured the pitcher over his head. He had a clean shirt on when his brother came back with a tray of cold meat, bread, cheese, and some fruit. "Tell me while you eat," he said, placing it on the bureau.

Will took a bite of pear. "Farming. Had to build some bridges, repair a lot of road. There's a castle, and a cross old lady, and as you saw, I spent most of my time outdoors, examining rooftops and building fences and arguing with stonemasons."

"A veritable festival of delights."

Will gave a mocking bow at his brother's sarcastic reply.

"So why did you stay?" Jack braced himself in the doorway.

He ate some ham before answering. "It needed doing. There hadn't been a capable steward"—*it's been thirty years since there was a duke able to care for it*, whispered Philippa Kirkpatrick's voice in his memory—"in a very long time. Once I started, I wanted to finish it."

"But running an estate is never finished!" Jack laughed in disbelief. "You could do it for the rest of your life and still leave things undone."

He almost choked on a slice of ham; everything he had done and learned in the last year would go to waste and he could never speak of it. But there was no way around it. He started in on the bread and cheese, wishing there was a hot cup of tea with honey to go with it. "Tell me about the crisis that demands my aid."

Jack explained the contacts he'd forged, the merchants he'd spoken to. There was a pent-up demand for shipping, after the American colonies—now states—had been cut off from the English markets. Everyone knew Massachusetts men were excellent sailors and shipbuilders, with acres of quality forests to supply their shipyards and a long history of not only shipping but running blockades and even a bit of piracy to prove their sailing mettle. Jack had managed to send three cargoes of goods to America so far, but this potential contract offered far more.

Will leaned back in his chair, done eating and now just exhausted. "Who is he?"

"A Frenchman named LeVecque."

"A Frenchman who wants to ship goods between London and Boston?"

His brother's eyes veered away. "And Le Havre."

Will's brows shot up. "In France?" Jack flushed and said nothing. "What does Pa think of that?"

"It's a very large contract."

When Josiah Welby had to report bad news, he did that. Even if it weren't his fault, the boy grew evasive and spoke instead of anything positive. Will had been trying to break him of it, saying he preferred to hear the truth, no matter how bad. "What's the cargo?"

"Meet him and tell me what you think," said Jack instead, deepening Will's apprehension.

He scrubbed his hands over his face, resisting the temptation to demand immediate answers. Jack wasn't Josiah; Will wasn't in command here. "Very well."

"There is something else I should tell you." He looked up at Jack's hesitant tone. "Pa wonders why he's not heard from you. I told him I was handling all the correspondence, but he's noticed that I don't mention you. I never betrayed you," he said hastily as Will scowled. "But you'd better have a good explanation ready."

He was so tired of subterfuge. "Perhaps I'll just tell him," he muttered. "Now that it's over, what can he do?"

Jack exhaled in open relief. "*Is* it over?"

He should say yes. He could write a parting letter to Amis and the duke, the only people who might miss him, and leave it with Mr. Edwards. What was left for him at Carlyle now?

"Nearly," he said. "I'm going to bed. We'll deal with the Frenchman tomorrow."

CHARLES-JOSEPH LEVECQUE WAS not the slippery charlatan Will had pictured. Urbane and stately, he presented himself as a nephew of Jacques Necker, who had been finance minister of France.

"My uncle is the only one who can save the king," he explained as they sat in a fashionable coffeehouse in Fleet Street. "The stability of France is in his hands, the future of the monarchy."

Will had no interest in French politics. "By shipping goods to America?"

LeVecque smiled. "Of course. Aiding your fight for independence from British tyranny was very costly. The French people would welcome the chance to increase our trade with your country. For this we need ships."

Will glanced at Jack, who nodded slightly. "You won't find finer ones than ours. The best craftsmen in Massachusetts, therefore in the world."

LeVecque laughed. "No doubt, no doubt!" He angled a little closer. "I must admit, whenever possible, I prefer to deal with a fellow Frenchman."

Will's pleasant expression didn't waver, but Jack stirred. "We are Americans, sir, though ones who deeply appreciate our brotherhood with France."

The other man made a gracious motion with one hand. "Of course. But you see. I knew a man who went to New France, many years ago. He was a military man but discovered to his great benefit that there was a fortune to be made in fur—the beavers, you see." He drew a circle on the table-top with one fingertip. "Your father was once a fur trader, was he not? My friend was also named Montclair." He glanced up at Will. "I wonder if your father knew him?"

Jack had grown visibly perplexed as the man spoke. "What?"

"No," said Will flatly at the same moment.

LeVecque paused. "You are very certain of that."

Will gazed at him stonily. "Anything that long ago has nothing to do with our ships today."

The Frenchman sat back and put up his hands with a smile. "No, no, naturally not! But I like to know with whom I do business. I have . . ." He leaned conspiratorially near. "I have responsibilities, you see." When they both said nothing, he rapped his knuckles on the table and rose. "I see you require more persuasion. Allow me to introduce you to some of my associates. Will you join me tomorrow at Bagnigge Wells? The waters are marvelously beneficial."

Jack stuttered an agreement. Will sat unmoving until the Frenchman was gone.

"I didn't know he meant to ask that!" Jack whispered in real astonishment. "He never mentioned fur trading before, or some other Montclair fellow." He lowered his voice even more. "But perhaps he's getting to the point? He teases about large shipments of the finest goods in Paris. Can you imagine the profit to be made from champagne alone? The furnishings, the fashions, even books. Elias Derby is straining to open a route between Boston and China. A stream of French delicacies into Boston would be a magnificent coup."

Will looked at him. "So that's what he's offering? Champagne and furnishings?"

Jack's mouth pursed in frustration. "He's been very cagey about what he actually intends to ship."

"And what would we send back?" Will wanted to know. Ships didn't cross the ocean empty unless they had no other choice. There was money to be made in both directions. Finished goods left Europe, and raw materials and resources left America.

"The usual things, I assume."

Will raised one finger. "Never assume. If this is a simple negotiation of these goods to America, these goods to France, why the theatrics? Why are we not already discussing contracts? Why his interest in Pa?"

Jack looked at a loss. "I've no idea. He hasn't gone trapping in ages."

No, so why was LeVecque so interested?

"He's not worth it, Jack," he said. "Anyone this slippery isn't."

"But he's mentioned large sums—"

"Until it's contracted and paid, with his signature attached, it's worth nothing."

"No, but—"

"I think he's leading you down the path," said Will. "Using your eagerness to extort better terms, or toying with you for his own purposes, I don't know. But tomorrow, either he spells it out with cargo and money, or we say adieu to the man."

Jack nodded, looking cowed. Will wondered if he'd have had the insight and willingness to say that if not for his year at Carlyle. There he'd quickly learned not to drag out a negotiation; to lean into his strengths; to pose a reasonable offer and stick to it. Having the weight and authority of Carlyle behind him was a tremendous asset, of course, but he and Jack weren't without assets themselves: they did have the ships and access to the American markets.

Still—he missed Carlyle, even arguing with the stonemasons. His interest in shipping, never deep to begin with, had faded almost to nothing.

BAGNIGGE WELLS LAY north of the river. Will had visited the pleasure gardens at Vauxhall before leaving London, but Jack had apparently been to several more. Bagnigge Wells was one of his favorites. "It was originally the home of a king's mistress," he enthused the next day as they rode up Gray's Inn Lane toward Clerkenwell. "The food is respectable, and the gardens have a skittles alley and a bowling green as well."

Will said nothing. It sounded as though Jack had enjoyed himself greatly without Will. Then he wondered if Jack had lied to everyone about his purpose and fallen for a woman wildly out of his reach, and decided he had no stones to cast. "Let us hope the pleasant surroundings bring LeVecque to the point."

They paid their sixpence admission at the door and found the Frenchman. He was with a crowd of dandyish-looking fellows, and first tried to induce Will and Jack to join them in the tea room. Jack began to say yes, but Will stifled it. "Business before pleasure," he said lightly but firmly.

LeVecque smirked. "But of course."

They went through the Long Room, where tables of ladies sipped tea from fine china cups at one end and rakish young men posed in front of distorting mirrors at the other, laughing uproariously at their reflections. Will's gaze slid over the ladies, elegantly clad creatures of London with their curled hair and gleaming silk gowns. Unwillingly he wondered if Philippa had come here, or if she kept strictly to fashionable drawing rooms and private gardens, an eligible gentleman at each elbow. She must be causing a sensation in town. Raw, bitter jealousy writhed in his gut, jealousy which had no salve and no remedy. With more force than necessary, he flung open the door to the gardens and stalked out.

He strode along until they reached a quiet spot.

"What is the nature of your cargo?" he demanded of LeVecque.

The older man raised his brows and placed a palm on his chest. "Monsieur Montclair—"

"Forgive me, sir, but we are busy men." Will was out of patience. "You've had weeks to take our firm's measure from my brother. If you are still so uncertain of us, perhaps you should seek another shipping merchant."

The Frenchman's eyes flashed but he nodded. "I see. You understand, in my position, I must have reassurances before disclosing everything."

"Have I not reassured you, sir?" Jack was somewhere between annoyed and surprised.

"No, no, young man." LeVecque gave him a paternal smile. "I do not fault you. You carried on admirably." He cast a speculative glance at Will. "But you, I think," he said thoughtfully. "You are the man to deal with."

Will spread his arms. "What is your proposal?"

LeVecque didn't look pleased, but he sidled closer, lowered his voice, and began speaking.

Five minutes later Will looked at his brother. Jack's jaw had sagged open, eloquently expressing how little he had guessed of LeVecque's intentions.

"You see my desire for confidence and discretion," said LeVecque.

Will jerked his head *yes*.

"Your father would wish you to agree," the Frenchman went on, his voice still warm and persuasive. "If he is the man I think he is—"

"If you want us to ask him," Will interrupted, "you cannot expect an answer soon."

LeVecque paused. "No," he said carefully. "But I would like to know. Wait a moment—my friends will add their voices to mine. Allow me to bring them." Without waiting for a reply, he hurried off.

Will paced away, seething. "Damn it," he burst out in a low voice. His instinct had been to run fast and far from LeVecque, and he'd been right.

"I had no idea." Jack was pale.

LeVecque didn't want to ship champagne and fine furniture; he wanted them to ferry shipments of munitions—not just muskets and gunpowder but cannon, bombs, and mortars—to France from America. What's more, he wanted them to recruit Americans to go fight for him in France. "He wants us to become French agents," Will said, but quietly.

"But why?" Jack frowned. "There's a treaty, shouldn't he appeal to the Congress?"

Will snorted. There *was* a treaty of alliance between France and the United States, but only to promote trade between the two countries. LeVecque wanted to outfit and command his own personal army. The rank and file of the French army had grown embittered against the nobility and king, and the officers—mostly aristocratic themselves—had little control. LeVecque was a wealthy man, with wealthy, aristocratic friends. He sensed an insurrection brewing and was looking to his own protection. Revolutions weren't generally kind to the elite, and LeVecque had a great deal to defend—or to lose.

"We'll refuse." Jack still looked dazed. "Mustn't we?"

Will hesitated. "Why does LeVecque seem so bloody confident Pa would agree to this?"

Jack shook his head helplessly.

Will couldn't explain to his brother his deeper dilemma about LeVecque. Partly because he sensed LeVecque still wasn't telling them everything, partly because he was unsettled by LeVecque's claims about their father, and partly because he knew things about their father that Jack did not— namely, that Pa had not been born a Frenchman named Montclair.

God. Will had wanted out of the shipping business even before this. Now he yearned to sell their ships and send Jack home to warn Pa that someone was asking dangerous questions about him. And then he wanted to go back to Carlyle, and keep up his charade forever.

They had been walking blindly and now came around a bend in the path. To one side ran a little river, burbling along in the sunlight. To the other side were box and holly hedges, with a fountain of Cupid astride a swan whose beak poured forth water.

And at the far end of the path stood Philippa Kirkpatrick.

Chapter Twenty-Three

❧☙

Philippa had virtually perfected the art of keeping her expression composed and polite while her thoughts ran a hundred miles away.

Diana had surrounded them with a party of extremely merry people, no doubt thinking to distract her from last night's debacle. Lord Ranley in particular made a point of being attentive, although he never once mentioned her uncle. Diana had probably warned him not to speak of it, for which Philippa was grateful. She didn't want to think about her uncle ever again.

It crossed her mind that Ranley might have been one of the gentlemen Diana had hoped would court her. He was handsome and charming, well-liked in London society. He was thirty years old, which Diana believed the perfect age for a man to wed, and he had a lovely estate in Hampshire.

Any chance of that had died the evening she politely asked him about his estate, and Ranley waved it aside and said his steward ran everything while he, Ranley, did more interesting things. That had begun a slow boil inside her, as she thought of how hard Will worked. At least the duchess wasn't off in London, spending all the income from Carlyle on horse races and new coats.

The duchess. She longed to see Philippa happily wed. Will knew it, just as he knew how little Daadee liked him—he'd cited the duchess when he told Philippa they had no future.

That was before he'd kissed her desperately and said she'd fascinated him from the moment they met, though. Before she'd seen the anguish flash in his eyes as he asked if she saw any future for them. If she'd said yes . . . If she'd said then that she was in love with him . . . If she'd told him the duchess would come around, because she adored Philippa and always gave in when Philippa insisted . . .

Would he have stayed? Would he have taken her into his arms and kissed her again? Would he have declared that he loved her, too?

She had to know. She *needed* to know. And to find out, she had to tell Marianne to pack all her new clothing and hire a travel chaise and—

A flicker of motion caught her eye. She glanced to her right and saw the man himself, standing at the end of the path.

For a moment time froze, leaving just the two of them staring at each other. He looked again like a pirate, *her* pirate, his hair loose and his coat bright blue. Her heart jolted so violently in her chest, she felt faint. He appeared as startled to see her as she was to see him.

The man beside him said something, and Will turned with a jerk and walked away.

At her side, Diana was telling some story about a viscountess and her spoiled lapdog, amusing the rest of the party. Without a word, Philippa turned and bolted after Will.

At the end of the walk she stopped; there was no sign of him or his companion. She scanned left and right, squinting in the sunlight, and caught sight of his blue-coated figure, striding along the river. She picked up her skirts and ran, keeping her gaze fixed on him. At one point he glanced over his shoulder; did he see her? Was he trying to avoid her or inviting her after him? He turned onto the footpath and disappeared behind a hedge, and Philippa's heart banged into her ribs. *Do not disappear*, she thought frantically. It felt like a physical need to see him.

She flew around the corner and he caught her arm, swinging her momentum toward a leafy hollow of the hedge and straight into his arms, where he silenced and answered her questions with a deep, desperate kiss.

It was like a jolt of lightning to her heart and mind. As if she'd been in a stupor since walking out of the trees beside the stables and only now fully woke up. She threw one arm around his neck and gripped his coat with her other hand, to keep him there, and kissed him back, opening to him and holding nothing back. It was what she should have done the last time he kissed her, and she wasn't making the same mistake twice.

"You're here," she gasped as he rested his forehead against hers, breathing as fast as she was.

He smiled wryly, stroking his thumb over her lips. "I didn't expect to see you."

She beamed up at him, too happy to care about that. "It was a glorious surprise to me, too."

He laughed and pulled her close, tucking her head under his chin and resting his cheek on her crown. Her hat must have flown off when she ran after him. Philippa hadn't even noticed it was gone, and she didn't care now. She pressed against him, never wanting to let go.

"What's wrong?" he murmured. She raised her head in surprise. "You were frowning," he added. "It was all I could do not to charge over and whisk you away."

She laughed. "I wish you had! Although, it was unnecessary, since I came running as soon as I saw you."

His smile grew warmer, more intimate, at that. He tipped up her chin and kissed her again. "We'll cause a public scandal," he breathed even as his fingers slipped around her neck.

"I don't care," she whispered, her head falling back to let him scatter kisses across her brow.

He laughed, then he sighed, and then he took her hand and led her a few steps down the footpath to a bench set in the greenery. Philippa sat indecently close to him, keeping a firm grip on his hand.

"Are you not enjoying London?" His thumb stroked hers.

"*No*," she burst out. "The parties are tedious, the streets are filthy, and the people are so frivolous. I wish I hadn't come." He was listening in sympathy. "How is everyone at home? How long have you been here?"

He hesitated. "I left only a few days ago. The duke has been unwell lately. Tired and weak, rather than ill. I've not seen him much."

"Oh no . . ."

"Mrs. Potter has been in close attendance, and Amis is always there. Neither seemed unduly alarmed. Her Grace is still in fighting trim, though."

From his tone, he meant it literally. She wondered why Daadee had even seen Will, in Philippa's absence. The duchess did not like him.

Well. That was going to change.

"I'm glad to hear she's well," she said, pushing all that aside. "What brought you to London?"

He hesitated a longer moment this time. "My brother needed me."

Instinctively she glanced back down the path. He'd been with someone when she spotted him. "Nothing terrible has happened, I hope."

He made a face. "No. I think it will prove to be nothing."

"Is that good?" She bumped his shoulder, trying to tease a smile from him. "A crisis averted? Or perhaps bad; an opportunity missed?"

He smiled slightly. "Certainly one of those."

"Selfishly I'm glad he summoned you. Is he here?"

Will seemed to be struggling with something. He frowned, then put his free hand on top of hers, already clasped in his. "Yes."

"May I meet him?" she asked shyly.

Two things had become clear to her: first, that she was really, truly, deeply in love with this man. Not a day went by that she didn't think of him and wonder where he was and if he thought of her. Not a night passed without him invading her dreams. Every gentleman she'd met in London fell short when she compared him to Will—and she *always* compared them to Will.

The second was that if she wanted anything to come of it—if they were to have the happy future she had begun painting in her mind—*she* would have to take action. She did not have the luxury of flirting and hoping he would propose marriage, not when he'd said he wasn't good enough for her. Everyone would believe him the most coldhearted fortune hunter, and she a fool, if she didn't actively create a better impression.

So for this mad yearning of hers to come to full fruition, they would need allies. The duchess would require extensive persuasion. The duke, she thought, would approve, because he already liked Will, and because he no longer had any sense of the rules of society or rank. Now she thought that if she could meet this brother and charm her way into *his* good graces, it might go a long way toward persuading Will they could make it work . . .

"Someday," he said. "Not now. I thought I must be dreaming when I saw you." He paused, then added in a lower, rougher voice, "I've missed you."

Now her heart did melt. Didn't see a future for them; nonsense. It was right here, waiting. All they had to do was decide they both wanted it.

"Come see me," she said on impulse. As much as she wanted to sit here for an hour with him, she was conscious that they were in a public garden, and that Diana was probably already looking for her. "Tomorrow. Hertford Street, Lady Beauchamp's house."

Will hesitated.

"Please," she begged, suddenly realizing how lonely she'd been since leaving Carlyle. Ironic, really, that she felt lonely in a city of thousands, and not at the isolated Carlyle Castle. But perhaps it was Will's company that made the difference. "I've missed you, too. Lady Beauchamp is wonderful, but London is an endless parade of pompous lords and featherbrained dandies. I want to see someone I know, who knows me and cares for me, and cares for the same things I do. I don't belong here, and even my uncle—"

His gaze narrowed as she stopped suddenly. "Uncle? What happened?"

To her disgust she felt her eyes prickle. Matthew Kirkpatrick wasn't worth that. But somehow she found herself telling Will. "We met him at the opera last night, and he shunned me."

He put his arm around her and pressed his lips to her temple when she laid her head on his shoulder. "He can go to the devil. Why?"

She took a deep breath. "He never accepted my parents' marriage because my mother was Indian." She held out one hand, slim and manicured but browner than any Englishwoman's. "I don't look like a proper English lady."

Will studied her hand, then took it in his own larger, scuffed and calloused hand. "This," he remarked, "is the hand of a remarkable woman. See how strong it is, just like the lady herself." He laced his fingers through hers. "See how soft and warm it is, like the lady's heart." He stroked his fingertips over her palm and her mouth went dry. "See how beautifully kept it is, like everything the lady cares for." He raised her hand to his lips. "See how exquisitely and finely made it is, like every part of the lady," he whispered, his voice low and rough.

"I've never seen a lovelier hand, or a finer lady." He cradled it against his cheek.

Her heart fluttered and whispered *yes, him*. She gripped his hand. Thank God she'd come here today.

"The search for a husband hasn't succeeded yet?" He spoke lightly but she heard tension. Or perhaps she just wanted him to be unhappy about the thought of her wedding another man.

"It's been a complete disaster," she said firmly. "Not a single gentleman I would go fishing with! Perhaps I'll just buy a cottage in Kittleston and live there. We could be neighbors," she said even as her heart skipped several beats. "You in Stone Cottage, I down the road in Kittleston."

Will said nothing, and didn't move.

"I envy you your place at Carlyle," she added. "When the captain inherits, he'll be certain to keep you on, but it will no longer be my home. I never want to leave, though."

"Ah, te voilà!" declared a voice. "LeVecque et ses amis veulent te parler."

Will shot off the bench and into the path so quickly, Philippa almost tumbled sideways. She sat up in surprise, peering past him—he had stepped directly in front of her, blocking her view.

He spoke to the newcomer very quietly, but she still heard. "J'arrive bientôt." The other man put his head to one side, trying to see beyond Will's shoulder. Philippa tipped her head, too, intrigued but also wary.

"Jacques, vas-y!" Will barked.

The other man put up his hands in surrender and backed up, hidden once more by the hedge.

Will turned back to her. "My apologies, but I must go. I will . . . I will try to call on you." With an impersonal bow he was gone, striding briskly away.

As he did, the newcomer stuck his head around the hedge again, looking wildly curious. Will caught his arm and then they both were gone, but not before Philippa got a good look at his face.

She knew him, she thought with a jolt, then realized no, she didn't. A little shorter, a little brawnier, but the resemblance was clear. His coloring was lighter than Will's, though they had the same nose. It could only be his brother.

For a moment she was too surprised to move. Philippa had been taught French, like most young ladies in England, but with no one to converse with, her fluency—such as it was—had waned. Not Will's. He and his brother spoke it fluently.

She had forgotten French was his native tongue. Ever since she'd told him the duchess didn't like the French, he had repressed all hint of an accent.

But why wouldn't he want her to meet his brother? It stung. Philippa had never ranted against the French, like the duchess, or declared provincials from New France even worse. She had never . . .

As if a Frenchman wasn't bad enough, echoed the duchess's voice in her head. *A provincial! One of those at Carlyle is more than enough . . .*

That's what the duchess had said after hearing that Lord Thomas St. James, the missing heir, had gone to New France—Canada—with his family. Fifty years ago, Mr. Edwards said.

Will's French father could be in his fifties.

Now she was sitting frozen. Will admitted this was his first employment as an estate steward; he'd left his family's shipping firm to take it. Why had he wanted this position?

Why had he been so very inquisitive about the duke and his health?

Why was he so cagey about his own family?

Why did he say she wasn't supposed to like him?

Some gentlemen came boisterously down the path, startling her out of her very disconcerting thoughts. She pressed one hand to her stomach, realizing her heart was racing. She took a deep breath and gave her head a sharp shake.

Madness. Will was not the son of the long-lost French heir. It was too bizarre a coincidence to happen by chance, and too unbelievable that he would know of his connection to Carlyle yet sneak in like a spy, wheedling his way into a grueling job where he was routinely scolded and reprimanded. Lord Thomas, or his son, could ride up to the front door and declare his claim to the castle, the estate, the dukedom itself, and no one could keep it from him.

But it was a good reminder that she still had a lot to learn about Will. Philippa said a quick, silent prayer that he would come to see her soon, and went back to find Diana.

Chapter Twenty-Four

❧✦❧

If Will had any doubts about what he wanted, they vanished the moment he set eyes on Philippa again.

One, he wanted out of the shipping business. Not only to avoid LeVecque and his dangerous questions, but because he disliked it entirely. He'd had to do just as much bookkeeping at Carlyle, and never hated it as much as he did the shipping books.

Two, he wanted her. Desperately, passionately, wistfully, perhaps even wrongly, but he couldn't deny it. The way she kissed him in Bagnigge Wells gave him such hope, as did the way she suggested she might buy a cottage in Kittleston and be near him. If she wanted him, too, there must be a way.

Will had no idea what that way might be, but he burned to think of one.

First, though, he had to put off Jack.

"Who is she?" His brother had been pestering him since they left the tea garden. "Where did you meet such a beautiful lady?"

"She's from the estate." Will picked up his hat

and pulled on his coat. "She wanted news from there."

Jack snickered. "At last I understand why you refused all my entreaties to return to London! Did you only come because she did?" He followed Will down the stairs from the office. "What's her name?"

In reply, Will slammed the door behind him and walked away, glancing back a few yards later to be sure his brother hadn't followed.

The Countess of Beauchamp's house was in the finest section of London, near Hyde Park in a well-kept street of elegant homes. He slowed as he approached, suddenly unsure what he would say.

He couldn't ask anything of her without first explaining quite a lot of things. He was tired of keeping secrets from her, but unfortunately some of those secrets weren't his to tell.

Face that later, he told himself as he rapped the knocker. Before he took any irreversible steps, he should be certain of her feelings.

Countess Beauchamp was a beautiful woman of about fifty, statuesque and regal. He could see at once she knew who he was and had been warned, but her scrutiny was more contemplative than suspicious. And she made no protest when Philippa declared it was so lovely a day, she wanted to walk in the park. Pausing only to summon a maid—Miss Marianne from Carlyle, who gave Will a grin when he tipped his hat to her—they set off across the street into Hyde Park.

"Tu vas bien aujourd'hui?" Philippa peeked at him from beneath the wide brim of her hat, smiling hopefully.

Will glanced at her, startled. "Trés bien, merci," he said slowly.

"Tu parles français, n'est-ce pas?" she said.

"Oui."

"Tu parles français avec ta famille?"

"Oui, ma mère vient du Québec, ce qui est une province francophone," he said rapidly.

She hesitated, clearly trying to parse the words.

"Why do you wish to speak French?" he asked.

"I noticed you spoke it to your brother."

Thank you, Jack, he thought darkly. "Yesterday we were with a Frenchman, so it seemed polite to do so."

Her head came around. "A Frenchman?"

Unease crept over him. "He inquired about doing business with my family, but I doubt it will come to fruition." He flicked one hand as if to brush the whole topic away. "What sights have you seen in London?"

"Several," she murmured absently. "What business? That's what brought you to London, isn't it?"

"My brother runs the business and he asked me to return to confer with him. Which sights in London do you recommend? Lady Beauchamp must know all the best ones."

"Will," she said, "what is the business?" He stared at her. "Why won't you tell me? Is it something . . . illicit?"

At that he smiled a little. Everyone with a ship had done some privateering during the war with England, his family among them. But now they were perfectly respectable merchants. "No. It's merely not very interesting. Merchant shipping."

A tiny line appeared between her eyes, as if she didn't quite believe it.

"We buy goods here, ship them home to Boston and sell them, then we ship cargo from Boston to London and sell it," he explained.

"Goods and cargo?" she echoed.

"Books and furnishings, bolts of fabric, soap. Panes of glass for windows and fine wines." She looked disconcerted and a little disappointed, and he went on with his determinedly dull description. "Then we ship back whale oil and bone, sometimes furs and skins. More bookkeeping than anyone should ever do."

"I see." She frowned. "And your brother is the agent for this shipping company?"

Usually a merchant employed an agent in every city he shipped to and from. Mr. John Hancock, the richest merchant in Boston, had agents in London, Manchester, and Liverpool and probably half a dozen other cities in Europe. Pa would dearly love to have a London agent but that required relationships, trust, a record of profit—exactly what he and Jack had been sent to create. For now, Jack was their London agent . . . although Pa thought Will was, too.

When Will hesitated, understanding dawned on her face. "You both run it," she said. "Or are supposed to."

He made a face. "Yes, we were both sent over to establish it. But my brother hasn't needed my help for months."

"But when he did, you had to return to London." She stopped in her tracks. They had been meandering along the path through some trees; ahead sunlight sparkled on a neat little pond. "Will," Philippa demanded, "what of Carlyle, when you are required by your brother in London?"

"Carlyle is in good hands."

"No, it isn't," she retorted in dismay. "It's supposed to be in *your* hands, but you're not there. Who do you think will see to it?"

"It bumped along well enough before I arrived, and will do so even more easily when I'm gone," he said without thinking.

Her eyes went round. "You're leaving?"

He drummed his fingers on his hip and took a controlled breath. *Idiot.* He hadn't meant to mention that, not today, not like this. "It's a miracle Her Grace hasn't chased me from the grounds already," he said with forced lightness. "It's only a question of time."

She seized his coat sleeve. "You're wrong. She won't sack you, not as long as the duke wishes to see you. Don't you see? He comes first for her; she would keep on even a terrible steward who amused and revived His Grace . . ."

Will said nothing. He didn't see any possible way he could stay at Carlyle.

Philippa's lips parted and the color faded from her face. She snatched her hand from his arm as if burned.

He inhaled deeply and studied the ground. "I don't want to quarrel about Carlyle."

"How can we quarrel," she said numbly, "when you won't be there?"

He had to clench his jaw to keep from baring his

soul and telling her things he should not. Why had he come today?

Because his heart kept hoping and wishing that the mess he'd got himself into would mysteriously, magically dissolve and somehow, some way, he would end up with Philippa in his arms—as his. Because he was still that helpless nail, unable to resist the magnetic lure of her company and attention. Because she'd said *please* and *I want to see someone who cares for me* and he understood it because he felt the same way. Because *she* was the person he wanted to see, always and forever.

Because he was an incurable fool.

A shout behind them interrupted his self-excoriation. They both turned to see a red-faced Mr. Edwards trotting toward them, waving one arm.

"Oh no," said Philippa in a low voice. She started toward the attorney, and Will followed.

"Miss Kirkpatrick, thank heavens I found you." Edwards gulped for air.

"What is wrong?"

"I had an express from Her Grace, just an hour ago." The attorney glanced at him, and then again, unhappily surprised. "Mr. Montclair! What are you doing here?"

"What is wrong?" Philippa demanded.

Will knew it was serious when the man immediately turned back to her, his face somber with worry. "The duke. He's taken a turn. Her Grace wishes you to return with all speed . . ." He trailed off as Philippa picked up her skirts and took off running toward Lady Beauchamp's house, Mari-

anne flying after her, pausing only to scoop up the
parasol Philippa had dropped.

Edwards put his hands on his knees and sucked
in a few deep breaths.

"How bad is it?" asked Will.

The attorney squinted up at him. His spectacles were askew and didn't gleam as pristinely as
usual. "Mr. Montclair, why are you here?"

"A family matter," he began.

"Not here in *London*," said the man cuttingly. "I
was informed of that and expected to see you in
my office—a visit I am still awaiting. Why are you
here, in this park, with Miss Kirkpatrick?"

There was no good explanation. Will gave a
small shrug.

Edwards straightened, having caught his breath.
"I am bid to ask you also to return to Carlyle. Her
Grace is frantic."

He started. "Is he dying?"

"I pray to God not." Edwards gave him a disgruntled glare. "But I do not know. Will you come?"

Will nodded. "Give me one hour."

PHILIPPA FELT AT once enveloped in fog and as
tense as a violin string.

Mr. Edwards had told Diana before he ran in
search of her, so the countess had already sent two
maids to pack her trunks. Philippa scoured the
duchess's letter, which Mr. Edwards had left for her.

Will said the duke had been unwell, tired and
weak. Now the duchess wrote that he had a fever
and wasn't eating; he had asked for Philippa. Her
letter verged on hysteria.

When the travel chaise rolled up, Philippa was

waiting by the door. She and Marianne came out as the servants loaded her baggage.

"Write as soon as you can and tell me how things are," implored Diana. She squeezed Philippa's hand. "I shan't sleep until I hear from you."

"I will. Give my love to Fanny." Philippa embraced her one last time and stepped into the carriage. Mr. Edwards was already inside.

It was early afternoon. There was no way they could make it to Carlyle today.

A knock on the window startled her. Philippa gasped as Will leaned down from his horse. "Shall I ride ahead, or stay with you?" he asked Mr. Edwards.

The attorney glanced at her. "Ride ahead."

For one taut moment Will's glance met Philippa's. Then he nodded, wheeled his mount around, and clattered off.

Their conversation of an hour ago felt like a distant memory, though she suspected it would haunt her later. "I assume she sent for him," she said in the silence.

Mr. Edwards rubbed one hand over his face. "She did. Anything and anyone who might restore His Grace."

Which told Philippa all she needed to know about the duke's condition.

Two days later, stiff and cramped from the rushed, jolting ride, she stepped down at the castle. Heywood swept open the door as she did, because of course they'd been watching for her, and her heart sank at his expression.

"Has there been any improvement?" She hurried up the stairs without even removing her cloak.

"Not much, Miss Kirkpatrick. Mr. Montclair arrived earlier, but His Grace was asleep. Her Grace
is with him."

The duchess emerged from the duke's suite,
ashen and somehow shrunken. Philippa flew to
embrace her. "Thank heavens you're here," whispered the duchess. "The fever hasn't broken."

Philippa's throat was too tight to reply. On the
endless trip home, it had sunk in on her how pre-
cariously her life was balanced. When the duke
died—*please, not today*—the balance would be upset and unleash a cascade of changes.

Captain St. James would become the new duke,
the new owner of Carlyle Castle. The duchess
would remove to the manor house she had chosen
decades ago. Philippa, with no husband or home of
her own, would go with her. But she feared, deep
in her heart, that the duchess wouldn't long survive the duke's passing. She was already seventy-
six, and the heartbreak of this final loss might be
too much for her to bear.

Philippa had known this for a long time. It
had all dwelt in the nebulous and misty future,
though, along with her long-promised Season in
London and an eligible husband and family of
her own. Now those questions bore down on her
without mercy.

She sat in the duke's dim chamber, the duchess
clutching her hand as she dozed. There was nothing to say, which left her mind at liberty to turn
over—and over and over and over—the questions
and choices facing her.

She couldn't leave the duchess. Not now, perhaps
not ever. That meant she couldn't leave Carlyle,

which was no hardship because she loved every stone and tree of Carlyle.

It was *how* she would stay that kept her mind mired in circles.

All her dreams seemed more like delusions. While she was painting fanciful pictures in her head of how they could have a future, Will was planning his departure. She heard how he spoke of the business that took him to London: *we* ship cargo. His brother may not have needed his help for months, but the moment he did ask it, Will went. Little things he had said, like not having enough time to do everything he wanted on the estate, came back to her. He had never expected to stay long at Carlyle.

Why had he ever come? Why had Mr. Edwards ever hired him? There had been months of discussion and argument over the hiring of any new steward, with the attorney all but begging permission, and then Edwards presented a man nothing like the steward the duchess wanted. Philippa remembered her mental image of that man: portly, bespectacled and graying, respectful and conservative, competent and dull.

She sighed. She didn't know why Will had taken the post. She only knew the thought of him leaving was almost unbearably painful. The duke might be dying. The duchess would never be the same. Was it too much to ask that she not lose everyone she cared about at the same time?

Beside her, the duchess jerked awake. "Oh, Pippa," she said, sounding weary and frail. "Go to your bed, my dear. If anything changes . . ." She trailed off, her grip tightening.

"Daadee, you must also sleep."

"Not yet," said the duchess, her gaze fixed across the room. A single candle stood on a table near the bed, casting a faint shadow on the motionless figure in it. The feeling that it was a death watch unnerved Philippa, so she got stiffly to her feet, kissed the duchess's cheek, and left.

She went to her room, where Marianne had already unpacked her things. For a moment she looked around, viewing it almost like a stranger. The tall bed, hung with yellow damask. The neat little writing desk by the window, with the view of the formal gardens. The portrait of her mother hanging beside the dressing table, her gentle smile perfectly illuminated by the glow of the lamp beneath it.

She sat at the dressing table and contemplated her mother. Noor's smile was reticent, shy . . . coy. The smile of a woman who'd wanted a man outside her faith, her culture, her parents' approval— and she'd got him.

"What would you do?" Philippa whispered.

Ammi's smile didn't falter. Philippa shook her head, exhausted and heartsick. She was talking to a painting, which could tell her nothing.

But Ammi's letters might.

She knelt beside the bed and pulled out a small trunk.

Chapter Twenty-Five

꧁ ❦ ꧂

The trunk's brown leather was cracked from age and salt air, the brass tacks tarnished almost black. Philippa raised the lid. The inscription on the paper lining was in her father's own hand: *Col. P. M. Kirkpatrick*. She'd been named for him, Philip Miles.

The tray fitted in the top of the trunk held his things, those he had left behind and those few items sent back from India. His spectacles, the left arm still slightly bent from when young Philippa had pulled them off his face. His compass, the steel case scratched and dented. His diaries, bundled neatly together, and a slim stack of letters he'd written home from India, tied with black ribbon. His pen knife, a gift from his second wife engraved with their initials on the mother-of-pearl handle: PMK intertwined with JSS.

As she always did when she opened this trunk, Philippa touched a velvet pouch in one compartment. It held the buttons of the coat her papa had died in. The buttons had come off in the hands of his frantic lieutenant, trying to drag him from the field, and the young officer had sent them to her with a condolence letter, abject in its grief.

She lifted out the tray and set it aside. Beneath it lay a shimmering pile of fabric, a cloud of pink and apricot, the colors still vivid and lustrous after all these years. It was her mother's, worn at her wedding. Her mother had been dainty; the clothing was too small to fit Philippa, who had some of her father's height.

Philippa pushed aside the trousers of cool slippery silk, the draped blouse embroidered in gold and silver thread, the swathes of muslin so sheer one could lay it over the page of a book and still easily read the words. Papa had said the Mughal ladies' clothes were made to be worn once and discarded, but he had persuaded his bride to save these, as the English did.

She ignored the beautiful box of ivory, carved in delicate leafy scrolls and flowers. It held her mother's jewelry, the pieces Philippa didn't wear on a regular basis—yards of gold chain and pearls, large ornate earrings that would have dangled to her shoulders, arm bangles, anklets, a large thin golden hoop that Papa said had gone in her nose. There were rings as well, for her fingers and toes; as a child Philippa had delighted in trying them on.

Tonight it was the letters she wanted.

There were two stacks. One was from Ammi to her mother, Philippa's grandmother. They were in Persian, beautiful script with illuminated characters. Her Indian daadee had sent them to her, and Papa had had them translated into English.

Philippa had read them all many times, but tonight she paged through until she found the ones her mother had written to *her* mother, when Philippa was born.

She is a beautiful baby, Mama, with dark hair and plump cheeks. I have never seen a child more beautiful. Miles is as much in love with her as I am, and we have named her after ourselves: Philippa Noor. I long for you to see her and bless her, as she is the child of my most heartfelt love. I pray she will once and for all reconcile your heart to my husband, Mama, for I do love him above all and know that he loves me. There can be no surer proof of our devotion to each other than this perfect child . . .

Her daadee had written back: *What joy is mine! Beloved child of my heart, now a mother. May god grant you and your child long life!*

Philippa looked up at her mother's portrait again. *Love fiercely,* Ammi seemed to say. *Do not be frightened of what love will cost you, be frightened of what you might lose if you deny your love.*

She clasped the letters to her heart. It always seemed to her that a trace of India clung to these papers, unlike anything in England. Philippa did not remember her mother's homeland. She had been raised in England as an English girl. But her father and Asmat talked of India and of Ammi frequently, not wanting her to forget either.

Noor had persuaded her parents that her happiness lay with Papa. Jessica had persuaded the duchess to love the man she chose. How could Philippa not do as much?

She swirled a gauzy muslin shawl over her head,

like in Ammi's portrait. The cloth was as light as a whisper, as insubstantial as woven air. A faint scent rose from the fabric.

Philippa breathed deeply. She'd known from the first moment she saw him that William Montclair was trouble, that he would stir things up and cause unrest. And now she was in love with him. Whoever he was, whatever had brought him to Carlyle. Whatever the future held, she wanted to share it with him.

Ammi would approve.

She studied her mother's curling script until she fell asleep on her bed, the long muslin shawl draped over her. She bolted upright, still half in a dream, her heart pounding. The feeling of something momentous weighed down on her, and she was terrified that it was the duke's death she had sensed.

She slid off the bed and made her way through the house. It was dawn; the light outside was gray, the shapes of the hills dark against the lightening sky. As she reached the duke's suite, the door opened and the duchess stepped out.

"Oh, ma'am," she said, then stopped.

The duchess's face, gray and haggard, lit up with joy. "The fever has broken. He has asked for something to eat. Oh, Pippa, I do think he will survive!"

Philippa flew to her, sharing a short bout of tears of joy. The duchess stepped back, dabbing her eyes. "I must go tell Mr. Edwards before he summons the captain."

"Yes, ma'am." Philippa smiled. Her heart, which had been in her shoes, now felt light and bubbly.

The relentless cascade of change had not been unleashed upon her today.

And now she knew beyond all doubt that she wanted Will.

WILL HAD RIDDEN ahead of the carriage, pushing his horse beyond sense, and arrived before noon. Amis told him the news in a low voice: the duke developed a fever, high and sudden. No appetite. Almost impossible to rouse from sleep.

On the duchess's order, Amis took him in. The change in Carlyle was shocking. Just a few weeks ago he'd been somewhat frail, but alert and engaged. Now he didn't move when Will sat down beside him, the chair pulled close.

"I'm sorry we haven't had a chance to finish *Roderick Random*," he said quietly. "He has such adventures on the seas."

No response.

"Amis will finish reading it. Perhaps I shouldn't spoil the ending, but you'll be pleased to hear Random is happily reunited with his father at the end, after so many years apart."

No response.

"It was my honor to meet you at last, good sir," he added almost inaudibly, then got up and left.

Stone Cottage was quiet when he reached it. He walked through the rooms, pausing in the study. There was the map he had put up, charting his progress as Carlyle's steward. Overall, he thought he'd done a creditable job.

The study was where he'd laughed and talked with Philippa. Her chair still sat there, at the corner of his desk, as if waiting for her to come visit again and tease him about tea. He contemplated that chair for a moment.

She knew he was keeping something from her. She'd tried to get it out of him in London, speaking French and asking about his family. His refusal to confide dismayed her.

His family was also not happy with him. Jack was furious when he bolted from London only a few days after arriving. There had been an argument.

"You swore it would only be a year," Jack had charged as Will crammed his things back into the saddlebags. "One year! And it's ended!" He tried to block the door but Will pushed past him. "You're like a ghost these days. Our parents and our sister are concerned that you've not written to them in an age. You should go home and see them. Speak to Pa about LeVecque. If one man will ask such a thing of us, another may as well. We should be prepared."

"We should say no."

"Will. *Will!*" Jack shouted as he headed out the door. "What are you keeping from me?"

Just like Philippa. And again, Will had no answer to that question.

What an arrogant fool he'd been, thinking he could keep secrets from everyone and not pay a price. No matter what he did now, he would hurt someone deeply.

It was dark when Mr. Edwards knocked on the door. Will let him in. "How was your journey?"

Edwards glared at him, but it lacked heat. "Exhausting. Miss Kirkpatrick was anxious to reach the castle as soon as possible." He hesitated. "No doubt yours was even more exhausting."

Will shrugged. He'd ridden through the night, one hand on his pistol.

The attorney came in, sinking onto the settee in the parlor with a sigh of relief. Will brought two glasses of port without asking, and Edwards gave him a grateful look.

"Is he dying?" Will asked again.

Edwards took his time replying. "No one knows, but His Grace is not a young man."

Will said nothing.

"It isn't supposed to be this way." The attorney tilted his glass and watched the light play on the wine. "Once a man inherits a title, his first task is to secure it, with an heir—or three or four, if possible."

"Why did the duke not do that?"

Edwards sighed. "He was young, not even thirty. He had little chance to wed before . . . the incident. The old duke was a tyrannical figure who wished to choose the lady his heir wed."

Will nodded. Philippa had told him about the old duke, cruel and dictatorial.

"I daresay I shan't surprise you by saying few grieved when he died. Apoplexy. If ever a more choleric man lived, I never met him. And for exactly eight months, it seemed a new age was dawning at Carlyle. A handsome young duke, eligible and vigorous. Decades of his father's tyranny, ended. There would soon be a new duchess, a houseful of children, a new presence in Parliament." Edwards sipped his wine. "He was an intelligent young man. Mild in manner but with a shrewd mind. He could have been a diplomat, a privy councilor, an ambassador." He sighed. "Such a tragedy."

"You were here?" asked Will.

Edwards nodded. "Mr. Norton had charge of the Carlyle affairs then, but I was serving as his clerk. The idea, of course, was to be Norton's successor. In much the same way a nobleman must have an heir, an attorney's clients must have a younger attorney in waiting."

"So you were raised on the estate," said Will slowly.

The other man smiled and raised his glass. "The far side of Kittleston. Near enough." He sighed. "It was a heady eight months. Rather like the end of a siege, and everyone eager for happier days."

Will tried to imagine the duke as a young man, nearly his own age. He would have known from birth what his destiny was. He must have felt liberated by his father's death, able to be his own man at last. What had he hoped and planned?

"When a man inherits a title, there are formalities to be observed," Edwards explained. "Petitions to submit, so on and so on. His Grace had gone to London to prove his claim, and, I expect, to sow some wild oats. He fell in with a crowd of other young aristocrats, and he simply wasn't prepared for their level of revelry. It was another gentleman's horse that kicked him." Edwards swirled his port. "The fellow was drunk—so drunk he could not sit the horse, though he insisted he would. His Grace was trying to persuade him into a carriage when the horse startled and lashed out. They brought His Grace back to the London house on a collier's cart. Everyone believed he would be dead by morning."

Silently Will got up and fetched the bottle of port. Edwards held out his glass and Will refilled both.

"As you might imagine it caused a terrible scandal. The other fellow fled London in disgrace. A few years later he broke his neck in a horse race. Drunk, naturally. But the duke . . ." Edwards sighed.

Will stayed quiet. This was by far the most information he'd ever got out of the man.

"A duke is not a typical man," said the attorney carefully. "As you've seen, he has responsibilities—obligations. Not merely to his family but to a large number of other people, in his generation and in those to come. Aside from the bereavement of his dear ones, his death would cause enormous upheaval. At the time of his injury, his only heir was his brother Lord Stephen, who was then a lad of fourteen—wholly unequal to the task. That is when Her Grace stepped in."

Will stirred. "Miss Kirkpatrick warned me the duke's condition must remain a grave secret."

Edwards smiled briefly. "She's correct. It has been carefully concealed as much as possible these thirty years. If the scope of his incapacity were to be known, there are . . . measures the Crown and the courts might take. As I said, a great many people depend upon a duke. If he is incapable, someone must be appointed to manage his lands and income."

"But not a woman," said Will slowly.

Edwards shook his head.

"She's managed splendidly," Will offered. He'd once been appalled at the conditions, but now realized how enormous the task had been. To ask it of a grieving mother, a woman who never intended or expected to manage it . . . Now he respected

how well she had done, to keep things going for
so many years without acknowledged authority or
control.

"She has," agreed Edwards. "Until last year it
was for the benefit of Lord Stephen. He remained
the heir." A faint smile touched his face. "He
was the apple of her eye. He wanted to remain
in Kittleston as vicar as long as possible, and she
couldn't deny him. But now . . . Now another will
inherit."

Will cleared his throat. "Captain St. James."

Edwards held out his glass for more port, then
settled back on the settee. "There are strict laws of
inheritance, Mr. Montclair. I mention this because I
believe Americans do things differently." He smiled,
and Will tilted his head in acknowledgement. "A
dukedom is not like a house or a set of silver; its de-
scent is precisely described. Carlyle descends to the
eldest legitimate son of the duke's body and to his
heirs. In this case, the duke has no sons, so we look
to the previous duke, and his other heirs. As long as
Lord Stephen lived, he was the heir. When he died
without a son, we trace back to the third duke and
his younger sons, then to the second duke, and so
on. Captain St. James is the great-grandson of the
third duke. Maximilian St. James, whose name you
also have heard, is the great-great-grandson of the
second duke."

"Miss Kirkpatrick told me," said Will. "Captain
St. James will inherit, and Maximilian is his heir,
until the captain has a son."

Edwards tipped his head back to stare at the ceiling. Will thought he must be getting on to drunk
by now, after three glasses of port. "Do you know,

it's not as certain as all that," the attorney mused. "The third duke had three sons. The current duke descends from the eldest, of course, and the captain from the youngest. But there was another, a boy named Thomas. His mother stole him away to France as a child over eighty years ago."

He went still. "Stole?"

"Disappeared without a trace," murmured Edwards absently. "But he would be an heir—the pre-eminent one, in fact, eclipsing Captain St. James's claim. I sent a man to France to look for him, and can you guess where Thomas went? New France, Mr. Montclair. Perhaps you were neighbors." Will darted a glance at the attorney. Edwards was smiling at him, his brows arched as if he'd just made a fine joke.

"So you found him."

Slowly Edwards shook his head. "Not yet. All I know thus far is that he left France with his wife and small son fifty-four years ago."

"That's a long time for someone to be missing. Can he still be alive to be found?"

"I do not know, Mr. Montclair. I only know that we must search for him to the best of our abilities." Edwards smiled again. "After all, he—or his son—would be a duke. Quite a stunning surprise that would be to an old French soldier in America, don't you imagine?"

Will grinned. "I imagine so."

They drank in silence for a moment. "What if he *is* still alive, but you don't discover him in time?" asked Will. "If the duke should . . . ?" He didn't finish the thought.

Edwards took a long time to reply. "The Crown

wishes to be certain, before a title is bestowed upon an heir. Do you know why?"

Will shook his head.

"Because once it is bestowed, it cannot be retracted." Edwards sat forward. "I don't wish to make a mistake because if another, nearer, heir should appear, but after the dukedom has been bestowed upon Captain St. James, it would be too late. Do you understand? They do not transfer dukedoms like property deeds. Lord Thomas or his sons could protest to the King himself of being cheated of their rightful inheritance, and it would not matter in the slightest. I am searching as hard as I possibly can for Lord Thomas and his children and his grandchildren, to prevent a grievous injury being inadvertently done to them."

Will cleared his throat. "Doesn't it seem likely that, if they haven't appeared in all this time, they have no interest in the estate or the title?"

Mr. Edwards leaned forward even more. He was on the edge of his seat now. "Perhaps they have no idea it's rightfully theirs."

"And what if they didn't want it, even if they knew?" he persisted.

Mr. Edwards's smile faded. He set down his glass. "Then I would conceal their existence, to provide the captain with an undisputed claim to the title."

"Really?" Will was taken aback.

The attorney stared at him for a long moment, his eyes piercing behind his spectacles. "Yes, Mr. Montclair. I would. The Crown would not retract a title, but the presence of another heir would cloud the claim of the captain's eventual son. It could throw the estate into abeyance, or back to the Crown entirely."

"How would you conceal . . . ?"

"Destroy every trace of them in the family records," said Edwards matter-of-factly. "Burn every letter and record from the investigators and pay them well to ensure their silence. Once the captain files claim for the title, I will make certain he gets it."

Will could only stare at him.

"My duty is to Carlyle, to preserve it for the tenants and family who live here and the generations to come." He stared at Will with ferocious intensity. "If there is another heir, he had better step forward soon, or he will lose all chance of Carlyle."

For a moment the words lingered in the charged silence of the room. Then Will blew out a low whistle. "What a remarkable story, Mr. Edwards."

"Yes," murmured the other man, still watching him. "Isn't it?"

Will nodded without meeting that gaze.

After a long moment of silence, Edwards got to his feet. "I should return to the castle. Thank you for the conversation, Mr. Montclair."

After he had left, Will prowled through the little house. Again he stopped in front of the map of Carlyle, his hand on Philippa's chair. He surveyed the estate, the fields and forests and rivers and roads. The mill, the shops, the houses, the castle.

Edwards had made clear what he had to do. Not what he wanted to do, but the right thing.

He sat down at the desk and uncapped his ink.

By the time he finished, the candles were burning low. His eyes stung, and when he stretched his neck, he saw the windows were gray with approaching dawn. He should sleep for a few hours. He pinched out the guttering candles just as there came a pounding on the door.

"Will!" cried Philippa. "Open the door!"

The duke. His heart like lead, he hurtled into the hall. "What?"

She burst in, hair falling down and dress creased and disheveled, but her face glowing. She seized his arms. "The fever has broken. He's going to recover."

Chapter Twenty-Six

He stared, uncomprehending. He'd been sure she was here to tell him Carlyle was dead.

"Isn't it wonderful?" She was smiling so widely her dimples were out.

"Yes." He cupped her cheek. "Yes! It's the best news I've ever heard."

And he kissed her.

Hard.

And she kissed him back, throwing herself against him so eagerly her feet left the ground. Will's back hit the wall and he pulled her tighter against him, and then he turned so her back was to the wall, and he kept kissing her there until the floor seemed to tilt beneath them.

"Oh!" She gave a startled laugh, clinging to his neck. "We're falling!"

He'd already fallen. Will's arms tightened around her. "I have you," he whispered against her temple.

Her arms snuggled closer. "I know," she whispered back. "And I have you, which is all I want."

The breath rattled through his lungs like a winter squall in a ship's sails. "Philippa, wait," he managed.

"Listen to me." She caught his face in her hands. "I know what I want," she said softly. "It's you. Not some London gentleman, not some country squire, not some nobleman. *You*." He opened his mouth, and she kissed him to stop whatever he meant to say. "I love you," she whispered. "Let that be enough for now. Please."

It was at once the best and the worst thing she could have said. Best, because it seemed to fill his heart with light, made anything seem possible, made him want to shout aloud for joy.

Worst . . . because it tempted him beyond bearing, beyond prudence and judgement and the last thin thread of his conscience.

He kissed her, letting his weight hold her to the wall. He cupped her shoulders and ran his hands along her arms to her wrists, and then he pinned her arms to the wall above her head. "I love you," he whispered. "I want you. God help me, but I do."

She nodded frantically. "God doesn't need to help you," she gasped. "I want you to have me. All of me."

Given how he had spent the night, there was only one honorable reply to this. But that last trembling thread of conscience snapped at her words, and he stepped into the whirlpool, letting it catch hold of him and drown him in desire for her.

He kissed her. A small thing, a kiss; it had been all the times he'd kissed other women. Kissing Philippa felt like drawing a breath of fresh air, like opening his eyes to a sun-kissed morning. She kissed him back as if she felt the same way. He still held her hands against the wall, so she hooked one leg around his, straining toward him.

When he broke the kiss to press his lips against the curve of her jaw, she arched her neck. She gasped when he nipped her earlobe. Finally Will released her wrists, so he could touch her face, stroke her shoulders, put his hands on her waist to lift her higher for more kisses, and she responded by gripping his hair and guiding him to where she wanted his mouth.

If she'd ever had a kerchief, it was gone. Her breasts were almost spilling from her bodice, a feast of velvety bronze skin, soft and warm under his lips and tongue. Her chest rose and fell rapidly, and her frantic whispers made him wild, and harder than iron. His entire body throbbed with wanting. He'd never wanted anyone or anything in his life more than he wanted to make love to Philippa.

Against a wall.

In the front hall of Stone Cottage, the door beside them standing open to the world.

He lifted his head and eased her back to the floor. Some of the haze cleared from his head. That damnable conscience feebly stirred.

Philippa slipped past him and took his hand. "Come," she whispered, her voice brimming with eagerness. She tugged him toward the stairs.

He took a step. His conscience rumbled again.

She paused on the first stair, pulling him close and winding her arms around his neck again. "Please." She kissed him softly. "Stop me only if you don't want to make love to me."

That would never be true. Down went his conscience again, for good this time, and Will closed
the door and let her lead him to his bedroom.

THE FIRST RAYS of the rising sun broke through the
windows of the bedroom as they entered, and it
felt like a good omen to Philippa. A new day, a
new *life* was dawning around her. Her heart beat
strong and true, no longer afraid and uncertain
but determined to choose boldly.

She chose Will.

Let there be a scandal. Let the duchess fret
and worry. To the marrow of her bones, Philippa
knew this was right; he was her love, her choice,
her destiny, for better or for worse. And whatever
secrets he was keeping . . . she would deal with
that later.

Right now, at this moment, there were more important matters.

He wasn't wearing a coat and his shirtsleeves
were rolled up. For the first time she realized he
must have been awake all night; his fingers had
ink on them, and his chin was rough with stub-
ble. She touched it, marveling at the texture, and
went up on her toes to kiss him as she began un-
doing the buttons of his waistcoat.

"It looks like neither of us slept much," she
murmured.

"No." His hands were in her hair, plucking out
what remained of the pins and dragging his fingers through the length. Philippa wanted to let
her head fall forward and moan at how good it
felt. No wonder Percival purred when the duchess brushed him.

"Then we should go to bed." She tugged the waistcoat down, and Will yanked his arms free before pulling her to him again.

She laughed even as she resisted. "Every laundry maid has seen you without your shirt."

He grinned as she worked at his neckcloth. "Envious?"

"Desperately!" She yanked at the stubborn knot. He reached up with one hand and pulled it loose, stripping away the long cloth. Philippa made a giddy noise of delight and reached for the neck of his shirt.

He caught her hands and kissed one, then the other. "That was only my second day at Carlyle. Have you been thinking wicked thoughts of me since then, Miss Kirkpatrick?"

She blushed, watching as he pulled the shirt free of his breeches. "Not wicked . . ." He gathered the shirt up and pulled it over his head, bundling it into a ball and tossing it aside. The breath left her lungs in a whoosh. He was magnificent. Pale sunlight, glowing late summer gold, picked up the sculpted lines of his muscles. Will had spent five months working long hours among laborers, and it showed. He was lean and strong, far more beautiful than any Greek statue.

Possibly just as wicked, though.

He went still when she reached out and touched him, gently, reverently. His skin was warm, lightly covered in hair. Unlike her, he was paler where the clothing covered him.

"Yes," she whispered, mesmerized by the feel of him. No soft, languid gentleman for her. "Very wicked thoughts."

"Excellent," he said, and picked her up by wrapping his arms around her waist and lifting. Philippa's hands landed on his bare shoulders, hard and rippling with strength as he carried her to the bed. His bed. *Their* bed, today.

He deposited her gently against the pillows, then sat back on his heels in front of her. Still entranced by his bare chest, she reached for the pins of her gown, burning to feel his skin against hers, but Will stopped her.

"I dreamt of this," he murmured. He propped her feet on either side of his knees, stilling her instinct to kick off her shoes. "In the schoolroom," he went on in a rough, sultry whisper. "When you fell on me."

Philippa shuddered, her stomach jumping at the memory.

"I imagined you like this." Lightly, delicately, he stroked her ankle. She inhaled; who knew an ankle could be so sensitive?

"And this . . ." Now his fingers feathered up the backs of her calves, sliding her skirt up along the way. Her head fell back on the pillows. She closed her eyes, concentrating on the touch of his fingers, wishing she hadn't worn stockings.

"My beautiful princess of the castle," he breathed. He rose up over her, bracing his hands beside her head and swooping down for a searing kiss.

"No princess," she managed to gasp. Her knees had gripped his waist on instinct and she ran her hands up his bare arms, entranced by the feel of him.

"My princess," he repeated stubbornly. "The lady of my heart. I pledge my love to thee." He bent his head and pressed his lips to the hollow between her breasts, the scruff on his face rubbing against her skin in a way that wrung a strangled moan from her.

She'd wondered what he looked like without a shirt on. It was better than she'd imagined.

She'd wondered what his mouth would feel like on her. It was beyond her wildest dreams.

And she was still fully dressed, not a stitch of clothing gone. For the first time she felt a deep vibration inside her, of anticipation, of primal longing to see how many of her imaginings and hopes he could surpass.

All of them, she guessed. Which only made her more desperate to find out.

"Are you mine to command, then?" She'd never known there was so much talking during lovemaking. She was both intrigued and impatient with it.

Will laughed, his mouth still moving over her exposed bosom. Her kerchief had gone missing somewhere, and her bodice had shifted down when he carried her. Her nipples felt hard and tingling, barely an inch away from his wicked tongue. She blushed all over—she must be thoroughly lost to wickedness to think of his mouth on her so intimately.

"I am." He looked at her, his dark gaze heavy-lidded but glinting with sparks of gold. "What do you bid me do?"

She opened her mouth, but had no idea. "Everything."

"Hmm." He ran one finger along the edge of her bodice, tugging it down until her aching nipples were bared. "Including this?" He ran his tongue around one dark pink bud and then took it between his teeth.

Philippa nearly bolted off the bed. "Oh my," she panted. "Oh my—"

"Stop?" He did it to the other side.

"No!" Her fingernails dug into his shoulders as he leaned down and suckled on her, making her legs shake and her toes curl and her stomach flex and twist.

He took his time, using his mouth until she felt knotted tight with anticipation. Every stroke of his tongue, every nip of his teeth, even the feel of his unshaven face and long hair on her skin seemed to send sparks through her limbs until she twitched at the absence of his touch when he drew back.

"Don't stop," she exclaimed.

His face was taut and focused. "I've just begun. What do you wish me to do?"

"All of it!" She tried to pull him to her again but he resisted. It was a surprise to her how immoveable he was even when she pulled. "I know what I'm asking for, I am not certain how to do it!" she burst out in frustration.

"Shall I show you?" That devil-may-care glitter came back to his eye.

"Yes!"

She had struggled upright, and now he pressed her shoulders back. Looking dark and almost dangerous, he spread her knees farther apart. His palms stroked up her skin, raising her skirt and petticoat over her knees.

"Like this," Will said in a guttural whisper, barely sounding like himself. His expression was fierce and his eyes seemed to singe her flesh as he looked at her, spread like a wicked wanton on his bed. "I dreamt of you like this."

Philippa swallowed. Her pulse began to throb between her legs, still beneath the skirts, but she knew he was staring at her *there*.

"So beautiful." Will raised his gaze to hers. "You should stop me." It was half snarl, half plea.

Philippa shook her head frantically, and pulled up her skirts the rest of the way.

Will went very still. His gaze roamed over her, hair spilling everywhere, breasts plumped above her bodice, stockinged legs spread wide invitingly.

"I want you," she whispered. "Want me." *Please want me.*

"I want you more than I've ever wanted anything or anyone in my life." His hand trembled as he touched her knee, then slowly slid up the inside of her thigh.

Philippa's eyes rolled back in her head. She knew enough to know he was going to touch her *there*, where her every nerve seemed to be tensed, waiting, anxious, eager. She bit her lip to keep from screaming.

The first touch wasn't *there*. His thumb ran along the crease at the top of her thigh. As light as a butterfly, his fingers skimmed her skin. Philippa held so still her bones ached. Leisurely, as if he meant to take all day, Will's fingers swirled over her thigh, her belly, finally, *finally*, drifting downward.

Then he stopped. She dragged open her eyes to see him hang his head. His hand was clenched in a fist, the sinews standing out on his arm. He pressed the fist to his mouth, his breath labored and harsh.

She sat up and kissed him, cupping her hands over his jaw and drawing him down on top of her. She hooked one leg, then the other, around his hips, ignoring the quake that rippled through her limbs at the feel of his body on top of hers. "Kiss me," she whispered, biting his lower lip. "Make love to me. I would make love to you if I knew how."

He looked at her, and a rueful smile curved his lip. "As my lady commands . . ." He laid his hand between her legs, his palm warm on her mound. Then he ran one finger through the folds, and Philippa jerked, her eyes going wide. Slowly he did it again, and this time she arched up into his touch, thrilling to the tremor that went through her body.

Then he taught her, his wicked mouth murmuring by her ear and his wicked hand between her legs, wringing gasps and shuddering sighs from her. She moved against him, impatient, eager, begging for more even as her insides twisted in unbearable tension.

"Let it go, ma chérie," he whispered. "Je désire te voir de cette façon . . ."

She bit his neck, too fevered to follow what he said and wanting to make him as frantic as she felt. He only laughed softly and pushed his finger inside her.

"Uhn." She threw back her head and dug her heels—sturdy walking shoes, still buckled on—into the mattress, and then she fell—like down a well, through a waterfall, into a vast and endless pit of pure sensation, sparkling along her nerves and singing in her veins.

Then she spasmed again as Will slid another finger inside her, in and out, seeming to touch something deep inside her that resonated like a harp string.

"That was . . ." She gulped for breath. "That was a lovely start."

He laughed, her earlobe between his teeth. He seemed not to be able to keep his mouth off her, which suited Philippa to perfection. "How so, my lady?"

She sat up. The rising sun lit the room with a rosy glow, exactly the way she felt inside. She pushed her hair out of the way and began pulling the pins from her bodice and yanking at the ties inside. "There are too many items of clothing."

He rolled onto his back and folded one arm behind his head, watching her.

She rose on her knees and stripped off the gown. Thankfully it was her sturdy travel gown, not a fashionably tight-sleeved robe. It sailed to the floor. She jerked loose the ties of her skirt and pulled it off, sending it after the gown. There was just a simple petticoat beneath, and she bundled it off.

She paused. Only her stays, shift, and stockings were left, plus her shoes. Will still lounged against the pillows, watching, but his carnal smile had faded. She propped one heeled slipper on his stomach. "Shall I be the only one disrobed?"

He undid the buckle and tossed the shoe aside, his hand caressing her foot. "I am savoring the disrobing immensely."

She blushed and began picking loose the knot on her stays. "You might grant me the same pleasure."

He was much faster than she was. By the time

she pulled her shift over her head, he was standing, completely bare, hands on his hips, watching. Philippa let her gaze rove over him.

More magnificent than any statue.

"What is it called?" she whispered. "The pleasurable thing you did."

"La petite mort." He pulled her to the edge of the bed and she wound her arms around his neck, shivering at the hot press of so much of his skin against hers. "The little death."

She smiled against his mouth. "Not death. I've never felt more alive."

"Really," he growled. His hand fell to her breast, cupping its weight in his palm.

"Perhaps I should try it again," she said. "I'll try to pay more attention."

He laughed as he bore her back onto the bed and propped himself above her. The sun gilded him gold and pink; even his hair glinted with colors. "If you pay more attention, I will have gone very wrong."

She beamed back. "Why?" She ran one hand down his chest, daringly touching his erection. His whole body tensed. "Perhaps you will be too lost in your own pleasure to attend . . ."

He jerked at her touch. "Oh my lady," he rasped. "How you do tempt me." His hand slid back between her thighs, spreading her open and stroking her again, this time firmer and with purpose.

Her breath bottled up in her chest. She reached for him, craving the feel of his skin. Feeling wicked, but also desperate, she reached down and touched him, testing the weight and length of him.

Will cursed and tried to flinch away, but she had her arm around his neck and held on tight.

"I've wondered what you felt like," she whispered. "All over. Please let me touch you . . ."

He tried to laugh. "As my lady commands . . ."

So she explored him, although her concentration flagged as he stroked her again until she was panting and bucking against his arms.

He rolled over her. "Do you feel it?" he whispered, his hand still between her legs.

"Yes." Her hips were rising, pushing into his touch, frantic again.

"I want you," he said, his voice trembling. "My darling Philippa, my love—"

She nodded, chest heaving, heart thundering. "Yes, yes, together . . ."

He moved over her, and then he moved inside her.

Philippa closed her eyes and inhaled. She'd never felt so full, so vulnerable, so connected to another person. He paused, and eased her legs up around his hips, only to sink even deeper, and she gripped his shoulders, feeling fully bared and exposed.

Nothing hidden. Nothing kept from him. She was his, entirely. It was exactly what she'd wanted, and she loved it.

He didn't move until she licked his chest. That made him twitch, and then slowly he flexed his spine. Philippa gasped and then moved against him, meeting his return thrust with her own.

She had dreamt of how he would make her feel. She'd had no idea at all.

She did not pay closer attention this time when

the whirlwind of sensation swept her up, too suddenly for her to catch a breath before she fell again, deep and far. She barely felt Will stiffen above her before he wrenched out of her clinging arms and legs and left her gasping and groping for him as she shuddered in pleasure.

For several minutes there was only the sound of their ragged breathing. Philippa opened her eyes to see Will sprawled beside her. He had torn himself away at the moment she wanted him closest. But now he pulled her to him, smoothing her hair back for a tender kiss that lasted until she sighed in contentment.

She rested her head on his shoulder. His arm went around her. Idly she traced circles on his chest and wondered how they would tell the duchess. The duke would be pleased. Everyone else at Carlyle . . . would be very surprised.

"I should take you home," he murmured. "Before you're missed."

She snuggled closer. "No one will miss me. The duchess will be with the duke."

His chest rose and fell. "You have named the two people who will be asking for you constantly."

She giggled. "And the two people who will forgive me anything!" She kissed his jaw. "But I am home now, right here, with you. Always and forever."

Will's smile died. He rolled onto his side, face-to-face with her. "Philippa."

She touched his face, unable to stop smiling. "Yes, my love?"

"I have to leave Carlyle," he said.

Chapter Twenty-Seven

For a moment she continued smiling at him. Her face shone with love and contentment, and he could see the euphoria still shimmering in her eyes.

But then his words began to sink in, and her beautiful lips parted in concern. "Oh, of course!" Her smile returned, surprised and a little shame-faced. "We left London so suddenly, your brother must be wondering—"

He put his finger on her lips. "No, my love." He paused as her smile dimmed. "I . . . I'm not coming back."

For a moment she was still, searching his face, an endearing quizzical line between her glorious, expressive brows.

Then she sat up abruptly, yanking loose of his embrace. "No! What are you saying? *No*," she repeated, more forcefully than before.

Will sat up. The sun was streaming through the windows now. It was morning, the bright light of a new day. No more hiding in the shadows of lies and half-truths he had told for so long, nor in the desires and wishes he had harbored in spite of all good sense. "I must. I gave my word."

She gaped at him. Christ, it was hard to tell her this, even if he hadn't spent the last hour making love to her, making her his, pretending she always could be. "To whom?"

He ran one hand over his head. "To my brother. One year at Carlyle, I swore, and no longer. The year is up within a few days." Tomorrow, in fact. He'd felt it approaching like the pale horse of Death coming for him.

"Tell him you must stay," she exclaimed. "He doesn't need you as we do!"

"I can't," he said quietly. "I . . . The rest of my family doesn't know I'm here. My father has grown curious—unhappily—that he's not heard from me in so long about the shipping business."

"Well—you must tell him!" She stopped, her eyes going wide and her face going pale. "Is it—Is it me you don't want to tell them about?"

"*No.*" His hands clenched to keep from reaching for her. "It has *nothing* to do with you."

She stared at him, her pink lips parted in dismay. With her long black hair curling wildly about her shoulders, all her perfect, copper-colored skin bare, she was the most beautiful woman he'd ever seen. The most clever and most intelligent and most sensible he'd ever known. She made him laugh and made him want to be a better man. And here he was, breaking her heart.

It *was* Death coming for him, of a sort. Leaving Philippa would excise a piece of his soul he would never recover.

"Will." She seized his arm. "Tell them. They

might yet surprise you. Write to them! Send it by the next ship. I will go with you to London and help persuade your brother that you must stay here—we need you. *I* need you."

"I can't." He shook his head when she started to protest. "Believe me when I say my father will be furious if he learns what I've done."

She released him, pulling her hand to her stomach as if to protect herself. "Why?"

He was silent for a moment. "I can't tell you why."

Her eyebrows wrinkled up in adorable confusion. "Then why did you come, if he is so implacably opposed?"

Another question he couldn't answer. He swung his feet to the floor to avoid the betrayal in her face. "I'll take you back to the castle." He rose and started to dress, heartsick.

Philippa also climbed out of bed and began sorting her clothes, but much more slowly. Will was completely clothed by the time she had put on her shift, stockings, and stays. Unfortunately, he could tell by her expression she wasn't merely slowed by the demands of her clothing; she was thinking.

"Did you come to Carlyle under false pretenses?" She tied on her petticoat.

"Define false pretenses," he parried, shaking out her skirt.

"Did you mean to do something other than the work of the estate steward?"

"No." He found her shoes and set them in front of her, red leather with steel buckles winking in the light.

"Did you lie to Mr. Edwards to obtain the post?" she demanded.

"No."

"So he knew you intended to leave after only a year?"

He grimaced, keeping his head down so she couldn't see his face. The last thing he'd done in the waning hours of the night was write to Edwards, resigning his position. It lay on his desk downstairs right now. "He didn't ask, and I didn't tell him."

"That might be construed as false pretenses!" She snatched the dress from his hands.

"It might be," he agreed. "On the other hand, Her Grace has longed to sack me since the day I arrived. She'll be delighted to achieve it at last."

"I told you she wouldn't dismiss you as along as the duke thrives in your company."

"That's no grounds to keep on a steward, and you know it."

She glared at him and turned her back, combing her fingers through her long black hair. Will watched greedily, knowing it would be the last time he saw it. She bent her arms behind her and coiled it, her neck arching, her ears peeping from beneath the heavy silken mass. He loved her hair. He could still feel it in his hands, against his chest. The satiny curve of her neck under his fingers. The arch of her spine as she moved against him in desire.

Without looking at him, she swept out the door and down the stairs. Will followed in silence. At the door she swung around to face him. "What will change your mind?"

His jaw clenched. "Nothing," he said. "I can't."

Angry tears sparkled in her eyes. "Not even if I plead?"

Will felt the icy fingers of Death slip around his heart. How he burned to say *yes*, to swear to do anything she asked of him.

At his silence, a tear slipped down her cheek. "Even after what we shared? Even after you made love to me? Will . . . I—I love you and want to be with you always. Did you not hear me?"

Death's fingers tugged, tearing his insides loose one agonizing bit at a time. "I heard."

She hit him, her fist striking right where his heart was breaking. "How dare you!" she said, her voice shaking. "How dare you? I *love* you. You said you love me and made me believe it—"

Something broke inside him. He hauled her into his arms and kissed her, one last desperate kiss that would have to last him the rest of his life. She pounded on his chest with one hand and gripped his hair with the other, holding him close and punishing him for hurting her.

"I do love you," he said fiercely. As if making one last bid to escape destruction, his heart was galloping inside his ribs, so hard his hands shook as he held her. "I will never love another as I love you—you own my heart for eternity, worthless and foolish as it may be."

"Then don't leave me. Please." Her lips were swollen, her eyes were sparkling with tears, and she gazed at him with such pleading, his nerve almost broke.

Will inhaled. "I'm not—I'm not the man you think I am. You deserve better. I tried not to love you, I tried to keep *you* from loving me," he said in agony. "I tried and I failed and it will haunt me to my grave." He brushed away her tears with his thumbs. "I have no excuse."

She backed away. "Then you can't love me."

He flinched.

"If you did," she said, her voice throbbing, "you would tell me, no matter what the reason. You would trust me enough to do that."

He didn't dare open his mouth.

The morning light reflected the bitter disillusionment in her eyes. After an endless moment she turned and hurried off through the cottage garden she had tended, one loose curl bouncing at her nape.

Death smiled and gave one brutal tug, wrenching his heart loose from his body, and he felt nothing but cold and empty inside.

PHILIPPA WAS STILL shaking when she reached the castle.

From the moment Will opened the door, she'd known she was right about him. His face had blazed with joy when she said the duke would live. He'd kissed her with passion and love, and even when he hesitated out of some notion of honor, the moment she took his hand he went with her. And then he took her to bed and made love to her like a lover. She was still glowing from the inside out at the way he worshipped her body to the peak of pleasure. Just thinking about his mouth on her skin made her toes curl. *Him*, sang her heart, ignoring everything but the feeling that he was hers and she was his.

Which made his intention to leave Carlyle utterly confounding. Leave Carlyle? He couldn't. He couldn't *want* to. Why? He cared for this estate. He was fond of the duke. He loved her. She'd seen his face when he spoke to tenants and Mr. Amis and even the maids in the laundry. Philippa would have wagered her very soul that he wanted to stay.

So why wouldn't he even try to persuade his family?

There had to be more, something she didn't know. A man who plunged into a river to save pigs, who faced down a duchess wearing servant's livery, who wandered into the duke's private garden against all orders and charmed him . . . He had done nothing to be ashamed of. Besides, he'd said his father was affectionate and loving.

Perhaps she *was* the reason. Perhaps Will had never meant to marry her. Perhaps his family wouldn't approve of her, or would be angry at him for making love to her. She'd instigated their love-making, but only because he hesitated. But that still didn't explain why he insisted on leaving.

What was she missing? How could she change his mind when she didn't even know the reasons he had for making it up?

She ran up to her room, startling Marianne, just bringing the wash water. "Miss Kirkpatrick," gasped the girl. "I thought you still asleep!"

"I went for an early morning walk," she lied without blinking an eye. "I couldn't sleep, after worrying about the duke. I want a bath."

Marianne goggled at her. "Right now, Miss Kirkpatrick?"

It was a terrible imposition on the staff, who

would have to heat the water in the midst of all
their other morning chores. Normally Philippa
didn't ask it. Today she said, "As soon as possible,
please."

Marianne curtsied and hurried off.

She paced her room, absently pulling off her
clothing. She was almost glad she had a pressing
problem to occupy her mind, because otherwise
she would sink into a bout of angry hysteria. How
dare he say he loved her and make love to her only
to say he meant to leave her?

Or, how he *thought* he meant to leave.

Philippa glanced at the portrait of her mother.
I'm not giving up, Ammi, she promised silently. *How
can I persuade him?*

When the servants had brought the tub and filled
it, Marianne bustled around as Philippa scrubbed
industriously. Papa had used to say baths were excellent for solving problems. Philippa suspected
he just wanted to persuade a stubborn little girl to
bathe, but she couldn't deny that he was right.

There were three steps, she decided. First, if he
wanted to leave, she would have no choice but to let
him go. But he would have to persuade her beyond
all doubt that he really wanted to go.

Second, convince him it was possible to stay.
Convince him the duke and even the duchess
wanted him to stay; convince him he was needed
and wanted here, by everyone from Gerry and Jilly
Smith to Charles Amis to Philippa herself. Convince him that there must be some argument that
could persuade his family to let him stay. Philippa
was conscious of the fact that she was asking him
to break his word to his father for her, but if Will

longed to stay at Carlyle, surely it was wrong for his father to make him leave.

The third step she hoped not to need, but it must be planned. Will said he was leaving soon. Assuming the first step was true, if the second step failed, she must have step three ready and waiting.

That was the simplest decision. If he would not stay, she would go with him.

She dressed and hurried off to find the duchess. Instead she found the attorney. "Good morning, Miss Kirkpatrick."

"Mr. Edwards. Have you any news of the duke this morning?"

He nodded. "Mrs. Potter says he's reviving splendidly, though it will take time."

"Of course. That is excellent news." She wet her lips. "Have you, by any chance, spoken to Mr. Montclair recently?"

The attorney raised his brows. "Just last night. Was there something you wished me to speak to him about?"

Philippa took a deep breath. "I wonder if he told you he intends to leave Carlyle permanently."

Edwards drew back, nonplussed. "No," he said sharply. "Did he tell you that?"

She nodded.

Mr. Edwards stepped closer, strangely intense. "Are you certain you understood him?"

"Unfortunately."

A frown snarled his brow. "I thought . . ." he murmured. He let out his breath, looking unhappily surprised. "I see I was wrong."

"What?" she demanded. "What did you think?"

He looked at her for a long moment, a long,

searching gaze that made her tense with alarm. What did he know? "I thought he had great promise," he said at last. "If he is determined to leave, however, it has all come to naught and I will have to resume my search. Was there anything else, Miss Kirkpatrick?"

"No," she murmured. "I suppose not."

He bowed and walked away. Strangely disconcerted, Philippa continued to the duchess's sitting room.

The duchess was usually to be found here, breakfasting in her morning dress and spoiling Percival with bits of bacon and toast, but today the room was empty. She must be taking her meal with the duke, which would be a good sign. Philippa ought to go see him, too.

Instead she dropped onto the sofa. Her burst of determination was being overtaken by worry. Mr. Edwards was irked at Will's planned departure, but nothing deeper. Philippa realized she had expected the attorney to urge Will to stay. If Mr. Edwards, Will's champion, would just let him walk away, it would be even harder to persuade the duchess.

A lump formed in her throat at the thought of leaving Carlyle. She wanted to be with Will. He called to her like a kindred soul, perfectly attuned in humor, desires, and passions. No one else had ever made her feel the way he did. Never had she felt the same connection and attraction—certainly not with any gentleman in London.

She would give up Carlyle for him, but she yearned to have both.

She looked up at Mama, painted on the canvas.

Jessica had chosen her family over love—until love caught her by surprise, and then she'd persuaded her family to love him, too. Love or family? *Why can't I have both?* she silently begged.

Philippa closed her eyes. Look at her, asking portraits for advice: first Ammi, now Mama.

And then her eyes flew open, and she raised her head.

The portrait had given her the answer.

Chapter Twenty-Eight

❧ ⚜ ☙

Will packed like a man heading to the gallows.

Mrs. Blake and Camilla arrived soon after Philippa left. He didn't have the heart to tell them he was leaving permanently, so he merely told them he wouldn't need dinner. He started to turn back to the house, then paused.

"Might I have a cup of tea?"

Mrs. Blake stared at him. He'd never asked for tea, not once. "Of—of course, sir."

"With honey," he added.

"Yes, Mr. Montclair. Camilla will bring it directly."

He was sitting at his desk when she brought it. Will murmured his thanks and she gave him a cheerful curtsy. Camilla was a good girl. He would miss her, and Mrs. Blake, and those tender little gulab jamun. Philippa had been right about those, too.

He sipped the tea, savoring the hint of honey. Damn. He even liked her tea now. He took a piece of paper from the drawer. On the corner of the desk was a thick packet, his labor of the night. It was a detailed summary for Edwards of the work both completed and unfinished, and what he had promised various tradesmen and tenants for the future.

He'd also sketched out his plan to begin a breeding program for the estate, not for racehorses but for strong, healthy cattle and other animals. He'd included the revised rent schedule he'd planned to implement, and his arguments for how beneficial a canal could be in getting goods to and from the estate. He'd even argued for a revision to the poor relief and greater investments in schooling for local children. If the estate paid the fees for educating its youngsters, there would be a capable workforce to manage and run Carlyle for years to come.

He hadn't quite managed what Philippa had charged him with—bring the estate into good order for the heir—but he'd made great strides. The next duke would inherit a vastly more modern estate, in much better repair. Of that, at least, Will felt some pride.

It didn't make up for the fact that he'd treated Philippa shamefully.

The blank page stared at him accusingly.

He owed her some sort of explanation. Christ, he'd taken her to his bed and made love to her. He'd pulled out short of completion, but he'd trifled with an eligible lady.

A lady who loved him.

A lady he loved desperately.

His mouth twisted bitterly. *My darling Philippa*, he wrote, and then threw the pen across the room.

He prowled into the corridor and saw his packed trunk. He veered away from it and went out the back, slipping past the kitchen, where he could hear Mrs. Blake calling to Camilla.

He would miss them all—Mrs. Blake, Camilla, Josiah, the Amises, Edwards, the duke, even the duchess in some strange way. He had grown to care about this estate and its people. But if not for Philippa, he would have already left.

Philippa.

He threw the saddle on Gringolet. There had to be a way, some half-truth he could tell that wouldn't destroy his relationship with his father. And perhaps, if he explained to Philippa just enough, she would understand and accept him as he was.

Mind working furiously, he wheeled Gringolet into the road.

THIS TIME PHILIPPA came to Stone Cottage on Evalina. She leapt off even before her horse stopped, earning her a snort of disapproval. With a brief soothing pat, she hurried into the house.

A trunk sat in the front of the hall. Her heart dropped. "Will?" she cried, lifting her skirts and running from room to room. The house was silent. Up the stairs she clattered, praying he was still there, still packing, fallen back to sleep—

The bedroom door swung open at her touch, and she knew at once it was empty. The bed was neatly made. The top of the bureau was bare; there were no spare boots behind the door. A breeze puffed the curtains, carrying a whiff of his shaving soap.

The lady of my heart, he'd said. *I pledge my love to thee.*

She ran back downstairs. The kitchen door stood

open, and she found Mrs. Blake tossing corn for the handful of chickens.

"Goodness, Miss Kirkpatrick!" The cook beamed at her. "I didn't know you'd called. Shall I send in another cup of tea?"

Philippa's brows went up. "Another?"

Mrs. Blake nodded, smiling. "Mr. Montclair asked for it this morning—first time he ever wanted any tea, miss. Perhaps he's taking to English ways."

"Perhaps. Do you know where he is?"

"He rode out an hour ago," piped up Camilla. "Looked right morose, he did."

Philippa's throat closed. "Dressed for travel?"

"No, miss," said Camilla in surprise. "Just as usual. He only come back from London yesterday."

She nodded, weak with relief. She hadn't missed him. "Of course. Tea would be delightful, Mrs. Blake. Thank you."

"I'll have it right in."

Philippa went into the study out of habit. The large map was still here, pinned to the wall. She went to it, touching spots where notes had been pinned as she tried to add up what he had repaired and rebuilt. The bridge that had fallen in under Gerry and Jilly Smith. Two entirely new bridges. Fences rebuilt, the mill pond dredged, numerous barns and houses reroofed and repaired. The roads that crisscrossed the estate, smoothed and graded. Philippa had even noticed fresh coats of lime in the service courtyard, and drainpipes all over the castle were being removed, repaired, and replaced. He *had* dragged this estate into good repair in just a few months, fighting the duchess all the way.

She spotted the letter on the desk. *My darling Philippa* it said, and nothing else. A good-bye note, she supposed. A folded page at the side, which Philippa opened without a single qualm, turned out to be a letter of resignation to Mr. Edwards. The thicker sheaf was a comprehensive catalog of all Will had done, and all that he hoped would still be done.

How could he leave this place he had poured so much of himself into?

She was sitting in her usual chair when Mrs. Blake bustled in with a tray of tea and cakes.

"Thank you," Philippa murmured. "Mrs. Blake!" The woman paused questioningly. "Do you think Mr. Montclair has been a good steward?"

"Bless me, Miss Kirkpatrick, yes indeed!" exclaimed the cook. "A very fine one, if I had to say. Young Josiah Welby worships him above all men. He takes the lad out and has been teaching him to be a steward. Josiah's none too fond of the milling trade and fancies a position like Mr. Montclair's."

Philippa nodded. "How do the tenants regard him?"

Mrs. Blake turned thoughtful. "Odd you ask that. He's had nearly all of them through here, reviewing rents and inquiring into the state of the farms. I've sent home more bread with tenants than I've ever fed him." She sniffed. "And I know Maria Amis is feeding him at the castle, as if I don't make perfectly good tarts here! But that young man works himself to the bone, miss." She gave a firm nod. "What he needs is a wife. Someone to tempt him to bed before he burns through all the candles every night."

"Does he?" Philippa smiled faintly. "Is he as capable as Mr. Grimes?"

Mrs. Blake hesitated. "Mr. Grimes were a good man," she said carefully. "But he'd got old. And Mr. Edwards . . . well, he's not a steward, is he? Mr. Montclair has been a godsend, ma'am, if you ask me, and most of the others about here." She winked. "And if he fancies a Carlyle wife, there's more than one girl on this estate who'd be pleased to have him."

At that Philippa actually laughed. "Well do I believe it. Thank you, Mrs. Blake. I hope Mr. Montclair has the management of Carlyle for a long time."

"We all do, ma'am," said the cook fervently, and went out.

Philippa closed her eyes. She hoped so more than anyone.

She sat with her tea and thoughts until a horse dashed by the window toward the stables. The bright flash of blue coat made her smile—her pirate. Her friend, her conspirator, her lover. Her love.

Whatever else she got wrong, she knew that much for certain. She pressed her hands together, feeling the unaccustomed weight of Ammi's jewelry, the bangles sliding up her arms, the rings on every finger clinking quietly. Today she had worn it all, to remind herself that love was not wrong and was worth fighting for.

There were voices outside. Mrs. Blake would tell him she was here, even if he hadn't noticed Evalina outside. Then his steps came, and Philippa rose, waiting until he filled the doorway.

Will hadn't shaved; three days of dark beard covered his chin, and his hair was in unruly waves almost to his shoulders. He looked more like a pirate than ever, and she had never loved him more.

"Run away with me," he said.

Philippa blinked, and then a smile started on her face.

"Damn my promises. I love you. I've not much to offer you, but everything I am and everything I have, I want to share with you." He held out one hand beseechingly. "If you'll have a poor merchant captain, my love, my heart and hand are yours."

Her heart began fluttering madly as she placed her hand in his. "For better and for worse."

He pulled her closer, kissing her hand before sweeping his arm around her waist. "For richer and for poorer, until death do us part." He grinned, his eyes beginning to glow. "Is that yes?"

She nodded. "I came to propose that, actually. If you won't stay here, I'll go with you. It's the only solution."

He laughed, and then he kissed her with a hunger that made her toes curl and her heart leap and her thoughts go quiet for a moment.

"I tried to go," he breathed. "Everything is packed. You'd left. I broke your heart, God help me. And I couldn't go. I rode out to delay until I could think of any way at all I could ask you to be mine."

She laughed. "Don't you remember? You've had me since this morning."

"I do remember that," he growled. "Fondly."

Philippa blushed even as joy bubbled inside her. "You've had me longer than that," she told him in a low voice. "Since you threw those walnuts at me. Since you dared me to wager on fishing. Since you invited me to the barn to see puppies and kissed me in the straw."

"I knew the puppies were a good idea," he said under his breath.

She wrinkled her nose and he grinned.

"I have one question," she said.

"Only one?"

He was teasing. Philippa smiled, too, trying to quiet the buzzing inside her head. She wanted to ask lightly, because she had one chance to catch him off guard and discern his real feelings.

"You said you don't much care for shipping. Would you consider taking a different position?"

Will looked surprised. "What do you mean?"

Philippa gripped his coat. Her mouth was dry.

"The position," she said, "of heir to the dukedom of Carlyle."

Chapter Twenty-Nine

❦

His brows quirked. "What?"

She held his gaze. "I know who you are."

"Of course you do," he said, sounding faintly puzzled. "They don't choose heirs by advertising at a register office, though. Edwards explained it last night."

She laughed from nerves. "I know how heirs are designated. Which is why I proposed you take the position."

Will paused. "Ah. Not you, too."

She blinked. "What?"

"Edwards." He grimaced. "He was throwing out hints that I might be from a long-lost family branch of Frenchmen. They disappeared into New France decades ago, he said. Coincidentally enough, where my family comes from. It's a romantic story, but also madness."

For a moment she paused, uncertain. But then she caught the watchful flicker of his eyes and remembered how well he had teased and provoked her, trying to make her dislike him to keep her at a distance. He was a good actor, but she had been studying him and trying to puzzle him out for too long to be fooled now.

"Of course that's madness," she said firmly. "I told you, I know who you *are*."

"I sincerely hope so, since you just promised to run off with me." He winked.

But Philippa had seen him twitch at her words; it was small but real, and sent her confidence soaring.

"I did. I will." She smoothed his neckcloth. "Will we go back to Boston and live near your father and your mother? I'm eager to meet Jack, too. I hope he'll help me practice my French." She gazed up at him innocently. "Will they like me? I hope they won't think me proud, coming from Carlyle Castle. I want to take them gifts from here. I hope you'll advise me how to choose. Perhaps a tea service from the Tate potteries? Maximilian and Bianca would be pleased to design one I could present to your mother."

He went very still.

"I shall miss the duchess terribly," she went on. "And the duke. Who will read to him once we're both gone?"

"Amis," said Will hoarsely, then cleared his throat. "He's taken up reading *Roderick Random*. I'm sure he'll continue."

Philippa nodded. "You've had such a restorative effect on him. I'll be forever grateful, as will the duchess. It won't be the same, only having letters from them, but I hope we can write frequently."

"Yes," murmured Will. She could almost see the thoughts flying behind his eyes.

"She'll want to know all about our new life,"

Philippa went on mercilessly. "Is Boston very different to London? I'm sure it is to Kittleston! I shall have to make sketches of everything at Carlyle to remind me, and to show everyone in my new home."

With a muttered oath he broke away from her and strode to the window, bracing his hands on the sides.

Philippa waited.

Finally he spoke. "What are you trying to do?"

"Nothing," she said, a tremor in her voice. "What could I be doing wrong, by asking about your family—soon to be mine—and expressing my hope that the duchess will write to me often in America?"

She *knew* she was right. But she didn't know why he was so determined to deny it.

She took a deep breath. "You'll be missed here, you know. The tenants are elated to have a capable, caring steward in charge of the estate. You know every inch of it now, better than Mr. Grimes ever did, I suspect, and you've impressed even Mr. Edwards—no small matter. He may miss you most of all."

Will might have been made of stone.

"The duke will be grieved as well. As you said, he's an old man, and he cannot take many more such losses. You see how desperately he misses his sister and brothers."

Will flinched, his shoulders tense.

"Even the duchess will be sorry to see you go," went on Philippa softly. "She has carried so many burdens for so long, not only the estate, but caring for the duke, knowing she might lose him as she's lost every other one of her children. She did so long for a grandchild—"

"Stop." He flung out one hand, then slowly turned. His expression was set. "I am *not* needed here, Philippa. There will be another steward. There are two heirs, groomed for the title and standing ready for it—"

"But they are not *you!*" she burst out.

"I am not who you think I am!"

She sucked in a deep breath for courage. "Prove it. What is your father's birth name?"

The color faded from his face.

"No matter. I know what it is." She came and laid her hand on his arm. "He told you not to come near here, didn't he?"

"I gave my word." He sounded numb. "I swore never to tell a soul . . ."

"I understand." Her throat felt raw, from tears and lack of sleep and the torrent of emotion raging through her. "But would he still demand the same promise if he were here now, standing where you are, where you have been for several months? If he knew what *you* know about this family and the castle and everyone around it?"

Will said nothing.

She leaned her cheek against his shoulder. "I still choose you," she said softly. "Always."

His arms closed around her. "Damn it," he said numbly. "I can't say no to you. I could leave all this without a shred of regret . . . but you." He rested his temple against hers. "You are a constant amazement and delight to me, love."

"Remember that when we argue," she said against his chest.

"Are we arguing now?"

She shook her head. "I'm hoping to persuade you, but if you are adamantly opposed, I'll stop." Then she couldn't resist adding, "But I think you're refusing out of fear, of what your father would say and what the duchess would believe. And I think you may be wrong on both counts. I know you're wrong about her."

"Oh am I?" he muttered darkly.

"I've known her almost all my life," she responded. "I know her heart."

For a long moment he just held her, stroking her back. Philippa had never felt so safe and comforted.

"Supposing you were correct," he said at last, "what was your plan for the rest?"

She shrugged, snuggling against him. "There's no plan. If you succumbed to my wiles this far, I thought we might sort out the rest together."

He laughed reluctantly. "You have found my great weakness . . . you."

Philippa grinned up at him. "And our great strength . . . *us*."

Will let out his breath. "It's madness, you know."

She gripped his coat for emphasis. "It's not. I think they will be more pleased than you think. They will listen. If they don't . . . then they aren't the people I believe them to be. I would want nothing to do with them ever again. If they turn on us with anger and disgust, I'll pack my trunks and leave with you immediately."

"I fear it won't go as well as you think."

She gave a little tug on his coat. "But imagine if it *does* go as well as I think. Isn't it worth trying?"

Will stepped back and paced away, one hand on his hip and the other at his brow. He circled the room without a word, deep in thought.

Philippa stood where she was, hardly breathing from hope. She had lived here all her life, and she would wager every last thing she possessed that this news would amaze and shock the duchess, yes—but then bring joy on a scale which had rarely been known in the castle.

At last he stopped, facing the giant map of Carlyle he'd pinned on the wall several months ago. For a moment he stared at it; Philippa saw his gaze move over the roads, the streams, the vast sections of land where there had once been pinned notes of needed repairs, which now were clear. Because of him. Because of his efforts, his labor, his unflagging determination to do right by Carlyle. She would never believe he didn't care.

"All right," he said, almost to himself. "Everyone makes a life-or-death wager now and then."

Her heart gave a great leap. "And would you stay, if they are welcoming?"

He stared at the map another moment, then turned to her. His eyes were dark and steady as he took her hands. "I don't expect it to happen, but . . ." His mouth twisted in a rueful little smile. "I've become rather fond of this place."

She beamed at him and stepped closer.

"Not as fond as I am of you, though." He wrapped his arms around her and kissed her again, until she was dazed and breathless, clinging to him with both hands. "God above, I love you," he breathed, his cheek against hers. "Tell me again . . ."

"I love you, I love you, I love you. And nothing anyone says or does will change that." Impulsively she bit his earlobe, and a shudder went through him.

"Even when they laugh in my face?" His voice was muffled against her hair. "When they order me from the property as a liar and an imposter?"

"We will decamp to London or America or any place where the name Carlyle shall never again be spoken aloud," she declared.

Will laughed. "That certain, are you?"

She nodded.

He pulled back and regarded her, his eyes warm and his lips quirked. "You love Carlyle. *You're* the one they need here, the one who makes the duke smile and who soothes the duchess's nerves. They would all despise me forever if I took you from them." He hesitated. "And you might despise me for it, too."

"Never!"

He gave her a look. "I'm only willing to try this for your sake."

"You should want it for your own sake," she began, but he shook his head.

"No. I wasn't supposed to take this position at all. But I'm glad beyond words that I did, and if all I get out of it is you, it will forever be the best thing I ever did." He clasped her hand and lifted it to his lips. "Philippa Noor un-nisa, you will marry me, won't you?"

"I will. Very, very happily." She bobbed on her

feet in elation. She must be literally radiating happiness.

His face split in a wide grin, and he kissed her again. "For my lady love, I would face sea monsters and dragons, let alone a duchess."

Chapter Thirty

They walked up the hill together, Evalina on a lead rope. Philippa clung to him as if he might yet vanish before her eyes, soaking in the pure pleasure of his hand in hers. Out in the open, where everyone could see. He was hers, and she was his, come what may.

But she saw no reason to face the toughest task first, so when they reached the castle she led the way to the duke's suite. Will shot her a look, but he went without protest.

"Is His Grace awake?" she asked when Mr. Amis opened the door.

He bowed. "Yes, ma'am, but in weak spirits." He caught sight of Will, and a flicker of surprise crossed his face. "Perhaps you've come to cheer him?"

Philippa smiled with determination. "We most certainly have."

The duke lay on the chaise, a white blanket pulled up to his chest. The variegated light from the stained glass fell across his form like an effigy in a church. His face was turned toward the window, his eyes closed, and his hand lay atop his chest, pale and thin. Philippa asked Mr. Amis and the footman to leave, then beckoned Will to come closer.

"Good day, Uncle," she murmured, taking the chair beside the chaise.

The duke stirred. "Ah, Pippa," he said feebly. "Have you come to read to me?"

"Not today," she told him. "I've brought you a visitor."

"I don't feel well . . ."

"You'll wish to see him, I'm sure," she coaxed. "He's come from Lemuel."

The duke's eyes opened. He turned his head and looked right at Will. "Oh," he said, his eyes brightening a little. "You! But Pippa, he's not Lemuel . . ."

"Though very like him, yes?" Philippa prompted.

Carlyle struggled to raise his head, peering at Will. "Come closer. Let me see you." Obediently Will stepped closer, still not saying anything. The duke began to nod. "Yes, of course. Lemuel used to look at me just so . . ." He smiled faintly. "You told me I was wrong, but I was right. I knew it!" He stabbed one shaky finger in the air. "You are my witness, Pippa. I knew when I saw him he was very like Lemuel."

She beamed and squeezed Will's hand. "Of course you were, Uncle. I'm sure Lemuel would admit it at once, wouldn't he, Will?"

The man beside her stirred. "Most certainly not. He would go to inhuman lengths to work out that he was somehow right and Joffred was wrong."

Philippa started, and the duke began to laugh—rusty, surprised, but full of glee and growing stronger by the moment. "He would! He was a devil when you called him wrong. That's why we had to record our wagers, because Lemuel would *insist* he won, every time." Carlyle's weak smile was triumphant. "He did not. We raced so many times, and I won more than half. My horse was better than his. You know the one, Pippa. My Nestor. Much better."

Will cleared his throat. "No horse was better than Hengroen. Not even Nestor."

Philippa almost leapt from her chair in astonishment as the duke laughed again. Hengroen—*that* was the name of the other wooden horse, the missing one whose name she had forgotten when they visited the nursery. She was sure no one at Carlyle had thought of Nestor and Hengroen in a decade at least. She looked at Will, speechless. The whole time they'd been up there, he must have been looking for Hengroen.

She'd been sure—*so sure*—but here was proof beyond all doubt.

"Mr. Montclair is Lemuel's son, Uncle," Philippa blurted out.

The duke patted her hand. "Of course he must be. No one else would dare try to claim that Hengroen was better than Nestor. And no one has called me Joffred in years . . ." He smiled. "Jessica did. Ah, I do miss her." He looked at Philippa, his faded eyes brimming with love and sadness. "I'm so glad she left us you, my dear."

Her throat closed so hard it hurt. "What does

Joffred mean?" she asked, trying desperately not to cry.

"John Frederick," said Will softly.

The duke was still smiling. "And I used to call him Billy Goat, which he despised even though he was as stubborn as one. So he became Lemuel. He yearned to explore distant lands and meet foreign peoples, like Gulliver . . ." He sighed. "Is he also here?"

THE CONSTANT DRUMBEAT in Will's mind for the last year had been one of caution: *do not give yourself away*. It took him by surprise how good it felt to drop his guard.

He'd heard tales since he was a child about his father's older brother; in Pa's telling, he was the wild, wicked son while his older brother was the good son, the sober and honest one who would never lie about stealing tarts from the kitchen or trying to scale the castle walls . . . but who still went along with every mad scheme. Pa had always laughed, talking about Joffred, but grew wistful and silent when Will asked why they never visited or wrote to him.

"No, sir, he's not here," he answered the duke.

Carlyle wilted into his pillows. "Ah, it was too much to hope. He did say he would never come back."

Will jerked, then leaned forward. "Why did he say that?"

The duke gazed into mid-air for a long moment. "The army," he said at last. "He went into the army, did he not? Mother was terrified he would be killed . . . And then he was." Carlyle frowned. "It must have been very bad. But Lemuel expected it. He said they were sending him to the edge of the world, and he didn't believe he would ever come back. He hated sailing." He looked at Will again. "But you're not afraid of the ocean. You came here. From far away, am I right?"

Stunned, Will nodded. That was true. His father had sent him and Jack because he didn't want to sail himself. Ironically for someone who owned a fleet of merchant ships, Pa hated ocean sailing.

The duke smiled again in triumph. "Another mark in my favor, Pippa! I shall tease Lemuel about it . . ." He trailed off, looking confused. "No, he's never coming back," he muttered with a shake of his head. He slumped back into the pile of cushions behind him, his face pale with weariness.

"We'll leave you to rest," said Philippa softly.

The duke's eyes opened and he groped for Will's hand, giving it a surprisingly strong squeeze. "I'm glad he sent you," he whispered. "You're a good lad to bring us word of him."

"Yes, sir," he managed to say.

Philippa leaned close and brushed a kiss on the duke's cheek. "Until later, Uncle," she whispered, and led Will from the room by the hand.

In the corridor she whirled on him. "Hengroen!"

"King Arthur's horse," he returned. "Didn't everyone name his first horse Hengroen?"

"No!" She laughed, pressing one hand to her forehead, looking both pleased and dazed.

"We weren't raised solely on tales from Gulliver, you know."

She laughed again, then went up on her toes

to fling her arms around his neck. "No one else would have known about that horse."

Will shrugged as he pulled her close. "Jack knows. Not that I'm switching places with him for anything, mind."

She laughed, he grinned, and then he kissed her. Who cared that they were in the castle, right outside the duke's suite, where anyone might walk by and spy them?

He had trained himself to be so careful about what he said and did. Even though he suspected the duke, with his shaky grasp of reality, would be the only person who believed his story, he found he didn't care when Philippa looked at him with her eyes glowing like amber and her smile so wide he wanted to kiss that tempting dimple. And when she leapt into his arms and pressed against him as if they were the only two people in the entire world, his brain tended to go out like a snuffed candle.

"Ahem."

By the time Will registered the sound, it had probably happened more than once. He raised his head reluctantly, and Philippa—very beautifully flushed—peered past his shoulder. "Oh," she said breathlessly. "Mr. Edwards."

Will growled in frustration and she gave him a twinkling smile. Slowly he released her and turned around to face the attorney.

"What a surprise to see you here, Mr. Montclair." Edwards sounded annoyed. "I understood you are leaving us."

"I intended to. I almost forgot something very dear to me and had to return for it." He hesitated, glancing at Philippa, and she beamed at him, still glowing with confidence and love, pressed close to his side.

Well, why not? He'd told the duke already.

"Mr. Edwards," he began, "I think you've suspected me for a while of being someone other than an ordinary fellow in need of employment."

The attorney raised one brow. "Why would I suspect that?"

"Because you're a clever and perceptive man," put in Philippa. "Even wily, some might say."

Edwards put one hand on his heart and bowed, as if gratified by a compliment. Will choked on a laugh. "Yes. And . . . because there was no earthly reason you should hire a lowly American sailor, new to England and completely devoid of experience, to manage a vast, landlocked estate."

"I required someone immediately," replied Edwards. "I took care to sound you out thoroughly on the subject before offering you the post."

"Yes," said Will. "You inquired about my family."

Mr. Edwards smiled slightly. "I wished to be certain of your character."

"And haven't you been pleased with how he's managed the estate?" Philippa interjected.

Edwards hesitated. "Yes, Miss Kirkpatrick. His work has been satisfactory."

She raised her brows, the lady of the castle again. "Satisfactory?"

The attorney's mouth twitched. "Thoroughly satisfactory, ma'am."

Philippa tried, without much success, to hide her

pleased smile. Will guessed what she was thinking: *How surprised Mr. Edwards will be when he hears
the truth.*

"I am delighted to hear that." Will found that he
was also enjoying himself. After a year of working
with Edwards, it was a pleasant change to know
something he didn't. "I'm well aware of how difficult it is to win your good opinion."

Edwards bowed his head, still wearing his bland
little smile that revealed so little.

"You're wrong, though. I'm not who you suspect
I am," Will said.

Edwards's smile faltered. "Who, pray, might
that be?"

"Some descendant of . . ." Will looked to Philippa,
who supplied, "Lord Thomas St. James."

Will nodded once. That theory had entertained
him to no end. How many heirs had the Carlyles
lost over the ages? "Through my mother, did you
think? Her family is French. Descended from old
French aristocrats as fine as any you have here, I
expect. But not St. Jameses."

Edwards's eyes flickered between the two of
them. "I suppose Miss Kirkpatrick told you that
name."

"Only the name. I guessed at the rest. You were
far too interested in my parents. Always asking
about my father's habits and how my family came
to be in Montreal."

Edwards opened his hands wide in a gesture
of innocence. "I'm a curious fellow. Forgive me if
I pried too deeply into your personal affairs, Mr.
Montclair."

Will hesitated. "It's stranger than you think."

Again the attorney looked between them, his curiosity beginning to show. "How so?"

In spite of himself, Will tensed. He inhaled a deep breath. "My father . . . My father is . . ." The words were too strange in his mouth, like a foreign tongue he barely knew. His hand tightened around Philippa's. It was one thing to tell the duke, who never argued or questioned. It was another to tell Roger Edwards, who would scrutinize and pick apart every particle of his story.

Philippa stepped into the breach. "Mr. Edwards," she said in reproach, "surely you cannot be unaware. I daresay you've done more than simply sit in your office and ponder it. Can you not detect the flaw in your analysis and see what's right before you?"

His eyes narrowed.

"In London I had the pleasure of meeting Mr. Montclair's younger brother," she went on. "At the time I thought he was familiar, but of course he couldn't be. That day at Bagnigge Wells was the first time he and I had ever been within sight of each other. Only today did I realize where I've seen him before."

"Where?" asked Edwards.

She smiled. "In Her Grace's sitting room."

Edwards blinked. Will looked at her in surprise.

"The portrait," Philippa said gently.

The attorney's head snapped toward Will, scowling as his gaze raked up and down before lingering on his face.

"What portrait?" Will asked.

Edwards sucked in his breath. "Merciful God," he breathed.

"What portrait?" repeated Will sharply.

Still locked in silent communication, Philippa nodded at Edwards. And Edwards began to nod slowly in reply.

What was this portrait? It was significant, Will could tell. He turned to Philippa, wishing she had told him about it.

Before he could ask again, she tucked her hand around his arm. "Come. I'll show you."

Chapter Thirty-One

❦

The duchess's sitting room was in the oldest part of the castle, in the south tower where Plantagenet ladies had stitched the tapestries that hung in the Tapestry Room while their lords jousted outside. It was far more modern now; a succession of countesses and then duchesses had improved the suite until it was the most elegant and comfortable in the whole castle. The window slits were enclosed with casement windows, a pair of stoves augmented the large hearth, and a thick carpet covered the flagstone floor. The furniture was elegant but still comfortable, upholstered in the duchess's favorite deep blue damask.

Philippa saw Will's eyes sweep around the room as they entered. She wondered what he thought of it. He'd seen the duke's suite of rooms, but even those paled in comparison to this. It had been the duchess's private domain for sixty years, refined and perfectly tuned to her tastes.

"This is the portrait." She gestured—rather pointlessly, as it was the only one in the room. But what a portrait it was.

It had been done by Thomas Hudson, the leading portraitist of his day, of the duchess surrounded by her children. Beneath their feet was a luxurious Turkey carpet, behind them an elegant satin drape partially drawn back behind a spray of ostrich plumes, providing a glimpse of rolling hills crowned with trees in the distance. The lands of Carlyle, Philippa supposed, although there was nothing specific about it. The duchess sat in a carved wooden chair that would have been fit for Henry VII, young and handsome and confident. The folds of her blue silk gown gleamed, the ropes of pearls around her throat glowed. John, the eldest son, leaned nonchalantly against her chair with his arms folded, his gray eyes sharp and clear and his mouth tilted indulgently. Stephen, the youngest, was a child of three or four on his mother's lap, his blond curls brushing his pink cheeks and one chubby hand clutching his mother's pearls. Jessica, the only daughter, had been about ten, still a girl but with the promise of beauty already evident. She looked ready to twirl off the canvas and fling her armload of pink and scarlet peonies at the viewer—in fact, that's what she'd often told Philippa she had longed to do, during the long, tiring sittings for this portrait. The artist had wanted her posed with her armload of flowers held out like an offering to her mother, and Jessica used to laugh that her arms grew *so* tired.

Jessica was the figure Philippa usually studied. She adored this portrait of her stepmother, and as a girl she had loved hearing stories of the sittings—how William had once slipped a mouse into John's pocket; how John had retaliated by persuading the painter to add the ostrich plumes which made William sneeze uncontrollably; how Jessica had lost her temper and stomped on all the flowers, and been sent out to pick more under the stern eye of her governess; how little Stephen had got into the artist's supplies and splattered paint all over an expensive carpet.

But Philippa knew Will saw only one face on the canvas today: Lord William St. James, the second eldest.

His father.

He had stopped in front of the portrait as if turned to stone. It was nearly full-scale, and as a young child Philippa had thought it so lifelike she'd sometimes spoken to the people in it. She wondered if Will was tempted to do the same. His hands hung at his sides, his head tipped back to take it in, and his face . . .

She looked at the canvas, trying to see Lord William for the first time, as his son might. He had been two years younger than John, a little shorter but broader. In the portrait he must be sixteen or seventeen, not quite a man, his arm flung around his elder brother's shoulders. Everyone always said the duke and he were the closest of brothers, the best of friends. Lord William had dark hair and brown eyes which shone with deviltry. There was a small, roguish smile on his lips . . . exactly like the one Will wore when he'd teased Philippa and made her want to tear out her hair and argue with him and then kiss him into submission.

It gave her a start. How blind she'd been. It was true that his brother Jack was virtually the image of Lord William, but she should have recognized Will long ago.

"What . . . ?" Will's voice was hushed. "When was this painted?"

"About forty years ago."

His throat worked. "Why isn't the old duke there?"

Philippa glanced at Mr. Edwards, who had followed. He, too, had been staring at the portrait, but not in dazed surprise—in fierce scrutiny, his forehead creased and his lips moving slightly, as if he were arguing with himself. At her look, he gave a violent start, bowed his head and hurried from the room. He was probably running to his office to look at the family records again.

She took a deep breath. "The old duke was cold and heartless. The duchess commissioned this portrait, not he, but he refused to sit for it. He thought the painter presumptuous and the whole thing a waste of time. I understand he spent most of his time in London, while the duchess and children were here." She paused, watching his face. "If you wish to see him, there's a portrait in the gallery."

"That's what I heard," he murmured, still staring at his father. "That old Carlyle was unfeeling and arrogant, immovable in his opinions and brutal in his dealings with everyone."

Philippa inhaled in sudden understanding. "Is that why he didn't come back?"

For the first time since they entered the room, Will glanced at her. "That is *definitely* not my story to tell." His gaze went back to the portrait. "But he said he could never return."

Her heart swelled and ached at the expression on his face—wondering, wistful, hungry, hurt. What had kept Lord William from England for thirty years, allowing his family to believe him dead all that time? And why had he told his son—one of his sons—the truth?

Behind her the door opened. "Philippa," exclaimed the duchess. "And Mr. Montclair." Her voice grew chilly and imperious. "What are you doing here?"

Philippa grasped Will's hand. The duchess saw it, and her eyes darkened with worry and anger.

"I brought him, ma'am," said Philippa. "There's something you must know."

She came into the room, her face set in disapproval. "I can hardly imagine what. He has resigned his post, has he not?"

"I have," said Will.

"Then I wonder why you are still on Carlyle grounds."

"Perhaps not for long," said Will under his breath.

The duchess heard, and her voice turned icy. "Pray, do not let me keep you."

"Stop!" exclaimed Philippa. "Both of you, stop it!"

Both gaped at her. Will recovered first; a hint of his cocky smile quirked his mouth, and he made a small motion as if yielding the floor to her.

"Philippa," said the duchess in deeply disappointed tones. "Listen to me—"

She shook her head, stepping away from Will. "No, ma'am. This time, you must listen to me. And to Mr. Montclair." She glanced at him again, still wearing his amused—almost proud—little smile, and warmth bubbled up inside her until she had to smile back, helplessly, adoringly. How did this man always make her smile? "To Will," she amended.

That stiffened the duchess's back. "He cannot say anything I wish to hear! And if he has cozened and seduced you, I will have him whipped from the property!"

"No, you won't." She ignored the older woman's indrawn breath of shock and sat on the sofa, holding out one hand in appeal. "Daadee, hear what he has to say, for my sake."

Her expression forbidding, the duchess stalked across the room and sat down. "Well?" she demanded.

Philippa patted the cushion beside her and slowly Will came to take it. For a moment he stared at the duchess, then he looked at the floor. He gripped his hands together, then rested them on his knees, then looked at the portrait again.

"If he will not speak, I shall." The duchess's voice was unsteady. Ignoring Will, she looked at Philippa. "Listen to me, my darling girl. Do not do it. Do not be fooled by the honeyed words of a man. You cannot know him well enough to—to throw yourself away on him. Please, dear Pippa, *please* do not say you are in love and mean to cast prudence to the winds . . . You know I cannot deny you anything but I beg you, don't ask this of me. It will break my heart."

Will looked up, frowning.

The duchess shot a venomous glare at him. "I knew it was a mistake to employ you."

Incredibly, Will grinned. He sat back more comfortably on the sofa and stopped fidgeting with his hands. "Wait until you hear the rest."

The duchess put one hand to her mouth as if she would be ill.

Philippa looked at Will in reproof. To the duchess, she implored, "Please give him a chance to explain. It isn't about me at all."

Will cast his eyes upward, but sobered. He drew breath, glanced at the duchess, then hesitated. "I must apologize, ma'am." He fixed his gaze on the carpet again. "I haven't told you something about myself."

"I doubt it can be anything of interest to me," she said, but without the previous ire; now she sounded defeated. Philippa saw a tear in her eye, and knew the duchess believed all was lost. She bit down on her lip to keep from bursting out with the news herself.

He seemed to search for words for a moment, then reached for his neckcloth without speaking. With a few short jerks he untied it and pulled open his collar. The duchess made a noise of shocked distress.

Will reached inside his shirt and pulled a chain over his head, a small silver medallion hanging from it. Philippa's eyes went wide as she remembered how he'd brushed aside her hands from his neck, how he stripped off his own shirt and flung it aside. There had been no chain around his neck when he carried her to his bed and made love to her.

Now he collected that chain in one hand and offered it to the duchess, who seemed frozen in her chair. Philippa leaned forward, trying to see what

Will had taken pains to keep hidden from her even in the heat of desire, and the duchess started out of her trance. She almost lunged forward to seize it, and gave a little cry as she studied it with frantic eyes.

"Where did you get this?"

Will cleared his throat. "From my father."

The duchess didn't move or speak. Her face was stark white.

"He wore it every day of his life," Will went on. "When I was a boy, he told me it was given to him by his mother."

The duchess made a strangled noise.

"He only took it off when my brother and I were about to leave for England. He said it had been a token of good fortune for him, and he hoped it would be the same for me."

"Good fortune," she whispered in a hollow tone.

Philippa couldn't restrain herself any longer. "Ma'am, don't you see—?"

"No!" The duchess looked up, fire in her eyes. "Where did you get this?" she demanded, holding the medallion in a clenched fist.

Will's gaze darted to Philippa's as if to say *I told you it wouldn't go well*. "From my father," he repeated.

The duchess leapt to her feet. "I'll have you arrested for a thief," she vowed. "As for your father, he stole this from a dead man and deserves to be shot!" Her voice cracked at the end.

Philippa jumped up and ran to seize the duchess's hands. "Look at the portrait," she urged. "Understand what he's telling you." The duchess squeezed her eyes shut and shook her head. Philippa gave their clasped hands a tiny shake. "Your William is still alive," she whispered, barely audible. "And his sons are here in England."

The duchess froze. Her eyes flew open. "Sons?"

Philippa nodded. "Will's younger brother is in London. They came together. I saw him—Jack—when I was visiting Aunt Diana. Daadee, he's the very image of his father. He might as well be your William stepping down from that canvas."

The duchess swallowed. "Pippa, I suffered his loss once. I cannot do it twice." She sounded old and frightened, and desperately hopeful.

"And I would sooner throw myself in the river than give you false hope." She bit her lip. "The duke knew him immediately. He simply didn't realize it must be William's son, instead of William himself. But Will—Mr. Montclair—knows things only William could have told him. He called His Grace Joffred."

The duchess's fingers dug into Philippa's.

"He named the old wooden horse, not Nestor but *William's* horse: Hengroen, after King Arthur's stallion."

The duchess inhaled a trembling breath.

"Let him send for his brother," Philippa begged. "You'll know the moment you see Jack."

For a long moment the duchess said nothing, just stared at Philippa as if trying to plumb her soul. Then she pulled free and stepped back. "Young man," she said unsteadily to Will. "You have made a very shocking and virtually impossible claim. What will you do if I say I do not believe a word of it?"

Will got to his feet. "I wouldn't blame you at all,"

he replied evenly. "It is indeed incredible. I would take my leave and return to London to join my brother."

"You would just leave?" she demanded. "And never return to Carlyle?"

He swept one of his flourishing, insolent bows. "As I planned to do all along."

She frowned. "What? Nonsense. How would that serve you?"

Will seemed to have concluded this was the end and he had no more reason to be deferential. "I've already got what I wanted." The duchess's gaze flew accusingly to Philippa. Will saw it and shook his head. "*Tsk*, madam, how indelicate. I've satisfied my curiosity about Carlyle, which was all I ever hoped for. My father told me just enough to make me wild to know more, and when a chance presented itself, I seized it. Now that I've seen it, I can return home in good conscience."

"Curiosity! No, I do not believe that. What do you really want from Carlyle?"

Will's gaze moved to Philippa, and he smiled— softly, warmly, the way he'd smiled at her in the intimate confines of his bed. "Nothing from Carlyle, ma'am. Nothing at all."

"You mean to seduce my granddaughter into running off with you!"

"If so, it worked," said Philippa before Will could speak. "If he goes, I'm going with him."

"What?" cried the duchess.

Philippa looked at Will. To anyone else he would have looked at ease, careless of what happened next: arms folded, feet braced apart, expression relaxed in indifference. But his collar was still open and she could see the rapid pulse in his throat. Oh, he was *such* a good actor. "I love him, Daadee. Whoever he is, wherever he came from. What's more, I believe him. I knew who he was before he told me. He never meant to tell you, or any of us. If you believe nothing else, believe that much."

The duchess looked between them, then down at the chain in her hand. A troubled frown wrinkled her brow and she rubbed her thumb across the medallion. Philippa was dying to know what was on it. "Why would he let us believe him dead?" the duchess asked in a numb voice. "The army told us he was found . . . brutalized beyond description." She turned the medallion from side to side. This time Philippa caught the Carlyle crest engraved in the silver. "But this was not on him," the duchess murmured. "I wrote to everyone from the generals to the lowliest lieutenant . . . Can it be? All these years . . . Not a word?"

Will looked down. "I don't know. All he ever said was that he could never go back." He paused as if wrestling with a decision. "I believe he did something unforgivable in the war."

"To a mother's heart, almost nothing is unforgivable." Her voice cracked.

"I don't think it was you he feared," muttered Will.

The duchess raised her head, as if something finally made sense to her. "His father. May God forgive me for marrying that soulless monster." She inhaled deeply as Philippa goggled at her and even Will looked taken aback. "Why did he never write to me, later?"

Now definitely off balance, Will cleared his throat. "He—he was French by then, ma'am."

"French!"

He shrugged at her horrified outburst. "When he came to Montreal and met my mother, he was simply another fur trader."

"His wretched father has been dead for thirty years!"

Will lifted one hand. "He doesn't know that."

Slowly the duchess walked to stand directly in front of the portrait. She gazed up at it for a long moment. Then she turned and stared hard at Will. Philippa retreated to Will's side, and he clasped her hand tightly.

"Wait here," snapped the duchess before she spun on her heel and stormed from the room.

Chapter Thirty-Two

❧❧❧

Will looked at Philippa; she looked back, eyes wide and lips parted. "I've no idea," she said before he could ask.

"Ah well." He shrugged to hide the sharp stab of . . . regret? Disappointment? "I expected nothing more."

That much was true. When Pa had sworn him to secrecy, he'd told Will that no one would believe the story anyway. *They've thought me dead for thirty years,* he'd said. *Even your mother barely believes it.* And Will had promised, despite all the questions burning inside him.

He'd meant to keep that promise, but when Roger Edwards told him the name of the family he served, all those months ago in London, and offered him a position on the estate, it had felt like a sign from the heavens. Fate wanted him to know more. He took the chance.

He had expected to be awed, impressed . . . and also disgusted by the rigid pomp and cruel demands of the nobility. Pa had mentioned loveless, arranged marriages, children who never saw their parents, young men who lived wild and rakish lives and young women married off before they were eighteen. Will had expected to come away fully convinced that his father had done right in leaving every piece of it behind.

It had taken him three months to realize that the duke wasn't the old tyrant whose wrath Pa had feared, but a man near his father's age. What was this younger duke like? Then there turned out not to be much of a family. What had happened? Every piece of instruction came from the duke's elderly mother. Why was she running the estate? Everything he learned only increased his curiosity beyond bearing.

And then he'd finally been sent to Carlyle itself, where he *had* been duly awed and impressed by the ancient stone castle and its rich appointments. But the people . . . He'd been entirely wrong about the people.

Still, he'd seen what he came to see. By rights he should be halfway to London now, with no one the wiser, his secrets undisturbed.

But his heart would be left behind.

As he rode the miles of Carlyle for the last time, he barely saw any of the things that had so consumed him. Instead he saw Philippa, leaning over a bridge with a little bit of silk ruffling around her face, curious and beautiful. He saw her advancing on him in high temper, vibrant in a dress the color of sunset. Memories of her battered at him from all sides—her triumphant little smile when she bested him, her expression when she bit into a gulab jamun, the resignation in her posture at Bagnigge Wells, and the joy that lit her face when their gazes connected.

The feel of her mouth against his.

The erotic little sounds she made when he kissed her.

The silk of her hair in his hands. The warmth of her skin under his fingertips.

The glow in her eyes when she moved closer to him, bare as the day she was born, in the worn linen sheets of his bed. The music of her laughter. The elation inside him when he made her laugh, and she wrapped her arms around him.

And most of all, the tremor in her voice when she said *I love you*. As if she knew he meant to break her heart.

He'd made a vow to his father, but Pa had also told him to live his life in a way that allowed him to die without regret. Since Will felt crushed by regret mere hours after leaving her, he wheeled his horse around and rode back to Stone Cottage. If Philippa would have him, he'd risk being disowned by his father.

The moment he saw her waiting for him, her dark eyes calm and bright with love, he knew he'd done right. He would never regret coming back for her.

The rest . . . he was still undecided about how much of that he would regret. But he was man enough to admit now, as he stood in the duchess's lavish sitting room feeling judged by his own smugly amused teenaged father from the canvas on the wall, that he did want to be believed. Carlyle had wormed its way into his heart and soul.

Against his wishes, he'd come to love it and he wanted to stay.

The chances were still slim. Her Grace was probably marshaling the footmen to forcibly remove him from the grounds. Edwards might be writing a lawsuit against him.

Ah well. He had something worth more than Carlyle. Philippa made every bit of this mad adventure worthwhile, and Pa would understand that.

Philippa was more upset by the duchess's departure. Her brows pulled together in worry. "No—no, I cannot believe she would disregard everything . . ."

Will took one more look at the portrait. *No regrets*, his father seemed to whisper meaningfully from the canvas. He nodded, then turned his back on it and took Philippa's hand. "Let's go."

"Where?" she protested as he led her at a brisk pace through the corridors.

"Out," he said over his shoulder. "Away."

"No." She tugged against him. "Here." She led him up, up, up a narrow stair of rough stone reinforced with ancient timbers, and then outside.

Will's breath caught. They were atop the highest turret of the castle. He'd seen it, obviously, from the ground; it towered over the rest of the castle. Pa had mentioned it: the tallest tower in the county, he'd said, built by a Norman ancestor who'd taken a Saxon bride and meant to keep her, even if an invading army should come.

Slowly he turned. The view was breathtaking. Philippa stepped closer to his side as the wind whipped at them, and he put his arm around her.

"You can see most of Carlyle from here," she said. The wind caught wisps of her hair, and she tucked them behind her ear. "There is Stone Cottage"—only the roof and chimneys were visible beyond the trees—"and the river. You can even see Kittleston, in the distance. And that is the road to London."

Will didn't look that way.

"I loved to come up here as a girl. For a time I fancied painting, and I would set up my easel and paint. Up here one feels how small we each are, and yet how important to this land and this place." She rested her head on his shoulder. "Seven hundred years of your family have stood on this tower, Will. They would want you here."

"Not without you."

She smiled. "They aren't my ancestors."

"No," he said. "But they'll be our children's, which makes you vital to them, too."

She pressed close to him; he folded his coat around her, and she put her arms around his waist, her head on his shoulder.

Her, thumped his heart. *She* was home.

He didn't know how long they stood there, holding each other, but finally a noise made them turn. The duchess stood in the doorway, Mr. Edwards hovering behind her. Dangling from her clasped hands was Pa's silver medallion, winking in the slanting sunlight.

"If you please, we would like to speak to you," said Her Grace stiffly. "William."

Chapter Thirty-Three

❧ ⸎ ❧

They made Philippa wait outside the Tapestry Room. After a few moments, Mr. Edwards emerged, holding up both hands as she leapt to her feet.

"Patience, Miss Kirkpatrick."

"The very thing I've none of!" But she smiled, and he came to sit beside her in one of the window embrasures.

"How did you know?" he asked.

She smiled wryly. "A chance encounter. Lady Beauchamp and I visited the tea gardens at Bagnigge Wells. It was rather tedious, until I spotted Will. I chased him down, and we talked . . ."

She paused, blushing. He'd kissed her half out of her wits in that garden. That was when she'd realized it was love. If someone had told her the sun came out and angels sang at the moment she'd looked up to see him at the end of the path, she would have believed it.

"His brother accompanied him. I had no chance to speak to him—now I understand why Will was so keen to prevent us meeting—but I saw him."

"And you recognized him?"

She shook her head. "I persuaded myself it was Will he brought to mind. They do look alike, as brothers. It was only later, when I sat looking at the portrait, that I realized Jack—or Jacques, as Will called him—is the image of Lord William. Then I understood."

Edwards shook his head. "Your understanding far outpaced my own, Miss Kirkpatrick."

"You thought he was one of Lord Thomas's descendants."

He smiled ruefully. "I did suspect something like that."

"When?" she demanded. "I've long wondered why you engaged him to manage Carlyle, when he had no experience, no connection to Carlyle, and was the precise opposite of the steward Her Grace wanted."

Something like a smirk played across the attorney's lips. "The moment I looked at his face, I suspected he was a St. James. *Which* St. James, I had no inkling. A descendant of Lord Thomas? His family was French. He sounded French, and confessed it was the language he spoke at home. And he displayed a marked curiosity about Carlyle from the moment I mentioned it. It would have been an incredible coincidence, but . . ." He opened one hand in apology. "I didn't want to let him slip away, on the chance it was something."

Philippa goggled at him. "You hired a man to administer this estate on a *whim*?"

He looked affronted. "I spoke to him for some time. I kept him in London for the winter, where I could assess and supervise him closely. I waited,

hoping he would betray some proof of his heritage.
I had him investigated—"

She made a sound of astonishment.

Mr. Edwards nodded. "I dispatched two men to
America the week after I engaged him. They returned only a month ago with information which
puzzled me exceedingly. His mother's family
was unlikely to be connected to Lord Thomas.
They had been in Montreal for generations. His
father was even more obscure, a fur trader from
the wilderness, and nothing could be learned of
his history. I feared I had been mistaken, or had
happened across a descendant of some previous
duke's illegitimate child."

"That wouldn't have made him an heir . . ."

The attorney lifted one shoulder. "Who knows
what Lord Thomas did in America? He was in debt.
A change of name, and he could have become a
new man, unconnected to his past. In desperation
I tried to provoke Mr. Montclair into confessing a
connection—"

Philippa gasped loudly. "When?"

"The night we returned from London." He removed his spectacles and polished the lenses.
"With His Grace so ill, perhaps dying, time was
of the essence. I explained to him the laws of inheritance. I all but told him to declare himself,
if he had any claim to Carlyle, and he did not."
He put his eyeglasses back on and smiled at her.
"Only you were able to draw him out. I feel quite
the fool, having neglected to examine his brother
for myself."

She smiled. Will hadn't admitted anything until she began speaking of taking sketches of the

castle and the town to show to his family. Now she understood why he had resisted so strenuously. There was no way to introduce her into his family without his father discovering what he'd done. Even an elopement would have exposed the truth, the moment anyone asked about her history. Will hadn't been willing to stake a claim to Carlyle, but he had been willing to confess to his father . . . for her.

After a long time, Will emerged. He glanced at Edwards, who fairly ran in behind him and closed the door.

Will came to sit by Philippa, his arm going around her as she slid close to him.

"How was it?" The duchess could be prickly; Philippa knew how to handle it, but Will didn't.

"I'm permitted to stay, on sufferance," he said.

Philippa gasped. "No! Surely she believes . . ."

Will grinned. "I said enough to convince her it was possible. She wishes to meet Jack, and of course write to my father. I think she cannot believe it until she hears from him."

"But she believes you." She couldn't resist smiling with some triumph. "As I told you she would."

"She waged stiff resistance," he exclaimed. "And once she began to believe, she grew indignant with me all over again, that I had tormented and provoked her so when I knew who she was. For a moment I feared she might conjure up a large wooden spoon and rap my knuckles, as Aunt Emilie used to do."

"No!" But she giggled as she said it.

"I intend to remain on guard, just in case," he told her. "And then . . . we spoke of you."

Philippa went still and quiet.

Will ran his fingertips down her arm. "You are her dearest treasure," he said softly. "She would trust me with Carlyle but not with you."

"But *I* would." She looked at the door of the Tapestry Room.

He held her back when she would have charged into the room. "I persuaded her. If she doesn't want me around, that's perfectly understandable. I offered to leave, but only with you." He turned his face into her hair and breathed deep. "From now on, where you go, I go. And I'll go nowhere without you."

"So . . . what now?"

Will glanced around, then pulled her into his lap. Philippa laughed, putting her arms around his neck. "You promised to marry me."

"Did you think I changed my mind?"

"Well, when you accepted me, I had very different expectations."

She laughed again. "And now that you're heir to all this, I might love you less?"

Will didn't laugh. "No. I might be heir to all this, but I'm still myself. I'll never be that fine, elegant London gentleman. I'll forever be out repairing roofs and mending fences with the tenants. I'm not the sort to sit back and let someone else care for Carlyle."

"I know," she said softly.

"And I'm *not* heir to any of this," he went on. "My father is, or would be, if he'll agree to it. I suspect he won't want it. That will leave me nothing but a glorified estate manager. But one who loves you desperately."

She touched his jaw. "That's what you were when I fell in love with you. The answer to your question is yes."

JACK ARRIVED FOUR days later, suspicious and annoyed. Will had written just enough to get him to come to Carlyle, wanting to tell the rest in person.

Jack looked dazed at the end. "Why didn't you tell me?"

"Pa made me swear not to."

His brother turned on him in fury. "*You* knew! Why did he tell *you* the entire story?"

Will held up one finger. "Not the entire story. No one save Pa knows that."

Finally a smile split Jack's face. A somewhat evil smile. "Yes," he agreed. "And fortunately for all, he'll be here soon."

Will went very still. "What?"

Obviously enjoying his predicament, Jack nodded. "The latest letter I had from him. He's had enough of our prevarication and said he would be taking the next Montclair ship to London. It's due in at the end of this month." He grinned. "How pleased you must be! You can present your new bride to him, and to our mother and sister." To Philippa he added, "They will adore you." He swept a gallant bow and brought her hand to his lips. "I suspect I shall, too."

Will looked at Philippa. Her face was bright with hope; he knew what she was thinking. She could put the St. James family back together, the son and brother who was lost, now come back from the dead.

While he . . . was in a great deal of trouble.

He turned to Philippa. "Will you marry me now? Tomorrow?"

"Before she has a chance to learn more about you?" Jack nodded somberly. "Good idea, Will." To Philippa he mouthed, *Run*.

She laughed. "And here I thought one Montclair St. James was bad enough! How will I endure two of you?"

"We'll banish Jack," said Will.

She gasped in affected affront. "Then who will stand up with you at our wedding?"

"Edwards," said Will. "He owes me that much."

"Will the duchess come, if I marry you tomorrow?"

"You'll have to ask her. She'll refuse for certain if I do." He kissed her. "Will you?"

Will I? she thought. *Every day, forever.* "I will," she said, and kissed her true love.

Epilogue

⚭❧⚭❧

The unfamiliar tolling of a bell woke Philippa. Her eyes flew open with a start, but then she recognized the bright yellow of Diana's guest chamber, and relaxed. They were in London.

Beside her lay her husband of fourteen days, staring at the ceiling.

"Good morning." She snuggled close to him, laying her hand on his chest.

He inhaled deeply and covered her hand with his. "That's to be determined."

Philippa pushed herself up on one elbow. She'd never seen him so quiet and tense. They had come to London to meet the *Mary Catherine*, the ship bringing his parents and sister to England. A messenger from Plymouth had brought word yesterday that the ship had put in the previous day, meaning it should reach London today. "Will he be very upset?" she asked softly.

"Excellent chance of that," said Will.

"What will that mean?"

He made a slight grimace. "Let us hope you're not a widow before nightfall."

Philippa raised her brows. Jack had assured her all would be well, but Will was unusually grim about the reunion. When she'd told him what Jack said, Will had retorted, "Jack didn't break his promise to stay far away from Carlyle. *Jack* will be fine."

She didn't like seeing him this way, not her teasing, laughing, cocksure pirate. She threw off the covers and sat up, unbuttoning her nightgown. "Perhaps you should stay here and I will go speak to him."

"He would find me," said Will, watching her hands with interest.

Philippa scooped up the nightgown and tossed it over her head, onto the floor. "If this is to be our last morning together, I should make the most of it."

"You should." His expression grew more focused and heated as she climbed on top of him, straddling his hips. He ran his palms up her thighs.

She braced her hands on his shoulders and leaned down to touch her lips to his. "I must try to inspire you to come back to me."

He grinned and kissed her. Philippa pulled the ribbon from her long braid and shook her hair loose. "God above," he groaned, reaching up to cup her breast. "I'd walk through fire to get back to you."

Philippa ran her hands down his stomach, still fascinated by his body. Men were such marvelously made creatures. His muscles were so firm. His skin felt so different from hers. At each pass of her palm over his erection, his stomach flexed and his breath caught, until finally he growled, "I see your plan is to kill me before anyone else can."

She laughed and moved, guiding him inside her. "Let us see if you survive."

He did. Will was a devoted and inventive lover. Philippa had had no idea her body could do some of the things he'd taught her in the last fortnight. She made love to him, moving atop him as his wicked hands stroked, pinched, gripped, coaxed, as he told her all sorts of naughty things she should do to him. His voice grew rough and guttural and she knew he'd switched into French but the blood was roaring in her ears too loudly for her to make out the words. Will's fingers dug into her hips, urging her to ride him faster—Philippa could hardly breathe—he threw back his head and she came, reaching blindly for him, lost to everything but him.

"Someday," she gasped between breaths, "I will learn French."

Will laughed as he rolled over, cocooning her beneath him. His chest was also heaving and he kissed her neck until she shivered. "Je t'aime," he whispered.

"I know those words." She pulled his mouth to hers.

"They are the only words you need to know." He kissed her.

DIANA HAD OFFERED to send breakfast upstairs, but Will thought the English custom of eating in bed was bizarre and he refused to do it, so they dressed and went downstairs to the breakfast room.

At the door he stopped. "I'm to meet Jack."

She pursed her lips. From inside the room came the sounds of silver on china and voices: Diana,

Fanny, and the duchess. "Won't you come in to say good morning?"

He grinned. "I promised to meet him half an hour ago. He'll be annoyed at me already."

"You should have said something . . ."

"I did say something. *Faster, darling, harder.*" He winked.

She laughed, then cupped his face in her hands. "Good luck."

Will touched his forehead to hers. "I'll need it."

He left and Philippa went into the breakfast room. "Good morning."

"Good morning." The duchess raised her brow at the empty seat beside Philippa's.

"Will had to join his brother," she explained.

"Of course. Fanny, ring for more tea," Diana directed.

Philippa appreciated her family; they let her fill her plate in peace. Diana had leapt to offer her home when they came to London. Will had argued against that; he wanted everyone to stay at Carlyle while he and Jack went to London to meet his father. The duchess had listened in silence, her face growing redder with every word until Will finally noticed. He'd fallen silent, and then, before Philippa could intervene, he asked the duchess to accompany him.

"This is so exciting," Fanny enthused. "Imagine, Pippa! They are your family now."

Philippa glanced at the duchess, who was sipping her tea with deceptive calm. "I'm very eager to meet them."

"How did I never suspect it?" the duchess burst out. "My own grandson, right in front of me!"

"He didn't want you to," replied Philippa, buttering her toast. "And really, who would have expected him to turn up as a steward?"

She had once suggested he try to charm the duchess. No wonder he'd laughed at her, when he was going out of his way to antagonize the woman for fear she *might* recognize him. His brash impertinence had kept him out of the duchess's sight for all but a few unpleasant meetings.

"He might have made himself more agreeable!"

Philippa couldn't stop a small smile. He'd made himself very agreeable to her.

The duchess frowned. "Do not laugh at me, Pippa."

"No, Daadee." She noticed the fine tremble in the older woman's hand. The duchess must be as apprehensive about this meeting as Will—perhaps more so. Her son had allowed her to believe him dead for thirty years, and none of them knew why. He had led an entire life apart from her; he was a stranger, but still her child.

After breakfast there was nothing to do but wait. Will and Jack planned to meet the ship at the docks, explain everything, and then bring their family here. Diana and Fanny wished them well before departing for the day to give them privacy. The house felt very large and empty in their absence, the ticking of the tall clock in the hall the only sound.

The duchess paced the drawing room, her hands clasped as if in prayer. Philippa tried to read, did a little embroidery, and toyed with the harpsichord before giving up when the clock chimed two. Will had been gone for hours.

"Shall I ring for tea?" she asked.

The duchess's head came up. Her eyes were dry, but wide with dread. "What if he will not see me?"

Philippa bit her lip. Will had worried about that very thing. He'd framed it as a worry that his father would be so busy thrashing him, they wouldn't make it to Hertford Street, but underneath it lay a real fear that William St. James never wanted to come home.

But he'd promised to send a note if that happened, and nothing had come.

"Perhaps the ship was delayed," she suggested. "We could take a turn in the park . . ."

Carriage wheels rattled in the street outside. Philippa's breath caught. The duchess froze. The wheels rattled nearer, then stopped. A horse neighed.

The duchess reached for her hand. Her face was pale.

There was a man's voice in the street. *Jack*, thought Philippa, her heart taking a giant leap.

The sound of the knocker made them both start. Diana must have told her butler to stand at the door all day, for it opened at once. More voices murmured, including a girl's. The duchess's grip tightened.

Several endless minutes later, the door opened. Will came in, followed by two women. "Ma'am." He hesitated. "Allow me to present my mother, Mrs. Montclair, and my sister, Miss Sophia Montclair. Mama, Sophie, this is the Duchess of Carlyle."

The duchess made a small sound. Sophia was *her* name.

The older woman was about Diana's age, tall and

slender and handsome. She met the duchess's gaze directly, and dropped a graceful curtsy.

The girl at her side had glossy dark hair and dark eyes that were perfectly round with wonder as her head swiveled to take in the room. Will gave her a look, and she hastily dropped a curtsy, too.

"Madame," said Mrs. Montclair, her voice distinctly French. "It is my great pleasure to make your acquaintance at last."

"And I yours." The duchess's voice shook. Her grip was so tight, Philippa couldn't feel her fingers.

Jack stuck his head in the doorway. He glanced around, then over his shoulder, and nodded.

Philippa held her breath. Will bowed his head.

A man stepped slowly into the room. He was as tall as Will, broad-shouldered and fit, his dark hair streaked with gray, his face tanned and lined. His eyes darted from side to side.

The duchess gave a strangled cry of joy. *"William."*

His wary expression eased, and a smile—so like Will's—broke across his face. "Mama," he said softly. "It is good to see you again."

*Next month, don't miss these exciting
new love stories only from
Avon Books*

Sisters and Secrets by Jennifer Ryan

There's nothing more complicated than the relationship among family, and the Silva sisters—tragedy-touched Sierra, seemingly perfect Amy, and free-spirited Heather—are no exception. As their secrets are revealed, each realizes that there is more to their family than meets the eyes . . . and forgiveness may be the only way to move forward and reclaim true happiness at last.

How to Steal a Scoundrel's Heart by Vivienne Lorret

Ruined debutante Prudence Thorogood lost everything when she was ousted from polite society, including her inheritance. Now she'll do anything to take back what's hers . . . even if she has to steal it. Accepting a scandalous offer from Lord Savage seems like the perfect solution. Until she discovers that there's more to this scoundrel than meets the eye.

The Bride Goes Rogue by Joanna Shupe

Charismatic and vivacious Katherine Delafield's father arranged an engagement to the much sought-after tycoon Preston Clarke ages ago. The only problem is Preston refuses to acknowledge it. But this isn't going to stop Katherine from living life to the fullest as she sets out to sample all New York City has to offer. Because no matter what happens, she and Preston will never marry . . . or will they?

Discover great authors, exclusive offers,
and more at hc.com.

REL 0422

*G*ive in to your Impulses!

These unforgettable stories only take a second
to buy and give you hours of reading pleasure!

Go to *www.AvonImpulse.com* and see what we
have to offer.
Available wherever e-books are sold.

AVONIMPULSE

IMP 0811